Milkweed

Also by Mary Gardner

Keeping Warm

A Novel

Milkweed

Mary Gardner

Papier-Mache Press
Watsonville CA

Firt Edition

ISBN: 0-918949-46-7 Hardcover

Cover art by Annie Aird

Cover design by Cynthia Heier

Photograph by Mike Woodside

Typography by Prism Photographics

Library of Congress Cataloging-in-Publication Data

Gardner, Mary.
    Milkweed / Mary Gardner.
        p.   cm.
    ISBN 0-918949-46-7 : $18.00.
    1. Eccentrics and eccentricities—Middle West—Fiction.
  2. Family—Middle West—Fiction. 3. Women—Middle West—
Fiction. I. Title.
PS3557.A7142M55   1994
813'.54—dc20   94-14469
                                                    CIP

This book is for my maternal grandmother, Mattie Day, and her children—Basil, Vivian, Marguerite, and Kenneth.

And for my cousin Claire McClellan Asher.

Milkweed

One

Her parents had settled on Mitty Creek where it flowed into the Wittimac River from the ridge that no one had given a name. Actually, the creek started from the tumbled rocks near the bottom of the ridge, welling up from so many places that the ground was spongy in springtime. Wildflowers almost like those in the East grew there. It was a short creek, four miles, but when it slid into the Wittimac, the blue water left its mark in the brown for quite a ways. The Wittimac was always mucky from the runoff where its banks had been cut bare for lumber so the houses in Valhalla could be built. Bank swallows had nested in the overhanging roots before the trees were all chopped down.

She remembered the swallows. Or her mother had told her. They must have gone somewhere else.

The first years when they'd settled the farm, there hadn't been any school. But she already knew her letters and could copy her numbers from the calendar before she was five. Her mother and father had brought a pile of composition books to North Dakota with them in the bottom of the trunk. One was for practicing letters; one was for arithmetic. One was for stories, but only on Sunday. Her mother always got out the one she needed. Each one had her name on it: Susan May McIntire. By the time she was seven, she could read the books in the bookcase with the glass doors, the right one cracked from when the train man had dropped it.

Then in that fall there was a school, and a good thing, too, because there were only two clean composition books left in the trunk. School was a long way away, toward Valhalla, where more of the farmers had settled. In the winters she couldn't always go, not if the snow was blowing, because getting lost was a real danger, and her parents wouldn't risk it. She wasn't scared at the prospect herself. But when the weather was cold, even when it was sunny, she bundled up in the blanket-coat and the mittens made from the Pritchards' wool, and set out. The way ran down to the creek, and then along it, and then across it on a log that had only gone halfway until her father had hitched the team to it and pulled it over so it made a bridge. In the middle, just where she'd begin to be frightened, two big branches stuck up on each side like handrails. She stood there for a minute every school morning, getting her feet shaped to the round of the log, getting her mind ready for the rest of the trip.

After that, she walked on, following the path her shoes had made over and over. In the winter, the brown grass stubs stuck through the ice glaze; in the spring, the path was a wide, green snake. After the creek, it was all straightaway. She was never late.

The June when she was nine, when she'd already been in school two whole years and could read practically anything, when she and her best friend, Pearl, won almost all the stars, the farmer next to the Pritchards sold out. He'd been there since 1902, earlier than any of the others. The fruit trees he'd planted on the south side of his house where they were protected from the wind were setting little plums. His name was Overbow; his wife was Mrs. Overbow. And all their babies had died, her mother said. They were going back East.

"It's so sad." Those were her mother's words. Her father was in the kitchen too, but he never talked about things like that.

"This will be the best summer in years. A fine crop. They should get the advantage of it when they've worked so hard all along." Her mother clanged pots under the open window, loud enough to make Susan jump even at the yard pump where she was washing Woodrow Wilson's tail. He was part collie. The tail was full of sandburs, the hair glued together in wads. Woodrow whined and drooled, but he loved his tail and didn't want to pull so hard that he'd hurt it. Susan washed more. The lye soap burned her hands.

"They'll be better off." Her father's voice was quiet.

"I hear the auction is Sunday."

"Saturday. They leave Sunday."

"I should have known." The pans clanked like swords. The smell of new bread floated out. Woodrow sat on his tail, his bottom pressing Susan's hand into the dirt.

Her father cleared his throat. "I offered on the land," he said. "They didn't take it," he added.

Her mother laughed and sent a washrag across the glass above the open part of the window, although it was perfectly clean. "What would you have done with it if you'd got it?" she asked, the washrag swabbing back and forth.

"Farm it."

"You need a son for that."

Woodrow rolled over, his feet batting the air. Susan gave up on the tail, sopping wet now and still lumpy with sandburs that hadn't come loose. She left him rolling in the dirt, dumbest dog in Mound County, and walked off to think. But she had already thought enough, so she decided to go see the Overbows while they were warm in her mind, and before it was supper. The walk was two miles, but that was nothing in the summer.

The first mile was like going to school, alongside Mitty Creek, but then Susan branched off to the left, over a tumble of rocks, and then down a smooth prairie hill where the grass grew like hair, just that tight to the ground. After that, it was flat. The wind came from the south in dangerous gusts. She could see its fat face, cheeks pouched out, lips suckered together. The big reader in school had a poem about the Wind Man and how he sent the air washing over the world. That was the last line: "The world is washed in wind." Susan said it as she skipped through the rough grass, pretending to be a witch who found the wind and fed him bread pudding until he blew out his other end. When she saw the Overbow house, she was giggling.

In the snapping breeze, Mrs. Overbow was hanging out clothes. The washtub steamed in the yard on a platform over the coals. "Susan," she said, her face smothered by a patchwork quilt so worn that the soggy batting stood out against her cheek.

"I'm visiting."

Mrs. Overbow stuck in a clothespin. The quilt snapped against her damp dress.

"My mother doesn't know."

"Aren't you the big girl."

"My mother says you're going back East." She had planned to wait longer to talk about it, but Mrs. Overbow had heaved another quilt out of the Indian-reed basket and was flinging it over the line. This one had a sun on it, split and draped down on each side. A golden sun.

Mrs. Overbow stuck in another clothespin.

"When you're gone, and Mr. Overbow, then there'll just be the Pritchards. And us. For miles." Susan rubbed spit on the scuffed toe of her right shoe. It darkened like the color would stay, but it wouldn't. She rubbed more spit on the left one.

With one hand, Mrs. Overbow shaded her eyes and looked hard at Susan. "You're the only girl around here, aren't you?" she said, pinning the final corner of the quilt.

Susan heaped dirt with both toes in turn.

"Where's your dog?"

"He didn't come." Susan began lacing her shoes over again, making them tighter. "I washed his tail," she added. "He's somewhat mad."

Mrs. Overbow didn't answer. The wind had stopped, too. In the June air, grasshoppers were clicking even though it was early. Two years ago they'd come and eaten everything. But this year would be a good one.

"I'd better go." Susan waited to be argued with.

Mrs. Overbow turned the basket upside down and shook it as if she might have missed something. But it was truly empty.

"I better go now, I think."

Mrs. Overbow ducked herself under the last quilt and then straightened up. Susan could see only her ankles and her shoes. Her skirt was completely hidden.

"I'm going," Susan said again, but she waited. She looked at the house, a cabin really, not like the houses in the East, not like the pictures in her parents' book. The curtains were down, the door open. Maybe they were moving sooner than Sunday. Maybe they'd be gone tonight.

"Take this with you."

Susan held out her arms.

"Mr. Overbow and I have enough. And they're all clean now." Mrs. Overbow draped a tiny damp quilt over Susan's wrists, then folded it. "Tell your mother I'll miss her," she said as she picked up the basket.

Susan waited until she was partway home before she unfolded the quilt, spreading it on the grass in as near a perfect rectangle as she could. The wind had come back up, and one end of the quilt kept flopping. It looked brand-new, not even faded. The corners were damp, that was all. She couldn't imagine what she'd do with it because, although she was only nine, she was far too big to sleep under it. It was like an apron, of which she was not overly fond. Or a big scarf.

But then she thought of Woodrow Wilson and how he got cold sometimes, in spite of his fur, and how he was probably still angry at her. He only had straw when he slept in the barn, and when he slept under the porch, he didn't have anything but dirt. She would get her father's saw and hammer; she would build him a bed and arrange the quilt on it for him. There would be a book somewhere with instructions, somewhere in the glass-doored case. They had brought a book for every need, her mother said.

Woodrow Wilson would have a fine quilt all to himself.

Two

Susan's mother held the bowl in both hands, tilted down so Susan could see into it. The batter lapped upward, golden as the sun.

"Would you like to finish beating it?"

The day was at that edge of time when things stopped moving. If she'd been standing in the yard, her shadow would have been a puddle that barely fitted her feet. Inside, the woodstove was chunking and crackling as the fire heated the square oven for the cake-baking. There was no cool anywhere, even in shadows.

"No."

Her mother hardly looked surprised. "Susan," she said. "No *thank you.*"

"No thank you."

Her mother began to thump at the batter in the bowl. The thud of her spoon against the crockery sounded like drumbeats. Indians played drums, only made of skin. No cakes came out of them, just sound. Susan began to thump the top of her legs to see if any skin would do.

"Susan, what are you doing?" Her mother flipped the batter out of the bowl into a tin, scraped the last bits loose with her wooden spoon. She wrapped her hand in her apron and opened the oven door. Steam burst through.

"Drumming." She raised her head. "Like an Indian," she muttered.

"You don't look much like an Indian to me."

Thoughtfully, Susan regarded her narrow, pale wrist below the flowered sleeve of her everyday dress. Her mother was nicer about Indians than most people. She said they had gotten cheated. She said white people sold them the liquor that made them fall down. She said they were an old, old people, not new like everyone else. The Overbows hadn't liked Indians, though. They said they were dirty.

"Did you hurt your wrist?" Her mother was shutting the oven door without even glancing at it.

"No."

"You're looking at it so hard."

Susan yanked her sleeve down as far as it would go on her wrist. "My skin is too white," she said.

Her mother laughed.

"Pearl's skin is like . . ." She had been going to say "dirt," but that wouldn't have been nice. And Pearl was her favorite friend at school or anywhere else. She had a book about the old gods. Thor was one. Sometimes they were women, like Persephone. The Indians must have their own gods. Or maybe they *were* gods. But what had happened to their thrones?

"Pearl's mother is part Indian."

"She *is?*" For once, her mother had surprised her.

"You shouldn't like Pearl any less because of it."

Susan stormed to her feet. How could her mother be so stupid? Pearl was a special person. Sometimes when Susan hated being an only child, she thought of making Pearl her sister. They would live in a mud cave next to the Wittimac. Susan would roll in the wet until her own skin was brown.

But her mother wasn't paying any attention. "Would you like me to read you a story?" she asked. "The cake will take an hour."

Nourishing her anger, Susan started to say "No." She could read for herself now, anyway. But her mother's presence, heavy and soft with the sweat of baking, surged through the kitchen and enwrapped her.

"All right."

"Would you like the fairy tales? Or the one about the Spanish–American War? I've never been sure how much history they teach in the schools in this state."

Outside, Woodrow Wilson was whining. He must smell the cake. Or maybe somebody was coming. Somebody from long ago, from underneath. Somebody who had special powers. Somebody who could be hurt and cheated but who kept the same skin.

"Read about Indians," Susan said.

Three

Mitty Creek.
Mound County.
Mittymound School.
Middleofthemound.
Moundmit?
Muttmutt.
Mickmack.Mitamac.Me.Me.Me.

Mittymound School was as square as a block from a building set.
All the fathers had painted it white on the day of the June picnic
after it was built, and it stood shining in a carpet of grass like a
block of salt for the antelope to lick. Its roof was blue. There were
two windows on each side but none in the back, then one on each
side of the front door. The steps were perfect for two to go down,
arms near enough so they almost touched. In back were the privies.
The fathers hadn't painted them. All around was the grass, worn in
paths from Run Goose Run and Prairie Tag, the kind you did on
your hands and knees. In the winter, the students made the same
paths through the snow. All around the edge they did cow-flop
angels, churning their arms in the snow until it came up their
sleeves and left their wrists chapped. Susan and Pearl made the
prettiest.

Inside, Mittymound looked just like any school. There were
exactly twenty desks, fastened to each other in rows of five going
back. They weren't new, hadn't been new in 1914 when Mittymound was built, either. They'd come from Blakeslee County over
near Pretty Valley where there'd been an old school torn down. So
the names cut into the tops were strange: *Sally, Olaf, Vivian.* That
was nice. *Jesse. Sarah* with an *h*. No one in Blakeslee had ever
carved anything bad. Someone in the back row had drawn horses,
though, and colored them in.

Susan's desk was in front, almost in the teacher's lap. Miss Vonnegut. She had come from the East looking for a husband. It hadn't
done any good. Not yet. But she'd only been there for one full year,
with this being the second. She'd had several prospects, but she set
her sights high. Anyone who had read all those books should.

That was what was best about Mittymound. On each side of the room under the windows, the fathers had built bookcases. They made them permanent, banging the nails right into the walls. The lumber had been given by the families that had extra left over from their sheds and homesteads. Some of the shelves were wider than the others, and those had the fat books on them. There was a reader for everyone; you didn't have to share. A whole shelf of poems. The encyclopedias with the alphabet letters in gold—the county had paid for those. The books with arithmetic, starting with counting and finally going into letters and shapes. The stories about people who lived in other countries. The ones that told you how your body worked. More books than you'd have thought in a school so far out in the country. Shelves full of books, like food.

On the Friday before Christmas, the first day of winter (though that was a joke because winter had started the first week in November), fierce gobs of snow like German planes started during the lunch hour. It was so grey and cold that only the boys had gone outside, leaning against the south side of the school with their caps sticking up above the sills of the two windows. Inside, the six girls put away their leftovers in their lunch buckets. Susan and Pearl. Judith and Alice. Alice was the baby, just six. Amelia, whose nose ran even when it wasn't winter. She was almost big enough to get married. Estelle. She had come from the East just last year. It would be her first Christmas out here, and she wasn't sure about it.

"I'm scared of all that snow."

"Silly." Pearl said it. But she was teasing.

"It's pretty cold."

"We'll maybe get a blizzard this afternoon."

"It's already started."

"That's no blizzard." Pearl cupped her hands around her eyes. "That's just snow like always."

Miss Vonnegut opened the door of the iron stove and dug around inside it. The sides rattled. Before they went home, one of the boys would have to haul the ashes out to the heap behind the girls' privy.

"My father says the cattle will freeze." That was Judith, whose father had been a clerk. He never stopped worrying about his farming.

"They never freeze."

"Who says?"

"Just look sometime. They all stand together."

"Even the boy cattle?" That was Pearl again. All six of the girls put their heads down and snorted. Amelia wiped her nose on her wrist, then wiped her wrist under her chin.

Miss Vonnegut threw in more chunks of wood until the pile by her desk was down to bark. She banged on the window where the boys stood until Billy Evering got the message and went to the woodpile for a new armful. When he brought it inside, the cold air spun out from him like an ice storm.

After lunch, when all the boys came in and sat down, everybody worked on Roman and Greek history. The little ones drew pictures of men wearing sheets. Miss Vonnegut practiced reading with Samuel, who couldn't, but he never gave up. His finger went from word to word, landing on each one like he could knock it through the page. Miss Vonnegut was very patient with him, maybe because his big brother was old enough to be a marriage prospect for her. Then she helped Billy.

Meanwhile, as the light outside lost its silver sheen and turned dead, Susan thought about Christmas. It was only four more days. She had everything ready, and she also know about the big Sears Roebuck box hidden in the empty stall since the first week of December. Her mother and father would both go to church with her even though it was a big trip to Valhalla. They'd already cut a tree down by Mitty Creek. The box with the ornaments was out. Pearl could come over, maybe, if her parents were willing to have their team make the trip. They could read princess stories together. They could make tepees out of blankets. Pearl knew she was an Indian and didn't care. They could stay up late like the gods.

Then the snow outside school came down harder. It was like her mother had shaken a feather tick. The privies disappeared. The sky joined the land in a white cover. There was almost no wind, and then there was a lot. The snow leaped up.

"Like eggbeaters," said Pearl. She had been watching, too.

The little ones in the front of the room stood up, and Miss Vonnegut let them. Billy stood on tiptoe so he could see, too. The schoolroom turned dark almost as if God had wiped a hand across the sky. Miss Vonnegut lit the big kerosene lamp so her desk lay in a golden circle. Without talking, all the children moved up to the edges of the light.

"Come around the stove," Miss Vonnegut said. She arranged them in a circle, the little ones on the inside, sitting on laps. Boys and girls sat next to each other, and no one giggled.

"I'll read to you," said Miss Vonnegut, and she took out the Shakespeare. They were doing *The Tempest,* which was really funny when you thought about it. Miss Vonnegut had already explained to them what was going on in the play, so even if some of the words were strange, they could understand. It wasn't really about storms at all, as you might have thought. It was about love.

And then, while the words flowed out, while Caliban made trouble for everyone, Susan kept her eyes on the window. Pearl was looking out, too, but they didn't say anything to each other. As Miss Vonnegut went on reading, twilight came down. No one could try to go home; it would have meant death. After Ariel got ready to be a captive spirit for the last time, Miss Vonnegut let them eat the very last of each other's lunches, sharing so everyone had something. They were on their own island. They might have to stay in the school all night. Alice whimpered like Woodrow Wilson, and Susan took her tighter on her lap with Alice's greasy hair tucked under her chin. She was so little. The room got colder. All the wood was burned or almost. Billy passed out the coats, and they all bundled up—mittens, scarves, everything.

Amelia snuffled.

"We are all right." Miss Vonnegut put her finger in Shakespeare. "Your parents know where we are."

"They can't come get us in the dark!"

"But they'll come when it's morning. The Schonfelds live just a mile away."

"It's cold," said Judith.

Someone else whispered the same thing, but Susan couldn't tell who. Alice was asleep, matted into Susan's front like a papoose.

"Well." Miss Vonnegut stood up. "Billy, get the ax."

"Here?"

"We can start on the table." You would never have thought she was scared. "It's very big."

"It won't burn good." That was Judith again.

"We'll use some books for kindling. Over there." In the dim room, her pointing arm was like a ghost's. "The old readers. They'll be adequate."

Susan couldn't believe Miss Vonnegut had said it.

"Get the scissors, Pearl."

Pearl struggled to get her feet under her.

Susan really couldn't believe it. To hurt a book was the biggest sin. But Pearl was already on her feet, hurrying toward the bookcase. She must have been scared to disobey. Billy was dragging the ax from the cloakroom, banging the handle against each desk. They were doing what Miss Vonnegut had told them to do.

So when Susan bowed her head over Alice's questionable scalp, it
was a desperate action. Because God had gotten left back East, if
the truth were known. And her family didn't go to church every
Sunday. But she did do all her schoolwork, and helped her mother,
too, and could braid her own hair. She had made Woodrow Wilson
a good bed. It wasn't her fault that he liked it under the porch better. God had ought to listen. Books were more important than a
sparrow falling, and he noticed that.

Susan started with words in her head, but they weren't strong
enough. She knew it. So she put her hands together in the well of
her skirt behind Alice. She pressed her fingernails in. It took what
seemed a long time.

But Pearl had hardly started cutting the first pages when one of
the boys yelled. Susan couldn't tell who it was because she had her
eyes shut.

"Look at that! I ain't never seen it that way!"

"Haven't ever." But Miss Vonnegut's voice was moving toward
the windows. And soon they all crowded there with her.

Outside the snow had stopped. Just like that. The moon, which
had been covered by the whiteness before, was glowing. The
ground was diamonds on a white skirt. All around, pouring from
the very top of the heavens, were rivers of silver that surged and
spread and swallowed back into themselves and then surged again.

"Them's the northern lights!" said Samuel.

"They're." But Miss Vonnegut had her arm almost around him.

And before they even stopped looking long enough to go back to
huddle around the ashy belly of the stove, the shosh-shosh of Mr.
Schonfeld's team came up to their ears, shifting the diamonds into
the path that would take them all home.

Four

They practiced writing in school all the time. Palmer penmanship, with every loop like every other loop. Susan couldn't understand why books were in print if all those loops were really
important. She argued with her mother about it.

"Just practice your penmanship." Her mother was wearing her
heaviest sweater to hold off the cold. It had been a ferocious winter,
though Susan hadn't minded it. She thought that as she got bigger,
her body made more heat. She could feel the extra waves around
her. She must have more blood, sizzling through the roadways of
her veins.

"Remember last winter? You didn't wear all those sweaters then."

Her mother looked at her and pointed to the pen, its tip resting
in a growing puddle of ink. "You're messing," she said. Then, "I
wore what I needed."

"The coldest was the day the blizzard came, and we stayed in
school."

"Well, nether of us will forget that."

Susan thought back. "It was fun," she said. "Except for burning
the books."

"Miss Vonnegut said you never actually burned any."

"But almost." She could remember Pearl's hands on the scissors.
It had been the purest luck that Mr. Schonfeld had come when he
had.

"I wonder if she ever thinks about it." Miss Vonnegut had married a farmer from Pretty Valley, where the desks had come from. It
had been very sudden, and everyone had talked.

"Why should she? She was a good teacher," Susan's mother said,
hugging her own shoulders. "The new one is too young."

That was probably true. The new teacher played games outside
with the children. When the boys wouldn't listen to her, sometimes
her eyes got wet. But Susan had taken charge of her own learning
and didn't mind. She did the work she was supposed to do and then
read. She had finished all the old geography books. She could draw
the world with every country and capital city. She could write perfect Palmer penmanship if she wanted to.

Susan's mother pointed to the tip of the pen. It was awash in black ink. "Take a new sheet," she said. The smile on her face stayed separate from her mouth but danced in her eyes.

"I don't want to write. I'll draw instead."

"With the pen?" Her mother began to rub the knuckles of her hands together as if she could heat them with friction. Then she opened the woodstove and threw in two more sticks of wood.

"Yes."

Her mother didn't argue. Instead, she looked out the window toward the barn. Susan's father was in there with the cows. Their steamy breaths would fog the edges of the hay bales, would blur their shiny eyes. Their fat udders would warm his hands.

"Why don't we have a horse?" As if it had a will of its own, Susan let the pen begin to draw a horse, refusing to lift it until the outline was done. It sprang out of the paper. "Pearl has a horse," she said.

"Just a pony."

"I'd like a pony." But the horse she was drawing was already too big to be a pony. It filled the whole paper, and she had to curl its tail around its hind legs to make it fit.

"I didn't know you liked horses."

Susan thought that her mother didn't know much about her at all, but she didn't say it. Carefully, she rounded the front hooves with the pen. "When I was little, I was afraid," she said. "Woodrow Wilson was enough. But now I'm big enough to ride."

"I suppose that's true."

Susan laid the pen down and held up the drawing. She stood up with it held in both hands. "Horses belong on the prairie," she said.

"What a wise young woman." Her mother's smile reached her mouth and twisted it upward.

"Yes." But she knew she wasn't a woman. Not yet. Soon.

Five

Standing at her window, staring through the wavy glass, Susan watched the sharp ridge blacken in front of the sun. It looked like the Day of Creation had ended before the last lump of North Dakota soil had been smoothed down into its place. But she knew that wasn't true, because she didn't believe in God or Creation either, and the ridge was just hard sandstone that the wind ate more slowly than the rest of the land. From their farm, from her window at sunset, it was only a black stripe against the red sky.

"Susan May?"

"Mother?"

They had the same voices. Woodrow Wilson never knew who to go to when they both stood on the porch calling him, and he would run around the yard trembling with confusion. Even though he was bigger than the coyotes, they confused him, too, and he huddled under the porch at night when they howled, brown fur ruffed up around his neck, his whimpers smothered by the board roof.

"Time for bed. Too dark to read." Even in the kitchen, the kerosene lamp would be dimming, licking the grey chimney. "Time for bed," her mother said again. But she waited for Susan to open the door.

When they'd first moved to the house, something Susan couldn't remember except for the brown snapshots, there hadn't been any inside doors. The openings between rooms had been roughed out in green boards which shrank and warped in the winters when the rusty stove poured out heat during the day and then died cold in the night. Her father had hung curtains down in the rectangle to Susan's room so she could have some privacy after she'd gotten bigger, but even then the drafts kept pulling the flowered cotton in and out. When she'd had her thirteenth birthday, in June, he'd finally made this door for her, using boards he'd dried in the shed. Her mother had painted it that same night, the kerosene lamp making shadows so muddling that she couldn't get the paint to cover evenly. But the door still didn't fit just right.

"Susan May?"

Susan shoved the door open. Her mother's apron was stained with berry juice—chokecherry and wild plum. The fruit cellar under the house had rows of purple jars, fruit riding at the top in its struggle to breathe, water-juice at the bottom holding it afloat.

"If you dream out the window when it's almost dark, they'll come get you." Her mother started on the looped buttons down Susan's spine.

"Who?"

Her mother laughed. "The Indians. The Gypsies. The old gods in the myths. Maybe even the preacher, if he'd recognize us anymore." Her thumbs dug into Susan's back, straddling her spine. "Do you know that you're growing? Hold tight and pull in. I can barely get this unfastened."

The dress was grey cotton with prints of lilies. Susan didn't like it. Under her mother's digging, the next loop popped loose. "Stop that," Susan said, without moving away.

"You never did like this dress, did you?" Three buttons popped out of their loops. "And you picked it out of the catalog too." Her mother might have been angry, but she wasn't.

"What I liked was the *picture* of the dress." The girl wearing it had been as juicy as apple dumplings, Susan's favorite. She turned away and stepped out of the cloth heaped on the rag rug, then smoothed down her shift and arched her front out to see if they were growing yet. A little swell, like the hills.

"Well." Her mother opened the bureau. "Don't stand there naked. You'll have bad dreams." She handed Susan a nightgown, tatting around the hem. "Put this on now and settle in, my dear. I'll say good night."

That was the way it was every night, and she never embarrassed Susan by watching her undress all the way. Her father was even more shy and stayed as far away as he could get, chair pressed back into the kitchen wall, or better yet, out in the barn with the cows. He was a private man. He didn't mind living almost two miles from the Pritchards. That was near enough for neighbors.

Susan pulled the feather tick to one side and lowered herself, thinking, then swung her legs up and slid down onto the pillow. The clean nightgown smelled of sunshine. Out the window, the red stripe of the sky turned to war paint on a brave's cheek, and she painted his other cheek in her mind, then his forehead, hair slicked back with bear grease. She couldn't see all the flat ridge out her window, but she could see enough. And she knew what Indians looked like, too. Pearl for one, but also the others who sat on the general store steps in town. A group of them had their shacks out past Valhalla in the hollow where the grouse danced in the spring.

She'd seen their children, too, standing in layers behind their mothers, but they didn't go to school with her. It hadn't always been like that, she knew. The old ones once had horses, and sleds for their dogs to pull. Woodrow Wilson would have hated it, he was so lazy. They had tepees too.

Like pinching out a sliver, Susan squeezed her pillow with her hand inside the case and oozed out a tiny, tufted feather. The stuffing was supposed to be pure down, but her mother hadn't done the plucking. All of the other ladies left in bits of quill.

Usually Susan couldn't hear much outside, because her room was behind the kitchen, but as she played with the fluff along her broken quill, a coyote gave a yodel from the hills, and Woodrow Wilson broke into moans in the yard. Next came the thump as he scraped the board opening by the steps and scrambled underneath the porch. The coyote went at it again, and his friends joined in. It was early—the moon wasn't up yet—so something must have been going on.

Lulled by Woodrow's lament, Susan started to drift away, half lying in her bed, half walking along the hills. She pulled her knees up as near her chest as she could and wrapped her arms around them. Under the tick, only the heart of the quill stayed intact between her thumb and finger. Susan touched it between her lips and went to sleep.

She didn't know how much time had passed. What she did know was that there had been a noise and now there wasn't any. It was so black in the room that she had to check her eyes with her fingers to be sure they were open. Her mother and father would be asleep, and the coyotes had gone about their foraging. Woodrow Wilson was dreaming of the things he could scare, like prairie dogs. She was listening to the dark.

It had to be a dream. Someone stood by her bed. All she could see was a body like a straight tree. There was a smell too, sharp like blood. When she turned her head toward the door, the smell got stronger.

He said, "Come." The word was in her head without any noise at all.

Again he said, "Come." This time he covered her face with his hand.

Susan turned her head just a little, and he lifted his hand higher, then slid it around where her hair was. She hadn't unbraided it. He held the braid like a rein. "Come where?" she asked, practical, not even frightened at something so new she didn't have a name for it.

He gave her no answer. Maybe he hadn't heard. So Susan got up, and his hand slid back from her braid as it fell down her back. She wrapped the feather tick around herself so it was like she was in bed again. Even her feet weren't cold. She thought of her shoes, but first there were the long stockings, wrong side out in the dark, and then the shoes themselves, and then the laces to knot. There was no snow, anyway.

She opened the door in front of her, following him, and they stepped into the kitchen. The window was whitened from the new moonlight, but Susan still couldn't see enough to keep a clear path, and she bumped the reed basket where her mother kept the plums that were too rotted to can. She must not have had time to bury them in the garden. The basket scuffed along the floor a little, and she thought he might mind, but only Woodrow Wilson, under the porch, had anything to say, and it was just a whimper.

She didn't know where they were going. When he lifted her up on his pony, Susan wasn't surprised, and he sprang up behind her so quietly that she didn't know he was there until she felt the pressure down her back. Susan knew she must be riding, but she felt more like she was sailing with the wind that blew her home from school—obliged to stay in the rhythm or fall off. The pony's mane was next to her, and she ran her hand over the edge of the hairs. They felt like her own.

They were heading for the ridge, past the graveyard with the moon on the stones, though how could she see them so well when they were going so fast? When they got to the ridge bottom, they didn't even stop, but swept up a trail Susan had never seen, walled on both sides by flat rocks. Already the moon was gone and it was dark except for the splash of the Milky Way across the sky. Someone was singing, an old song, "Scarborough Fair" she thought, but the words were still "Come, come."

Should she go on, or go down, or stop for a while? Whatever happened would be all right. The tick was just as warm underneath as on top, and the air was warmer than she'd thought. When she looked straight up at the stars without tilting her head back, they filled her eyes, all the gods sending her their old light and telling her she was a good girl no matter what.

And when the dream was over, she was supposed to wake up in bed, go sleepily out to the kitchen to eat the breakfast waffles her mother had cooked on the old, black waffle iron that hung on the wall behind the stove. Susan used to take cold waffles out to the field for her father, each square wrapped in a scrap of flour sack so it wouldn't dry out. They would sit under a tree at the fence line together, the horses sweating in their traces behind the cultivator, and he would break off each crispy corner for her, because that was her favorite part. They would drink iced tea out of the same stoneware crock without even bothering to turn the lip around.

But that wasn't the way the dream ended. When she woke up in the morning, she was in the yard, as if she'd gone out looking for something, lying pressed up tight against the fragmenting boards by the steps of the porch, and Woodrow Wilson was lying next to her. His head was heavy across her chest, and when she reached out to shove it off so she could breathe, it flopped onto the ground without his waking at all. Her front was bloody. The coyotes had got him, she thought, or maybe even the wolves her father said were around. She didn't move except to turn her head to see if any animals were there and coming for her. The yard was empty, though. She rose and stepped over Woodrow, going up the porch steps on her hands and knees, because it was hard to straighten out so early in the morning, and she was cold. Her head hurt, too, as if she'd banged it on something.

The kitchen door was open, but the house wasn't warm at all, though her mother always got up before anyone else to poke the coals and bring in some new wood. Nobody was in the kitchen, but the calendar that usually hung over the table, the one with the children fishing on it, was on the floor. She stepped over it carefully because she had always liked the picture.

It was a long trip across the kitchen and into the living room and then to her mother and father's bedroom. The door was open, so she went in. In all her life, it had never before been open to her if they were inside.

At first, Susan thought her parents must have been asleep under their tick because it was still so cold. Then she saw the mess on the floor from the trunk, all the papers spilled by the bed. Her teeth were chattering. Nobody had built a fire yet. She said, "Mama," and then, "Daddy," but her voice was croaky in the morning, and she couldn't speak loud enough to wake them. They always slept soundly.

The blood was barely visible on him because it had all soaked into the mattress underneath. Her mother's throat was all cut open, though, and there was a lot of blood from that. She must have been rubbing her eyes awake when it happened, because one arm was over her face, and the soft white underside of it was sprinkled with red, like chokecherry juice.

A part of her wanted to climb in their bed and wash in their blood. A part of her wanted to die with them. But another part knew that something needed to be done, and that was the grown-up part. She walked out of the room, through the kitchen, down the steps, and started up the path toward the Pritchards' house. Already the flies were buzzing around Woodrow Wilson, but they left her alone. When she reached the dirt road, she turned and walked where she knew she should be going, but now the hard ground hurt her feet. She went to the side where the grass was softer, only it wasn't soft enough. The sun burned her hair, and finally she slid down into the ditch and crawled along it. That was easier. She didn't have to be grown up in the ditch. The grass above her covered the hot sky, and if she cried, the tears fell straight down. The earth soaked them in and never noticed a thing.

They never found out who'd killed them, even though the sheriff came out from Bismarck to check everything over. It could have been a farm worker, or a crazy man, or a strange Indian, or one of the group of foreigners who were building the branch railroad on the other side of the county. Sometimes, in the years that were to come, it seemed as if it might have been a force beyond them all, something from under or over the earth, because it changed her life so much. But then how did she know what her life might have been? No one could know that.

People tried to be nice, though. They lined up to take care of her for months afterward. The Kirschmeisters even brought a new puppy to the Pritchards' farm where she was staying. He had white fur with grey at the bottom of all the hairs, like shadows in snow. She drowned him the rain barrel.

Six

Every sunset was different. When the sky had been filled with clouds, grey swatches, the grey world would get thicker, pushing down toward the horizon. But sometimes the melting glow on the edge of the world would break through anyway—a great orange ball, cut off by the layer of grey. Then the black, quicker than ever. She mourned because the light was gone.

Now it didn't get dark until ten or eleven. The unnatural day of midsummer. The sky seemed a china bowl: blue, blue, licked like an ice cream cone, each tongue-curl fading the top until the blue grew into pale blue, memory of blue, white with blue memory behind it. The trees around the bottom stood out like a bulletin board border. No ridge, no Valhalla ridge.

Then, before she could put on her nightgown or put her book away or plan her dreams, one long cloud, lit orange underneath, moved over the horizon like a roof against the gods. The old ones who had dangerous powers. But they broke through anyway because they could fly or crawl, up or down. They could do anything.

In the marsh out back, redwings squabbled like third graders. They swayed on cattails, parabolas of feathers. Geometry, like last year in eighth grade. Her book still lay on her desk, opened to the page where she'd stopped studying on Memorial Day.

Her own room, almost like the old one. But not the same. Not far away, but she'd never gone back.

Tonight there had been Mrs. Pritchard's stew, carrots and turnips, soft bits of onion. Apple dumplings for dessert. She had taken hers upstairs. Crust like a starched bodice. And inside, the juice, the apple slices cut separately, thicker in their middles, crystallized in brown sugar and cinnamon, yet under the fork opening themselves to their own tart, earth-flavored hearts.

Seven

At first, Susan hadn't wanted to travel. But the Pritchards were obsessed with making her forget what had happened. They didn't even talk about the money she had inherited—little enough once the farm had been sold—but kept it set aside for her in the Valhalla bank until she should be old enough to spend it without pain. Susan knew it was there, but she had no interest in it. She had no interest in travel, either. When the Pritchards bought a Model T, already used but still functioning bravely, she felt as if they had done it to distract her.

She began to take long walks before the rest of them awoke. That meant getting up before dawn. It was easy in the summer when she could shift her bed so that the first lightening of the sky would wake her, but in the winter it was harder. When the sleet cracked against the window, she didn't even try. Instead, she read whatever book her hand fell upon in the dark, huddling next to the lamp on the table by her bed. The Pritchards had come from Minnesota and were powerfully drawn to its more civilized attractions. They had a small library about its geography, its places of interest, the history of its development. When they realized that Susan was a reader, they put the books in a case in her room. Their own children, grown now, had read exactly what they had to and no more.

The first trip that she finally conceded to take was to Itasca, where the Mississippi began. Just a little stream it was, flowing out of a grassy swamp as if it might end as soon as it turned out of sight. That wasn't so bad. It didn't even look like the Wittimac, or Mitty Creek either. The Model T had clattered along above the road so high it was almost like a covered wagon, and when they stayed with the minister's widow, who ran a boardinghouse in Sunset along the way, they'd had fried chicken to eat. The pieces didn't come out even in terms of how a chicken was designed, but afterward the widow had told Susan that she had gotten three chickens at once from her daughter and had cooked just the pieces she wanted. The ones that were left over, she had canned. Then she'd taken Susan down into her fruit cellar to show her the jars, the meat packed into brown gravy until it hardly looked like flesh. She was so matter-of-fact about it all, that Susan dreamed the next night of a line of women, some with five arms, some with none, dancing happily together.

So once the trips got started, they continued, and often. Susan knew the Pritchards felt they were doing the right thing. They visited Minneapolis and went to a concert. The music sounded like wind to her, or grasshoppers, or something falling and clattering all the way down. Sometimes it sounded like all of those things at once. She read her program over and over because at least the words made sense without sound. Not being musical didn't bother her. None of the old stories had been accompanied by music.

Then a relative of the Pritchards died and left them some money. They were frugal with it, but they did hire a girl to help them in the kitchen and do the laundry. She had grown up on the Standing Rock Reservation, but she was only part Indian. Like Pearl had been. Susan hadn't seen Pearl for a long time.

Sometimes they cooked in the kitchen together. The girl made fry bread, greasy little balls in the pan until suddenly they exploded into airy circles. If you put sugar on top, it was dessert. If you filled one with meat that you cooked with lots of pepper, it was supper.

"How can you make it so light?"

"All Indians can do that."

"Who taught you?"

Mary smiled. All the girls who went to the reservation school were named Mary, she'd said. No one called them by their own names anyway. They were just Indians.

"Who *taught* you?"

"My grandmother."

"How long ago?"

"Before I was born."

"That's not possible."

Mary smiled again. "I know," she said. She dropped another dollop of dough into the grease. "The boys learned how to shoot arrows from their grandfathers. It didn't matter who was alive. The girls learned fry bread."

Susan reached out her hand to the brown elbow. "Tell me the truth," she said.

Mary turned her head toward the window, where a wind was stirring the curtain. Before that, it had been hot and silent. "The old ones teach us whether we know it or not," she said and lifted the fry bread from the pan, light and hollow as the breath of God.

Eight

"We know only the minimum about her."

"Parents dead." Mr. Olsen set the folder aside.

"She did extremely well in high school."

"Wants to be a teacher."

"An appropriate ambition."

"Perhaps the Fletcher Fund would be better used for a young man. Of whom we could be sure for a stated number of years. She may marry. And then . . ."

"Of course, no one knows what the future will bring." Miss Maak thought extensively about the future of education. It was indeed difficult to predict.

"That's true."

Mr. Olsen opened the folder again. "Taylor's Studio. Most of them are satisfied with a snapshot. Vain?"

"Perhaps only young."

"She reminds me of my niece. Good to see that they don't all bob their hair." Mr. Oliphant was bald himself, resignedly so.

"An attractive young lady."

"Very strong chin."

"But that is no indicator of any specific negative trait."

"Of course not."

"Exactly how much does the Fund have available?"

"For the first year, two hundred. Two hundred fifty after that. Conditional on academic achievement, of course. Renewable until the degree."

Miss Maak fingered the photograph. "Other resources?"

"Hard to determine. Her home is North Dakota. Her high school was Valhalla."

"The gods must approve."

"Hardly a matter with which they would concern themselves, I might guess."

"After all, at Belfontaine Normal, we should hope that the Norse spirits would accept their due honor in the classroom without excessive intrusion otherwise." Mr. Oliphant was United Brethren, however scholarly in other ways.

"Her required essay shows considerable sophistication."

"Perhaps a dangerous sign."

"But if sophistication in both thought and grammar exists in one essay, then one is allowed considerable hope."

"I would agree."

"The final list?"

"If you include the young man from Minneapolis."

"Of course."

"Perhaps a personal interview?"

"I would confirm that."

"Full name?"

"Susan May McIntire."

"A Scotswoman."

"No doubt."

"An intelligent people, the Celts."

Nine

"You wouldn't dare do that, you devil, Susan. Don't even try. Oh, all right. Try. That's right. Try again. Yes. Yes."

Flat on her back on the quilt, arms out straight to the sides, Susan's very best friend, Lucianne Allen Bowles, turned her head and smiled. Around her hair, the pink ribbon was mashed against the pillow. God was watching. They didn't care.

"I not only would dare, I would do."

"If your mother was alive, she'd die."

"She isn't, so she can't."

"*If* she was."

"*And* she isn't. I like doing what I want to, not what I have to." Susan flung her braid over her shoulder. "I don't have-to anything. That's the way I want it."

"You have to breathe." Lucianne arched her back, her blouse tightening. She was one of the flat-in-front ones, even in Belfontaine Normal. But not entirely.

"And shit."

"Bad!"

"*You* say." Susan farted, giggled. She had taught herself to do it whenever she liked. Then she sat up. "Your parents expect us to be lining up the rows out there, girl. Putting in the lettuce, too. Before the wind changes. It's cold, my dear Lucianne, and snow is a distinct possibility." Out the tall window in the corner, the clouds answered yes. "We're on the outer margin of safety. Our tongues could soon be frozen to the pump handle if we keep on being wicked."

"All right." Lucianne bounced on the wobbling mattress, got up, burrowed her feet into her outdoor shoes tucked half under the bed. From the wardrobe, she yanked out her garden coat, the raggedy one with the big plaid print. "Let's plant. I'll hold the string and you unreel it. I can't believe my father plowed that patch up already. He must have had to chop through ice. I want to go back to Ohio."

"Iowa."

"Indiana."

"Pennsylvania."

"New Jersey." Their faces were straight as sticks.

"The Universal Universe."

"The Popperding of Mankind."

"The Witch's Womb."

"Let's go plant, dummy." They both put their spring mittens on, one layer of yarn instead of two, yanking them up over their palms. The wool was grainy from not having been carded properly before it had been spun. There were still farm grandmothers who sheared and carded and spun and knitted, and one of them was Lucianne's, although the old lady was half blind and dribbled when she ate. Grandma Bowles knitted like she breathed and had a whole pie chest full of accumulated products, layered like woolly ears on top of each other. You could choose as many as you wanted.

"Let's go." They were big girls, women, too old to run down the stairs with the brown carpeting, brass rods holding it flat at the inner angles, too old to race through the living room and the front hall, giggling and pushing at each other. Susan brushed a Boston fern, which wobbled on its stand. She felt its fronds tickle inside her.

Outside, the wind was sharp, stirring up the leftover berry clumps on the black ash and spinning the shrubbery twigs. Along the fence to the plowed garden, a series of bushes had sent up new, succulent red spires. Susan tried to break one, but although she tugged and twisted, even spitting on her woolly palm for a better grip, it ended up staying attached. She shrugged and moved on.

Lucianne and Susan. Twinned but not sisters. Tangled in sheaves of gardening string and pulling so hard to mark the row straight that they both ended up sitting in the dirt. Both in normal school at Belfontaine, studying to be teachers, favorites of their own teachers with their test scores, their pinafores, their hair shiny from being washed in beer and rainwater. Susan lived on campus in the dark-framed dormitory by Old Main. She'd been boosted back in the first-floor window so often after evening curfew that her good shoes had scuffed toes. Lucianne lived just outside of town and had a big bed of her own. She shared it without asking. Susan had been to Minneapolis and Duluth, had waded in the Mississippi where it started to be a river, had sopped her hem and made damp lines in the sand with her skirt.

Lucianne pointed up, holding her billowing dress down with her left hand. "Look, Susan." The wind snapped and walloped, the cloth beat against her arm like a flag. "I think the sun's coming out. Shall we cheer?" She flung both her arms above her head and hopped in the air, the toes of her outdoor shoes together off the ground. Caught in the whirlwind, her skirt flew out in a circle with her petticoat layering under it. When she landed, she skidded down flat on her back, and Susan made twins next to her.

"Not the sun! He doesn't shine till June!" Their faces were polished from the wind. Underneath them, the careful string they'd hooked up for the first lettuce row twanged into the dirt. Susan beat her heels. "Mud angels!" She ground her shoulder blades deeper, hands flung out in the sod, wet and cold and molded full of blackness. A last dry leaf blew across her lips and then on up into the air.

"Susan May?"

"What?" Underneath the yielding earth, there rested a layer of warmth, but she could feel it only if she held very still.

Lucianne watched the leaf. "We're crazy."

"Of course."

"We shouldn't."

"Who says?"

"That's why people get married."

"I'm not marrying."

"Don't you want children?"

Susan ran her finger down Lucianne's mittened palm. "No. I want to hunt free. Like Diana. Silver as the moon."

"Can I visit?"

"You're the nearest star."

"There's that boy in Educational Practices. He likes you."

"He doesn't know me in any important way."

They rolled toward each other in the mud. Noses together, they blinked into each other's eyes.

"His name is Richard. He's been after you a long time. But you always had a book in front of you. You should let him get a word in."

"I only listen to my own words." Susan cupped her hands by her ears.

"He might turn into a parfit gentil knyght."

"Or a parfit gentil ogre. With a warty chin."

"He could support you. Then you wouldn't have to teach school after next year in some shack at the end of the world. No blizzards to fight. No ashes to dump." Lucianne tested the wind, cooling her finger in it. "Just give him a chance. I'll bet he's got it all planned out."

"You can take care of me."

"*You* can take care of *me*."

"I *can* take care of you. If I want."

"Do you?"

"Maybe."

They lay together. Then they both giggled. Susan took Luci-anne's hand and pulled her up.

"Richard Carson."

"He's probably Swedish."

"English. Welsh. Irish. Watch out for those people."

"Shoulders like a coat hanger going down the hall."

"Blond eyebrows, black lashes. Bad luck, that." Lucianne fur-rowed her forehead.

"How good are his grades?"

"Middling. Probably wants to be a farmer."

"He wrote a letter to the school paper once, I do believe."

"*You* wrote eight times. And they were all published."

Susan pulled away, bent to the row. Richard. Did he dream her? All she dreamed was a spring garden with Lucianne, pressing the clay lumps, damp from the melted snow between her fingers, until they transformed into paste. What she dreamed was the two of them flat on their backs at the end of the tangled row, looking up at the Minnesota sky. She didn't miss anybody, hardly, so how could she want a new person to miss? Especially somebody with white eyebrows. Susan and Richard. Susan and Lucianne.

"Penny for your thoughts."

"What?"

"Penny for your thoughts." Lucianne's finger lined the row, a tiny trench with lips on each side. The seed packages stuck out of her coat pocket.

"None, dummy."

"I'll bet."

"None that I'd tell you." The thoughts were sliding over the ridges in her brain. Richard started across from the other side, just above her left ear. Fog swirled, and he was gone.

"Well, if you're not thinking, then I'm planting." Lucianne pulled out the seed packets, two to start with, and gave Susan one.

"All right." Susan yanked off her mittens. "You want them?" she asked, turning to Lucianne.

"Absolutely." Lucianne took the two mittens and wedged them into her coat pocket. "I'll do this end. You start the other." She shook her seed packet, ripped the top open, then slid the seeds, black as pepper, out in her hand. "We'd better hurry up, Susan. I'm freezing."

Susan walked to the other end of the row, the turned soil clogging the edges of her shoes. Her feet straddled the black line; somebody looking would have thought she'd grown a tail that dragged in the dirt behind her. Richard Carson, Richard Carson. Snapshots of teaching rose from the book of her brain. A rural school, alone on the prairie. Then the furrows leading to it, farmers' children marching along them like lettuce seeds. Inside, a wood-burning stove with silver letters beaded into the iron around the door. Sopping boots steamed. But Richard had oozed into the furrows, flat colorless hair a doily on the mud. She flattened it with her dainty teacher's boot, giggling. The children applauded.

Her hand cupped the black seeds, slid them out between finger and thumb. She was bent over, the wind whisking against her legs and into the slit of her skirt. Naughty. She pushed the skirt back down with the hand that wasn't dealing out lettuce, but the cloth kept flapping. Lucianne was coming down the row toward her, hair in a stew around her head. Her fingers walked an inch above the wet earth. The seeds fell.

Then Susan found the arrowhead. Everything was black: the seeds, the soil, even the stubs of last year's plants that hadn't gotten plowed under. The clouds were darkening too, wrapping the sun away. The trees along the windbreaks below the garden stood like black turkey-feather dusters. Only the arrowhead sent the colors back instead of soaking them up. She picked it up in her right hand, and then held her left hand crosswise underneath. Against even her own light flesh, the arrowhead was whiter yet, as if it had never been born in the black dirt, as if the spring rains had washed it clean to its core of whiteness. The point was so sharp that when she touched it, she felt a pricking chill on the edge of pain. Every flint chip lay layered on the next like fish scales. At the bottom it had a tiny shaft, just enough to knot a willow-stick arrow with a buckskin thong.

"What do you have?" Lucianne's voice touched her ear like a dry leaf.

"An arrowhead."

"Oh, you lucky thing! I never found one so near home." Lucianne held out both hands. "What color is it?"

"It's white."

"Show me."

"On Halloween."

"Susan!" Lucianne made a grab but came up short.

"I said Halloween. When we haunt. When we dress up like the

old gods."

"But I'm your best friend!"

"Not until you tip over a privy with me."

"Boys do that!"

"Then I'll ask Richard Carson."

Lucianne put her arms around her friend and nuzzled her shoulder. "Please, please, please," she said. "Richard's no good. He has crooked teeth."

"But don't you want me to marry him?"

"Yes. Maybe. Because . . ."

"Because why?"

"Because the other way is the hard way. Now will you let me see your arrowhead?"

But Susan didn't, not even after the lettuce had been entirely planted.

Ten

Miss Retherath was uncomfortable. College was for the accumulation of knowledge, for the transfer of that knowledge to young minds who would then transfer that same knowledge, slightly freshened, to even younger minds on the outreaches of civilization. In the classroom, firmly anchored behind her lectern with its oak boards fronting her bosom, her voice rose, the sacred chariot freighted with the names of poets, the births of heroes, the heath and heather of blessed England. Outside, prairie roses transmogrified themselves into Wordsworthian daffodils about which the beloved poet himself had written so eloquently. In the previous decades, she had dreamed herself Dorothy to his William. Foolish, of course. The sacred sisterly bond.

But all could not be spiritually attuned. It was, for instance, a necessary professorial obligation that she perform less attractive duties such as tonight's judging of the Belfontaine Normal Halloween Costume Contest. Her lack of athletic ability, traceable to her ample physique, prevented her from direct supervision of girls' basketball, while Miss Polgowski had done the French Club since its origin. This specific Halloween assignment had fallen to her as if fated.

Planted on her foolish judge's throne, Miss Retherath allowed her eyes to circle the school gymnasium. The maroon velvet curtain on the stage was pulled tight as a backdrop for the contestants, and the gym itself was more than half full even though it was a Saturday night. The costume contest, well publicized as wholesome recreation with posters and newspaper editorials, drew dozens of student participants, cheered on by their compatriots. Extensive chaperonage attempted to keep it seemly, and appropriate judging was guaranteed. Miss Retherath took even forced responsibility with the utmost seriousness.

However, despite the normal school's efforts at organization, the evening had elements of tomfoolery. More than thirty students were waiting to have their costumes judged, and the gymnasium held a good number who, while not officially contestants, considered themselves participants as much as observers. They sat on the bleachers, several among them, Miss Retherath was stunned to observe, in bloomers and fragile linen tops. A number carried paper jack-o'-lantern faces elevated on sticks. There was constant noise and a riotous aspect which Miss Retherath was hard put to relate to anything literary, especially in the British tradition. Irish, perhaps, where the more primitive impulses were rife. She was uncomfortable without her lectern and without her yellow lecture notes, benisoned by age.

When the announcements had been made and the noise somewhat suppressed, the costumed lineup began to emerge from the locker-room door to the right. Each student was greeted with ardent cheers from his or her supporters. Because the administration had imposed the theme of "Great Figures from the Past," some conformity was required, and among the first to parade across the stage was a George Washington, white peruke askew, and a rotund little girl with a blue waistcoat, Napoleonic hat, and sword. Miss Retherath recognized her as a home economics major from Videla County. The sword clanked against the stage floor, occasionally stabbing at her ankle. Even at the considerable distance, Miss Retherath could see her wince.

After the first dozen or so, Miss Retherath found herself relaxing. They had been reasonably creative. A few were whimsical, including a Puck with a pointed cap and the Spalson twins portraying Jacob and Esau. Esau wore several sheepskins, which hung loosely against the kettle of pottage which he was clutching. Miss Retherath marked them a seven on her ballot, then changed the rank to an eight. She felt a quiver of ambivalence since there were, after all, two of them.

Perhaps because of her preoccupation with careful judging, she did not immediately notice the young woman who stalked out of the locker-room door after the twins. Nor did she hear the footfalls on the steps to the stage, the feet being bare. But when she raised her eyes, expecting a Julius Caesar or a Robin Hood, she saw a silver figure, slim as a boy, with a loose drift of brown hair that floated around it. To her horrified eyes, it became stunningly clear that the figure was wearing nothing, or perhaps something fitted so tightly to the young body that it was as good as nothing. However, with the hair, the upper part of the body was sufficiently covered. The lower part was another matter. Over the *mons veneris* (she had read the expression in the Sonnets, yes she had, though of course she had never taught anything so daring) was a pair of large green leaves crossed as swords on a heraldic shield.

"Susan!" came a voice from the audience, but everyone else was paralyzed into silence. The figure glided across the stage. From behind its back, it pulled a scrolled paper, unrolled it. With thick green letters, it read *Paradise Lost*. The silver arms held it high.

Eleven

The snow fell. Great gobs, whipped cream, hitting the dormitory window. Then sometime in the night, the temperature having fallen, the snow changed to an icy sweep that clattered along the glass. The shrubs under the window were gone, not even twigs sticking through, and when morning finally arrived, a sullen grey that didn't mark out the world so much as obscure it, Susan knew that the true spring blizzard had come.

She was hungry.

Down the hall, slippers sluffed along the linoleum. Someone banged the door, giggled, banged more gently. From so deep down in her pillow that its white walls fluffed up on each side, Susan said, "Come in."

"It's locked!"

"Don't come in, then."

More giggles. Theresa.

"Tell me what you want through the door."

"I'm making popcorn."

"For breakfast?"

"Yes, I am, Susan. They canceled classes. This morning, anyway."

Susan rose to her feet, plucked her clothes from where she'd deposited them around the room. "I'm going to Food Hall," she said over her shoulder. Theresa was running her fingers along the edges of the door like mice.

"You're crazy. It's freezing out there."

"Not even zero."

"How do you know?"

"I've made it up."

Theresa tapped once more, ping-ponging on the doorknob. "I'll save some popcorn for you. Dessert." She padded off.

Dry early-morning mouth. Licking behind her teeth, starting the juices, Susan bent over the end of her bed to the window, rested her hands on the sill. Sinfully dark for whatever time it was. Sleet-strings rasped the glass. She slid herself into her dress, buttoned on her wool coat, unearthed her boots from under the bed. White bands of mold, borders of former damp, marked circles around them. She zipped them on, the hard rubber on the tops digging into her calves. The spring mittens from Lucianne's grandmother. A woolly headpiece, knotted under her chin. Her uncombed hair zigzagged out in front. In back, she tucked in her braid, not unraveled yet.

One last thing. A scarf. She wrapped it around the bottom of her face, snuffling in the damp warmth.

Outside it was truly impossible to see a thing. Like the books said. The Arctic, death in an igloo. A child would have been swept away. Because the flakes were so icy, it hurt to look up into them, and Susan found herself peering through her wrapped fingers, funneling the snow away from her eyes. Down the steps first, her feet anchoring themselves in the heaps of snow. Had everyone else given up on breakfast? She could go back and eat graham crackers from the box under her bed. Drink tea from the hot plate in Theresa's room, gobble inappropriate popcorn.

No. The hedges on both sides of the walk gauntleted her like spear-bearers. She had to stay between them. At the curb, she stepped off into the carpet of whiteness. Not a horse, not a car, nothing except the wind and a solid greyness blocking the light. Like being in a mouth, chewing and chewed. The ribbed sky pressed down through her skull.

The breakfast bell? It was only the whine of the wind.

Food Hall, the cafeteria, was a block away, round behind Old Main. She'd shortcut it, go down through the corner park designed for the training school children. Her feet had already stopped being; she walked on silent space boxed in below her ankles. When the slide ladder loomed in front of her, she pulled back. Snow ate at the tops of her boots, nuzzled her kneecaps. Inside her coat, inside her skin, her organs yearned toward each other, nudging into the narrowing warmth.

Past the slide stood the merry-go-round, cake on a pedestal. Then the jungle gym, roofed over. The swings were the last, next to the street that ran in front of Food Hall. Each one was loafed in snow. The wind danced them like friends.

She saw Richard just when she sat down, perching herself in the middle of a loaf. Crazy, too, stalking in the snow like he owned it. Going the other way, not cutting across. Not looking her direction. Couldn't see her unless—her move.

She pumped up, snowplowing the ground. He stopped, mummied in white. She pumped up again, giggled. Snow filled her mouth. Like biting cotton, swabbing all her teeth. Like eating clouds.

"Who's that?"

Susan let the question float.

"Who's that?"

The swing lifted free. Her boots pushed into the flakes, cutting tunnels. They touched the air on each side of his face.

"Susan?"

His eyelashes were roofed with white.

"You're crazy!"

She pointed her toes to see if she if she could touch his ears on each side.

"Get *off* there!"

She pushed higher. She could sail over his head, snowball herself into the crusty clouds.

Richard stopped, lunged for the swing. It batted against his grasp. She slid back, her knees hooking over the board seat. Her bottom dragged in the drifts.

"Get up!"

"No!" She pulled at him, laughing. Food Hall was curtained off with white. A blurring gust, then the top of the slide sliced through the white air.

"You shouldn't be out in this."

"Don't tell me what I should do."

They stood in the snow, hands up like boxers. Their breaths circled their mouths, cloud in cloud. The spring snow fell like it would never end.

Twelve

"We could buy the one in Arenbergs Jewelry. Or the one at Evershams. They were both good values."

"I know."

"I thought you liked the one at Arenbergs better. The one with the pearl. I thought you liked that one."

"I did like that one. But the other one was all right, too."

"No matter which one we decide on, you'll have a gold band for the wedding."

"Yes."

"That's all right with you, isn't it?"

"It's all right."

"When we decide, what will you do with that old ring?"

"What?"

"The old ring you wear."

"I haven't thought about it."

"Wear it on your right hand?"

"Maybe."

"Did you get it from your mother? It has that old setting with the filigree. Now they do it solid."

"No. Not my mother."

"Did you buy it?"

"No. You know I never buy jewelry for myself. It's Lucianne's. She lent it to me."

"I didn't know that."

"No, you didn't."

"She'll probably want you to give it back."

"I don't think so."

Thirteen

"We should have gotten her pot holders. The best shower present."

"Just how many pot holders would anyone require?"

"You know what I mean. Kitchen things. A soup ladle. A decent eggbeater, so she wouldn't have to use a whisk. Not crazy old books." Julia crossed her eyes in an effort to see as she tapped powder on the blur of her nose.

"I don't think she cooks. Might spill something on Shakespeare."

"Well, not in the dorm, of course. But Susan will learn what she needs to know. I have no doubt that anyone who could persuade Miss Retherath to cough up the only A in three years of British Literature could learn to conquer a sponge cake if she didn't already know."

"I think Retherath just got tired of arguing."

"Susan never raised her voice."

"Never lowered it either. Every paper on time, too."

"Jealous, Theresa?"

"Not in the least. All those poets died of consumption anyway. I'm going to live forever."

Outside, the air was transparent with sunlight. Any eye could see through the window all the way down to the Belfontaine River. Food Hall glimmered as if its brick facade had candles in it. The thermometer had been on ten below zero for a week, steady as a faithful lover. No January thaw yet.

"We should have had this in a real party place. A wedding shower is a real party."

"I think this room is perfectly respectable."

"Did you sweep up the graham cracker crumbs?"

"Susan's the one with the crackers. You know that." Theresa tossed her hair, huffed, then grinned. Lucianne grinned back. Merwyn and Cecily tapped the edges of the little table, a teapot next to the neatly arranged cups. It did look like a real party, almost. Tea, cream, lump sugar, each lump wrapped in ornamental tinfoil. Imported from England. Julia's father wholesaled them.

"Will she be late?"

"What's late? She'll be here after she gets her activity fee back."

"How long can that take?"

"It depends on how hard she has to argue."

"She's not the first person to leave midyear."

All of them were quiet.

"Well, she isn't. She can finish at any Minnesota state normal. All her credits transfer."

"If you don't wait too long."

"How long would she wait?"

"Why don't you ask her?" Merwyn rearranged the cookies, gingersnaps on the outside, fat macaroons heaped together in the middle. Fingers of crisp coconut thrust out from them. Lucianne's mother had baked them even though it meant grating a real coconut. Mr. Bowles had brought one from Minneapolis the week after Christmas.

Lucianne stood at the window, the light slicing down her front. "I don't ever want to get married," she said.

Everyone was perfectly silent.

"I don't want to sacrifice myself to some man." She pulled her hair back. "I don't believe they ever sacrifice themselves for you."

"Pessimist."

"Richard's as positive a prospect as any."

"They're doing it now because of him." Theresa sat on the bed, sandwiched between Cecily and Eleanor. "He's got enough credits for *his* diploma. Then his uncle got sick and couldn't run the hardware store. I told you already, Julia."

"It's a good professional opportunity."

"I never was in Manatee."

"Well, it's almost to Wisconsin. I never was, either."

"Where will they live?"

"Didn't Susan tell you? He rented a house. Probably has the drapes up already, linoleum down, cupboard hinges oiled. Susan didn't have any say. They can move right in as soon as they get there."

"They were going to wait until June to get married."

An icicle fell, crashing off the eaves like a blade of glass. Everyone jumped, shifted, settled back.

"Susan said being married in January has to be good luck because it can only get warmer."

"I still think we should have gotten her kitchen things."

Lucianne stood up. The crystal light burned through her hair, frizzing it like wire. "The important thing is that she knows we know what she really likes. Now and forever. She can carry the encyclopedias with her no matter where they end up."

"They aren't even new, Lucianne."

"They sure aren't."

"That's the point."

"She'll think we're crazy."

"No, she won't."

"They're valuable because of their antiquity. The ninth edition. 1889. The *Britannica* at its best. Even Retherath would approve."

Eleanor, wrapped in a plaid skirt that hung on her, asked the essential question. "Do you really think she'll like them?"

"You know Susan."

"Of course she will."

"Well, then." They waited. "Bring them out, Theresa."

Theresa went to the closet, opened the door. "I worried all week that she'd want to borrow a dress. Even in the back, the box stuck out. I draped my underwear over it." She rummaged. "For Susan's shower, I was willing to collect room demerits. But crazy Miss Shelton never checked."

Wrenching, Theresa maneuvered the box out. All twenty-five volumes were inside. Their bindings were padded leather. The nearest girls poked them.

"I like the gold on top."

"This is the deluxe edition. Not the cheap one."

"Weighs more than pot holders. Or eggbeaters."

"Consider them brain furnishing. Shower of gold. Zeus and Athena."

Lucianne peered out the window. "Stop," she said. "They're coming. He's with her."

All six young women crowded against the window. Lucianne heaved it open, sat herself on the sill, leaned outward. Theresa grabbed her hips and braced her own self back into the room. Merwyn and Eleanor flanked her. The frame was full of cloth, bodies, crowded solid. They blocked the light like an eclipse.

"Are there enough?" Merwyn reached out for a spear of ice.

"Plenty," grunted Lucianne.

"Hurry up!"

And as Richard and Susan rounded the corner, came down in front of the dormitory, raised their eyes to the giggles that had coalesced into a chitter of noise like vagrant January birds, they were greeted by a shower of icicles, plunging spearlike to the pavement, shattering into wisps of silver, glittering on the frozen ground.

Fourteen

"Some people carry bricks in the trunk on purpose in winter, Richard."

"Not twenty-five giant-sized ones."

The landscape was all white and grey like a book illustration. Rolling farm hills touched the sky and melted into it. On both sides next to the road, lumpy with January ice, the snow fences stretched on to the horizon. In Minnesota, in winter, they held the drifts in line as much as anything could.

"Actually, it's only twenty-four. I've got the first volume up here." Susan's foot touched her carpetbag on the floor under the dashboard.

"Some women carry clothes."

"Richard, I've got plenty of those."

"I know." A smile came up between his cheeks. "It's not your clothes I'm interested in anyway." His eyes stayed on the road.

"I suppose not."

Last night they had stayed in the Jeffritz Hotel on the north edge of Belfontaine. He had wanted it that way; they could have set right out. After they were done and he'd gone to sleep, she'd washed, but in less than a minute after she'd turned the water on, the hot had stopped running. So she had scrubbed herself with cold water, raising goose bumps from one end of her body to the other. The radiator clanked and moaned, struggling with the impossible burden of bringing June to a Minnesota January.

It had been past midnight when Susan had walked to the window. Richard slept on, a clean line down the middle of the bed. His hands were straight at his sides, his legs tight together like a diver's. Even his toes were aiming somewhere. Manatee? His uncle's store? Their future together?

Well. She'd know soon enough.

Outside the hotel window, Belfontaine had showed not a sign of life. Across the street paraded a line of frame storefronts. Campbells Dry Goods. DRUGS in neon. In the next block was Barney's Bar, dim at that hour except for the Magic Water Beer sign. Snow plowed from the street had been piled along the sidewalks where it had solidified into small mountain ranges. Under the dim streetlights, their ridges and crevices had caught the shadows.

In the morning, they had eaten breakfast in the hotel restaurant. The sky was still black. When she had laid her hand on the table next to her coffee cup, Richard had put his over it. The waitress, bringing their eggs, had pretended not to notice. Steam rose from the plates.

But now it was only grey, no longer black. And they must be at least halfway there. Susan opened the encyclopedia, which she had hoisted into her lap. "Aberdeen," she said.

"What?"

"Aberdeen. Abyssinia. Achilles. Acts of the Apostles."

"Do you plan to educate me?"

"Africa. Agrarian Laws. Agriculture. Richard, there are pages on agriculture."

"I wouldn't mind running a horse farm. Breeding stock. Once Uncle John's store is on an even keel."

"Algae."

"I'll let that one pass. Susan, this is one book full of useless information. And twenty-four more in the trunk."

Susan moved the volume closer to her stomach. "Alchemy," she read. "Abelard."

"You're not following the alphabet."

"I'm flicking back and forth." She shifted her back against the seat, moved her head forward. "Richard, remember him? In Medieval History?"

"The one with Heloise? That was a dead course in every way."

"See what it says here. 'Taking him defenceless, perpetrated on him the most brutal mutilation.'"

"Sounds mighty unpleasant. Go back to Agriculture."

"It really happened, Richard."

"Served them right."

"They loved each other."

"I doubt the *Encyclopedia Britannica* says that."

"Well, it gives him two full pages. Their bones mingled, did you know that? And 'marvelously preserved.'"

"For God's sake, Susan, read something else. Or don't read."

Susan looked out the window. Minnesota went on forever. It seemed like they should be in Michigan by now, at the very least. Yet they were still passing the little farms, each farmhouse skewered by a straight line of smoke on this cold, windless Sunday.

"How far now?"

"Two hours. Three. More like two."

"Will we stop to eat?"

"Nothing's open on Sundays except the hotels. And there's only one more town big enough. Rogersville. We'd better hold out."

"Can we eat in Manatee?"

"The house should have what we need."

"How can you be sure?"

"Susan, I arranged it. I won't starve my bride. I take care of my things." The Ford hummed as if casting a vote in affirmation.

"Body and soul?"

"Yes."

"Mind?"

"You've got the ninth edition of the *Britannica*. I wouldn't compete with that."

Susan held Volume One across her lap, its comforting weight pressing permanent wrinkles into her going-away skirt. Going away. And still the Minnesota farmhouses marched across the grey, each perfectly separated from the next.

"Alphabet. Altar. Amazons."

"For once and for all, settle the breast issue. One? Two?"

Susan skimmed down the page. "It says here that the word *Amazon* really means 'strong-breasted.' Like Diana, their goddess. Or from a Greek word that means 'not touching men.'"

"Women and men were meant to be together. No Amazons in Minnesota."

"They're hiding."

Richard reached for her knee, but the book covered it up. He burrowed, then moved his fingers back to the steering wheel.

Susan kept looking. "Adam," she said. "Ammunition. Aesthetics." She touched the gold leaf on the tops of the pages, matching it to her ring as best she could in the grey light that filtered into the Ford.

"Anatomy."

"Anesthesia."

Fifteen

The McMillans lived next door. No one in Manatee knew Susan was a Scotswoman too, and she had never confessed.

Peter McMillan had a face like a dried apple doll, though he was only forty. He was a cabinetmaker. "Not a carpenter," he said the very first day they arrived, as he stood in their cold kitchen with his arms around his wife's gift of two loaves of bread, a chiffon cake, sweet rolls still giving forth waves of hot cinnamon. "I build the inside things." He had turned his garage into his shop, and on sticky summer nights when the air held moisture, the sliced woods he'd been working with scented the breeze that tracked between their houses. He never seemed to pound, only to scrape, to sand, to drill with the big manual bit that sent lines of shavings out of the holes like dancing snakes. People brought old furniture to him and stood over it with pleading eyes while he touched every splintered joint, checked angles, stroked wood that still held solid. When he couldn't make it perfect again, he only charged half the usual price.

Mrs. McMillan was named Bertha. Her face was so firm over her skull that sweat popped off her forehead when she baked. Through their hall window, with the stained glass in the top half, Susan's eyes looked right into Mrs. McMillan's kitchen where her red face rose and fell like the sun as she peeled, dunked, mixed, molded, kneaded, steamed, sliced.

"You don't eat enough to keep a bird alive, Mrs. Carson," she said on the third day when she came to collect her cake pan, bringing a loaf of banana bread along. They sampled it together, and Mrs. McMillan's eyes counted the crumbs left on Susan's saucer. Then, two days later, "You eat like a sparrow, Susan." Which was true, by Mrs. McMillan's standards. But the food kept coming, every week, sometimes every day. Richard developed a small round belly from trying to keep up. At night in bed, he tapped it gently with his fingers. Susan stayed thin until the baby started to grow. Then all her body woke up, blooming from the inside out. Mrs. McMillan bounced with the news until she had to hook her toes on the side rungs of Susan's kitchen chair to keep herself from rising, like yeast. She had none of her own.

On the other side were the Togenroths. Their three boys, twelve, thirteen, and fourteen, slept all summer in the backyard, curled under an oilcloth roof rigged between the two elms that framed the back of their property. When the fireflies came out, the boys chased them around the yard, cupping their hands around the captured glows. They slept out until the frosts started coming two or three times a week. Then they gathered everything together, the summer's worth of firefly jars, the old blankets, the oilcloth faded into a mottled checkerboard. Their parents hardly seemed to notice that they had moved back into the house.

Across the street were the Zittners, retired since before the World War. She had a wheelchair, the kind made with a woven cane back and wooden wheels. Her husband pushed her to church every Sunday and on Wednesdays, too, during Lent. In her hands she held a large blue purse with a golden clasp. It covered her entire front, and she held her chin out above it with such pride that Susan often considered the possibility that something magic was inside—a silver crown, a book of spells, an arrowhead.

That first fall, before the Togenroth boys had moved inside, when the Indian summer filled the days with a golden sunlight, Mrs. Zittner sat outside every afternoon. Her husband came home from the post office for lunch and then pushed her out to the front sidewalk when he went back to sort the afternoon's mail. She stayed there until suppertime, occasionally rotating her head with such slow control that Susan would watch her with fascination from the front window. On Wednesday, when Susan was watching her legitimately because she had to leave for the library to return her nine books ("No one takes out as many as you, Mrs. Carson"), Mrs. Zittner got out of her wheelchair as if she had been resting there briefly between tasks and knelt in the perennial border along her walk. For half an hour she garnered out the dead stems, snapping them off with both hands. Occasionally she smiled. Susan watched for the entire time, the books towering under her breasts, and when she finally moved to set them on the table, her cotton front was imprinted with their bindings.

When she had finished, Mrs. Zittner got up and sat back down in her wheelchair. She was a neat woman, and when Susan greeted her on the way to the library, the books in her carpetbag this time, there was not a gardening mark on her.

"Mrs. Zittner?" Richard just stared at Susan when she told him at supper.

"Yes."

"Maybe she fell out."

"Amazing that she landed in the best position for gardening."

He snorted and began to read the paper, back to front. That way he never had to worry about finishing it.

There were others she knew besides the McMillans, the Togenroths, and the Zittners. On their side of the street, the backyards ran down to farmland, planted to alfalfa now because the soil was right, and the man who owned it, Mr. Retzlaff, had a cattle operation. Mostly beef, but enough dairy cows to provide milk for his family, of which there were forty-three members. That counted children's spouses and grandchildren. They were all Roman Catholic and proud of it.

Only the youngest son, Elwin, had anything of interest to offer. Susan had met him at Richard's hardware store, which even had Richard's name on the lease now that his uncle was sinking fast. It had been Susan's third spring in Manatee, and she wasn't showing yet. Elwin had been buying seeds, even though it was too early for seeds, despite it being March and officially spring. Standing on opposite sides of the rack, the two of them had both spun it against each other at the same time. Then they had hesitated. When the had attempted to turn it again with the same result, they had both stuck their heads out and peered at each other. He had laughed first.

"You know it's too early to plant, don't you?" he said.

"I'm feeding my soul."

"Would it prefer broccoli or sweet corn?"

"It would prefer climbing roses and bachelor's buttons."

He moved her hand to the flower packets as if it were the most natural thing in the world to do. "That's a package of petunia seeds," he said. "Would they satisfy you?"

"If I start them in the house now, they'll be ready to transplant in May."

"Their seeds are so small that they'd slide right through my fingers." He held them up for her to see.

"They're not all that big."

"How can you insult my fingers?"

"What matters in a man is not how big he is in any part." She realized what she had said as it came out, but she never took anything back.

He looked at her, laughed. "You're right," he said. "Benjamin Franklin probably said that."

"I thought it was Charlotte Brontë."

"Perhaps Emily?"

"They deserve their full names."

"You're right again." He stepped back. His eyes peered at her around the edge of the seed rack as if it had amused him to bring their worlds together. He bought gardening gloves and kohlrabi seeds, paying for them with a handful of quarters.

After that, just before Easter, he went off to Duluth to sell houses. His father replanted the alfalfa not long after, and the refreshed blossoms hung purple with scent until the next haying late in summer.

Sixteen

She would rather keep on dreaming, thank you, because the bed was lovely and warm, the Hudson's Bay blanket tenting her round stomach. Morning hadn't come either, not yet, although the sky in the gap between the curtains on the window across the room was greying a little. An unhappy grackle had a word, then another. She pictured a line of them, black grackles, tight to her under the blanket, woven into her crevices. Under her flannel nightgown, her nipples retracted and hardened into her flesh. She clapped her hands over them for protection, knowing it was a dream, but not wanting to take any chances.

Away from the chain of birds, she edged against Richard's arms.

"Susan?" The bed creaked and swayed.

"Hold me."

"What?" His legs spurted out between the sheets.

"Hold me." Her eyes were shut so she couldn't tell exactly where his head was. She clutched at whatever was available. "Hang on. I don't like this dream."

"Wait a minute, wait a minute." She must have been on top of his arm, because something under her was struggling to get loose. She tried to pull herself up, but her belly was too heavy, and she spilled back into the sheets.

"Are you having the baby? Isn't it too early?" He sought her hand, groping through the rumpled cotton.

Was she? Her mind ran over her body, checking its parts. She couldn't imagine ever having been thin. "No, of course I'm not having the baby. It's supposed to hurt, isn't it?" Black feathers edged her vision, then departed. "I was dreaming about grackles."

Richard had extracted his arm, and she went down with a soft collapse onto the pillow. "I don't know what in God's name you're talking about with those grackles, Susan. There hasn't been one around here in weeks since I took the gun to their tree." He was whispering, but his normal voice broke through at the ends of sentences, like Lucianne's had. She would have to write to her after breakfast. If she had time. Time got eaten up like butter horns.

"Oh, it doesn't matter."

"Then why did you bring it up?"

"It mattered to me before. While I was sleeping. Now I'm awake." Under the blanket, her hands climbed the ridge of her stomach. Was her belly button still there? She couldn't find it with her left thumb, but the right one hunted out a little soft curve that might have been it. She poked tentatively. Oh Lord. She tunneled her head into Richard's neck, making him grunt, and then rolled back across the bed to where her arms could dangle down and touch the rug. This was it, this was the moment of getting up.

"Getting up?"

"Watch me." She lunged erect. The bed swayed like the sea.

"Be careful." He was folding back the Hudson's Bay blanket.

"I can still do it myself." She did it. Then, sitting upright with her toes in the woolly rug, she knocked gently on her belly with one fist. Who's in there? she asked, almost aloud. On the other side of the bed, Richard's naked rear shimmered gently in the early morning light. As if he knew what she was thinking and didn't approve, he hoisted his boxer shorts up his legs and anchored them safely around his waist. She giggled, but through her sleepy mouth it came out a snort.

"What's funny?"

She snorted again and let her belly push her backward. Richard was sorting out his undershirt sleeves by feel. The tousled blond hair on the top of his head was just erupting through the collar hole when she tipped over and plopped back into the mattress.

"Jesus!" He hardly ever swore.

"I'm all right," she choked out, knotted with laughter.

He knelt down next to her, one arm hanging out below his undershirt bottom. "Do you want me to lift you up?"

"No. I'm going to lie here until the baby is born."

"What?"

She convulsed with laughter again, and an ooze of tears started out of her eyes, stinging her vision.

His breath all sheets and underwear, Richard bent over and touched his mouth to her forehead. She let him—he was too strong to fight. For a moment his head hesitated over hers, his lips with those funny vertical lines sliced through them. There had been a time when she'd thought she could drawstring him together and capture the whole bundle: her husband, store manager, Manatee citizen, future farmer perhaps, good provider. Good provider every inch of the way from Belfontaine. But he was too strong.

"Do you want anything?" He was at the door.

"Not a thing. Not a thing you could get me." A line linked his eyebrows. "I mean, I don't need anything except for you to go to work. I bought fresh coffee," she added, because he'd use the grounds of the old over again if she didn't remind him.

"I could have bought it."

"I know. But this came from Minneapolis, and it smells like Christmas. A special flavor." He winced. "I thought you might like it," she said, knowing he wouldn't.

"Well, I'll give it a try." He was tying his shoes, heavy immigrant things like his uncle had worn, with a leather tab up the ankle where the stitching finished off. He was meant to be a farmer of some sort, no doubt about it. "Should I bring you a cup?" he asked.

"Yes." She paused. "No." Over her belly arched the colors of the Hudson's Bay blanket. "I'm going to sleep."

"It's seven." He stood in the doorway looking at her.

"Go to work, Richard." She turned on her side and rolled back. "Let me live my own life." Levering with her leg, she tried for the other side of the bed, his side, and reached it. Would she ever lie down in free will again?

Then it was later, safe. All hers. She sat up, pushed the blanket aside. Her hair snaked down her back with one loose end of the disintegrating braid reaching around the waist of her nightgown like a prying brown finger. When she lifted her hands to smooth the fringes back from the sides of her face, all the weight in her lower body pulled her elbows back to her sides. She gave up and rose, walked to the window and looked out, belly resting gently against the sill. With her right index finger, still thick with sleep, she touched the flannel over where the head might be. Could it see out if her skin was stretched thin enough? Now? Next week?

The sky was a quiet blue now, still smoky along the edges where the low clouds of dawn lay. They could both watch. The grass in the yard had frosted over last night, and white lines spidered across the blades. The basil was dead in the herb garden, the parsley still green. Beyond both lay the yard, the sidewalk, the town. But the fields pulled at Richard. Her, too, in another way. If a buyer came for the store, they'd be gone to some outlying farm. She knew it as well as breathing.

Susan shifted her weight. The row of poplars waved toward her, then back. In the spring after they'd first moved to Manatee, Richard had cut them all back to stumps when she'd been out shopping. She'd seen the destruction when she'd walked back through the gate. "But they were all dying anyway," he'd shot back when she found him putting his tools away. "The only way to get new growth is to cut them way back."

And now they were back, sending up ten foot high shoots from their stubs. Autumn had barely touched them yet. But the mountain ash was emptying except for the hard berries at the twig ends, and the peony foliage flamed golden, richer than when they had bloomed those funereal heads in June.

Across her belly a wave buckled, straight from the right to the left, filling her up. Then it subsided. Down near her left hip the skin popped out momentarily, sank back. Even the loose nightgown rode tight on her now. Flesh popped out in a hard lump. She put her palm on the spot in the cloth. Like a knock on a panel of flesh, her own skin hit her hand and retreated.

"You've got the wrong door," she said. "Stay home. Nobody's ready yet." She pulled the cloth up, let her stomach taste the cool glass. Then she answered in a new voice, "I'll do what I want, thank you."

In the kitchen, the oilcloth on the table had half a damp circle on it from Richard's cup. Coffee steamed quietly on the stove burner. She poured a cup, stretching her arms out to replace the pot at the back. Sitting down, she held the cup with her sleepy finger through the handle and extended her arm to set it down in Richard's mark. Then she moved it back. He hadn't tried the new coffee after all. Or had he? Her mouth was so full of morning fuzz that only the heat penetrated. Pushing against the table, hands braced flat out for balance, she thrust to her feet and walked out the door. The screen slammed behind her.

The air was cool. Blue arrows slid through the wide neck of her flannel nightgown and chilled her nipples. Blue arrows came up underneath and iced her thighs. The sun on her hair was thawing, though, down through the reborn poplars. She ran one finger down the sky, testing the wind.

They didn't have a real porch, just a cement slab that marked the step-down from house to yard, only big enough for two small clay pots of marigolds sitting on each side during the summer. They had frozen brown-dead the day after Labor Day. Below the slab ran a cobblestone walk that angled out to the picket fence. Nettles that she had chopped to submission everywhere in the yard sent their new recruits between the stones, stubby and vicious. She had to be reconciled to them. Richard had wanted to tear the walk up, of course. Cobblestones weren't part of the furniture of his mind.

Susan walked out, leaned against the fence, stomach firm on the pickets. Quietly, she undid the tarnished silver cone that fit into the gate latch, stepped out onto the Manatee sidewalk. A car moved past the corner, and she raised her right hand up to where her nightgown puckered at her full breasts so she could twiddle her fingers down the street at it.

She should get properly dressed. Then she could go downtown. Smiths Grocery Store, Farmers Bank, Richard's hardware emporium. It would be warmer downtown where the wind didn't reach, but she would hold to the sunlight anyway. Testing, she placed one bare foot into a golden spot in front of her and noted that it fit perfectly. There was another one next to it, quite a lot of sun, as a matter of fact. She had to crane her neck down over her belly to see the golden lily pads, but it was possible. A neighborhood black cat, striped down its chest with white as if it had spilled its saucer of milk, scurried alongside her from under the next-door hedge. It had its own business on its mind.

"Where ya goin'? Where ya goin', lady?" A little boy, hair matted, appeared by the curb, his square face turned toward her. Not a McMillan. Not a Zittner, a Togenroth, or a Hofberg. A visitor. Boys didn't pay attention to what ladies wore.

"Play ball?" He teetered one foot on the curb, scraping a toe of his high brown leather shoe on the cement. "Play ball, lady?" One finger explored his nose in a patient circle.

"Where's that ball? If you find one, I might play with you." She had been good at playing ball long ago, out in the yard just before sunset when the chores were done—awfully good for a girl with her hair in a braid, just as good as a boy. Her father used to tell her so.

"Looks like *you* got the ball," he said, eyes narrowing until his seedy blond lashes touched his cheeks.

"What?"

The boy sat softly down on the curb. "Lady's got a *big* ball," he murmured, taking his finger out of his nose so he could dig at the tar between two sections of cement.

"I've got a baby in there," Susan said.

He was silent.

"I've got a baby in there, and it's going to be born pretty soon." The little boy looked away. "I'm a baby," he said sadly.

"No, you're not." He was just a grubby little boy, maybe Polish or Hungarian, and he picked at things. "You're too big."

"Yes I am." He dug at the tar again and got a little piece loose. Balancing it on his lower lip, he tasted it with his tongue. "Yes I am." He rubbed his eyes with one fist, not convincingly. "I *was* a baby."

Susan rocked herself down next to him on the curb in front of her house. The dead leaves in the gutter were still night-damp and gave her feet a chill, even though the sun was getting higher. Her stomach knotted.

"What's that?" The boy sat up straight.

"That's the baby." She spread her palms across her belly, pressing down. "It's planning for a visit." A hard knot rose under her right hand, and she took the little boy's arm, not even noticing that he was leaning away from her. "Want to shake its hand?" She felt around on her nightgown, trying to locate a marker. The little boy sat tight, waiting.

But Susan was waiting, too. "I don't actually know if it's his hand or not," she said. "Or her hand. I don't know that, either." She shifted on the curb, moving away from the boy, then looked up as a car passed, crunching stray leaves under its wheels, slowing down. "Sometimes I think that being married to Richard isn't what I really wanted. But I don't know. It seemed like it would be easier to belong."

The little boy shifted on the curb, too. "Who's Richard?" he asked, turning away as if he might be thinking of something else.

"My husband," Susan said. She put her hands on her belly, spreading the fingers. "But he matters less than you might think."

Seventeen

Inside her belly, the light surged. She held on to it even while it was scorching her.

The doctor had a green suit on. Like a goblin. He wanted her to wait. How could he know what she should do?

Richard was too far away to hear. And she wouldn't have given him the chance, anyway. This was her private affair. If she couldn't squat in the ditch, drop it into the dry grass with the sun on the back of her neck, she could at least keep her mouth shut.

Someone behind her head had a mask. She didn't want it. She said so. She screamed it.

The goblin was telling a joke about hunting. Deer season hadn't opened yet. When it did, he'd be ready. Rifle from Daniel Boone, hunting knife. He had one in each hand. They were for her. The light shone off them.

The ridge blocked off the stars. Her teeth were chattering. But she had asked for this. It was as much her fault as his.

She would bear it.

Eighteen

"Slide over."

"I am over."

"More." He gave her an inch, pushing himself against the driver's door.

"The baby can't breathe."

"He's asleep."

"Richard, there's no *room.*"

He breathed in, shrinking a millimeter. Susan edged against him. Frankie's eyelet spring cap lay against her arm, and in his sleep his eyes tightened, then his lips. He sucked the air, smiled a dream smile, and sucked again. His feet, toes sticking out from the blanket like miniature sausages, pushed against the piles of bedding and books. Comforters and sheets. Encyclopedias and a volume of Shakespeare's tragedies.

The door on the passenger side shut without her touching it. Outside, a hand checked the edges for tightness, then waved. Peter McMillan, their good neighbor. Would he miss them? It didn't matter; he would have loaded the car of a stranger and tucked a set of carved bookends, properly initialed, into the glove compartment as a gift. He might even drive out to see them in the new place, four miles from town. He might even bring Bertha. Fifteen years they had been married, and nothing more than banana bread. She had looked at Frankie as if she could have eaten him.

It was spring. Through the open windows of the Ford, Minnesota birdsong trickled in like water over a rock. Snowmelt. Frankie was still dreaming, his hands twitching, then his feet.

"Mrs. Murphy will have the place cleaned out." Richard put his free hand on Frankie's head, rumpling the bonnet.

Susan's foot tapped the floorboards. "If she just does something with that sink, I'll be satisfied."

"She promised."

"Yes, she did." Fifty years of artesian water, piped from the well to the kitchen wall and up into the sink, had left a swatch of iron red all the way around the drain. Sandpaper wouldn't get it off. But perhaps Mrs. Murphy's scrubbing was without human limitations. And Richard had paid her five dollars last week, with five more

coming if she aired the carpets. Susan dug her toe into the floorboards, jouncing Frankie. She would do it herself if she had to.

Richard tried to kiss her. The Ford never wavered.

Richard tried again. She pushed him away. Frankie sucked air.

Outside through the windshield, flawed with one gravel nip
exactly in the middle, country rippled away on each side. They
were past the backyards of Manatee. Charcoal blankets from
burned-over pasture were changing already, first grey, then brown,
then a green so fine it was like a girl's satin dress on the clothesline,
airing in the sun. Lucianne's fern. Where the lumbering county
road-grader hadn't scraped flat last fall, the road held dishpans of
springwater, specks of sky, pieces of cloud wobbling in them like
meringue. The car couldn't go very fast, not with Frankie asleep.
The pile of books and bedding next to her hardly jostled.

Without awakening, Frankie wet himself. Her skirt soaked it up.
What had happened to his diaper? She searched. Wadded between
his knees where it didn't help at all. Gently, she pulled it upward.

"Another mile." Richard laid his hand over Frankie's head again.

"It doesn't seem as far as it did at first." She shifted the baby's
rear, smoothed out the damp wrinkles of her skirt. He sucked air
again, mouth working dryly. His hands moved back and forth,
kneading like a kitten's paws. She'd heat his bottle on the stove
when they got there. If Mrs. Murphy had gotten the pipe cleaned
out and the wood in. No fancy gas burners for a little while. Not
like town. But she had lived this before.

"Are you sorry we're moving?" His finger walked around
Frankie's earlobe.

"It should be all right."

"But are you sorry?"

"Richard!" She hoisted Frankie upright, then put him back
down on her lap. "You wanted to do this. I'm coming along. If
you're not cut out to be a storekeeper forever, fine. If you want to
farm, fine. Raise horses. Whatever. I can do what has to be done."

This time his kiss bounced off the side of her nose. Frankie
gagged and threw up.

"Stop it!" She swabbed the baby's smeared face. The smell
wobbled up her nose as the car turned up the dirt driveway, hanging onto the middle. Frankie turned his cheek against her leg and
smiled at her, his two bottom teeth gleaming. His knees dug in as
he hunched up on her lap, then launched himself against her front,
both hands in her hair. Richard laughed. The car stopped.

"We're here."

Unlike their old rented house in town, built all at once in 1906 by Peter McMillan's father, this farm home had been put together in sections over the years, one birthing the next when the need arose. The driveway curved around next to the porch, then swung between the barn and the house, ending at a grey shed, the garage. Its door hung crooked. Around the bottom, late spring grasses nipped through the brown, wet leaves of winter. No ruts. Hardly anyone could have driven here since the April thaw.

"The windows are open." Richard stepped outside the car; the pressure in the front seat loosened. Susan let her body melt. Frankie, jacket sodden down the front, chewed on the steering wheel, his eyes swollen shut with pleasure. She looked beyond him at the waving curtains.

"Mrs. Murphy must have been airing out the house."

"Like I said."

"Nice to know somebody does things like you say."

Richard only smiled. Then he opened the passenger door and boosted out the linens, disappearing behind the uneven tower. The foundation rested comfortably against his chest. Susan felt the Shakespeare tumble next to Frankie. "Get out," Richard said, turning back. "It's still light. We can look around."

"Frankie's hungry."

"He can wait." Frankie gnawed lustfully at the wheel. "The truck will take an hour, and his crib's the last thing on it. You can feed him and put him to bed then."

Frankie stamped his feet in bliss, spit smeared over both cheeks. He stank.

"I should change him. He stinks."

"No one to smell him except us."

That was true. The grasses didn't count. Or the birds in their twilight song. Rain must be coming; robins edged the driveway with their demands for it. They always got what they wanted. A brown thrasher too. Wrens. Marsh wrens, so there must be cattails somewhere. Richard would wrench them out, of course, and haul in fill for another corn patch. But not yet. Not until next year.

Suddenly, Susan didn't want to see the house, or the stovepipe, dirty or clean, or the curtains up close. Not one bit. Her toes curled in her shoes like bird claws. Feathers layered her shoulders. Frankie could sleep under her arm, head tucked down. She could feed him gnats of her own catching.

Richard put the sheets down gingerly on an old picnic table weathering by the back doorsteps. Then, his nose wrinkling, he took the baby, prying him loose from the wheel. Frankie's face went serious, head back, and his hands jerked straight out. Richard blew at him, ruffling his frizzy hair. He blinked. Richard blew again. Frankie giggled and burrowed into his chest.

"Come on, Susan."

Without Frankie, she could almost fly: angel, snow angel, mud angel. Inside the open window of the house next to the back door, the fringe of the curtain flapped with an audible rustle in the rising breeze. Mrs. Murphy's flag of welcome. In the west, beyond the tight vertical corner of the garage, the sky was orange, blood orange, pouring down to the black line of the earth underneath it. A straight slash, then a ripple of trees. A hill, edging up to the left, curved like a breast. No flat ridges. They were a good ways out from town, a good ways.

"Who's the nearest neighbor?"

Frankie a package under his arm, Richard bent over, stretched the barbed wire apart, birthed her through. The posts sagged, weeds shoving at them. Once the planting was done, they'd be swallowed up in endless work.

"Is it Mrs. Murphy?"

"Not her. She's on the other side of the rise. It's the Stanislaus sisters. They farmed with their brother until he died, so now they run the place themselves." Balancing Frankie on his hip, Richard moved next to Susan, their ankles circled by the new grass along the margins of the field. "Look over there. See the tree that branches, that big elm? Look down the trunk." He put his free hand on her cheek, twisting her head. "Almost at the bottom. See that catch in the horizon?"

She did. "No," she said.

"No?"

"Now I do."

"It's their house. It's nearer than you'd think. Maybe a mile, maybe little more. I just met them once. A nutty old pair, tough as nails. They cut their own calves, would you believe it? Never hire a soul for help."

Susan smiled, shook her head. It was like she was shivering.

"Cold?"

"We should go back."

"Truck won't be there yet."

"It might be early." She took Frankie, placid as whey, out of Richard's arms.

"I doubt it." But he turned with her. She waited at the barbed wire for him to pull it open for the both of them. A snag caught her skirt, then snapped loose.

Her feet were wet. She and Frankie smelled, though the evening breeze was pulling the odors out beyond them. The house looked grey now, the nearest open window a dark eye. Down at the gravel road, a car was coming, comet tail of dust marking its way. Wasn't it too wet for dust?

Richard had the door to the house open. "Come on in," he said.

Frankie chewed her pocket. She came in.

Nineteen

The Gypsy lady was dancing under the elm. Like in the stories. From the mailbox down by the gravel road where she stood with Frankie, Susan could see the woman's skirt swaying toward the ground, a splash of dried blood color. She bent in front of the caravan, castaneting her fingers with tiny chops, the sound of which carried on the wind. Her hair was black, hanging down both sides of her face. Near her a horse grazed, an ordinary bay with three white feet. Three was bad luck. But maybe he had a fourth anklet, buried in the creek grass where it couldn't be seen.

The Gypsies passed through only in August, the first part of the month. They never came into the town of Manatee itself during the day—not the women, not the children. The men sometimes. The women stayed in the fields, camping. Campfires glowed at night. They fixed pots, melted copper, waterfalls of searing metal. Part of the land Susan and Richard rented had always been a Gypsy campground, people said, and it still was. They set up their tents and carts where there was water, trees. The corner of the lower pasture was perfect for them, cool in the afternoon, but near the road so the men could tramp off to Manatee together, talking some language that wasn't Swede, wasn't German, either. They held their arms around each other like women might, heads tilted until their bushy mustaches ran together. The children huddled to watch them go.

Not many this time, people said. A few families. From here they'd head south, down toward Iowa. By the time winter came, they'd be in Florida, pulling oranges off the trees, camping on the beaches. In the summer, this was the farthest north they got.

There hadn't been any mail, not even a Sears catalog.

The Gypsy lady kept dancing. The black hair hung over her face as if she didn't have one. A white bone in it would have shown like a star. An arrowhead would have done the same.

Susan began moving down the road toward her. In his mother's arms, Frankie raised his own arms to the sun. They were people, too, the Gypsies, even if their English wasn't good. You had to talk slowly, that was all. And all women loved children.

As she stepped into the grass, the bay neighed, shifting feet. The Gypsy lady tossed her hair back. "How long are you staying?"

Susan asked, making sure not to sound pushy. They could stay forever; Richard wouldn't plow here. She wouldn't let him.

The woman tossed back her hair again. It wasn't necessarily clean. The Indians had used bear grease, but all the bears were gone.

"Two week." She laughed. Frankie laughed back. The woman reached into her pocket in the folds of the skirt of blood and held out cornbread. It was yellow in the sun.

"He had his breakfast already." Susan's own mouth yearned, though she had eaten too.

"Take it." The Gypsy lady laughed again.

Susan reached out, balancing Frankie in her elbow. The Gypsy placed the cornbread in her hand. "Thank you," Susan said.

"You like?"

Susan nibbled.

"Your man like?" They were supposed to have perfect teeth, but hers were greyed in front. She saw Susan looking and smiled wider.

Susan licked the crumbs from her fingers. "He's not here," she said, moving Frankie to her hip.

"Big boy," said the Gypsy. She took Frankie onto her shoulder, holding him against the side of her head. He beat his legs against her collarbone, smiling back at Susan. "You got girl, too?"

"No girl yet."

"Come," said the Gypsy. She pulled Susan to her caravan, really just a farm wagon with canvas slung over it like a tent. Thin poles held the cloth up at the ends. With Frankie clutching her, she moved the material aside, stepped back for Susan to look in. "Mine," said the Gypsy, laughing again. "Mine."

Inside, on a pile of quilts, rags really, slept three little girls. Older than Frankie. All the same size. They had black hair, too, like their mother, but it curled around their heads in damp knots. One was sucking her thumb, her mouth fat around it. The other two slept with their arms out straight as if they were leaping down from the sky.

"They're yours?"

"Two year," said the Gypsy, giving Frankie her little finger to work on.

"Are they triplets?"

The Gypsy lady set Frankie back in Susan's arms like a chubby doll. She must not have known the word.

"Did your husband want a boy?"

Under the big elm, the bay whinnied. The woman turned, lifting the heavy sweep of her skirt, and stepped up into the wagon. All three children heaved in their sleep, resettled. "I give him girls," she said, looking around at Susan with a smile so wide the ends tangled in the blackness of her hair.

Twenty

"It's just the wind."

She turned her head against the pillow. "No, it's not."

"What else could it be?"

"I don't know."

"Should I go look?"

"Wait."

The house breathed in, mice in the walls, loose shingles, the dangling kitchen ivy twisting its pot against the window. Frankie turning over in his crib. The house breathed again.

"Do you still hear it?"

"It's out there."

"Susan. Please."

"I don't mean *that*. It's of this world."

"The one we happen to be in." He turned on his pillow, toward her. His hands plucked her breasts.

"Please, Richard."

"Lie still. There's nothing out there."

"If we wait long enough, I'll hear it again."

"What kind of book were you reading today, for God's sake?"

"I didn't read."

"What did you do then?" His shucking hands grappled with the hem of her nightgown.

"I went to the Gypsies."

That surprised him. His hands left the cloth. "I thought they'd left," he said. He began on the buttons.

"Not yet. Two more weeks."

"So did they tell you that?"

"She did."

"You met one?"

"We talked." Susan put her arms out to her sides carefully, as if she could fill the bed by herself.

"I didn't think you knew Gypsy language."

"I know enough."

"Susan." He rose against her, she against him. "You're cold."

"I'm cold in August?"

"Sure feels like it." His toes grappled with her ankles, slid further down. The sound came again, far away. Mice scrambled. The ivy danced.

"Perhaps they're going sooner than they thought."

"Where?" His words breathed in her neck.

"Wherever they go."

"Then maybe I'll finally get to plow down by the creek."

"It's too late now. August."

"For next year. Hold still."

"I am still." The stillness covered her like a tent.

"Then move."

"What do you want, Richard?"

"Can't you tell?"

"Ask me what *I* want."

His tight belly with its bar down the middle dug into hers. She said the same thing over again.

"What?"

"Ask me what I want."

"Let me guess. More books. A new dress. That the muskmelons won't freeze. Twin foals next spring for Babe, so your husband will be happy. Shoes for Frankie."

Soon he wouldn't hear her. "Ask me what I want, Richard," she said, not making a question so much as a demand. She hardly ever demanded.

Burrowing, he turned his mouth to the air. "All right. What do you want?" One ear was free, too, so he might be able to hear her answer.

Susan thought, her arms stretched so far out that her hands hung off their respective sides of the bed. Or almost. Her mind rose toward the ceiling like milkweed fluff, blown loose when it was time. The pod of her body opened.

"I want. I want." Loose hair from her braid tickled her ears.

"I don't know what I want."

Twenty-One

No one had used the privy since the indoor bathroom had been put in the farmhouse. Spiders had woven the inside corners into a gummy mist. The rich ammonia smell of urine had faded into the general damp of earth, and around the two holes the boards were warping back in irregular humps against each other. Rain had washed in through the half-moon on the door. The roof still held. But not for long.

"He's going to start crying."

Susan anchored her palms against the boards on the side and heaved. "No, he isn't," she said. "He thinks he's home in his crib. If he's thinking at all." She heaved at the privy again, panting. She'd laid her coat aside, and the back of her dress was dark from sweat, though the October night was full of winter on the edge of every wind. It was a perfect Halloween, couldn't have been better if they'd had a direct pipeline to all the old gods. Over the scudding clouds rode the fat-cheeked moon. His cold light touched the elms around the farmhouse, safely distant.

"They don't do this in Duluth."

"You bet they don't." Susan heaved again. There was a definite give. "Work," she said. "Why do you think I told you to come?"

"I've been wondering all evening." Elwin Retzlaff stood next to her, placed his hands flat against the weathered boards. On a comforter in the grass, wrapped in a cocoon of warm blankets so thick that he could have been an overturned stump, Frankie made a tiny squeak.

Susan looked around. Frankie was quiet again. He must have been dreaming.

"So why am I here?"

"For your manly brawn." Susan shoved again, Elwin beside her. He was visiting his parents in Manatee for a week before he went back to the real estate business in Duluth. The mailman had told her on Tuesday. There had been time to transmit the gossip into action.

"What about your husband?"

"He's looking at another horse in Norwood."

"On Halloween night?"

"He's staying over. It's too far."

"Isn't he afraid to leave you by yourself out here?"

The two of them had developed a pushing rhythm, and the privy was beginning to rock back and forth. Overhead, the moon balanced on the clouds. It wouldn't take much more. Frankie wouldn't even wake up.

"No one ever uses this privy." Elwin was panting.

"I know it."

"So why are we doing this?"

"It's a symbolic gesture."

"Symbolic of *what?*" The old boards let out an unearthly crack like a witch's voice, but Susan refused to break the rhythm. Elwin grunted and pushed harder.

"Symbolic of what I want."

"And what's that?" He had slivers in both palms.

Susan didn't answer. "Push!" she said. And with a final shove, the boards cracked loose from the nails holding them to the foundation slab. Teetering for a moment, the wooden rectangle shifted to the right, then went slowly over with a clatter. The roof split down the middle as it hit the ground. In the silver light, the platform with its two seats truly stood like a throne.

Susan clapped her hands and hooted, then scooped up Frankie. "Now we can trick-or-treat."

"What?"

"Trick-or-treat."

Elwin looked at her. "How old are you?" he asked. "You don't look ready to put on a costume to me."

Susan had Frankie in her arms, her face nuzzling his neck. "I'll be the Virgin Mother," she said. "Look, my coat is blue. I'll pull it up over my head. All you have to do is drive."

Elwin looked toward his Packard, its top gleaming in the moonlight. "You want me to *drive* you?"

"The farm's too far from Manatee to walk."

"That's for sure." Elwin picked his way through the remnants of the privy, kicking a board aside. He wasn't sure what he'd see if he looked back. "Maybe we could just go back to your house," he said. "If your husband isn't home."

"That's not what I feel like doing."

He stopped, still looking at the Packard. Nobody would be able to see it from the main road. "We could have a good time," he said, not at all sure that it was the right thing to have passed his lips.

"I'm having a good time right now."

"What're you doing?"

"Peeing."

Stunned, he turned back. Susan was sitting on one of the exposed seats, her blue coat in her lap, her skirt circled around her like a cushion. The lump that was Frankie lay next to her on the platform. Night wind raised the loose hair that had sprung free around her face. She was smiling.

"Jesus."

"I do what I want."

"I guess." He didn't know which way to look. The Packard seemed to have distanced itself by leagues of fields from where he was standing.

"Women don't show anyway. Theirs is secret."

"I guess." His voice had turned to sandpaper.

"Take me in the car. Frankie can sleep in the backseat."

"All right." He felt himself giving up.

"I just want to drive around. Then you can go back to Duluth. I'll make my own Halloween candy. I don't have to beg it."

Devils rose in him. "What if your husband finds all this out?" He was sorry before he'd finished saying it, because then his father was sure to know, too, and that would be the end of the inheritance, if there was going to be any. And a lot else besides.

"I don't care if my husband knows. He gets what he wants from me." She had risen, put on her coat, gathered up Frankie. Bundled against the moon, she could have been a refugee from some threatened country, except for her smile. Sparks came off that smile.

"Well, come on then." They headed up the rise, down toward the car. The roadside ditch opened before them, grassy with what had been left uncut after the last fall mowing. "Careful," he said, as if she were an ordinary woman.

"I like ditches."

"Ditches?"

"Yes. They hold you. They're where the bottom is."

"I guess."

"I like ridges, too, but you're never the same after you've been there."

"Who told you that?"

"I just know it." She shifted Frankie, laid him against her shoulder with her chin tight on his blankets. Then she was running.

"Hey!" He started after, but it was hopeless. "Hey, wait!" he shouted, knowing only the moon would hear, sure that he'd never catch her. "Trick or treat!" he yelled, figuring he'd show her he could play, too. She might like that. She might like it that a man was trying.

Twenty-Two

They'd done a lot of fixing up. But around the sink in the farm kitchen, the floorboards had rotted from the years of splashed water, and she'd stood there bouncing gently as she washed dishes, dried dishes, put away dishes. Bounce, bounce. Frankie had dug out cheesy bits when he banged pans next to her on the floor, until she had finally laid a slice of plywood over the spot, and a linoleum scrap over that. The bounce seemed further away, faint as a heartbeat.

It wouldn't be as bad this time. Not like the last time, when she hadn't been ready. The green wash of the Manatee hospital walls had splashed around her head as if she had been inside a paint jar. The horse hammering her back with his hooves. People. She'd kept her eyes shut so the green waves wouldn't wash her away. Hanging on when the pains came. Hang on. And the baby, Frankie, so red, indecent, so covered with flesh torn from hers. Amazing that love grew out of blood and lasted forever.

In the downstairs bedroom, walled off behind the stove, Frankie called out. Not awake yet, but speaking from his nap-dreams. A giggle. Nothing. He was good for another half hour. Then she'd have to get him up, hold him over the porch railing like a faucet. Toilet training was easier that way. But maybe he'd soaked through already. The old mattress was mapped with yellow cauliflower ears, outlines on top of each other. Babies on babies. Yellow, white, tiny waterfalls.

And now a new one coming. A Christmas present she couldn't send back.

Twenty-Three

"So you're happy being a farmer's wife," said Bella Stanislaus, her hand whisking the egg whites into spume, both feet balanced on the rung of the kitchen stool, shoes crumpled into creases over the base of her toes.

"Wouldn't be *anyone's* wife." That was Eura, in the maple rocker, her feet on the attached footstool, nudging the chair toward the cupboards by the sink, forward, forward, and then back with one rigid plunge when the footstool nuzzled the edge of the wakened boards.

Susan didn't reply to either. Rubber spatula angled, she sliced through the sponge cake batter, cutting in the flour and salt. The eggy mixture slid over it. Slice. Under the yellow liquid, the untouched white softness barricaded itself. Slice, slice. The green bowl had a crack down the side, white chip in the top edge. Frankie, grabbing it off the counter. In the crack lived the little people, clustered in the crumbled china dust, spawning dirt in their tiny pronged hands. Not germs, though. As real as any of us.

"These don't whip right." Bella held the whisk aloft while she stuck her thumb down into the egg whites, then pulled out a gob from the foam. She lifted it, inspected it. Eura nudged over and watched. Both of them had green eyes, cat green. Wrinkles cut through their cheeks like war paint. They were the same height, smaller than Susan, whose nose brushed their hair when she stood next to them. Bella had breasts like a roller inserted from arm to arm. No wobble, they seemed boxed. Eura had nothing at all. Flat as a pancake. Lucianne.

Eura saw her looking. "I cut 'em off," she said, rocking. Her green eyes rippled.

From the sofa across the house, the baby cried, a dribble of sound. Silence. Another cry, tuning up, this one not stopping. Breath. A downright scream. EuraBella turned their heads.

"Mar's awake."

"She's awake."

"You can pick up her if you want." Eura? Bella? Susan had been looking at the sink, packed with naked apples. Four piecrusts lined the counter, fluted into their tins. The woodstove steamed red.

Now she could pare the fruit down, press in the cinnamon and sugar, stripe the latticework across the tops. Four. EuraBella. One for Richard and Frankie and herself if she felt like it. Two for the church supper, if they went.

The rocker nodded, empty. Eura had gotten up. Bella held out the bowl, stiffened into white hills. Apple pie and sponge cake, bread made yesterday, tomatoes still in the fruit cellar, canned from last summer. Preserves. Preserved.

"Here's Chicken Little." In Eura's arms, rolled across her flat front like stuffing, Mar in her blankets was surprisingly solid. At one end, the fluff of dark curls stuck straight out, bobbling in the daylight. One small foot protruded from the blanket, little toes in a line, the big one stretched back away from its sisters. Eura held her with total attention. "Chickchickchick," she clicked, edging herself back into the rocker.

"Margaret is not a Norwegian name," said Bella, patting the top of the stool through her spread skirt.

"We're not Norwegian."

"We're not, either."

They were silent. Mar began to smack her lips, fervent. EuraBella smacked theirs back.

Leaning against the counter, Susan looked down. The sponge cake spread its thick, golden soup in the tube pan. She set it into the oven, fanning her hand to check the heat. Gas next year, if they were lucky. Back to the apples. She opened the silverware drawer, tugging at its handle, looking for a paring knife. Not in front. She felt in back, delicately, not risking her fingers. Mar made sucking noises while the chair creaked.

"Where's Frankie?"

"Outside, in the barn."

"Alone?"

"With his father."

"Doing what?" The vertical lines of the stool legs were tree trunks around which the thick vines of Bella's ankles had twisted themselves.

"Getting the other horse stall ready for the new one." Had she lost the paring knife? Above the creak of the rocking chair, the stove crackled.

"Hope he doesn't kick." The two of them said it in chorus. Susan squatted halfway down, bending her head so she could see deep into the drawer beneath the edge of the counter. The wadded braid on her neck thickened against her skin. She nudged the fingers of her right hand around inside the drawer. Had she thrown the knife out, burned it in the trash by mistake?

"You know," said Eura, Mar's curls sticking out between her fingers like coiled rings, "when Bella and I were girls, we decided the only difference between men and women was the boots. Not the clothes, but the boots. Heaven knows why."

Bella looked straight ahead. Mouse tracks puckered her eyelids.

"Well." Eura patted Mar's tummy, then flipped her over like a pancake and patted her bottom beneath the baby blanket. "Heaven probably does know." She looked up. "We had those shoes with buttons and loops, but only for winter. In the summer, we were barefoot. Then in the fall before Daddy died, we found this tree with bark that looked like leather."

"Two falls before he died." Bella's eyes were closed and came loose only a slit as she walked to the sink. "Give me a knife," she said. "Those apples are ready to rot."

"Here's one." Susan's fingers had caught it. She pulled it out, handed it over. Reached in again. Cool point in the jumble of string at the back. Arrowhead.

"Can't cut that with that," Bella said.

Susan touched it to the edge of the counter.

"You didn't find that one here." Bella hoisted up her skirt to a platform around her hips, readjusted the waistband, smoothed it down again. Shrugging her shoulders, she started on the apples. "These held together pretty good for a winter in the cellar," she said smiling.

"It was a sycamore tree," said Eura, on her own track.

Susan held the arrowhead up to the light. So long ago. Outside now, the soil was the wrong color, not the rich black where the Indians had camped. Here, most places, you couldn't even have seen a flint arrowhead, white on white, another pebble among the sandstone remnants. Nothing to be proud of, no message. But then. The angels. The spring wind.

"Got these pippins half pipped," said Bella. Steam from the sponge cake crept out the lines around the oven door.

"Bark like sunburn," said Eura, Mar dangling over her lap.

Bella made an apple-skin ring, uncoiling the red carpet with her paring knife in a fragile spiral that grew over her forefinger. The red-and-white tickled the shelf of her breasts. Bella raised the parent apple higher, naked against the brown cupboards. The knife slid further, then notched it loose. The coil rested across her bosom like a military decoration. Three or four triumphs in the field.

Susan touched one end.

"You look like you won the war."

"Civil," said Eura. Mar's arms hung limp. She was asleep again.

A brown smell surrounded the oven. Pot holders wadded in each hand, Susan opened the door. The sponge cake had risen over the edges of the tube pan in a tight circle. Holding it in front of her like a treasure, Susan elevated it toward the countertop. Bella wiped her hands on her front and began shoving the pies to one side. She had a hairy mole on her chin, and its longest hair swayed energetically.

"Make room for the King of the Sponges." But the royal path had already been laid bare. Susan balanced the cake to cool on the tube of its pan, upside down as it had to be. What if it fell out? But of course it wouldn't. It was stuck tight to the tin walls, safe as salvation.

"Five more minutes," said Bella, laying the strips of raw crust across the apple mountains, pinching the dough into edges, her right thumb and forefinger like little teeth. "Then we can bake them." Her crust strips were graded roads over apple valley, apple cliff. Elves could have marched along them, toes flirting with cinnamon.

"Let's take this baby outside to learn to know the world." Eura hoisted Mar to her shoulder and headed for the door. The chair rocked on, emptied. The last strip went on the last pie, the oven door slammed open. Pies in. Then it shut, more gently, and Bella opened the top of the stove, digging down into its innards with a poker. Sparks braceleted her wrist. She slammed the cover back down.

"All right."

Above the backyard, the sun balanced on a horizontal strip of cloud like a gold coin. The air was lemon yellow. Susan stood in the middle between the two old women, her head back, her belly pushed forward against her apron, a small, soft pillow. After babies, it never quite went back to where it had been. Mar's dark curls wobbled against Eura's neck.

"If we go down to the barn, we can get Frankie and take him, too."

"Pie time, three-quarters of an hour. Better not plan any trips into town."

"No need." In the same moment, EuraBella reached out their flanking hands and took Susan's, linking them all together. Their old skin was papery and warm. They exerted no force. Mar's head bobbled as they all edged across the driveway. Against the north side of the garage, where the raspberries were planted, dirty snow still piled. Dead canes stuck through like witches' fingers. Goose bumps covered Susan's upper arms. It was only April, and a late spring, too. Mar would freeze.

"She'll freeze."

"Babies are their own little furnaces." Eura's hand tightened. Nail edges danced across the pillow of Susan's palm.

Together, all of them marched the path to the barn, the ruts pushing their insteps. Around the edges of their world, the farm still slept, Minnesota spring with snow still piled on all the north sides, machine sheds frost-heaved and leaning toward each other. Ahead of them, the barn leaned too, nuzzling the slow hill that rose up and stretched along behind, then down to the creek where the Gypsies had camped. In the spring, frogs talked the waves deaf with their mating. In the real spring. Now the ice still covered them while they shoveled themselves deeper into the chilly mud, their throats bubbling in and out. Over their brown roofs, the water pressed quietly down. Weed strands laced through. On top, winter nested, except in the corners by the undereaten banks where wave tips nibbled their way through the doilies of ice, tasted the soil, nourished themselves for spring. Next week. Soon.

Inside the barn, the floor was damp with mulled straw and manure thinly carpeting it, but above at knee level, the warmth from the cattle layered the air. The women stood in a row by the stanchions, dusty rays from the hayloft slicing through, looking for the men. At the end of the row, a pail clanked. Richard was cleaning up. Then Frankie saw them, his wool scarf wound around his neck, boots flopping. His cheeks were chapped; his lips were chapped, too. He stood by the new horse stall, ready for the Percheron bought a week ago, soon to be delivered, and he plunged toward them, arms out. "Maaaa," he said, like a foal himself.

EuraBella purred like tomcats. Susan slid back, hands in her apron pockets, exploring for broken seams. Eura reached out and caught one of her hands again, holding it warmly in her own while Frankie sucked himself into them. "MAAAA!" he shouted, giggling. Dust motes from the straw danced in the air as they hugged each other as if for the last time.

Twenty-Four

Mr. and Mrs. McMillan would come out from town. Because of how they felt about children. They'd have been out already, but Susan had said no. Only when it was time to finish it.

EuraBella had come, gone, would return.

Elwin was in Duluth. He had no part in it, anyway.

Susan held on to the edge of the table. She counted the circles, ovals really, of the grained wood. But then the first board ended and another one began. No way of knowing how many there were.

"Don't touch it, Mar. Listen to me."

Usually she kept the pretty dishes on the table, pushed toward the window where the light hit them. The blue saucer with the color swirling in it. And the silver snuffbox, antique from way back. The inlaid top latched so tight you had to use two hands to open it.

The vase with eucalyptus.

The china dancer. No one had ever danced like that.

"Don't, Mar. Don't."

The room was too small, even for a parlor. Everyone would suffocate when they arrived. Already the air oozed sweet like canning syrup, clinging to the pan bottom, scorching into caramel. Lucianne couldn't come. Her mother was sick. She was too far away.

"Mar. Please."

Susan looked around, her eyes passing sentinel. She knew everything there. The walls were plaster over lath, white roughened swirls from floor to ceiling. Pine boards surfaced the floor she'd swept so many times around the edges that her broom had walked scratches into the finish. In the middle, the big, braided rug was their history book, every spiraled layer defined by the fabrics from worn-out winter coats, flannel shirts, the vest she'd made for Richard that had never fit. Now it was under her feet forever. And her good dress from just before they'd been married.

The little clothes, too.

Kaleidoscope, the rug swirled in her brain. Would all the feet fit on it? They'd need to put four on the sofa, two on the horsehair couch. Perhaps three. They could use the big chair. Move the rocker in from the kitchen.

They could have had it in town. But Frankie had been a farm boy all his years.

"Don't touch. Don't touch him, Mar."

The little girl, head snaky with curls that shot out every which way, turned toward her mother. On her face, all her childhood freckles had concentrated themselves into a brown explosion on her nose. She shook her head so fiercely that anything less firmly anchored would have shot off. Then she shook it again. Her blue eyes, blue like winter ice, focused on Susan's brooch at the neck of her black sweater. Mar grabbed at it. No luck. Without pause, Mar turned across the room and toddled to a pine chair in the corner, seized it, and wrenched it forward with all her strength. When the chair had moved far enough, Mar climbed on the seat, first the chubby hands, then one knee mashing the air, then the other knee. Like thrusting sparrows—no, chickens, grackles, hawks—her hands shot out for the bar on the chair's back, and her whole person, curls erupting on top, stood up. She grabbed for the brooch.

"*Don't touch.*" But already Mar's fingers were tugging at it.

"Oh, Mar. Don't. Don't do it." Stooping, Susan hoisted the little girl up against herself, propping her on the curve of her stomach, trying to mold the straining body to her. Mar relinquished nothing.

Then, down by the road, through the window with the drape swathed across it, Susan thought she heard them coming. That was all right. That was the way it should be. Richard was in the kitchen, waiting too. For the food they'd bring. He liked to eat. He could swallow anything, the angel food, the devil's food, sponge, marble. Banana bread, fig cake, chiffon. In the pantry, he would gather the tomato jars until they glinted against his chest like buttons of blood. In the bedroom. On the porch with the trellis next to him cut in wooden triangles like butter cookies at Christmas. Like pie tarts from the leftover crust. Like hooves on a little boy's chest.

Mar sucked at the brooch, her pink mouth surrounding it in a damp circle. The thick smell of the room caught in her curls. Susan pried her loose, set her down, unpinned the brooch, and pressed it into her hands.

There were a million things to do in the time that actually remained. The floor should be swept again, and there were still fingerprints along the bottom of the parlor door, from Mar's fingers, and his, too, old ones, last week's. Overhead, the parlor chandelier was webbed with dust. She should take care of these things.

"Peekaboo," said Mar, fat on the rug. "Peekaboo."

Susan turned to the window, her belly against the heavy drape.

No eyes, no eyes. No eyes yet. Mar banged the braided rug with both fists. Did they just keep coming? Was one supposed to be as good as the last one would have been?

At first Susan thought Mar must have banged her hands too hard, but when she looked down, her own winter-reddened hands were half over her own open mouth. Mar hadn't made any new noise at all. Who had made that sound? She forced herself to listen. The air whined like radio static.

Then the door opened. It was too soon. It was much too soon, even for the preacher. It all came back to her.

She had read somewhere, in some important book, that if you went to an undertaker in the big city, a real professional undertaker, he could make a little boy last forever. She didn't know just how they did it, but they took the blood and shit out in a special way, put something in that didn't rot, pushed it through all the veins until it roped itself permanently around all the highways of his innards. People who had the money did that all the time. It was almost as good as real if you didn't look too close. Though it might not feel right. But his hands would be the same for a very long time, with the nails almost as soft as the flesh. Of course, she wouldn't be able to hold him right, because he'd be stiff, but she could learn to look at him like a picture and just run a finger around his outline. She was smart. She could learn that. She wouldn't have to think that whenever she gathered the October windfalls for the old cider press, the soft brown undersides would have come up from him, his rotting warmth circling them like a swollen hand.

Her hands were on him. Now Mar was screaming too. Susan just wanted to see if he had softened in the woodstove heat, but he hadn't. One eye showed a slit under the white lid, curved like a fingernail moon. His curls, so much lighter than Mar's, disappeared into the crocheted pillow. When she plunged her head down next to his, the other eye jolted open, too, but there was nothing behind it. The little box shook, drumming the table, and she held it against her front with both arms as tight as she could, the table edge slicing her belly and whoever was inside. There wasn't room for anyone else in there. She didn't want anyone else.

Twenty-Five

"That's my pretty baby." And EuraBella swung her between them up the farm driveway.

"That's my pretty Mar." They swung her over a fat bush, flying her down through the golden air and then up again before her feet could touch. EuraBella were too big themselves, but they could fly her like an angel.

"Want some candy, Marbaby?"

"You said you didn't got any!"

They looked at each other.

"You said!"

Eura put both hands over her apron pocket.

"You *said!*"

"We shouldn't tease." Bella took out a peppermint stick. It wasn't wrapped, and when Mar took it, the sticky rubbed on her hand. Eura lifted out jawbreakers, two of them, fat as a cow's eyeballs.

"You save those for later."

Mar wedged the jawbreakers in her cheeks, chipmunking them away. She stuck the peppermint stick in the front of her blouse between the buttons. Her mouth was too full to answer back.

"Your mama plugged your ears before she brought you over to us."

"Your mama needs to wash out your ears all the way down."

"You be wicked, Marbaby." They were both kneeling with their hands all over. Bella kissed her hard. Eura straightened her collar and tickled her chin. They smiled and smiled.

Mar swallowed, the sweet juice skidding down off her tongue. The end of the peppermint stick tickled the line between her ribs. She could save it if she wanted. Or eat it now. EuraBella made a magic circle around her so she could do anything. Even now, turning away from her, they held her safe.

"Milkweed's ready to blow."

"This one's still green."

"All the ones on the north are.

"South ones are ready to blow." A little crunch. "Look here. Soft as silk."

Over Mar's head, white feet trod the wind. She held up her

hands. In the peppermint stickiness, one touched down. Its wisps
looked sharp, but they were no sharper than threads.

"Your daddy will want you back."

"He said four o'clock."

"Your mama will be coming back from the doctor any minute."

"With Baby Jimmy."

"That Dr. Collins, he's a baby himself."

"Jimmy's a spring runt by nature. He'll grow out of it."

"Your daddy will want you back, Marbaby."

"Want EuraBella to ride you to Banburycross first?"

Mar giggled. She blew at the milkweed fluffs, coming faster now.
EuraBella giggled too, snorting like horses. They held her up between them.

"See? There he is."

"Driving fast."

"Must of dropped your mama home first. With Baby Jimmy."

"Probably had his heart listened to."

"Your heart is a strong heart. Pump-pump."

"You'll be his big sister all your life, Marbaby."

"Big, big sister."

The car pulled up along the driveway, smothered in old lilac
hedge. The purple flowers. Not there now. Only milkweed.

Twenty-Six

"Come on, Jimmy." Mar tugged at her little brother's hand, pulling him until he rocked unsteadily, then letting go. Before he tumbled, she yanked him forward again with her hand that wasn't holding the food bag. In his oversized shirt, the sleeves rolled until they ended in wads above his elbows, he staggered against the brambles at the edges of the path. He whined.

"Don't whine."

He whined again, both eyes shut.

"Don't whine!" She thought for a moment. "Only puppies whine."

"I do, too!" Startled, Jimmy looked up at his sister, his eyes bluer even than hers. She had to laugh—it was such a big sound for someone she could still carry, if she ever wanted to be nice, which was never. Startled again, Jimmy grinned, his empty gums on top pink and rubbery. Six months ago, he'd had front teeth, then he'd fallen on Daddy's forge in the shed when he'd been messing in the nail heaps. The teeth had gotten pushed right back in, they all thought, because they'd never come out in his BM or anything.

Jimmy chugged ahead. He wasn't whining anymore, although he rubbed across his forehead with his fist, digging into the skin. Mar could look right over his head, she was so much bigger. She was stump solid, too, and she knew it.

"Once upon a time there was a girl and a boy and they walked. And walked. And walked." Mar's feet still hit the ground with purpose as she started a silly story. She knew how to keep him moving. "Then when they got there they knew it for sure. When they got there." Without slowing down, she reached out and bumped Jimmy in the back with her fist, then lowered her hand to grab his belt for a better push. He accelerated.

Ahead of them was an iron gate, painted and then painted again so that the bars were thick. From the narrow wrought-iron pineapples on top, broken streams of rust edged down, disappearing into the cracked black surface. Chocolate-caramel, Mar thought, as she picked off a hardened glob and fractured it between her fingers. But no good to eat. The lock was a flattened bar shaped like an arrow. It wasn't hard to lift, even though it was above her head, and once she had it out of its socket, she shoved the gate back into the weeds. The hinges made a noise like chickens.

There wasn't much inside, just the high grass. The gophers thought they owned the territory; there were dozens of holes plugged into the earth, starting straight down from their rims and then angling off beneath. If you ran your hand down one, it might get stuck. Nothing could nip you, because the teeth were deeper down. Jimmy stumbled in one, only it was too big to be a gopher hole, and it had a heap of sand thrown up to one side. A fox? More likely a woodchuck. The two old stones, fronts flaking off, were deep in grass, and there were others further back. Up front was the new stone with the peony behind it. There hadn't been any buds this year, or last year either. But her mother said it took a long time because peonies were like people, had to get used to things first before they would awaken into blossom. Mar didn't believe that. The gophers had eaten its roots for breakfast.

"Mar?" Jimmy dropped to the ground. "We're far enough. I'm hungry, Mar. What you got?" When he finished talking, he left his mouth open.

"Well, wait. I have to take it out." Mar sat down beside him in the grass, her back up against the new stone, shoulders brushing it through her dress. If she curved forward, she could feel it in her backbone too. It was hard, harder than bodies. But it wasn't a piece of him anyway.

Mar set the paper lunch bag in the grass. She had packed all the food she had been able to locate without being found out: curds mashed together on two chunks of bread, three carrots from the root cellar, the last of the angel food, dry-edged, an apple, one foil-wrapped toffee she had saved in her drawer since Christmas. While Jimmy watched, she set it all out in a row between the two of them, balancing the bread on her skirt so the curds wouldn't get tracked on by the ants. Ants were always there in the grass, and she scratched her ankle. Then Jimmy, watching her, scratched his.

"I'm thirsty, Mar."

"You have to wait. We'll drink after, at the creek."

"I'm thirsty now." But he began rubbing the curds off his piece of bread with his fingernail, rolling them between his fingers and stuffing them into his mouth like peas. It wasn't polite, but no one was looking.

Over their heads, out of reach, the summer clouds slowed their passage with the wind and began to group. By the time Jimmy had finished his curds, a thick grey curtain had drawn across the sky to

the north. Although any number of birds had been chirping beforehand, as they always did in the scrub woods around the farmsteads
outside Manatee, now there came a quiet edged with grasshoppers
and the rubbing of twig on twig as the breeze picked up. Jimmy bit
into the apple with whatever teeth he could find. Then a robin
came back, and another one answered from somewhere by the back
fence. Jimmy looked at Mar, then up at the sky. Mar looked up too.

"Birds."

"I know."

They listened. The cloud bank moved a little to the south. Next
to them the peony leaves touched each other and then moved back.
Mar began to toss the crumbs out toward the tall grass where the
birds would find them, and Jimmy helped.

"Are you dead, Mar?"

"How can I be dead. I'm *here*."

"He's here too."

"No, silly. His *meat* is here. Like when they kill the pigs."

"Did we eat him?"

"*No*. The bugs ate him. And the worms."

"Did Mama cry?"

"Of course. Like when I got lost in the corn that time. And I
wore my prettiest dress too. Everyone said I was a big help." Mar
stopped. She wasn't at all sure about any of this. "And I *was* a big
help," she finished defiantly.

"Where was me?" Jimmy crawled nearer and began to rub the
base of the stone where the grass was growing.

"You were a glimmer in the eye of the Almighty." Mar wasn't sure
where those words had come from. "You weren't here."

"Was I at EuraBella's?"

"No. You couldn't go there by yourself."

"Maybe Mama took me."

"No. She stayed with me."

Jimmy pulled himself to his feet and leaned against the stone.
"Maybe I was dead, too."

"You were *never* dead." Then she grabbed him around both
knees and pushed him down into the grass where she tickled him
until he started to cough as well as scream. She stopped because Ma
would be mad if he threw up and messed his shirt.

Mar did remember some things. While Jimmy lay flat in the
mashed grass with the grasshoppers, drumming his heels as he
caught his breath, Mar settled herself against the stone again, her
shoulders and bottom pushed back for support. Her nose itched,

and when she scratched it, it was like a little bubble burst, drib-
bling pictures into her head. Her mother with a ball under her
dress. Woodstove heat. Then, in the back of her eyes, she saw a slab
of brown wood, and her hands felt it too. They had touched it for
sure. For a moment that was all, the feeling moving from her fat
palms right up her wrists, and she finally had to push her arms
over and rub her hands against the stone to bring them back. Then
the sun went under a cloud, and everything was gone except the
parade of ants crossing her knee and Jimmy's blue-eyed accusing
stare from half down in the grass.

Frankie. There had been a Frankie, and he wasn't there anymore.

She was on her feet. "Come on, Jimmy," she said, yanking him
up so hard that the air jumped under him. "We gotta go home, and
that's no joke." She bent for the last leftover, tossed it away, and
tugged him down the path behind her, his head wobbling. "We
gotta get home real quick."

"Why?"

"Because." Already they were through the iron gate. "Because we
have to eat."

"We ate, Mar." He hopped on one leg, then the other, trying to
keep his balance.

"Not like supper. We had a lunch."

"It was big, though."

"Not big enough." They were past the edge of the woods, looking down the ditch and then up at the gravel road on the other side.
It hadn't rained for weeks, and the dust coated their ankles.

Overhead, the sun balanced between two clouds, each one round
as a puffball. The grasshopper noise had been left behind, but now
at the road's edge a new drone of singers started. One green fellow
sharpened his leg on Mar's anklebone, then twitched aside.

Next to her, Jimmy was whining again, tinny like the grasshopper. "I need to pee," he said. She ignored him except for the series
of shoves between his shoulder blades. The whine became a whimper. *"I need to pee,"* he whistled out.

"You can pee when you get home."

"Home is *far.*" She ignored him. "Home is *very* far, Mar." He
listened to himself with his lips hung open. "Farmarfarmar," he
muttered, his feet shuffling along the edge of the ditch. "Farmarfar-
marfarmar." Then, "I'm wet." The damp, salty smell rose. Although
she could see the edge of the cornfield now, even where their path
to home began and, therefore, where the edge of the yard would
turn up in hardly any time at all if they hurried, she clipped Jimmy

hard across the side of his head. It was too far for Ma to see, and she'd be hanging clothes or hoeing or snapping beans. Or reading, something with no pictures.

"Waah!" He hit the ground at her feet.

"Get up, dummy." Jimmy had his hands over the back of his stubbly head. "Get up, super dummy. Get up, kingfish baby." Jimmy's wet rump stuck up further than any of his other parts. "Get up, dummy," she said, but he wasn't moving except to clench his hands tighter around the back of his head so she couldn't get at him. She pulled him up and shoved him where they had to go.

Like a fairy-tale wall at the edge of the kingdom, the green corn stood up in front of them. Knee high by the Fourth of July, her father always said, and it was August. Now the tassels that were spurting out of the tops of the stalks waved over her head like Indian feathers. It wasn't good corn country anymore, her father said, because the soil was worn-out and sandy. But if the season was good, and if it rained right—not big downpours that gulleted all the slopes, but day-long drizzles instead—then the green spears shot through the soil like bullets. In the hot nights they grew and grew, even if only good girls could hear them. And now, even though the stalks were browning at the bottoms, with the leaves that were blocked from the sun cracking toward the earth, the tops were richer than ever, higher than castles. Inside, along the rows and then crisscrossing between them, you could lose yourself for hours, sheltered with a green fence that shut off bulls, wasps, big hooves, voices in the night that came into your dreams and tore them. When she grew up, all her dreams would grow along green stalks with fuzzy heads touching the blue, and pollen, pollen everywhere, golden on her hands and down her front where she rubbed them. She would wake in a bath of golden ears covering her like sand, and when she moved from side to side, the corn would move along with her. Jimmy could jump in too. They could both drown in the green and the gold. They would be children of the corn.

But they hadn't even gotten all the way out of the ditch, hadn't stepped into the first soft furrow between the green stalks, when their mother grew up beside them. The sun hit behind her head, making the loose bits of her hair into candles, and she grabbed them both by their hands like she loved them enough to hurt them bad. With a squeal, Jimmy banged up against her side, but Mar, indignant, pulled away.

"You!" That was what her mother always said.

Jimmy hung on to her mother's apron with his free hand. He

didn't say a word.

"You." Her mother let her go. "You are always the one to take him off. Aren't you big enough yet to know where you should go and where you shouldn't?"

A grasshopper at her foot took up his fiddle. All the greens came together. Mar hunched. Then, in the silence before anything exploded, she raced off into the cornfield, scuttling between the rows.

"Mar!"

Mar scrambled on. With Jimmy to hang on to, her mother might not move fast enough to catch her.

"Mar!"

Deeper in the corn now, Mar dropped to her hands and knees. Like Indians. Her sweaty face dripped. Another grasshopper centered itself where a leaf joined the stalk. She swatted it down and kept on crawling toward home, a path as familiar as hymns. She was six; she knew the way.

But her mother let her be. Instead of chasing after, Susan lifted Jimmy up into her two arms so he sat on her elbows like a throne, and started the long way round to the farmhouse. A quarter mile of grassy bank next to the ditch, then a turn along the pathway that cut across the field toward where they lived. Jimmy sniffed occasionally but didn't say anything. Her long skirt brushing against her legs, Susan kept on. Halfway up the pathway, she stopped to check the blackberries, their thorny canes spilling down into the grass, green and red nubbins tangled together like necklaces. A few were black; she held Jimmy so he could grab them and gobble them down. When she put her face up close to his hand, he dropped one between her lips.

Richard was haying at the far end of the field. The second crop was half yellow rocket, hardly worth the getting in. At the edge where the fence started, with Rural Electrification wire that frightened the cows just by its presence, they watched him furrow the distance, a Monkey Ward straw hat pushed back from his forehead. He never looked like a farmer; even the white forehead over his tanned face didn't count as it would have on another man.

He didn't see them. Or hear them. The racket from the John Deere blotted them out. The tractor jolted along, the cutter behind it slicing the grass and then moving on. From the little rise Susan stood on, with Jimmy held against her, the field stretched like green fabric, darker in a line behind the tractor. Above it all, the blue sweep of the sky, splashed with white along the edges like soapsuds, deepened and shallowed with the waves of the sun.

She didn't think he could see her now, either. But perhaps? The tractor hesitated, coughed into neutral. His right hand was on the gearshift. Was he planning how to catch her if she were to take off running, arcing through the field with Jimmy on her shoulder? He had the right. They were joined in holy matrimony. He wasn't a bad man. He provided.

"Susan!"

She pretended it was a voice in her dreams. Jimmy was asleep.

"Susan!" He even owned her name.

The tractor grumbled into first gear, swung around, started down the last swath toward her. Then the motor switched into neutral again, and he stepped down, his right foot moving onto and then off the pedal, which was grey with crusted dirt in all its grooves. He came to her through the hay, stirring the cut smell, walking through it without sinking in, moving in the mowed part where it all lay in swatches against the soil, a roof for the mice who trembled underneath.

In their Belfontaine wedding picture, which Mar kept taking out of the drawer and staring at, they had stood facing the camera with the tops of their heads exactly together. You could have laid a ruler across them. Of course, she had held hers up high. He had parted his hair in the middle then, still did, though there wasn't as much of it now. His eyebrows striped across his forehead, a roof for his eyes, that impossible glass-blue like Jimmy's. And Mar's. Her eyes weren't like his; they were brown all the way inside.

"Susan, I thought you were in the house." He smiled.

"No."

"I thought you were there. Did you see EuraBella? They wanted to take Mar to town."

"No." Suddenly Jimmy weighed a ton. His bony head collided with all her ribs no matter how she shifted him. Stooping, she laid him down in the grass, brushing aside the fronds that bent over his face. But as she made him comfortable and straight, hands flat on his stomach so they wouldn't go to sleep with his weight on them, she couldn't get up herself. She couldn't capture her body to make it rise.

"Are you all right?"

She couldn't answer.

"Are you all right, Susan?" He stepped over Jimmy's legs, already sinking into the ground, and knelt beside her. His eyes drew a rectangle around her, and she knew she was supposed to stay in it. She even pulled her skirt in so it wouldn't spill beyond the boundaries.

Since it was being done to her, since she surely wasn't doing any of it herself, no one could blame her. Her linen was clean, she knew that, although it wasn't linen, just cotton. Her mother would have had linen. There had been drawers of it, all smelling sunny from the clothesline, and then the sachet bags packed underneath. Lace and tatting and crocheted patterns of daisies along the legs and tops, and even along the seams. When you ran your hands through it and heaped it up over your mouth and nose, it had been like being buried in transparent wings.

His leg came up against hers. The pop-pop of the tractor motor hesitated, coughed, then sputtered out as if he had turned the key. He laughed. "At least we won't waste gas," he said.

She put her hands behind her, but he caught her by the elbows and moved her arms out to where he could grasp them. "You can't say it isn't warm enough." His boot arced along the grass, pressing it down. He looked over at Jimmy, asleep, the bending stems tenting his face. "Where's that Mar?"

"Home." She might be by now, stamping into the kitchen or climbing the elm by the porch. It wouldn't make any difference anyway. "Richard, anyone could see," she said. And the time was wrong.

It was like planting seeds in the house garden, one, and then one, and then another one, spaced by eye but still accurate. First the right shoulder buckle, the strap darker where the metal lines had cut across it. Then the left one. Two buttons were missing from his shirt, but that wasn't her fault. He hadn't put it in the sewing basket. The empty buttonholes were frayed, and the raveling bits came into her eyes and brushed across them again and again until even closing her lids couldn't still the rush, which was all mixed up with the sunlight by then, and the hay, half cut and half grown, and Jimmy's knee, a hard irregular lump against his dirty pants, raised just far enough off the ground for her hand to slide under it if she had tried. She would have tried, too, because there was something about the way he was sinking into the dirt, pulling the grass down across him like a lid, that urged her hands out. Only they couldn't get loose. Richard had them pressed down against the grass so hard that they were molded into sticks, into slender fans of bone that would brown with the fall rains and then crumble into fertilizer. What was it? Phosphorus? If she had read more, then she'd know. But you couldn't put words into the bowl and whisk them into froth, you couldn't bake them and slice them into sweetness on the plate. Words weren't alive, they weren't her body that felt the nubs

of the soil all the way down, even through her loosening hair that
pancaked out from her skull and must be choking him, his breath
came with such a rasp. Her dress was a great wadded blanket all
along her backbone, forcing the arch even higher. She would con-
centrate on her back. While he worked, chugging like his own
tractor with the core of his body, she started at her shoulder blades,
checked them, moved down her spine and counted the small
bones, swept into her waist, running now as she curved inward,
then swooped her mind-fingers next to his, now on her hips, and
over them, marking them with her own mark. On the top of his
head, down now so she could see it, the spilling hairs uncovered
where he was getting bald, pinking in the sunshine. Pink like a
baby's behind, her mother would have said. In the middle of the
pink doily, the skin with its fragile pores moved up and down. In
her own center, she moved too, faster, answering him whether she
wanted to or not.

She hadn't even noticed he was done until the little loose throb
came out inside her. He whimpered with the loss. Then the sun she
couldn't see slipped behind the evening band of cloud, and she
knew that was true because a cool layer passed her face. It must be
going to rain. In the elm grove at the edge of the field, an evening
robin called anxiously, called again, began to tell the sky exactly
when the rain should come down, because he was thirsty, because
the land was dry, because it was an August evening in Minnesota
and the corn was heading out at the right time, only it needed
moisture to pack the kernels full and golden, water for the brown-
tipped annuals in the kitchen garden, water for the ditches to
muddy the dust layers on the trodden grasses, water to fill the barrel by the side of the house, water so soft that when she filled a
dishpan with it and dipped her hair in, the suds sculpted around
her face like a coif. Like a coif.

In the corn, Mar was listening to the robin too. His silver thread
pulled her through the tunnel, and at the end of it, lower than she
was, her Ma sat in the grass with her skirt swaddled up around her
belly. Jimmy wasn't there, but then he was because she heard him
cry like he did when he woke up. The tractor screeched from somewhere near them, and then her Ma pulled Jimmy up from where he
had been hiding in the grass and bounced him into the air. Then
she hugged him. Mar didn't want to be bounced or hugged either,
so she turned and trotted through the corn to the edge where the
ferns grew up, and then snuck down to where the tractor had cut

and she could get to the farm through the side yard. If she kept
going the right way, she could get there before anyone.

Twenty-Seven

Dear Lucianne,

I've been thinking all year about leaving him. If I could get the money for a down payment, I could buy an old house in town and take boarders. There's a factory outside Manatee that makes boat cushions, and they're expanding. There'll be new people. Jimmy will be in school half days.

Dear Lucianne,

I think I have to stay on the farm with Richard. He isn't a bad man, like you said. He still wants my body. Some women don't even have that. He doesn't drink, at least not much, and he's only hit me once. It was my fault.

Dear Lucianne,

I don't want to have any more children.

Dear Lucianne,

It's the hottest summer in almost a decade, the farmers say. I canned sixty-two pints of beans. They just kept coming and coming until I thought I'd get heatstroke. Richard talks about getting Jimmy a regular horse. He talks about it all the time.

Dear Lucianne,

If I go, he could make me leave the children with him. But I don't think he will. He'll probably move to some other town, or go off to war somewhere. I think this Hitler will make trouble soon enough. If Richard were a soldier, then he could shoot someone and not be blamed for it.

Dear Lucianne,

Tonight the sun was drawing water, and I sat on the porch watching it. Mar has two kittens from the barn, and she dresses them up in her doll clothes. She has scratches from top to bottom. Jimmy hardly ever pees in his pants anymore. I miss it.

Dear Lucianne,

   I feel as if something is the matter with me. I can't go to
Frankie's grave. I don't even know if the peony bloomed this year.
Sometimes I have to keep my hands behind my back so I don't hit
the children. I never have hit them for no reason, but the reasons
get smaller and smaller. Richard sees me as just one of the useful
things on the farm.

Dear Lucianne,

   I've read all the encyclopedias straight through more than once.
They don't have the answers I need. I wish you were here to tell me
the answers.

Twenty-Eight

"In ten years, you'd expect something to have changed, wouldn't you?"

"Has it been that long?"

"Ten years, eight months."

"And it might have been even longer if I hadn't told myself I was just going to up and come."

The two women sat against the back of the barn in the last light, skirts swept up under them on the grass. Lucianne's hair was marcelled into waves over her skull. Susan had let her braid down. The tail of it hung over one shoulder, curving down her breast. They were holding hands like schoolgirls. Which, after all, was what they had been.

"Don't you ever wear gloves to protect your skin?" Lucianne's thumb mapped its way along Susan's palm.

"Are you crazy? I'd have no time. Or if I did wear them, they'd have to stay on forever."

"Coconut oil is good for skin conditioning."

"Your hand feels like you have a monopoly on it."

Lucianne laid out their hands in a row on the browning grass. The sun was so low in the sky that only the tips of their fingers were lit. "Well," she said. "I'm exaggerating. Skin doesn't matter. Soul matters."

"I don't know if that's a compliment."

"It means you've won out over life."

"I've won an occasional battle."

The two of them moved closer together. "I missed you," Lucianne said.

"I missed you, too."

"I couldn't come when Frankie died."

"I know it. I know you would have if you could."

"My mother had pneumonia. She was flat on her back. I didn't leave the house for two weeks."

"Couldn't she even water her fern?"

"I did that." Lucianne leaned back against the barn, her feet straight out. Her toes bumped up into the horizon. "So you still remember that fern?"

"I never forget anything."

"Not even me? Not even when I don't write?"

"Lucianne." Susan stretched her legs out parallel. Above them a firefly twinked on and off. Then he was gone in the last light of the sky. "There were times." She spread her skirt, neatening it down around her legs against the mosquitoes, though it had been dry, and it was late in the season for them anyway. "There were times when the remembering got me through. When they were born. When I saw Frankie in the horse stall, stretched out like he was asleep. And sometimes at night when Richard holds my wrists out so I can't move my arms. I think snow angels, mud angels, and I can manage."

"Do you still want Richard?"

"Is that what it is? He wants me. Or something."

Lucianne was silent.

"I wouldn't necessarily call it love."

"No. Not the way we'd define it."

"I think it was like someone came who had a title to the property. The Susan May McIntire property. That was Richard. No use combating a legal document. So I said yes to him."

"He's not a bad man."

"No, he isn't."

"He's given you children."

"They're not a gift."

"Jimmy has your face."

"He stole it. When I wasn't looking. Now when I put my hands up under my hairline, it's blank as an egg."

"And Mar has your spirit."

"She stole that, too."

Lucianne turned toward Susan, reached out. Her forefingers slid up the sides of Susan's jaw, across her cheekbones, scooped up against her nose and smoothed her eyebrows. "Your face is still there, my dear. And I didn't notice any absence of spirit."

"How long can you stay?"

"A week, altogether. Then I go back to work."

"Do you like clerking?"

"If I can make the store rich by my competence. Which perhaps I can. But after Christmas they're going to let me manage. Not *let* me, exactly. I demanded it with fire in my eye."

"In Belfontaine?"

"No. Omaha. The home store."

"So you'll move."

"Yes. My mother is going to her sister's in Fairfax. She'll be better off, actually."

"Who gets the fern?"

"I'm going to send it to you in an enormous barrel with three pickled turkeys and a gross of darning cotton."

"Why don't you include a set of reference books?"

"You already have the encyclopedias. And Shakespeare."

"But I know them by heart."

Three fireflies sparked on and off as accurate as clockwork. The evening star made a fourth. Off to the right, the upstairs light in the house came on, the electricity they'd finally become accustomed to. Richard had driven off after supper, so it wasn't him. Mar was probably beating Jimmy into submission before she showed him his picture book.

"Do you still have time to read?"

"I take time."

"Such a strange wedding present we gave you. The *Britannica.*"

"I read an article every week. At least. Did you know that some ancient tribes worshiped the grass because they thought it was the hair of their ancestors?"

"Some people read the Bible."

"That would be far down on my list."

"Do you miss normal school?"

"With my very soul."

Lucianne took Susan's hand again.

"I feel as if I live in an afterthought on the rim of the known world."

"But you still have Mar and Jimmy."

"When Frankie died, I knew what hostages to fortune meant."

"Susan."

"When I look at them, all I see is the space that would be there if they were gone."

Lucianne bent over, holding Susan against her, her knees lifted up so her lap made a nest as soft as a nest could be.

"Then love them while they're there."

"I sometimes think I can't take one more thing."

"Another Indian summer? Another winter? Another round of life?"

"Another empty space. Another day of living with what isn't the same as me."

"You'll see your grandchildren. Think of that."

"Lucianne, you know what I want?" Susan turned her face upward, lifted her hand, tickled Lucianne's chin where the jawbone made a perfect triangle underneath. "I want to see if I can do it on my own."

"What else did you ever do?"

"Like if I woke up on my own cloud, absolutely alone in the sky. With no one. No Richard to love me or whatever he does. No children to rub little pieces off of me. Or on the earth, with the grandmothers buried underneath. Nothing in my body that wasn't mine."

"Then you'd be God."

They looked up together, waiting for the bolt. Then they laughed.

"He's off duty tonight."

"Maybe he needs a partner."

"I'm not going to be a partner. All or nothing."

They held their linked hands against the sky, waiting.

Twenty-Nine

All around her, the dry leaves crackled. The sun was just coming up, and the horizon was grey whenever she got peeks of it through the trees. What time? Six? She hadn't checked the kitchen clock. Richard had left at two, heading for the North Dakota border and then on to Mitchellsville for the livestock auction. They must be doing all right if he went to Mitchellsville for an auction. They must be able to run more cattle, buy another horse, maybe build a second machine shed.

Mar and Jimmy would sleep late. They'd been up till all hours, popping corn, gobbling it. Jimmy chewed on the sides of his mouth now that his front teeth were gone. Mar stuffed the brittle fluff in everywhere.

The road turned. Susan went up the bank. Soft as a lawn, because EuraBella's goat, Mary Queen of Scots, always grazed there. She relished nettles best of all, then the big thistles, then sandburs, and finally the grasses, green drool in her beard. Her udder left its own trail along the stubble. EuraBella milked her together, one behind squeezing, one in front pillowing her bony head.

Beyond the bank was their picket fence. In the grey light of dawning, it was hard to see, but she knew by heart that it was painted lavender. Sears had been having a paint sale. As she passed through the pastel gate, she caressed the nearest picket. Mist, early morning mist of almost-winter, hung in webs around the windbreak behind the house. She went up the steps and across the porch. Eura's rocker was swaying just the least bit from the wind; Bella's was wedged against the railing and didn't budge. Susan shoved Bella's loose so it could get some exercise. She went in.

The first room was the kitchen, the floor covered with newspaper, spread clean every evening. No one from outside had seen the linoleum. "Not missing a thing," Eura said. They had three stoves, the big Acme from Ohio with its gut full of ashes, the regular gas stove corded to the bottled gas tanks leaning against the wall outside, and an electric hot plate built into a platform Bella had made years ago. It was painted lavender too. The three stoves nudged each other in genteel friendship against the far wall. Opposite them, the door to the parlor was closed and padlocked, with a molasses-bottle doll, face painted black, wedged up against it. On the kitchen table—oilcloth checkerboarded across it—were their next morning's breakfast plates, napkins folded into triangles next to them. "So they're ready if we wake up blind," Eura always said.

Susan went upstairs, up ladder steps so steep she had to lean a little backward to form a triangle of balance. In the half-dark, the opening at the top glowed with the beginnings of the day. They'd carpeted the stairs; her feet were silent as her mouth.

At the top, she could see better. Her pupils must have sucked up the darkness. EuraBella's bed was in the middle of the room, sloping walls protecting it like a canopy. They'd built the frame themselves and it was monumental, a square ship with the remaining floor just a ripple around it. Over the mattress, which they'd sewn from corn shucks as if they'd just gotten here from the old country, they'd stretched a gigantic patchwork quilt of their own making. The pattern had started out to be Double Wedding Ring, but then it had evolved into Garden Path, and finally the Pineapple. Bella had finished it off with a Star of Bethlehem in the top corners.

Yes, up here it was lighter, above the windbreak and the dark earth. EuraBella's heads were neatly centered on their pillows, apple-doll faces leathered against the tatted cotton. They both wore nightcaps, elasticized around the edges. The Star of Bethlehem border bisected their necks at exactly the same spot on each. A little ways further down, Bella's front humped up; Eura's was flat as a pancake. Near the bottom, their toes peaked the quilt like two little roofs.

She hated to wake them. Maybe if she just waited.

Through the left-hand window, a horizontal cloud blushed on its underside.

Her muscles ached in her thighs. It had been a quick walk. She hoisted her legs up onto the bed, wedging them under her, but quietly. The shucks whispered, but neither nightcap twitched. Balling herself up like a caterpillar, Susan lay down.

She never did have to wake them. The warming dawn came around her like a blanket. Only her nose, sticking out the farthest into the leftover night air, prickled with damp. All the rest of her was under the Star, and the Pineapple, and the Garden Path. The Double Wedding Ring had ended up all on Eura's side. Susan was as warm as a June lamb, born at the height of noon. She had never been so warm. All her blood, smiling, tasted the insides of her flesh. She could have tindered the stove by her own body.

"Such a surprise." Eura's voice contradicted every word.

"Not such a surprise." Bella's apple face looked right up at the ceiling, beaming. She held out her hand.

"Of course we'll have to get the things we need first."

"Like before, with your others."

"How far along? More than two?"

"They never get enough, these men."

"Can't help themselves."

"Should keep it wrapped."

"They never think."

"Comes from the wrong end for thinking."

"Yes, indeed." Eura giggled. Outside, dawn birds answered on the same pitch.

"I'll bring the children over. We'll do it while they nap."

"All done by evening."

"You can all sleep here after."

"Hardly any blood, the way we do it. You know."

"Hardly any."

"No need to be frightened."

"A fall cleaning, you might say."

"That's a bad joke, my dear."

"There are no bad jokes."

"And I'll make apple dumplings for supper afterward," Eura said happily.

Thirty

The popcorn chain reached all the way to the door of the parlor. Chuckling, Jimmy hopped along it, clapping his hands in front of him.

Mar sat next to her mother in the kitchen, balanced on the top of the stool. Next to her on the counter was a yellow pottery bowl, little Indian designs under the rim. Inside, the bowl was yellow halfway down, then white, drifted with popcorn. Next to it was a tray of cranberries. Mar had sorted out all the bad ones. They didn't have enough; the store in Manatee had been almost sold out. Daddy should have taken them shopping earlier. Everyone bought cranberries for Christmas.

"Want me to thread your needle?" Her mother's voice was soft. She stood behind Mar, arms beside her, hands resting on the counter. It was like being in a warm box. Mar pulled her arms close to her own sides.

"See, like this." Susan took the needle Mar had almost threaded and held it up to the light. "Good. Now take the ends. Lick your fingers, see." Mar did. "Then roll those threads together. That's right." She circled Mar's wrists with her hand. "See, there's your knot. Now start again. Three whites, one red. Or more whites. We'll try to come out even. There aren't enough cranberries to cook anyway."

Jimmy's giggles were getting louder. He was coming back along the popcorn chain. Around the corner, in the niche under her mother's elbow, Mar saw the end of the white road where it snaked into the kitchen. Jimmy must be stepping on it because the end kept jerking.

Outside, through the window over the sink, the snow spread white as soapsuds. The sky was white, too. Only the edge of the garage was grey, and the edge of the barn at the corner of the window, and the patch of trees by EuraBella's, though you couldn't see their house no matter how hard you tried. Flakes were coming down, little wisps that dandled the air. All Daddy's footprints to the barn and back were eyeholes in the white carpet. When you walked in them, you slid to the sides because they'd iced over in the bottom.

"That's good, Mar. That's a good chain. I could wear that one for a necklace." Her mother picked up Mar's string and held it against the light of the window, stretching it out between her hands. Then she wrapped it around Mar's forehead.

"You look like a goddess. Or a princess. Maybe you'll find a prince in your stocking. Or slippers to carry you away to his castle. Remember Cinderella? Glass slippers like hers."

Mar looked at her feet. At the ends of her legs, they stuck out like little pillows. Over the black toes of her slippers that Daddy had given her, the flesh arched in tight rolls. She scrunched her toes together inside, wedging their tips down to the soles. Then she jabbed her needle into the brown spot of a cranberry, one from the wrong pile. The needle wobbled in the slush. She pulled it out and put the berry in her mouth.

"Mar!" But her mother couldn't grab it away because it had already gone down the little red lane.

Outside, her daddy appeared by the edge of the barn. He had buckets. Behind him, the newest horse snorted and stomped, steam rising in the cold air. Her daddy rubbed the horse's mane, his hand circling in the stiff hairs. Her own hair prickled.

Her mother bent toward her. Mar stabbed at the popcorn. Jimmy came across the linoleum, the popcorn chain wrapped against his stomach. Her mother kissed him.

"Shall we put it on the tree?"

In the parlor, the Christmas tree was anchored in its stand against the window toward the road, its slanted trunk artfully arranged so it leaned toward the wall. Mar had seen her mother do it. It didn't look crooked that way unless you crept along behind it, which nobody would. On the floor underneath was an old cotton sheet, heaped up on curves like the snow outside. They had a few presents already, from EuraBella, but they'd had those since Thanksgiving. EuraBella liked being first. And Aunt Lucianne's package had come yesterday, too big for Jimmy to carry, but Mar had no trouble with it. It rattled a lot.

Her mother wound the biggest popcorn chain around the bottom branches of the tree, dressing it out like petticoat trim. It reached around once and then half again. She wedged the end into the branches up near the trunk. "Let me have yours, Mar," she said.

Mar handed it to her, keeping one chubby hand on her own end. For a moment, they held it taut. They draped the string around the front of the tree a foot above the long one.

"Which ornament do you like best?" Her mother sat in the big chair with her feet out, toes together. Jimmy got up and climbed on her lap.

"I like the clock."

"Is that right, Mar?"

"Yes it is." To prove it, Mar stepped firmly to the side of the tree and put her hand around the glass ball, painted white but chipped so that the pure glass showed through in places, with the black numbers in clusters and the hands made out of wire that hooked around the lump in the middle. Someone had tied a ribbon around the loop on top, and that was what it hung from.

"Who tied this ribbon?"

Her mother looked at her.

"Did you tie this ribbon?" It was smooth, silky on one side. Mar felt it again.

"My mother must have."

"My grandma?"

"Yes."

"She's dead."

"Yes."

Jimmy dug his heels into the chair cushion on both sides of his mother's lap and scrabbled himself upright. "I want candles," he said.

"They aren't safe."

"Why not?"

"Because we're too far from town. The fire department could never get here in time."

"But there's a fire in the stove."

"That's different."

Mar let the clock bang back against the branch. "You don't need candles, Jimmy," she said. "Candles are old-fashioned. We have tree lights. I'll turn them on right now." She followed along the black cord, pieced with electrical tape from her daddy's toolbox, and stuck the plug hard into the wall socket. The tree sweetened with light.

"I want candles," whined Jimmy.

"Get him one," said her mother, her face sliding further and further away. "At least he can hold it."

That was dumb. That was really dumb. Mar stamped off to the kitchen for the stool, then through the door into the little pantry room with shelves all around. The cold put its arms on her stomach under her dress. She wrenched the stool next to the north shelves and climbed up to reach the box on top, digging into the stool with her toes while her body balanced against the shelf edges. The candles were beeswax, pale brown and slender. She took a pair, linked together by their wicks, and put them between her lips so she could use both hands for balance as she clambered down again. Landing safely, she stomped out to give the candles to Jimmy.

Except she couldn't. Inside the parlor, Jimmy had disappeared. Instead, her father and her mother were talking, sitting across from each other. Her father had his yard boots on, and he kept one foot on top of the other so the rug would get only half dirty. When there was a space in the voices, he'd exchange feet, and his whole body would shift a little. Her mother sat tight-quiet. Mar heard words, the words she always heard, but this time there were more openings between them, more spaces when the mouths weren't moving and there were only the boots exchanging places, thump-and-shuffle, and maybe the sound of her mother's fingers on the hard-stuffed arm of the big chair, tapping like crickets. Mar peeled bits of beeswax from the bottoms of the two candles where nobody could see and sucked them.

"I don't know what you want."

"If it were possible to tell you, then . . ."

"Seems like nothing satisfies . . ."

"Sometimes it's like I gave up all the . . . or they were taken . . . or . . ."

"What matters is what's . . ."

"Oh, how would you know what . . ."

"Susan, you're acting like . . ."

Mar caught the last words in her mouth with the beeswax. Sweet and salt mixed on her tongue. She felt like eating the popcorn chain from beginning to end. In her chair, her mother sat thin as a fence post, but she wasn't crazy. People said that EuraBella were crazy, but that was because they had mixed up their patchwork quilt. Mar *liked* it the way it looked. She herself might be fat, she thought, her free hand wedging her belly back underneath her waistband, but she knew what was what.

Jimmy came up behind her and grabbed the candles. She forgot to hang on, but he still yanked them away so hard that he fell down. His rear hit the kitchen linoleum like a shovel on rock, and all the voices in the parlor swooped down to nothing.

Later, in the cold night, Mar remembered Christmas the year before, and how cold it had been then, too, and how she had worn her long underwear to bed under her nightgown. It was a good thing the Baby Jesus hadn't been born in Manatee. Huddled up under her quilts, all of them ordinary, each telling one story, Mar tested bits of sheet with her toes, first warming up the parts by her bottom, her legs tucked up tight under her. When the sheets had heated up a little, she explored further with her toes, inches at a time. Down to Iowa, then Kansas, then New Mexico. She wasn't supposed to know that yet, but the sixth graders were learning it in school, and she listened. Down to Guatemala. Outside, the cold iced the edges of the windows like white paper dolls. Moonlight made the ice dance. Moonlight danced along the inside of her lashes, poked and splintered by the sharp hairs. Her toes reached Bolivia.

The next bed, jammed into the corner of the room by the door so anyone could have crept over the foot and out into the house without even creaking the mattress, was empty. Holding the candles in both hands, the wax softening, Jimmy was in the parlor, sitting with as much of himself as possible on the sheet under the Christmas tree. The matches from the pantry were damp, but they might work anyway if he did it right, so he scraped them with extra care on the tree stand. When one sparked and held its light, he lit both the candles, apart now since he'd chewed the joining wick in two. They were pretty, his own moon.

He didn't touch, because fire burned. Christmas fire burned too. His hands stabbed the candle bottoms into the floor, but they wouldn't stand up. The flames dipped like August fireflies. Jimmy leaned over, his head on Aunt Lucianne's box. It was hard. One candle went out.

Thirty-One

The snow blanket had a tiny flame underneath it glowing through. Around its piercing tip, the soft white had thawed, dripped down, then frozen again as the flame flickered to one side or the other, frozen into ice so clear, so hard, that it was metallic, prismatic, fairylike. From the top it was just snow, white hills stretching like banners settled from sky to earth, ripples in the fabric, creases, swirls, coverlet of an unmade bed for the giant creatures from the heart of the world, no horizons, or rather, white horizons, white sky, swirls of clouds, all one, all white, all cold. But underneath burned the flame, alive, yellow at the tip, then red, and then the heart, blue, blue as veins, the liver of a new-killed deer, the flesh of a horse's foot within the circle of the metal shoe. Bluer than eyes. And it had a sound, too, yellowredblue together, a sound going in and out like breath, like the pumping of a squeeze-box, through the colors and then back, the whole color wheel, art class, normal school, Lucianne's picture on the easel, snow angels, dirt angels, only she couldn't catch any of them, she couldn't get out from under the snow. The flame burned and burned, one side, then the other. She saw it, or was it behind her eyes? And he was in her way, on her, heavier than snow, like earth, not part of the sound at all, swallowing her breath, and on top of him the snow, now with pictures, and on top of that, up where she couldn't see in the dark on both sides of her head, the sky as white as the snow, as black, and that tiny light too near for comfort. Much too near for comfort. And the sound!

Miles from Manatee. Miles from Manatee. Her dreams had closed, gate barred, clangclang, couldn't get back in. Even with the "whatisitwhatisit" barreling along the side of her head, she battled out from underneath, feet skidding on the linoleum, hair hanging, crystal-nosed, and hit the door with such force that the latch sprang without a finger on it. In the parlor, the air was full of vowels, scraping, and an on-off light that snapped in the air. The tree was burning into the sky, Christmas candle, and on the floor, crawling, asking, was a half fire, *Mamamama*, that was known to her, that was indeed known to her, that was melting the air into salt, that was the flame under the snow.

Thirty-Two

Dr. Collins had red hair. But there had to be grey in it some-where, maybe at the hairline where the wave swept down over, or buried behind his ears. Because he was a doctor, after all—college, medical school, no plain normal school for him. If he knew what he was doing, he couldn't be as young as he looked.

And Jimmy was getting better.

The hall footsteps skittered against the tiles. A laugh, profes-sional voices. Knock-knock, but not on their door. Muffled words. Footsteps again.

Susan looked at her hands. All her fingers waved in her lap like weeds under a lake surface. Her nails were pale green shells, each one neatly tucked into its bed, nothing sticking out, no flurried sheets, no wadded pillowcases. Nothing.

Jimmy was sleeping, his shaved head mottled against the pillow. All his bandages were off except for one arm. His burned skin had been red, then bubbly, and now was brown and pink in a patch-work across his chest and up under his chin and down his shoulder and up the side of his face. His one ear was a tiny pink flower, bud-ded against his skull. His other ear was fine.

"Mrs. Carson?"

Who was that?

"He's sleeping, Mrs. Carson. That's good."

And the red hair came in.

When they'd brought Jimmy to the hospital in Manatee that night three weeks ago, wrapped in the throw from the back of the sofa, his screams worn down to a grating whistle that went off and on with his breath, she and Richard had stood side by side inside the entrance. Like jigsaw pieces they'd stood, like the continents, inserted into each other and then set adrift by the surges of the great waves, but each still holding the impression of the other. In the space opened between them, the rattly cart with Jimmy on it had skidded down the hall. They had told the doctor what had happened. The doctor had replied. They had stayed, but not till morning. He wouldn't die. The doctor said. Not this time.

So they had gone back to the old Ford and driven off in the cold dawn, spines arched against the icy air that made their bones brittle as glass. From each to the other a long wave slid, and slid again, while bits of their insides crackled within their frosty flesh. They had gone back to the farm, to the house, to the room with the scorched tree and the braided rug half-mooned with soot. A wonder that it hadn't all gone up. But they could not be melted by the flame, could not flow toward each other again.

"Everything is going well. By the time he's grown, you won't see most of the scars."

Yes.

"We'll keep him another two or three days to make sure the new skin is coming in right and get the bandage off his arm."

Yes.

"It was lucky you got to him when you did. It could have been much worse."

Yes.

Susan stayed in her chair, head tilted, listening attentively. The one part of her. The other part knelt at Dr. Collins's feet and flung her arms around his thighs. That part burrowed its head between his knees, neck thinning like a heron's. If he would only tighten on her, then everything inside her would flow out, bear her away in moonlight. She would be emptied. There would be no more reaching into her, no more growing. The juice, the pads of flesh, no more. Dried and blown away. Pemmican. On the top of the ridge, she could ride the fingernail moon to where even the air would be gone. She was strong. Having children made a woman strong. She had borne them. She could bear it.

"Mrs. Carson?"

Susan rose from her chair and looked up. She hadn't done an untoward thing. Nothing untoward at all.

"Do you have any questions?" Dr. Collins wasn't even looking at her as he listened to Jimmy's heart, touched the scars, lifted the bandaged arm. Jimmy's eyes opened, and he curled himself under the sheet. The top of his bare head stuck out, stubbly against the pillow.

"Any questions?" Dr. Collins was looking at her now, up close. In his right eye, a red web danced through the white. Inside there, somewhere inside there, were all those words, all the bones and muscles, all the knowledge. *Femur. Trapezoid.* All the pills, pellets that could say yes and no. Shelves and shelves curving gently along the inside of his skull.

"Thank you very much, Dr. Collins."

That was safe.

"Thank you very much for doing what you did."

He looked at her as if he might have more to tell her. But already she knew where she was going, and she had her heavy coat hunched up against her back as she thrust her arms into the sleeves. She had said good-bye appropriately enough, even remembering to lay her hand on Jimmy's knee under the sheet as she went out. Dr. Collins was already talking to some nurse in the hall, their voices clattering out into the cold as she stepped into the stairwell and started down. Around her head she tied the brown scarf from her pocket. Her feet clumped in their galoshes, steady like hooves, and by the time she reached the bottom door, by the time she was out in the hall, she knew what she was going to do even better than when she had begun.

Outside, the cold filled the air like a fierce voice. It crackled her ears, then set them to burning. Smiths Grocery Store was near, on the block next to where Richard's hardware store had been. She still got groceries there sometimes when they drove to Manatee. The store on the other side of town was bigger, but she never felt at home there. Smiths had wooden floors, the boards worn down to the grain, and a barrel of crackers, although it wasn't hygienic and hardly anyone kept to the custom anymore. Mr. Morrison (there had never been a Mr. Smith as far as she knew) was there all day and often into the night, his hands so solid when he leaned on the counter that when he lifted them she always expected to see five-pointed dents left behind. A tiny American flag stood in a toothpick holder on top of the cash register. You could get credit if you lived anywhere within twenty miles, though she and Richard had never used it.

As Susan reached the right corner, she opened her mouth. Her breath shot out in a cloud. Her teeth hardened into ice. It must be below zero, with windchill to match. She anchored her eyes on the door, pulled herself toward it by the line even as the cold ate at her. No one else was on the street. Over her, over everything, the sky was an oval of grey of which she was the core.

When she pulled the door toward her, the brown and golden light from inside the store broke in her head. Mr. Morrison was in the back on a ladder, lining up canned goods on a high shelf, so he didn't see her until after she had begun to gather.

"Shopping?" he asked as he came down, rung by rung, even though it was a foolish question, even though he might as well have said nothing.

"Yes," she replied. Then she moved up the aisle and behind the bags of flour. He wouldn't follow her in any deliberate fashion. This was Minnesota.

She made her selections carefully, but she had already made them in her head. Not more than she could carry. As she gathered the items—dried apples, raisins, walnuts, the expensive winter tangerines—she piled them in an ornate pattern on the counter. It was so cold and so windy that not another soul had come out. Mr. Morrison would have been glad if she had chatted, but she knew how to turn him off. He probably thought she was sorrowing for what had happened to Jimmy, and perhaps she was. Though she wouldn't have called it sorrowing. When you had offended the gods, you had to pacify them.

Once Susan had made her choices, she paid Mr. Morrison, whose eyes were steamy with curiosity. She had the correct change, which was a sign. When she left the store, she made sure her whole foot touched down at each step, to send the ground a message. It was magic, and magic might be true. Halfway back to the hospital, she passed the Retzlaff house, but she kept her head turned in the opposite direction. Elwin was in Duluth, but it was still important not to allow him in. He wasn't right.

Her left hand, pierced by the cold through her store-bought glove, had numbed into ice across her fingers where the shopping bag handle dug in. Her hands hadn't been properly warm in winter since Grandmother Bowles's mittens. Her hands hadn't been warm since Lucianne.

As near the hospital as possible, but where the town was still country on the edges, she turned past the corner of the block and walked to the winter fields. The last houses were ramshackle with unshoveled walks. Beyond the final garage, its door open to show an old Chevrolet up on blocks, the road ran between open land. She walked along, timing herself, until a grove of bare trees came up on her left, and then she walked further to where they blocked her or any other passerby from the eyes of town. Three steps off the road, big steps that brought her past where the sidewalk would have been had there been one, she knelt in the snow. With her bare hands (it was important that they be truly cold so that there would be no doubt of what she was willing to give up), she made three holes, deep past her wrists, and in each one she placed a little pile of food: dried apples, a tangerine, some raisins, a walnut. She covered them over, scooping the displaced snow back together until it was smoother than it had been before, packed to the beginnings of ice. Another cold night and they would be planted as firm as the grave. Then she bent her body to one side and slid herself out flat, her arms spread as far as they would go, her feet poised like a diver's. She shut her eyes against whatever was up there and concentrated on what was below. She could deal with the buried ones. If she were to save Jimmy and Mar and herself, she would need the powers from underneath.

When she got back to the hospital, the receptionist noticed her snowy coat, and Susan noticed her noticing it. "Snow is everywhere," she said, not explaining beyond that. She took the elevator up to Jimmy's room this time, and spread the remaining feast on his blanket with such flourish that as he woke up he couldn't help but grin. First, she dropped the raisins and dried apple slices into his mouth, one at a time, until he began to giggle as he chewed. The walnuts she cracked open on the bed table with the heavy drinking glass. For the tangerines, she dug in her thumbnails, and the orange cover came away as if the fruit were undressing itself. When she touched Jimmy's forehead with her sticky fingers, she made it seem as if she were checking for fever.

Dr. Collins came by on his way to make his house calls, stopping at the door to see what was going on.

"What are we celebrating?"

"The new season," Susan said. Her cheeks were flushed.

"Nothing new about January."

"I define a month by what I can do with it, not what it does with me."

Dr. Collins looked to one side as if he had been taken aback. Doctors weren't used to patients who made statements. "You sound as if you have control of things," he said.

"Some things." Soon.

Thirty-Three

"Do you think we have enough?"

"It depends on what she needs to do." Bella knitted sturdily on an afghan of all the off-colored yarns Sears sold from their bargain bin.

"Susan's proud."

"No surprise."

Eura stirred the soup, which was slapping the sides of a vast kettle. It took up the back half of the Acme stove. "She may not take it, you know," she muttered. The dumplings were drifting on the top of the broth like chickens, fat and white. They veered to the middle, clustered together. Eura slammed at them with the wooden spoon. They spun apart, reunited.

"We never talked about it with her."

"She may think we live on the old-age pension."

"Susan's no fool."

"I never said she was."

Bella heaved the afghan to one side, dug her needles into a new ball of yarn. "There's what we saved in the pillowcase," she said.

"Both pillowcases."

"And the green vase in the parlor."

"Inside the skirt of the black mammy doorstop."

"I thought we didn't use that anymore because the bills always fell out."

"Remember? I sewed an inside pocket a year ago."

"That's right."

"On the shelf in the pantry."

"In the Crisco can. That's right."

"Clabber Girl rusted too fast."

"Next to lard, Crisco is best for everything."

"Didn't we used to use the Bible?"

"Not since Roosevelt got himself elected."

"It wouldn't have been polite, him swearing on it and all."

"Lay not your treasures on earth."

"Lay not your treasures *up*."

"You know what I mean."

"And there's the silverware box, too."

"But only under the serving pieces."

"And inside the hat ribbons."

"Protects against the heat. We must have two or three hundred dollars in those hats." Bella rose and draped the afghan over the back of the chair. She swatted her needles into it. "I'm ready for a dumpling," she said.

Eura peered curiously into the pot. "They all fell apart," she said cheerily. "You can have the pieces."

"Three carrots, too. You dish it up."

"We already own the cemetery lots."

"Right next to Daddy and John."

"With an extra one so we won't be crowded."

"She really would be happier leaving that man." Bella blew on her soup, white with collapsed dumplings. She blew again.

"There're the children to consider."

"Won't be any left soon, the way things are going."

"Susan needs to think of herself."

"She tries to. It's an uphill battle."

"And some hills are very big," said Eura. Her face lit up. "We must have at least a thousand saved."

"More than two." A dumpling mustache lined Bella's upper lip. She rubbed it in with her finger.

"Will you tell her?"

"Why not you?"

"We can do it together," announced Eura. "Next time she comes by."

"Richard could be worse, actually."

"Some women aren't meant to be married."

"Not in this world."

"No marrying in the other."

"I guess that tells you where we all ought to stand on that topic," said Bella.

Thirty-Four

He could run like always. When the tractor chugged by, Jimmy ran toward it like an army, elbows pedaling. Further behind him where the hedgerow held back the wind, the farmhouse stuck its roof up, chimney snipping out a square of the sky. Under his shirt, half of him sweated.

If he ran fast, he could catch up. His daddy would see him and call the bombers back. They would swing through the clouds in a proud turn. Spitfires.

The tractor was coming nearer now, with the cloud of dirt behind it racing forward. Up on the seat, his father stuck through like God. The dust hid his cap and smoked the edges of his tan shirt. He and Jimmy had the same bib overalls. The very same.

He got nearer. His father swung the wheel, his shoulders sliding. The dust stayed where it was, then sank. The cultivator teeth hung over the dirt like a friendly dragon. Jimmy looked up so far his neck folded backward.

"You hungry?"

Jimmy hugged himself as he ran the last steps.

"You hungry, boy?"

Up above the two of them and the tractor and the hill of dust that was exploding back down into the earth, the sky was blanket-blue. Jimmy bounced into it and came down, plunging both heels into the fat furrow. His father laughed.

"You do that, I won't need any cultivator. Just send you jumping."

"*Yes.*" His father was so far above him on the seat that when he reached up his arms, it was like praying.

"Ride?"

If he said yes, that was pushy. If he said no, that would be a lie. You got licked for both. Jimmy shut his mouth tight, tasting the scales of dry skin on his lower lip. His tongue watered them.

"Ride, boy?"

The hot blue washed his eyes, and he shut them to keep from drowning.

"Get yourself up here, then."

Still wordless, Jimmy jumped toward the tractor, one foot on the furrow, one foot in the plowed valley below. When he reached it, he scampered to the side where the lined pedal was fastened and held out his hand. The work glove came down and swallowed it. He went up like horses.

"Where's your mama?"

Jimmy was thinking about clouds. If they never came, would day stay forever? The metal rim of the tractor seat sent his legs on each side of it shooting out like firecrackers. His overalls rubbed.

"Where's your mama, son?"

The sun was right there.

"Where is she?" The tractor droned off into the new ground.

Jimmy thought. Maybe his mama had walked the wind to Manatee. Maybe she had wrapped herself in a wet sheet torn from the wringer. She was making apple pie at the sink, the fall apples soft in her hands. She was hitting Mar because Mar talked back. She was in the barn with her needle, pricking Old Maude in the soft skin where the bit went in.

"I don't know." Dust from the cultivator edged down inside his collar.

"Well, I don't either."

The tractor surged down the furrows, its belly ruffling the leaves of the new corn but never flattening them. Jimmy felt his hair, long again, except for the one side where specks of fuzz peppered the funny pink skin. He pulled a chunk of good hair down over it. It was like tissue paper underneath, crunchy against his skull. When he drilled it with his fingers, it didn't hurt. The soft bounce of the tractor jabbed his finger against his head, away, back against it. He shifted to one side. The metal saddle spooned between his legs.

Two big blackbirds flew by, then came back. He twisted to see them. They began making circles around the tractor. Once he heard their wings, like beating rag rugs on the line. He kept them in his eyes so they couldn't get near. They had sharp mouths.

"You're getting big enough for a real horse, son. Old Maude's not much for riding."

That was true. She was fat as a sausage.

"Alf Rollins has a little Morgan he's tired of feeding, now that his kids are gone. I was thinking." His father's voice came out with spaces between the words. "I was thinking I might look him over. Not today. Friday, maybe. If the old fool doesn't change his mind." His father looked up. "Damn, look at those birds. They must think I'm planting."

"Mama doesn't like horses." Jimmy slid his left hand inside his bib, edging it down. "She only feeds Old Maude because I forget."

"That's nothing new to me, son."

Morgans were leather-brown, all of them, mane and tail. They only kicked if you snuck up on them. They were for princes. Jimmy's bottom hummed against the seat, and the dust tickled. The field was almost done, but not quite. He hung on.

"But I like Old Maude, too," he said, being polite.

His father didn't answer.

The tractor jolted down the row. Behind them, the cultivator combed the field, digging in. Dust rose. His father rose up behind him, too, like a warm pillar, like the front wall of their house straight up to the roof. Back against him, back to bib, nothing could touch Jimmy except the warm air, hand-of-God, and nothing could stop the warm nuzzle down where he split off, the warm egg coming out and in at once, the good fire that got hard and popped and then got soft like ice cream in the sun, like apples, like Mar's hand at night when they huddled together under her quilts so they could make their own voices, not the ones across the house, not the sounds with sharp edges, just the pretend-sleep, just the hands like summer earth, just the horses' hooves shaking and shaking until they all got there together.

Thirty-Five

"Susan, it makes no sense."

"Sense isn't the issue."

"I could hire someone to help with the housework. The harvest cooking."

"That's not the issue."

"Why do you have to make a mystery out of everything?"

"It's no mystery, Richard."

"I miss Frankie too, you know."

"Yes."

"We could have one more boy."

"You can't replace people."

"You'd rather read than be with me."

"Sometimes that's true."

"Jimmy and Mar don't want to go."

"How would you know?"

"They've lived here all their lives."

"They'll do what I do."

"Do you expect me never to see them again?"

"Richard, you'll have to decide that. Manatee's not Minneapolis. Anything you want to find out about us, you won't have any trouble doing. I'm not going to the Sahara. We won't live in a cave."

"I can't believe you're planning this."

"I have to."

"You're not a story in one of those books, you know."

"It would be easier if I were."

"Is there someone waiting for you?"

"What?"

"You know what I mean."

"Richard, you would think that."

"What if I don't let you go?"

"The truck is coming tomorrow. Were you thinking of lying down in the driveway?"

"God, Susan. You used to be a gentle woman."

"I was never a gentle woman."

Thirty-Six

At first she'd kept thinking that boardinghouse must mean a house made of boards, even though she knew better. But the boards on hers were real enough, covered with a rough layer of paint smeared on after somebody's second-rate scraping of the old coat. At a distance, the sun caught the roughness and made tiny shadows. All the windows had their own storms and screens too, stored off-season in the garage. The house had twenty-eight windows, not counting the half-circles below the peak, and every one had to be dealt with at the proper time. When she'd moved into town more than two years ago, not a storm or screen had been labeled, and putting them on was an incomprehensible jumble because the fit was tricky even if you had the right one, and impossible if you didn't.

Susan leaned against the rake. It was too early to rake, April, with the crusted filthy snow still humped on the north side of everything as well as under the garbage cans where it hunkered in icy circles. Inside the house, the air was thick with smells from the closed-up winter. Outside, the air came from somewhere else, more and more of it, wind-fresh. Even the damp ground, yellow-green with grass nubbins just awakening, renewed her feet, and the wet that soaked in where the heels of her shoes had worn down and opened was a refreshing chill.

The row of wet rubble she'd raked together lay in front of her. Leaves not gotten last fall, dead grass, sodden candy wrappers from Mar's snacks. One of Jimmy's toy horses, rusting where the paint had chipped. Part of a dandelion, sprung too soon. The bushel basket stood to one side, so she gathered as much as she could from the debris and dropped it in. Scraggly brown bits hung over the top. She leaned the rake against the willow and carried the basket halfway around the house, dumping it on the discard heap.

At first it had seemed simple. She could cook, she could clean. The old house had been for sale for a year by the Collins family, who didn't need the money anyway with their doctor boy and their lawyer boy too. EuraBella had insisted. No one had troubled her at the closing, though the heat of August had stuck her blouse to her like wallpaper paste. By September, when Mar and Jimmy started school at the Greenbriar Grade School four blocks away, she'd already gotten the inside painting done. Before the real cold weather, her first two boarders had settled in upstairs. Mr. Rawlings sold trading stamps for a four-county area, and Mr. Keopek worked in the boat cushion plant on the edge of town. Only now they made life preservers for the sailors, and the children earned pin money from the ripe milkweed pods they sold the manager there. Mr. Keopek was from somewhere in Europe and had an accent. Mr. Rawlings was from the East. The other two boarders she had taken in talked normal English, when they bothered to talk at all.

Susan raked some more. Too wet. She'd tear up the ground more than it was worth, and it would take a long time to heal itself.

Under the bushes along the porch, her rake hit ice. Discarded pine needles were thawing out of it like fish bones. Soon, she'd have to get the chairs out, lining them up far enough from the porch railing so the boarders could rest their feet on it. Mr. Keopek never sat. Mr. Rawlings sat when he got in from his rounds. His old Pontiac would cool in the driveway along the side of the house while Jimmy asked him why he didn't use a horse. The two new boarders sat most of all, especially on Sundays when the people walked by for church. Watching the ladies. They didn't dare talk when she was around, but she saw the newspapers' corners bend down and their eyes stick out. But both Mr. Devonshire and Mr. Jacobs were prompt with the rent. So it was all right.

Her rake jerked free. Jimmy was riding it. Her hands still cupped around the air where the handle had been.

"Morgan Champ!" He swatted his own behind. Head down, mane flying, he trotted to the end of the porch and back.

"How was school?"

"Clippety-clop." The rake clanged on the sidewalk.

"That's not an answer."

"Clippety-clop!"

Susan moved toward him. He was in second grade, but he couldn't read yet. Maybe if he ever sat still to try.

"Where's Mar?"

"Cleaning blackboards."

"She did that yesterday."

But Jimmy was crawling up the porch steps on his hands and knees, not answering.

The blackboards must need cleaning every day. They wrote all the time in fourth grade, the children did. Memory dusted the inside of Susan's nose and throat. She coughed. Hair lifted from her bun, freeing her neck, and one frazzled streak cut across her right eye so she could see it. Not entirely brown anymore.

Susan shoved the strand back in, burying it. Then she grabbed Jimmy down from the porch, riding him on her hip with his legs circling her body. He clutched her under her arms, his head back, and she could see his new front teeth coming in, white lines pushing through the gums. He put his head in her neck, and she smelled his salty hair.

"Doodah, doodah," sang Jimmy. He bounced on her hip like a papoose. "Go ride for Mar, Mama."

No fence to go up to, no gate to go through. After their yard, a dirt path that ran along next to the curb, beaten almost as hard as a sidewalk. Its edges were damp. Down the curb, across the street, up the curb again. Susan's body skewed to one side because Jimmy was pulling it down. She jerked herself even. Jimmy laughed. "Giddyap," he said, leaning back, spreading himself to the wind. He twisted himself around further until he was riding her back, legs hooked around so his feet banged each other on the cushion of her belly. She bent down, neck arched, but not so far down that she couldn't see ahead. She felt the bit in her mouth and the reins pulled back against her ears.

Trotting, they conquered the blocks and sighted the school-house. It had been set back behind a wire fence with blacktop inside it. The town had added to the building twice as the population expanded, and the front part went up like a tower, taller than it was wide. The stairway was steep as a ladder in the middle, Susan remembered.

"Giddyap," said Jimmy. He petted her braid.

Because it wasn't all that late, the school door hadn't been locked. Inside, the fat janitor was sweeping, pushing the brush as if he were swabbing a ship's deck. They trotted past. Susan caught her breath and began the stairs. Because Mar's room was the first one on the right upstairs, they could hear the little eraser plonks before they'd reached the top. They sounded again, stopped. Two voices, Mar's pitched higher. *Plonkplonk.*

Jimmy squirmed down and got away.

"Mrs. Carson?" Mar's teacher, tall as the blackboard herself, stepped forward. She had sheer stockings on, a rarity. "You've come for Mar."

Susan raised the corners of her mouth. In front of the room, Mar danced two erasers against each other out the window.

"Mrs. Carson, you must have thought that she was never coming home. But she's been helping me. And now we're almost finished anyway, so I'll turn her over to you."

Plonkplonk went the erasers.

Jimmy peered around the door from the hall. If she didn't hurry, he'd be hiding somewhere. Mar had put down the erasers on the shelf and was buttoning her sweater. White chalk streaks from the heels of her hands mounted next to the buttons and buttonholes. She went to her desk, took two books, came to her mother.

"She's such a big help."

"Thank you. She helps in the house too." Susan urged Mar ahead of her, caught Jimmy as they stepped out of the classroom. Down the hall, down the stairs, out the door. Jimmy's pants pleated in front and back because he was so skinny, and his gritty hair almost covered both sides of his head. She had looked at his burned ear for so many months that it didn't seem strange anymore. Mar had chalk sprinkled across her curls.

"We'll go to the gardens."

The children's mouths opened like traps.

"The gardens. Jefferson's Gardens." It wasn't much out of the way. It could be a treat.

"Mom! It'll be wet and cold." But Mar was already moving. Jimmy hopped along beside her.

The gardens were around the other way from the school, on Hickory Street, set back behind an iron fence and then down a gravel path through a wicker archway planted in the damp lawn like an upside-down Easter basket. They were famous, for Manatee. In the spring, people began to come from all around to look at the plants blooming, first the snowdrops, ice-specks on ice, then colored balls of crocuses splashed through the muck and across the dead grass left over from October. Violet and yellow and white, never a red or an orange, only the fairy colors. Jonquils then, and daffodils, lacy cups yellow as God's breath.

They walked through the Easter basket. A few jonquils, a few daffodils, not many yet. "Please Drop What You Can in the Box for the Perpetuation of These Gardens" said the sign fastened to a post of grey wood, box nailed underneath. The post was anchored deep in the black soil. Mr. Jefferson must have been mulching the whole garden for years.

Jimmy was pulling her skirt. He had a stemless tulip in his hand, circled by his thumb and forefinger. "Here, Mama," he said, stuffing it into her pocket as she bent down. "For you."

"You can't do that." Mar pulled it out and threw it on the ground.

"Don't, Jimmy. Come look with us." Susan took his hand and walked past the tulip. "Over here. There are rows of them. They're just starting. Mr. Jefferson would be angry if you picked any more."

But Mr. Jefferson wasn't there that afternoon, or at least they couldn't see him. The early tulips cupped perfection, icy dew at their centers. Fierce colors burned. At the summer fair, the flowers from Jefferson's Gardens always won the most ribbons. The tulips were gone then, but the summer flowers would have come through, gloriosa daisies and phlox, sweet william with its wadded flowerets, the alyssum, not a bouquet flower but a white cloud in a fragile dish, and the roses, death-rich, rising out of their bud vases like cannonades.

It was late. Susan turned. "Come on home," she said.

The two children had been giggling at something. When they heard her voice, they stopped.

"Come on home, Mar. Come on, Jimmy. Supper will be late for the boarders."

They walked through the wicker archway and out. Each child took a hand. When they got to their own front walk, Mr. Rawlings was watching them from the porch in his own chair, fetched down when they hadn't been looking. He poked Mar in the ribs as they marched past.

By nine, after the evening meal and Mar's help with the cleanup, the children had gone to bed and the boarders to their rooms. Susan sat emptied. Tulips were opening in the heat, clotting the room. She could smell herself; Woodrow Wilson would have smelled her already, anyone could have. Soaped herself every night, she did, cold water and hot, not touching too hard, always decent. Clean underthings, straight from the line with the golden northern blowing them out tight until they kited into the blue, fabric crunchy as crackers. The soft cushion of her belly, two, three, four, she'd lost track, and did you only count the ones that baked brown? Had there been a time when she could beat a tune on herself? Now all of her was like quicksand, suck, suck. And inside her the fleshy purse. They all had it. Mar? A year, two, three, the same.

She got up, went to her room. Even the bed wasn't hers with Mar blocked in on one side, solid as a dam. The boarders had the other bedrooms, with Jimmy packed into the sewing alcove. The quilt she flung aside barely covered. Mother-squares, stored, then pieced with Lucianne. Easter vacation. Spread on the kitchen table, a cloth landscape. Star of Bethlehem, like that part of EuraBella's. All of it stitched together with the needles walking through the softness.

Now she dreamed it when the fall came and the quilts came out, spilling their warm bodies on her bed. Only not the same. Not like before. Not her, not her, not them either, not even him, all gone now, all gone like they all were, just her own body, moon-flattened, all the pieces breaking in her, suck and crack. All the pieces breaking.

Well, there wasn't anybody. Mar didn't count. There was nothing except emptiness and need and bunched cotton and her own fingers, tender as tongues.

Thirty-Seven

"Why can't we go?"

"They didn't want to have one."

"Why not?"

"I don't know why not. They always wanted to choose their own way."

"Won't I ever see their house again? Won't Jimmy?"

"I don't know."

"What happened to Mary Queen of Scots?"

"Don't you remember? She died last year. They buried her by the back porch."

"I thought they ate her."

"They wouldn't have done that. She died of natural causes."

"Were they sad?"

"No."

"Did somebody kill them?"

"Mar, please. Forget the war. People aren't always killed."

"But what happened?"

"They ate something."

"But they were such good cooks!"

"They planned it that way. Bella was sick. Dr. Collins told her. She was getting thin."

"You mean they poisoned themselves?"

"Mar."

"You mean they killed themselves."

"Mar, please. They didn't want to wait. They always did everything together."

"Did you tell Jimmy?"

"I will. Later."

"Do you think they died like soldiers?"

"I don't know what that means. They were in bed. They had their nightcaps on. The table wasn't set for breakfast. That's how the bottled-gas man knew something was wrong."

"Do you think they went to heaven?"

"If they did, God will have to move over. And paint his throne lavender."

"Oh, Mother."

Thirty-Eight

It was a terribly embarrassing place for a single woman to go, though heaven knew there were enough of them in the parking lot, talking to each other like clutches of chickens, powdering their faces, checking the seams of their nylons. The transition between daylight and dark had come about so subtly that when the fluorescent light saying KILROYS had blinked on, the illumination had come as a surprise even to Susan, who had been watching for it. Underneath the glass tubes, the double door banged back and forth, and the music from the band spilled out, choked back, spilled out again. There weren't very many men, and the ones that were there all had something wrong with them: limps, bald spots eating their way down to their ears, a youth so extreme that the cigarettes they smoked looked like they must surely have been candy. She didn't like to think of herself as critical, but what else could she be? The good ones were all gone, choking on seawater as they floundered up the Normandy beaches. It had become a world of women.

Kilroys was in Fletchersville, fifteen miles from Manatee. Susan had taken the bus, the last one, which ran at seven P.M. She had no idea how she'd get back home. But then, it wasn't her responsibility.

She wasn't sure she'd even recognize him. Yet, it hadn't been that long. He'd come every week at first, had even offered money. She hadn't taken it. Mar had kept herself to one side, but Jimmy had always hung on him like a puppy. Then it had been every two weeks, or three. He'd left to sell dry goods on the road, turned the farm over to other renters They'd let it go to rack and ruin. Now it was almost a year since the last time, and Jimmy didn't talk about him anymore. Perhaps he was too young to remember.

He'd called three or four times, always late. The children were sleeping. She wasn't sure he'd been sober. Over the phone his voice crackled, high in pitch. It had reminded her of Charlie McCarthy, and the image of him as puppet, wooden jaw clacking, stayed with her even after he hung up.

But she had never been fair to him. It wasn't Richard's fault. Of course, who was to say?

A little ways to the side of her, a woman with dyed blonde hair was carefully pouring her bottle of beer into the dirt. She had tipped it so that the stream was as slow as it could be without sputtering. When it hit the ground, it pierced the center of the spreading puddle, which had reached the toe of her pump and was beginning to encircle it. Her face was composed, her eyes heavy, but she didn't seem drunk. The bottle had an infinite amount of beer in it. When it was finally empty, the woman turned to her companion, a thick man with grey in his sideburns, and took another bottle, which she began to drink.

Susan looked at her watch, which she normally never wore. He was an hour late. Of course he had to drive in from Rampart, half-way across the state. Perhaps he had run out of gasoline coupons. Or perhaps he had simply decided not to come.

"Waiting for someone?"

Susan raised her chin before she spoke, sure that the gesture would be needed. "Yes," she said.

"Been here a long time." The burly voice seemed friendly, though of course you could never tell. "Gertrude here said I should check just to make sure everything was alright."

It took Susan a moment to focus on Gertrude, who stood to one side, her grey dress blotted into the beginning night. She was a farm woman, clearly, legs and arms coming straight down from where they were attached, shoes solid and just barely acceptable for dancing, if that was what they planned on doing. Her hair was as long as Susan's, pinned on top of her head in concentric braids like circles of the moon. She was as tall as her husband, if you counted the braids and the moderate heels on her shoes. And there was no doubt that he was her husband; they stood by each other without the faintest sense of flirtation. They had clearly been standing by each other for a long time.

"I'm all right."

"If you're waiting for someone . . ." He stopped. It was not alto-gether polite to pry, even in the parking lot of a country dance hall, even when a single woman was involved.

"It's all right."

"If you needed a ride somewhere?" Even though most people dressed up for a Saturday night dance, he was wearing a plaid flan-nel shirt that was buttoned tight to his neck, out of which prelimi-nary wattles hung and dabbled around his collar.

"No, I'm all right."

"My wife here thought that . . ."

Susan looked at the woman again. If Richard should come now, he wouldn't have any reason to complain if she had left. Being made to wait over an hour was a justification.

"Thank you. But I guess not."

He turned away, though not with anger. He had done his duty, Susan thought. His wife turned with him, a half-smile on her face. When she turned back momentarily, her left eye closed and opened again, as unrelated to her other features as if the wind had moved against it. Could it have been a wink?

Leaning back, Susan watched the both of them walk toward the door, then open it to a wave of piano chords. The piano was the only instrument she could be sure of recognizing. It spoke with its own voice, which even a dance hall couldn't disguise. The tune itself was bouncy, with swoops of passion every now and then, and even when the couple had let the door fall shut behind them, it sounded through and out into the parking lot with pieces of melody.

Around her, most of the people had gone. It was late and getting later. Her upper body moved to one side, then the other. Behind her, a pickup lumbered slowly out onto the road, conserving gasoline even in the reluctance of its departure. Susan waved to it, then continued the wave with her other hand. Her hips moved in the same pattern. She tilted her head back while her body swayed and allowed the heavy braid anchored to the back of her skull to keep her facing the stars. She couldn't see them, of course, because there was too much light from the Kilroys sign, and because the clouds were coming in. Who was to know if they were dancing, too?

Thirty-Nine

Thunk.

Hit it square on the steps.

Thunk. Off the tree and on the walk. Them's winners, them that bounce.

Old Mathison. Thinks he's so tough, can't even pee straight. *Thunk.* Under the bush. Never find it.

Thunk.

All the others had bikes, double damn it. He could have one, too, if he wanted. She'd buy it for him. Maybe. But them bikes was lousy as shit. Town kid stuff. Bikes like nothing next to a horse.

Thunk again.

Long ago. Never got the Morgan. He must not of had the money, after all. Or just too pissed. But he hadn't been a bad boy, not me-Jimmy. Ugly little sumbitch, maybe, but not bad. Now he'd never. Have one. Unless the stable would let him. And no good in town anyway.

Thunk.

Didn't look like her, that's for sure. Not Mama. Looked like his dad, for sure. Long time. Maybe he was making it up.

Where'd he gone to? Could at least be sending postcards!

Thunk. Two stars in the window.

Thunk. Old lady owed him three weeks' worth.

Around the corner. A big tomcat lay drooped around the top of the fence pickets. Something the cat dragged in.

That was a good one.

Thunk.

The tomcat batted at his ear, balancing with his legs stretched out. Jimmy ran a paper along the fence, drumming up a racket. The cat blew up its fur, stood up. Little eyeteeth gleamed like Halloween.

Thunk, thunk. Wilson sisters. Same house, two doors, two papers, never talked to each other. Crazy.

Dr. Collins's place. *Thunk.*

Jimmy heard the fire whistle and stopped to look back. Maybe it was the boardinghouse, tinder, ready to go anytime. He'd never dared to light more than a couple himself. Charred sticks under the alcove rug. Maybe somebody else had dropped his weed. Maybe they'd all burn up, them old bastards. Then they could go somewhere else. Maybe the farm was still there like before. The barn, anyway.

The whistle was still blowing. Behind him, two doors slammed almost at once. He looked back. Like Kewpie dolls, the two old Wilsons were hugging each other, balanced over the bush between their little porches.

Across the street, his last year's teacher had stopped her car. She sat in the front seat wiping her eyes.

The whistle ended, then roared up again. The whole damn town must be burning.

Jimmy reached for one more paper. Before he got a good heave going, somebody grabbed his arm. He spun around.

"Giveyaadollarferthat."

Jimmy hung off the pavement, his nails in the wadded-up paper. "Two bucks!"

Jimmy hit the pavement. Into his shirt pocket the man stuffed two bills. Jimmy dug for them.

The Wilson sisters were still hugging each other in a ball like caterpillars.

Horns were honking along with the whistles.

The war was over.

Thunk.

Forty

It wasn't really her room, of course, but Mr. Rawlings had gone back to visit his old aunt for three months, and he'd been such a good boarder for so long that her mother was keeping it empty until he came back. So Mar could use it. Mr. Rawlings hadn't left a trace, anyway, except for two shiny blue suits pushed way to the left of the closet, and something hard that had glued itself to one corner of the dresser. It might have been Juicy Fruit at one time, or a gumdrop that had melted and stuck. She had scraped at it with her fingernail until one corner had lifted just a little bit. From that, she knew she could get rid of it if she wanted, but the finish might come too.

Mar brooded about the finish coming too.

And they had to paint the walls, anyway. Before he came back, which wouldn't be until Thanksgiving. Not because he'd been dirty or anything, but because the walls had been pretty dim even when he moved in. But there was no point in painting this early before he got back. Besides, Sears always had a sale in early November, and their inside paint would be half-price. That's when her mother always bought her paint. You could save it until spring if that was when you wanted to use it. In the basement, where it wouldn't freeze.

So it was all right to tape up the pictures on the wall. Even if it was crazy, like her mother said. As long as her mother didn't come in and take them down.

Not until they painted, anyway.

She hadn't put up very many. First there had been the big colored picture of President Roosevelt from the newspaper. She'd saved that one for more than a year. The color printing was funny, and the edges of his head were in layers like he'd moved when they took the picture. Only it was just that dumb Manatee newspaper that didn't know any better.

He had been a good man. They said he'd limped. Lots of people probably did.

She didn't like all those movie star pictures, so she only had one. Clark Gable. He was a hero too. All the ladies were too thin.

For a while they'd subscribed to *Life* magazine. Her mother didn't care what you did with them after everyone had a chance to look them through. There was room in the boardinghouse attic to store everything, but there was no point in accumulating, really. It wasn't as if this was their home.

Life had good pictures, though. Most of the others on the wall had come from it. A koala bear from Australia, looking like some-one had bought him at a toy store. They'd found him right in the woods and taken his picture. The other animals were from the zoo.

On top of them all was the one of Princess Elizabeth, which was appropriate since she was going to rule England someday. They must be training her already. Was her sister jealous? People bowed to her too, so it probably didn't matter much. Elizabeth was stand-ing with her arm out like she was stopping a car, though she was probably blessing people. Lights burst all around her.

Life had lots of soldiers, of course. All the time. Some of the earlier ones had been bloody. The last issue before the subscription ran out, there'd been a big picture that you had to fold out to get all the good of, it was so long. It was a Liberty Ship coming home from Europe with soldiers all along it. They were lined up everywhere, and the ones that couldn't fit on the deck were sticking out from the portholes down below. They were throwing their caps and ev-erything else. Their faces were little white dots.

If you used a magnifying glass, you could see quite a bit, though. Most of them were pretty young, but some of them had to be fa-thers. Mar couldn't see every face clearly, even when she held the page up to the sunlight. She probably would never know for sure where he was.

They were all coming home now. For some people, things might be able to begin all over again.

Forty-One

When Mar came home from high school that day, she saw the red dog next door roped to his stake by the new sidewalk. The circle of his freedom rolled out into the street, then back again up through the parking lot with its tired grass, and on to the fence around the Ramseys' yard. He didn't bark at her, but his throat rumbled, and from the very front of his mouth where the white teeth overlapped each other on the bottom, a rag of pink tongue heaved threateningly. His collar was as tight around his neck as the belt on her Sunday dress.

"You're home," her mother said as she entered the house. Red Dog's tail stuck up by the curb where he'd lain down in defeat.

"Yes."

"It's near supper. Slice the apples."

"Where's Jimmy?"

"At the stable." Her mother handed her the little knife.

"He's silly about those horses." Mar waited to see what the response would be.

"Better he be happy." Her mother always defended him.

The two of them stood by the sink, porcelain with a network of greyed lines where her mother had rubbed the metal pad. Two sides, one of them full of apples. Both she and her mother began to peel, dropping swirls back down on the apples still in the sink. The wallpaper, yellow with daisies and smiling suns, had begun to curl up from the back of the drainboard; her mother had stuck Scotch tape at the corners when they'd spring-cleaned in April. Now when the wallpaper began its upward march, it carried the drying tape circles with it.

"Where's Jimmy?" Mar couldn't help herself asking again.

Her mother kept peeling. "I told you already," she said.

"It's late."

"He'll come when he's finished mucking out."

"They should hire someone bigger."

"He's big enough. Better he do that than fool around getting in trouble." Her mother banged the bowl with the apple slices, settling them. "He likes to work at the stables. Let him be."

Mar did. Though he could have been home cutting grass. Or

putting on the storm windows. This house was bigger than the one on the farm, more work. All the houses on this street were big, but set on lots so evenly divided that no one was allowed to be better than anyone else. Their boarders sat on the porch in a row in the evenings—Mr. Devonshire, Mr. Jacobs, Mr. Rawlings. Even Mr. Keopek sat sometimes now. His English never got any better.

Mar slammed the point of her paring knife so deep into an apple that it stuck out the other side. Would Jimmy ever turn up? The stable had shiny tack from England hanging on the walls, even though it was mostly for decoration. He polished it for hours, humming. People didn't need horses anymore. Keeping a horse there was a luxury. Letting the pithy core slide into the cup of her hand, Mar finished the last apple. The perfect brown seeds poked against her skin. She rubbed her thumb along them.

When she looked up, her mother had turned to the door. At first, it was empty, then it filled up. Mr. Rawlings. Or Mr. Devonshire or Mr. Jacobs or Mr. Keopek. The pretend fathers. But this time it was Mr. Rawlings, leaning over and laughing. Because he was leaning over, she could see where he combed his hair across the bald spot on his head and watered it down in a curve behind his right ear. He combed it every morning over the sink upstairs, looking at himself in the mirror, practicing little smiles. She'd peeked at him many times.

Mr. Rawlings leaned further. "You cut that last one right down to nothing," he said. To her.

She should be polite. She knew it.

"Fritters or pie?" he asked.

"Applesauce," her mother said, shucking the apple slices into the pot on top of the stove. They mounted; she banged them down. She blanketed them with cinnamon, then sugar like a November snow flurry. "It's for tomorrow. Tonight we have pot roast and white cake. Baking powder biscuits too, if I get time. I don't starve you."

The two of them, Mr. Rawlings and her mother, looked at each other. He smiled. Her mother didn't. But she didn't not smile, either. Her apron had a damp streak across it, and when she wiped her hands on it, they didn't dry. She held them up to the light. Her nails were short, not peeking over the backs of her fingertips. Pushing back the bits of hair that edged her forehead, her mother touched her ears, her eyebrows. An apple seed had caught near her hairline, but she couldn't see it, and it kept hanging there.

"Well." Mr. Rawlings looked at his watch, his wrist pulled from his sleeve. "Well." He checked his hair over his ears with his middle fingers. "Biscuits," he said, his eyes moist.

"In a little over an hour," her mother said. She turned down the gas under the applesauce, smacking and bubbling in the pot.

"Well, let me take this young lady out while we're waiting. Car shopping. She can tell me what I should buy next." Mr. Rawlings had been promoted to office work every other week, but the trading stamp rounds still wore out cars.

"Not much choice in this town."

"McGinleys got four in."

He and her mother looked past each other. Her mother was slamming flour into the yellow bowl, measuring it in fistfuls. "Take her," she said. Mar wasn't sure what her mother meant.

"Go on." Her mother smoothed her collar. "Are you deaf? Go on."

"All right." Mr. Rawlings looked at the bowl, flour clotted up the sides. "Not too brown now," he said.

"Leave me to mind my own business," answered her mother, flour across her nose like a whiplash.

Mar and Mr. Rawlings walked down the hall, out the door, onto the porch. The geranium basket, hung above the railing, was waving in the wind. Red Dog was on his back in the gutter, legs curled toward his midsection like flower petals closing. In his sleep he gurgled at their footsteps but didn't wake up.

"You're in what grade?"

"Ninth."

"And what's your teacher's name?"

"I have a different one for each class." Mar said thoughtfully, "Mrs. Larson is the one I have for homeroom."

"Is she a good teacher?"

"She just makes announcements." Mar measured her footfall on each sidewalk crack. "She eats Tootsie Rolls for breakfast," she said, looking back at the outline of Red Dog. They walked on.

McGinleys Car Dealership faced Water Street five blocks away with three plate-glass windows tinted green against the sun. Only there was no sun today. The big overhead door where workers drove the cars inside was creaking open as they came up, spitting out a blue Chevrolet pickup, its silver aerial bobbing as the truck edged out into the lot. That machine had never carried a thing in it yet, didn't have a speck of rust. But Mar was sure Mr. Rawlings wouldn't want a pickup. Like the next scene from a movie, the blue swam into green, then orange, then red, and the truck from the old farm pulled together its outlines in the middle of the color in Mar's

mind. That truck was always dirty, she remembered. When her
father had taken her and Jimmy to the fields, she'd made balls of
loose straw bits clinging to the corners. Jimmy had wanted to eat
some, and she'd let him. Then he'd thrown up over the tailgate. She
remembered. Long before Mr. Rawlings.

"Want a ride?"

"In what?" She was still looking at the pickup.

Mr. Rawlings laughed, then smoothed back his hair, such as it
was. He pointed into the lot at a maroon car. "That one. More in
style. President Truman probably has one like that."

"Yes." The maroon car had chrome belted around it, reflecting
the attentive salesman who was watching it so closely that he was
practically attached. Mr. Rawlings said some words, got the key,
swooped her in. The seats were soft as pillows, and their new smell
soaked the whole inside. Mr. Rawlings read her mind and opened
the window as the car purred out of the lot and bumped over the
edge of the driveway into Water Street.

The two of them set off toward the edge of town, hardly a hop,
past two gas stations and then the high school with its stone front,
bleak without the yellow buses that fed it every morning. Red Dog
was far behind. Mar petted the seat between her legs, letting the
smooth upholstery tickle her palm. Out the window, she could see
that they had turned onto the old highway, then down under the
railroad bridge where the pigeons nested, and around the Catholic
cemetery. The cemetery near the farm had been much smaller.

"Do you like it?"

Mar didn't have anything to say.

Mr. Rawlings smiled, then rubbed the dashboard. "Do you think
your mother would like it?" He swallowed his lower lip and moved
his hand over the stretched-out crease in his chin.

"Maybe."

"Do you talk more than this in school?" He had circled the car
around all four sides of the cemetery and now was driving through
the metal gate toward the Armistice Memorial with the drooping
angel. She was solid granite, really, but the sculptor had made her
droop because so many men had died in that war. Mar and Jimmy
hiked out to visit her at least once every month.

"Yes."

"I sure hope so."

The car, heavy as a hearse, circled the Memorial, jouncing in the
ruts from yesterday's rain. They drove on, past the dripping faucet,
past the stack of pretend urns that you could help yourself to if

you'd brought flowers and didn't have a vase. No frost yet, so even the patch of zinnias by the grave that said NOEL HOPKINS was still aflame. Sometimes zinnias lasted past hard freeze-up, and even when their leaves went, the flowers flared like pom-poms. Noel Hopkins had an angel on top like the Memorial, a boy angel with a Bible in his lap. His marble curls looked like horns.

Mr. Rawlings was testing the brakes, slowing down as if his foot were dragging, then letting it out. Mar held her stomach, restlessly buried under the stretched waistband of her skirt. She was too old to throw up. When the car bumped over a branch in the cemetery path, she looked at Mr. Rawlings's plastered hair, anchoring her uneasy stomach by concentrating. He put his hand on her knee.

"You like it here?" One piece of his hair hung down his cheek like a tail; the path where it had been stuck gleamed white across the front of his head. Mar imagined armies of little people marching along it.

"It's all right."

"Want to sit and watch the leaves fall?"

That was silly. There was nothing to watch. Mr. Rawlings's fingers spotted her knee; inside her skin, the bone was melting. "They're not falling much yet," she said.

"They will if we wait long enough."

Mar looked at the boy angel. He had turned into twins. The other one was colored, though, and acted alive. The live twin kicked the marble twin, then hopped up on his back so that the marble face stuck out like a cluster of cauliflower from between the legs in his brown pants.

"Giddyap!" said the live twin, his voice coming through the open car window. Then he ran toward them. Mar bit Mr. Rawlings on his upper arm, right through his shirt. The stiff cotton tasted like farina.

"I'll tell your mother, bitch!"

"I don't care!"

The car died in the next roadway rut while Jimmy propelled himself onto the hood like a steeplechaser. Flat on his back, he attacked the windshield with his feet. Mr. Rawlings lunged against the door so hard it sprang open, one of his hands grabbing the steering wheel about hard enough to break it off. He let go, stumbled out. Mar, tight in the middle of the front seat, yanked her skirt back down over her knees, but it popped back up again. Jimmy leaped down and ran to her side, pulling her door open. Shoulder to shoulder, they raced off together, not even looking back. When they finally slowed down, almost to the railroad bridge with the evening pigeons chortling through the heavy air, Mar could hardly catch her breath.

"What was he doing?"

"Nothing." Jimmy smelled of horses.

"Nothing?"

"Well." Walking that close together with him, she'd soon smell of horses too.

"Didn't look like nothing."

"What do you know?" They were out of sight of the boy angel, the cemetery, the car, everything.

"I get to drive Tom Nelson's trotter in the race Saturday."

"In the race?"

"Not *in* the race." Mar could hardly hear him through his grubby hand, which was under his nose. "Well, almost in the race. Around the track for warm-up before Florin takes over."

"You're pretty small."

Jimmy looked at her and tapped her stomach. "*You* ain't," he said.

Mar could have punched him, but she didn't. He had straw behind one ear and a wad of it in his belt too. He looked funny.

They walked on for quite a while. In the distance, Red Dog appeared like a reassurance. Jimmy whistled through his teeth, and Mar put her hands behind her back. They rested comfortably, and she only needed to link the tips of her fingers. As they got nearer, someone came out of the Ramsey house and took Red Dog in. He moved slowly, as if he expected the worst.

"How's school?" Jimmy sounded older than he was.

"It's all right."

"I think it's shit."

"That's a bad word."

"Everybody says it at the stable." He scratched his head hard. Mar looked down at his scalp, which was questionable. He must have nits again. Their mother would kill him.

"You got any friends?" He was still scratching.

Mar took that seriously. Elizabeth, who ate crackers while sitting on the toilet? She had a yellow front tooth that she petted with her finger during math class. Melinda? She came on the bus, so she must live on a farm, like Gerhardt. But Mar had been invited to the sleep-over at Elizabeth's house on Saturday, so they must at least know who she was.

"Gerhardt," Mar said. The name just came out.

"Who's that?"

"A boy." Up ahead, the boardinghouse blocked the sky.

"He must like 'em *fat.*"

"Shut up."

Jimmy stretched out his leg and pretended to kick a tree with it. "I'm sorry," he said.

In the kitchen, the applesauce was bubbling in the kettle, slow bubbles struggling to the surface, clustered like blisters, then popping while the juice foamed. In the dining room, the table was set and their mother was glaring like God on his throne, but she didn't slap. Mr. Rawlings never did come.

Forty-Two

"Why didn't you bring me a pillow?"

"But you were supposed to bring your own!"

They all collapsed in giggles, rolling their eyes, tossing their hands. Even Mar, her goose-feather pillow covered in a flowered percale case, let out a little snort. If she did what everyone else did, even if a half-second later, then she'd be safe. It just required attention. Paying attention was something she could do.

Elizabeth, her blond hair wrapped around at least thirty fat pink curlers, thrust out both her arms. "If we were witches, then we could fly," she said. "We could zoom over there when the team is practicing and scare them to death."

"Scare the *shit* out of them," stated Shirley, her bangs aloft. The giggle rebounded. Elizabeth leaped off the mattress into the air, practicing witchhood. Peggy Sue leaped beside her. Mar let herself off the sheet in a timid pounce. They all landed on the bed together, rolling and bouncing. It wasn't really that hard to do. Pillows banged around them.

"Boys are so dumb."

"Football boys are the dumbest of all."

"But they're so *cute*."

"Ohhh, they're not *cute*. They're too *big*."

"The big ones are the *cutest*."

"Did you see that boy with the curls? The one on the Black River team?"

"My brother knows his sister. She says he sets his hair."

"Ohhh!"

"That's the *truth!*"

"My father uses witch hazel."

"To set his *hair?*"

"No! Because he's getting bald! It's supposed to make it grow." Elizabeth replaced a curler in her own thick mop.

"*My* father lost all his hair before he was thirty."

"*All* his hair?" Jeannie lay on the floor, embedded in the pretend angora rug. Her baby-doll pajamas barely covered her. She pulled the bottoms up even higher.

"Every single bit!"

"Every *bit?*"

"Jeannie, you are *terrible!*"

Mar rolled off the bed to the little chintz rocker. She'd tested it out and knew she'd fit. "My father never lost a hair on his head," she said. Her heart banged so hard the rocker surged forward. The words had just popped out.

"*Your* father?"

"Well, who else's father would she be talking about?" said Elizabeth. She checked over her toenails, her head bent.

"I never met your father."

"He doesn't live with us." Mar crossed her legs. That made it impossible to rock, so she uncrossed them. "Jimmy is the man at our house." That was so silly she got up. The chair quivered.

"Do you know where your father's at?"

Mar hesitated. "Somewhere in Illinois. Outside Chicago." Practically anywhere in Illinois was outside Chicago.

"I wish *my* father wasn't home when he smells up the bathroom with that old witch hazel!"

"He wishes *you* weren't home when you chase after that boy from Black River!"

They were being polite. But that was all right. Mar risked a little smile.

"What time is it?"

"Late."

"Too late?"

"For what?"

"Oh, I don't know."

"Ask your *father.*" They all giggled, then giggled more. There wasn't room on the bed for Mar. Downstairs, Elizabeth's mother banged on the ceiling. They choked their giggles into the pillows. The bed shook.

"I'm escaping!" Jeannie put the angora rug over her back and crawled toward the window. Mar watched from over by the bureau, wrapped in her own flannel nightgown. Jeannie's bottom slid in and out of her baby-doll pajamas, but she didn't look so bad. She almost looked like she could turn into a friend.

Forty-Three

The closet was under the stairs where you came in. It went back and back, the same width, until it hit the wall to the dining room. Above, the reversed stair treads hooked down zigzag against the ceiling; at the back wall, you had to stoop so low you might as well get down on your knees and be done with it.

Susan was on her knees. She had taken everything out, and the living room behind her, one illuminated rectangle framed by dark, was piled with the boxes of discards and books that had followed them in from the farm and that they'd kept even though nobody but her had used them or read them, or ever would. The closet itself was like a tomb, straight sides, body high, slight damp, sowbug shells curled in the corners. One light bulb, screwed in the ceiling, lightened the brown on the edges toward the door, and its cord hung down straight beside it with a frayed tail on the end. In the back where she squatted, it was womb dark. Her pupils soaked in what light they could. But cleaning didn't take any light to speak of; the hands did it all, the hands, the rags, the buckets of soapy water, dirty or clean, ammonia bite dissipated, drained out, swallowed up, swallowed down.

She started in on the ceiling. Dirty trails trickled down the walls; she caught them with her rag, sweeping across continents. The walls did themselves. The floor, muddy puddles, lay quiet under the rag when it was its turn. She wrung filth into the bucket, pulled out clean. Then less clean. She duckwalked toward the door. Sweat caught in her widow's peak. She sat back.

Already the floor was drying, back where she couldn't see it. The air was gobbling up moisture. Through the floor vents, the unnatural oil heat buffeted the air and cracked the floorboards with its dryness, soaking up spit in the mouth, tears, anything. Down to the bottom and out the river, down to the sea, never staying long enough, never enough water to fatten the little cells like balloons (she remembered, she remembered normal school biology, shiny paged textbooks that begged for your fingernails, and Lucianne's laugh no matter who got the highest mark, no matter), never enough. Somewhere there were ocean people who were never deprived. But she didn't know any.

Susan started putting things back, snowballing them ahead of her along the floor, shoving them against the wall. All the boxes were full of useless things. The biggest she pushed in first, then the smaller ones on top against the back wall. A corner of a farm box, the oldest farm box, had gotten wet sometime, then wrinkled, then dried, but inside nothing was damaged. She dug her fingers down next to Frankie's picture, the one she knew even with just her fingers, but there was no damage, not even mildew. The encyclopedias, heaviest box of all. Documents, in a legal folder. What did she own anymore? Who owned her?

The closet was half filled, with a little pathway down one side so she or Mar or anyone could get to the boxes piled against the back. A flat mountain path up their history. And in what box was the arrowhead? Or had she cut a throat with it? And was it now mixed with the gravel somewhere, not just somewhere but on the bank of Mitty Creek, only the tip showing, hard as a horse's hoof, but buried from the attack, never to be found, except by whom? The Indians were gone.

They all left, didn't they? Even when they weren't grown up yet, the dead and the living, even when their heads smelled of salt and hay, even when pieces of them weren't perfect anymore and would never be, even when they loved you.

Forty-Four

"Where'd that Jimmy go?"
"We don't know."
"Your whole family takes off, don't they?"

Forty-Five

Margaret Carson
English 3
March 14, 1950

My Life

I was born on a farm a good ways outside of Manatee. Actually I was born at the hospital in town, but it amounts to the same thing. You got to the farm by going under the Burlington Northern overpass, then right on the gravel road to where the trees start. Then right again. That's when it got tricky because the road looked like a driveway with grass in the middle. But it was a road. In the spring, summer too, there was sweet clover and alfalfa growing on both sides, and the bees were so thick that they'd get hit by the car going by and their bodies would be in the bottom of the ditch. Sometimes their wings weren't even broken.

I don't know if anybody lives there now. We haven't been there for a long time.

Over the years I have come to be an only child. First I had a little brother who died. I don't remember him. Then I had a brother named Jimmy, but he just up and left not long ago. He ran away from high school during his first year. He didn't like school. He used to work with the horses at the stables after classes were over, and then he started acting like they were getting over earlier and earlier until he was hardly going to school at all. Maybe he's with my father somewhere, but I don't think so.

I am seventeen years old and plump. My mother says I was always plump, but in the pictures from when we still lived on the farm, I was just square. I've stopped belting my skirts so tight now. I will just be what I am.

My mother's name is Susan May McIntire Carson. She runs a boardinghouse in this town. She bought it when we left the farm a long time ago. I think Dr. Collins gave her the money, or maybe EuraBella, or Mr. Keopek. I don't really know. My mother tells me every summer that I should earn my keep and paint it, but if I tried she wouldn't let me climb the ladder anyway because she thinks I'd collapse it. We usually have four boarders and there aren't enough bedrooms, so my mother and I sleep in the double bed in the room behind the kitchen. Jimmy's old room is too small.

I am a junior in high school. Next year I will graduate. I have people to talk to at school but nobody I can talk to for very long. Elizabeth is a friend sometimes. I don't have a boyfriend, but Gerhardt teases me. He lives in the country on a farm.

I don't know what I want to do when I graduate. If I get married, I will never leave my husband. He will never leave me either.

Forty-Six

The phone rang. She was baking pies. Apple and blackberry, the apples wrinkled like old grandmothers from the cellar where they'd been stored since fall. She'd canned the blackberries, but they had lost their cheekiness, too.

The phone rang.

The phone rang again. Susan topped the second crust, floury fork in her hand, etching with its tines the juice-releasing slits into the dough.

The phone rang one more time. She didn't wipe her fingers, but let the doughy whiteness dust the mouthpiece as she lifted it.

"Hello."

"Mrs. Carson?"

"Yes." But she wasn't really. Her body was the apple grandmother, wise in the wheat fields, light as a feather ball.

"This is Mrs. Collins."

"Who?"

"Mrs. Collins."

"Yes."

"I'm Dr. Collins's wife. We've met at the office."

"I remember." She did, too. A short woman, shoulders curved as if she were closing a box on her breasts, only not so closed that you didn't know what was inside. Passing through on her way from shopping, she'd been, and she'd spoken to the nurse with a snap in her voice as if she'd known how to give orders for a long time. That had been a year ago, when Mar's stomach had started to hurt. Dr. Collins had given them a prescription, which hadn't helped. And then everything had gone back to normal in the summer.

"My husband asked me to call. We've got a complicated situation here, and we were wondering if you could help."

"What is it?"

"Dr. Collins's practice has expanded so much in the last year that he's having trouble running the office." She spoke so smoothly that she must have had speech training. "He needs someone to help settle people in when they come, keep records, straighten up a little. I've lent a hand over the last month, but I don't want him to get to depend on me." She laughed just a bit, then coughed daintily into the phone.

Susan looked upward at the plaster ceiling with the crack down the center. Futile spackle clotted each side. "And you called me?" she asked. But perhaps that wasn't polite. "And perhaps I can help?" That "perhaps" was delicious, much more sophisticated than "maybe." She was an educated woman, too, even without the certificate.

There was a pause on the line. "Yes," said Mrs. Collins, her voice poised. "Could you help? I think we would need someone three days a week. Monday, Tuesday, and Thursday are the busiest. We can discuss wages when you come. Dr. Collins will do what is appropriate, I'm sure."

The package of words sat on the palm of Susan's outstretched hand. She shook it gently. Nothing rattled, but a heavy weight inside shifted. She felt it nudge the side of the box. Her hand compensated.

"When would you want me to start?"

"As soon as you can. Would it be any problem with your children? Or your . . . boarders?" She hesitated a moment before the final word.

"No."

"You're sure?"

"I'm sure."

The silence of the line between them had a hum in it. Gremlins. Atoms of static. Susan waited.

"Good. Tomorrow? Nine o'clock?"

"Tomorrow. Nine o'clock."

In the living room, the air was so solid she could have moved handfuls of it from one side of the place to the other. Had she never aired this place out? She knew what the Collins house was like; his office was an addition on the first floor. There had been a time when she and Jimmy had spent hours there: measles, chicken pox, pneumonia. All the ceilings were twelve feet at least, edged with gibbets. No, that was for hanging. What was that plaster strip? Molding. With designs on it. To dust them she would have to sit on his shoulders, and even then . . . Would she need a costume? Would Mar be able to get the pot roasts going at home, the pies, the laundry churning in the tub, munched in the wringer? Mar was almost done with school. Mar was almost grown up.

But she wasn't thinking of Mar. Under the corner of the carpet, her stiff shoe traced the outline of the postcard Jimmy had sent. She didn't need to lift the rug to see where she'd buried it. Jimmy'd gone farther than she ever had, for sure, down to Missouri, that strange square neither west nor east in the heart of the nation. The card had a picture of a horse pulling a sleigh on it, pulling it through an old-time village, high snowbanks smothering the houses so only their chimneys stuck out. Jimmy could have jumped off into any of them and not been hurt. Like he'd jumped out the high-school window, down the drainpipe like a monkey, teacher and principal on his shirttails, children screaming. They'd told her. He had been too young to leave home, but by the time she'd figured it out, by the time she'd realized he wasn't late because he'd been mucking out the stables, he was gone for good. And not a word of warning.

The edges of the postcard burned through the sole of her shoe. Like the flame on his silly head. And his writing was so bad. He had never learned even to join the letters together right. Couldn't do math, either. Couldn't do anything in school. But when he had run his stubby brown hands down the sides of a horse's face, that nag, whatever nag, would open its mouth, arch its lips over its green teeth, and take on the bit sweet as butterscotch.

She kept expecting him in the doorway, flannel shirt half buttoned, not as tall as she was but eyes straight on hers anyway. No books, no comb, but runaway eyes.

She outlined the card with her toe. He'd never learned to spell. Had the weather been good or the welfare? Had he been happy or hungry? Was that word before his name really *Love?*

From the kitchen, a burnt sugar smell was clouding the doorway. By the time she got there, Mar had pulled the oven open, daisy pot holders in each hand, and was yanking the pies loose. She held them far out from her school dress. Both women looked at each other through the smoke, eyes burning. Blackened juice rimmed the piecrusts.

She'd have to tell her. About Dr. Collins. So she did, while Mar scraped crust edges and deposited the worst parts in the garbage. It was all right with Mar.

That night in the bedroom they shared, Susan sat on the edge of the mattress listening to Mar picking up after the boarders' supper. ("Go on, Mother, I can just as well. I can manage.") She had gotten a Russian novel from the library, translated of course, but the names were so confusing. Outside and down the block, Red Dog was whining. She pulled her nightgown on over her head, then began to loosen her hair, tugging it out from its braid. The Indians hadn't got it. She still had it all, rooted into her skull. Hard to scalp a woman. Hard to bury one. Hard, hard, hard.

Forty-Seven

"We'll die of the cold."

"I'll keep the motor running, goddamn it."

"Then we'll die of carbon monoxide."

"You sure make things a lot of fun, Mar."

"I don't want to be here in the first place, Gerhardt."

"Stop calling me that."

"It's your name."

"Gerhardt, Heinrich, Horst. Sounds like some bunch of Nazis. My mother was crazy."

"So what should I call you?"

"Gary. Or Gar."

"Sounds like a fish. That's too far down. Get away."

"Just want to see what you got in there."

"Nothing you'd want."

"Enough of it, that's for sure."

"Get your hand *out.*"

"OK, OK. You like your name?"

"No."

"What's it for? Martha?"

"Margaret."

"That's not so bad."

"My father picked it."

"How'd you know that?"

"I just know."

"You never see him. Is he even around anymore?"

"Get your hand out, Gerhardt."

"Gar."

"Oh, for heaven's sake, Gar."

"How much do you weigh?"

"What do you care?"

"Just want to know."

"How much do *you* weigh?"

"Enough. Come on. It won't hurt."

"I'm cold. Will this car start?"

"Should. I tuned it up last week. Come on, Mar."

"Don't *push.*"

"You the only kid your mother's got?"

"For now."

"You figure she's planning more?"

"Of course not. Gar, that tickles."

"No it doesn't."

"All right, it doesn't. But don't do it anyway."

"OK. See, I listen to you."

"Sometimes."

"You say it, I do it. Gotta be smart if you're a senior."

"Do you think you're going to college?"

"Hell, no. The army."

"At least Hitler's dead. Gar, you're tickling again."

"You going to college?"

"Maybe."

"You just want to hang around that doctor's house with your mom."

"I don't hang around there. I take care of the boarders at home."

"Bunch of dirty old men."

"Gar, I'm freezing. Fasten that up."

"Bet they all want a taste of that."

"Gar!"

"Yum-yum. Banana cream. Pudding."

"Gerhardt, *stop it.*"

"Can't."

"You're crazy. I'm walking home."

"I'll come over and carry you over the threshold."

"Gerhardt!"

Forty-Eight

"Mr. Dalloway? The doctor will see you in fifteen minutes."

Mr. Dalloway. A short man, lump in his neck. "Had it for years, Susan, had it for years; never gave it a thought. Then it was like I couldn't turn my head right. The wife said to come in and have it checked. Can you see it from there? Doesn't seem like much, does it?"

He sat down, twisted back toward her in his chair. "That girl of yours in college? Heard she came back. Probably need her at home, right?" He reached for a magazine, thick fingers fumbling at the corners. "Ed Rawlings finally headed for the Twin Cities, heard that, too. The wife said she wasn't surprised either. Lots more opportunity there. Nothing the same here after the war."

Anxiety made him babble. "Dr. Collins pulled me out of it when my appendix was acting up," he concluded, feeling inside his collar.

Susan turned. "Mrs. Wochinski? The doctor will see you next."

Square lady, farmer's wife. "Don't I know you? From the last time, I guess. Must be nice working here. Oh, I get checked twice a year. Sugar in the blood. I could never give myself those shots, but my daughter does. I've just about gotten used to it."

Mrs. Nelson and Jeffrey. White head, white hair, resting on his mother's shoulder like a grapefruit. Eyes shut, arms dangling back and forth in the air. Nose running.

"He'll see you. Just a minute."

The wind. Blowing hard for March. No, March was right for wind. Almost April. Soon the apple blossoms would be combing the sidewalks. No, that was May. Sparrows fluttering with dry grass in their beaks, caught in a gust, stuck in the blue above the sidewalk like pinned butterflies. Clothes flapping on the line. The office door banging when the wind snatched it from a patient's fingers. Silver clouds butting like goats.

"The doctor will see you now. The doctor will see you."

Only three more left on the list. Two. Mar back home, making beds, doing what had to be done, doing it over and over, baking, the pages of Fannie Farmer stuck together with yellow spots. A great help. A great help to her mother. They didn't sleep in the same bed anymore. Now there was room.

"The doctor will see you. Would you please fill in your address on this card? We don't have it on file."

But Jimmy always got away. Flesh, fire, nothing could tie him down.

"My God, I thought we'd never get done!" The red hair had dimmed through the years, but the bushy fluff of his sideburns still hinted of it. Dr. Collins unbuttoned his white coat while behind him his nurse, Rebecca Cassiday, preened as she tied her mink hat with the pom-poms on the cords that went under her chin. Even in Manatee, a mink hat worn in March made a statement.

The phone rang. Mrs. Collins checking in from the house. Dr. Collins's sideburn compacted against the receiver. Rebecca, mink-cuffed face agleam, slipped out the door into the sunshine, her coat belted crisply around her miniscule waist.

The phone clicked down. "She wants eggs," Dr. Collins said.

"What?" Susan's coat was a good brown, permanently styled. She had one arm in it.

"She wants country eggs. From Mabel Tourette out on 82. Ridiculous."

Susan paused. Mrs. Collins washed her hair in egg yolk. She obeyed the suggestions in the women's magazines.

"Goddamn." He looked up. "Sorry." Then he beckoned with his whole arm. "Come with me while I pick them up."

"What?"

"I'll drop you off on the way back. Give me some company. You can tell me what you think of old Dalloway's growth. I think it's some kind of cyst, myself. I'll have to check it out at the hospital."

Susan stood erect. She still could not call him "Robert." "Bob" was much worse, of course. The "Doctor" was a protection, like an electric fence. She had been grateful for it more times than she could remember.

"I have to be back by six. To feed the boarders."

"How many of them do you still have?"

The Buick smelled of new carpet, fresh-cut fibers. She settled in. "Three."

"Enough to cook for."

"After next summer, only two. Mr. Jacobs is buying a house in Black River. His mother is coming to join him."

"Well, if you can still manage, I must be supporting you properly."

Susan didn't know how to respond. She supported herself.

Dr. Collins accelerated. "Forget it," he said.

To their left was a series of brick-fronted stores from the time when the downtown had been built, dates set in medallions on top: 1893, 1904, 1908. Slomans was having a luggage sale. Beyond Slomans was the druggist—more bottles, every color, and the soda fountain where Mar ate ham sandwiches between layers of Taystee bread. Then the park, half the swings out for repair. A little girl was putting her puppy on the teeter totter, chin drilling its back as she pressed down. Someone had cut her hair with a bowl like they used to, like they used to on the farm.

Outside of town, the car followed the road beyond the railroad tracks. Dr. Collins was humming. Susan wondered what they used the leftover egg whites for. Mrs. Collins didn't bake. The Buick purred.

Then they hit the familiar road, rutted gravel. The grader had been by, though, and the edges were heaped with lines of loose sand. In the center of the road, the surface had been scraped hard. A few more farms, grateful that they'd survived another winter. Where the grass started at the edge of the gravel, a gopher rose, warned by the rumble. When the waves of air from the hood moved by him, he scuttled for the ditch.

"You used to live out here?"

"Yes."

"Land's all gone to hell. Chickens are about the only thing left you can make a living off of, and not much of a living at that."

Susan didn't answer because they were nearer than he knew. Then the Tourette farm loomed up, house on one side of the road, barn on the other. A hound dog tore for their car, leaped at the fender, disappeared, reappeared snapping at the hood. His movements were as well planned as ballet. Dr. Collins swung by him into the yard.

"She better have them ready," he said as he opened the door. The dog snarled, leaped, keeping a tight circle of safe air between himself and any possible contact. Dr. Collins kept his hands in his pockets, stalked to the back door. He disappeared inside.

Behind her and down a ways, in the very corner of the rearview mirror if she stretched, Susan could see where the long driveway turned in. Or almost see. It was still early, but the grass was greening up. Inside her clothes, her body came alive against the layers of fabric. She tested her feet against the floorboards, felt her muscles tighten all the way up. "You are one tough lady," Mr. Rawlings had said before he took off forever. Maybe for once he had gotten something right.

She climbed out. Let Collins figure out by himself where she'd gone. He didn't pay her overtime. She started down the driveway slowly, the dog torn between her presence and the bulk of the car still to be attacked. She turned at the end of the drive, started along the gravel. She ran. Her practical office shoes adapted surprisingly well. Next to the creek the Gypsy camp had been plowed up, and the elm was gone.

Richard hadn't been a bad man. He had tried to keep contact. Visits at first, then less and less frequent. A few calls. Fletchersville, where he'd said he'd meet her, but hadn't. After that she hadn't read the letters, willing them to stop. Which they had. Maybe he was dead, like she had let everyone think. Maybe she had hurt his pride beyond what a man could live with.

There was a different name on the mailbox this time, a different mailbox, of course, painted glitter-white with its red flag shining. The dirt driveway was raked clean, gravel tramped down until even the little stones blended with the dirt. Around the corner of the house, she could see the steep edge of the barn. The new people this time hadn't painted it, either. The house, however, even from down here by the road, gleamed a sharp white with green around the windows. This farm wife ruled.

"Mama, this ear don't look right."

"Don't worry about it."

"Mar says it looks dumb."

"Don't listen to Mar."

"Where's Daddy, Mama? He don't come no more."

"I don't know."

"Is he dead, Mama?"

"I don't know."

"Does he still have horses, Mama?"

Susan stood looking at the grass in the ditch that ran along the road. The driveway rose over it. A spring jungle, old and new, woven with dandelions, quack grass, pigweed, pussley, clover, nettle, all entangled. She could have lain down in it and sunk in, like Ophelia, let her brown coat be soaked into the new green of spring. She could have made a spring angel in it.

She turned around, moved past the mailbox. Past the fences, one with shiny electric eyes. Past the new house down the road with the two dogs yapping in the front window, lined up like carnival prizes behind the glass. Past the field, then up the pathway still mucky with snowmelt. There was still time for a new downfall, but not today. Today spring was in the air.

Inside Susan's head, the old time rose like a bubble, a balloon floating inside her skull, bumping her hair from the underside. She'd been back before, yes, but when? Long ago. Had the grass never stopped growing? It must have, in winter, when everything stopped. The fence had very little additional rust, though the paint was squared off into loose chunks cracking out from the iron. She picked off a piece and put it in her pocket. Ahead of her was a path through the wet weeds, still visible.

At first she thought it wasn't there anymore. No, but the old grass was so high. And it was already growing in the dampness of spring, growing like crazy, tangling with the alfalfa that had thundered in from the field beyond the fence around the graveyard. Roots would cling to his hair. The smell like sodden perfume. Never to be free of it.

Her hands found the stone, tilted halfway back. They should have set it in cement. Her fingers sought out the letters, but the shaking ate at them so that they wobbled away. Her hair bending forward in a bird-wing swoop across her cheek where the hairpins had loosened, Susan touched her face to the very edge of the stone near the top. Holding on with her left hand, she bent the clotted grass with her right, tearing it off. The season being so early, it was the only possible bouquet to give Frankie.

Forty-Nine

Good heavens!

Even though the Methodist parsonage was a sturdily built structure, the woman's sobbing came through the walls of the pastoral
study directly into the sewing room where Rosa Bellamy, the
minister's wife, was sitting. It distracted her from her mending,
though heaven knew that by this time she should have been able to
darn a sock in her sleep. It sometimes seemed as if she were mending not just for her children and husband, but for a bevy of tattered
parishioners as well. When she opened the front door of the parsonage first thing in the morning, looking for the milk bottles
necked in yellow cream, she half expected the steps to be festooned
with holey socks, frayed collars, pants with the zippers gaping. Her
index finger was reddened from holding the needle, though one
wouldn't have thought that its slender spear could mar human flesh
that way at all.

Rosa dug into the mending basket and shut her eyes. Whatever
she came up with, she'd do next. It would be a signal of need and
necessity, lightly tempered with whim. Against the insides of her
eyelids, red circles expanded, then dwindled off into black space.
Her fingers acquired something grainy and long. She knew it had to
be her husband's wool sock, and it was.

It was silent in the study. Perhaps they were praying together for
guidance, although usually she heard her husband move back his
chair when the prayers were about to begin. Over their four years
in Manatee he had evolved a ritual for everything.

Over their four years in Manatee, Rosa had evolved a number of
things for herself, as well. Three children were enough, and the cap
did work if you made a point of putting it in every single time. No
need for anyone else to know. It was possible to make one Bible
verse substitute for many if you chose carefully. For example, "To
every thing there is a season" from Ecclesiastes served the purpose
for Sunday school scheduling, nursing home consolations, and
Circle meetings. Tithing was less painful when grocery expenses
were taken out first. And no one interrupted a darning woman very
often, not even a minister's children. Darning had the power to
make whole again. Everyone respected that.

She had finished the hole in the heel. On the ball of the foot was a second hole, a smaller one. How was that possible? She had just readied her needle when the sobs broke through again.

There was no particular pleasure in being a minister's wife, especially a Methodist's. The Episcopalians brought more prestige to the position. However, she enjoyed having the parsonage as a home, since it was in surprisingly good condition for a structure provided by a church. The Circle ladies had hung hand-sewn lace curtains on each window when the Bellamys had moved in, and replaced them with even nicer ones three years later. The house was carpeted throughout the downstairs rooms with a maroon wool marked in a lighter colored pattern like leaves, and it had been new enough so that not even a path had been worn from the front door to the study when they arrived from their previous assignment. In the children's rooms upstairs, the pine floors were islanded with rag rugs which the Circle had also donated, and at the slightest sign of wear, a new one would be presented at the monthly meeting held in the parsonage parlor. She suspected scouting expeditions on the obligatory journeys to the upstairs bathroom when the ladies were visiting. No doubt they looked over her dusting, too, and bed making, and the condition of the doilies on the nightstands.

That was a scream.

She rose quickly, the sock tight in her hand. A door slammed. When she reached the window, there was no one to see, simply a swaying branch on the crabapple tree where it overhung the walk by the front gate. The gate was open. Whoever it had been must have gone with the speed of the damned.

Her breath rising in her throat, Rosa looked toward the sewing room door. Her husband stood there, his hair ruffled, his familiar face arranging itself into the demeanor of one who provided consolation for a living, whether it was accepted or not. He stepped toward her.

"Who was that?"

"A woman who needed answers."

"And you didn't have them?"

He looked at her, taken aback, then reached out his hand, his wrist extending from his shirt cuff, which was frayed. Turning cuffs was as complicated as turning collars, neither of which she enjoyed, but both of which she did with regularity. It wouldn't have been seemly for the minister to have threads dangling from any portion of his anatomy.

"Do you know her, Rosa?"

"I didn't see her leave."

"She runs that boardinghouse in town."

"Oh. Yes."

"She was distraught about something. Or someone. I couldn't understand most of what she said, and she didn't say much." A spasm of discomfort moved across his forehead. "She didn't want to pray or hear the Bible. She said they weren't listening. I heard *that*."

"I think she left her husband."

"I heard that, too. But her children are grown now, or nearly so. Her life can only be getting easier."

An answer was on Rosa's tongue as quick as spit, but she swallowed it back. She folded the sock into thirds and laid it on the careful mound of the mending basket. He would have asked the woman to join the church before the interview was finished, she knew that. Perhaps that had brought about the final outburst.

"I asked her to join the church. The Circle, anyway. You know the Rebecca Circle can use every member with the Lilac Sunday dresses to sew. I thought she might like to help. But by then she was out the door."

"Perhaps she doesn't sew."

"It's hard to imagine a woman her age who doesn't." He looked fondly at his wife, the needle, the basket, the folded sock. The discomfort drained out of his face.

Rosa moved her head carefully from side to side in what might have been acquiescence but was not. Her own voice seemed propelled by a force not usually hers when she said, "Perhaps you can ask her again. If you see her." She pulled the sock from its triumphal position and with both thumbs began to scrape away at the darn on the patched heel. Her elbows trembled.

The minister didn't notice. Then he did, as he was turning back to the door. "Not mended to your liking?" he asked without waiting for an answer as he stepped to the hall carpet, feet anchored among the leaves as if they, too, had grown there.

Fifty

All the browns. Grey too, with dapples. Pintos. Palominos,
creamy manes and tails like meringue. Little huffs from chocolate
nostrils, tiny pink roses inside. The frog, flesh circled by hoof,
fenced in safe. If a pebble got lodged there, you could flip it out.
The limp gone.

In the richness of summer, the horses all romped. When the July
thunderheads belched up over the top of the sky and let the rain
down, soaking the air, the great heads shook and whickered, all the
colors transformed by the damp. Animals you couldn't eat or gather
eggs from. For the delight of man. He'd heard that somewhere. For
their own delight in delighting man. For movement itself, long
muscles snaking in their velvet sacks, thrusting and tightening.

Jimmy sat on the fence and looked. He was always looking.

Eighteen was a good age. Nothing he couldn't do. Mucking out,
grooming, trimming hooves when the blacksmith took one look at
a rolling eye and quit. Walking and cooling and throwing blankets
over sweaty backs, gold dust rising in the brown sweep of the stalls.
Breaking. Feeding treats, hauling buckets of oats cool as silver in
the hand, grains sliding through his curled fingers. When he
banged the bucket, the horses came from everywhere, soft noses,
lips blubbing at the metal, tasting, sucking it up.

He might get bigger yet. But he didn't want that. All jockeys were
little men.

Remainder was watching him from under the one elm left in the
pasture. Tail switching. She whinnied, flicked her ears, started toward him.

He'd never owned one. Not for himself. Just the pictures. The
only good thing about school had been the pictures, but the old
witches always made you look at what they wanted. He could read,
though, had picked it up finally. Never had owned a book, either.
Didn't want one. No.

Jimmy climbed down off the fence. Sweat ran down each side of
his nose. He smeared the drops together at his lip crease with the
back of his hand. Bristles. Not just a kid anymore.

Remainder had stopped part way, looking him over, too far for
him to grab her halter. He made a sound, starting it far back in his

mouth, then tapped his heel on the hardpan, hinting. He reached out. Nothing. Her eyes swirled, absent from this world, but one ear tilted. In the middle of her forehead where the map of the soul was—where they'd shot Billy, and Redbird, too, when they were no good anymore—light brown hairs whorled over her skull. He held out his forefinger. Remainder arced in a half-circle around him.

Down the fence line, in the trotting path along the edge, a yellow Jeep humped and coughed. Kelly would be in it, looking, looking for him. She said he smelled like horses, then laughed. How old? Older than Mar. She said she liked them little and young, ran her hand inside his belt, laughed some more.

"Jimmy!"

He didn't answer. Looking away, he sidled toward Remainder, leading shoulder down. She might think he had something. He closed his hand in a lumpy fist, black hairs like ink scratches behind his knuckles. Crabapple, sugar, baby carrots with the green tops circled around them. He lifted his closed hand gently, like a precious nibble too secret to be let loose all at once. Remainder drooped her eyelids, stayed put. Flies slid from her sides like pepper flakes when she shrugged.

"Come on, Jimmy." Kelly had let the door hang open, her white legs sticking out. "I'm here."

"Gotta catch Remainder first."

"She's not on your list for today."

"How do you know?"

"You told me yourself yesterday." Her voice had a whine in it. He didn't look back. "Gotta catch her anyway."

"Old Issom'll be mad, you messing with his filly."

"Let him." Remainder had pulled back her upper lip, delicately split and then velveted together under her nostrils. Her front teeth gleamed yellow like October corn. Green froth emerged between them as she breathed.

"I'm driving into town."

"Go ahead."

"You're not coming along?"

"Gotta catch this filly."

"It isn't going to take all year." She was right behind him, her shirt where it rubbed her breasts touching his shoulder bone. He anchored all his body against it. The filly cocked her ears forward, two pointed cups lined with satin. They were so beautiful he wanted to lick each one.

"I'm catching her, I told you." Remainder nipped at his collar, her lip curious. As she pulled away, she left her spit on his chest. He could have caught her halter; the brown straps had been right on top of him. But he had kept his hands at his side.

"All right, you fucker. That's it." Kelly pounced into the Jeep, slammed the door, revved the motor. He didn't turn around. The filly dipped her ears together, raised them, dipped them again. A new collection of flies was building a blanket on her flanks.

Jimmy couldn't remember before horses. Old Maude, in his father's barn, her hooves like wastebaskets spilling over with handfuls of heavy hair, white, snarled around sandburs in such deep wads that he had to dig for them with both hands. The false nail buried underneath, toe they'd lost back with the dinosaurs. Galls on the insides of their knees, hard white walnuts. Brown faces lowered to his, eyelashes out straight at the sides. Nudging his crotch with that fabric nose until he'd come up along the skull, off the ground, arms around the forehead, hands into the mane. Bones on his bones. Just that giant face, lifting him. Until he was big enough to ride like the wind. No. People who said that didn't know horses. *Be* the wind. The rider's feet growing through the ribs and joining together, toes edging through the folds, feeling the hot hay, heels resting on the liver. All of him growing like a spirit in the blood.

Remainder danced off. One lifted foot reminded him of Mar, back before, walking all over him while he huddled in the corn rows and she danced down from the edge of the field to stick her toes into his ribs as she charged over. She was probably too fat to do it now.

He wasn't. Could swing over the fence one-handed like always. And land with his knees bent so his legs would hold. One break in '51, one in '52. Couple of sprains. One ligament pulled. More bruises than he could count. What the hell. Jockeys didn't need to walk much. He could still make it to town one way or another.

The Jeep had disappeared, but the dust hung in the air. Jimmy hurdled the fence, started along the loose gravel. He stuck out his thumb, unpuckering his forehead so he looked thirteen, fourteen at the outside, just a kid finished with his part-time job, ready to head back home. Pick me up, ma'am, please. Give this boy a lift back to Mama.

He might even beat Kelly into town, if that was where she was going. Get it on with her like she wanted. He might do that. He might do that if it was his own choice.

The pickup that went by first was so new that it gleamed. But it didn't stop. Jimmy stuck up his finger.

Then a dusty Chevy. '39. No luck.

Motorcycle. The guy on it had an old-time flying helmet on. No hitching there.

A school bus, some fat grandpa driving. Up too high, couldn't see him, anyway.

From out of a clump of clover, a bee zoomed loose, aiming for Jimmy's sweaty head. Goddamn, he hated bees. Against his instincts, he held still, pretending he wasn't there, but the bee knew better and kept circling. Didn't dare swat it either, make it mad. The zooming got louder, sizzling like grease in the hot air. Jimmy put his fingers in his ears, then took them out, yanked the back of his shirt up over his head, and jumped into the roadside ditch, squatting tight against its side. He shut his eyes. In the darkness, humming with his own blood, he tried to think of the Derby field. The Santa Anita Handicap. The big ones. He'd muck for months if he could watch.

"You sick?" A big station wagon had pulled up on the edge of the ditch by him.

He yanked his shirt the rest of the way down. "No. Bee." Christ, only a baby would hide from a bee.

"You hitching?"

"Yeah. Going into town?"

"If I can make it before the bottom rusts out of this tank." They looked at each other through the half-open window. "Are you?"

Jimmy reached for the door handle. It was locked.

"*Are* you?"

"Yeah." Was this bastard going to take him or not? Jimmy peered at the face, split under the nose by the glass. Then the door opened.

"Get in. Don't expect too much, though. This heap is a wreck."

"It's OK." Jimmy climbed in, dwindling into the upholstery, legs dangling. The station wagon didn't look so bad. Better than walking.

With a snarl of the motor, they took off. The man didn't say a word at first. His lips were pressed together so tight at the midline that they lay flat on his chin. But his eyes were the opposite, crinkled like tissue underneath in pouches, spearheaded with wrinkles at the outer edges.

He winked. "Name's Jelico Roberts."

Jimmy nodded.

"Yours?"

No words came out.

"Kid, for a ride you owe me at least a name." The bags crinkled, wrinkles tightened.

"My name's Jimmy Carson." Nonsense words began to race around the back of his throat. He coughed.

"Glad to know you, Jimmy." The station wagon swayed underneath them both. "You're one of the kids at Generalissimo's stables?"

"Who?"

"G. G. Issom. You know who I mean. The old man." His fingers circled the wheel.

"Yeah, I work for him."

"Long?"

"Year." Between the two tendons behind his right knee, an itch nibbled. Jimmy rubbed it.

"Earn enough to live on? Not that you'd need much."

"I guess." The wagon leaned into a curve, wheels tight on the road, chassis edging to one side. The door rubbed Jimmy's shoulder.

"Probably can stay alive on hot dogs and horse shit, little guy like you."

Jimmy checked the door lock. Another corner and he'd be sliding out into the ditch.

"Not that old Issom hasn't won his share."

The station wagon had passed all the Issom property and nudged south. Riverrest Lake was next, and six miles further Dunkirk. Hardly a turnoff on these roads, a few little trails to houses set back in the woods. The Shining Pike Resort, its entrance arched over with logs like a dude ranch. Clumps of daylilies, gone wild, anchored the two sides of the arch. Behind them, the trail led down to the lake, he knew, two sandy paths for the tires, grass tickling the muffler in the middle. Poplars. Jack pines at the edges.

"You don't talk too much, kid."

Kelly said that, too. "Guess not," he muttered.

Behind him, the backseat had been laid down like a hospital bed right through to the tailgate. An empty bucket and a fire extinguisher rolled against the door whenever they took a curve. There was a cardboard box wedged against his seat back. Open. He diddled in it with his fingers, the bottom half of his arm a free spirit, his shoulders still held frontward.

"You ever raise them Shetlands, Jimmy?"

"Just the two for Issom's kids."

"Mean little buggers."

They were passing the Gypsy camp. Half a dozen old house trailers jammed against the side of Hummer Hill. Washing draped on the grass, rocks holding it down. A lady in long skirt, bare feet, was pulling a baby by one arm away from the road. She looked up as they passed, one hand wiping the spill of hair away from her forehead. Both her front teeth were gone.

"Know a good trotter I could look at, kid?"

"Issom doesn't handle harness stock."

Jelico Roberts snorted, shook his head. Sweat laced his cheeks. With his free hand, he grappled for his window handle, wedged it one way, then the other. The window didn't move.

"Goddamn. Open yours, kid."

Jimmy did. A wave of pig moved through the car. The smell was so strong it ate at him.

"Goddamn! Shut it before we both puke."

That was all the conversation. They drove on. At the peak of the next hill, before the road angled down again, the station wagon stopped.

"Gotta take a leak." Jelico's head popped up. Outside, birds scattered.

"Me too." Jimmy didn't, but he could feel a little knob of warmth halfway along his prick. He could negotiate it into a trickle. Yanking his fingers out of the box, he stepped out of the car, bending weeds with his feet. One last bird rose.

They tromped to the side of the road. In two miles there'd be a Texaco. Gotta go, gotta go. Jimmy jammed the rhyming back into his head.

"Wait a minute."

"What?"

"Wait a minute, kid." Jelico had turned back to the station wagon, stamping through the dry grass. He opened the tailgate and pulled the cardboard box toward him until it balanced half over the edge. Jimmy held his hands next to his prick. He did have to go. Under his nose, the bristles itched, like teeth pushing through. Hell, he didn't have to wait. He unzipped, reached for his buddy, edged the tip through his underwear. A whiff of old urine came up to him.

"Lookit."

"What?" He hadn't done it regular in the pot until the week he'd started school. His mom hadn't cared. He could wear his pajamas all day, too, eat milk toast for dinner, splash around in horse shit up to his knees. He and his dad in the trough, cooling off after the fields, white cigars floating next to each other. "You're about as big as me." Had he imagined it?

"Lookit. Better'n what you can buy in a drugstore, let me tell you."

The pee hung just above his slit, pressing hotly.

"If I was selling again, like I used to, this is the line I'd have. Make a fortune." The four box flaps hung open, and Jelico ferreted inside among the papers. Jimmy hung fire. "Lookit this, kid." Jelico's baggy eyes beamed, crepy skin wobbling.

The two blotches of white on the postcard moved from snowballs into women, wearing ballet slippers and nothing else, lying front up on what looked like a pan of fudge. They were holding hands.

"Ain't that something? Makes you want to try the old swimming hole one more time, don't it? And this one." Jelico pulled out a postcard with a frayed corner, his thumb imprinting it tenderly. A heavy woman supported her own breasts, one hand under each. The nipples were dark. Another woman, squatting with her bum toward the camera, knelt in front of her.

In Jimmy's hand, his prick turned steel.

"Best ones is these, though." Carefully, Jelico moved a pile of postcards back to the box's furthermost corner and brought out a brightly colored folder, glossy-fronted. He held it up, then flicked it open so the pictures moved in an arc through the air. "Lookit. Make you wanna grab your gourd, don't it?"

Jimmy shifted, trying to will his gourd back down. It refused. In the first picture, a girl with a flouncy skirt and curls like Kelly was walking down a country road carrying a basket of flowers. Then came a fence. Then the girl at the fence. A roan horse was checking her out from the distance. Next, the distance had diminished. Close-up. The horse butted her bottom while she waved her hands. The horse reared.

Next frame. While the girl hung over the fence with her skirt up, the horse mounted. Jimmy twisted in embarrassment. As if in answer, Jelico's piss spattered off the gravel in the bottom of the ditch. The smaller stones jiggled under the impact.

"Amazing, ain't it? I bought those things in Chicago, practically back to Dillinger. Some folks like the ladies together best, but the horse makes everyone real excited." He flicked his pecker from side to side. One golden drop hung at the tip.

"Well? Peeing or jerking off?"

Jimmy squirmed, wordless.

Jelico looked straight at him, his hands holding it in front like a machine gun. Ratatatatatat. Every cloud in the sky curled tight. Jimmy couldn't find a hole in his clothing to put his prick back through; even his pockets had clamped shut. Protective, he put his right hand over it. He pushed, and the tip bent. Jelico was laughing.

"That hard-on'll win the blue ribbon at the fair, kid. Right up there with the Polish dills."

Desperate, Jimmy yanked at his prick with both hands. He managed to wedge it inside his pants. The next thing Jelico said was too far behind to be heard.

Afterward, running along the road like Remainder herself, the station wagon shining in the heat far behind him, he held his mouth shut with his right hand so the noise wouldn't come out. He was good at running away, had been doing it forever, and even though his one foot had hit the ground crooked, numbing itself along the outside edge, it wouldn't be too far to Dunkirk, mile maybe, couple of miles, and if he wanted to turn around and go back, Kelly might pick him up. She practiced every road in the county with that Jeep, never went anywhere straight, and even if she had gone to town, she might be heading back by now. She'd figure he'd been walking a long time, served him right, lippy jockey, and she wouldn't look at him for miles after she picked him up, just stare ahead like a homecoming queen. Then she'd shake her curls, sorting them out, and she'd say, "God, you stink." The smell would rise off him, horse funk, it was rising off him already, marking him like his scars, like the suede muzzles that pillowed his dreams, and the colors, too—War of the Roses (he'd jumped out the window and left when the teacher was still talking about it, so he didn't know who won), white on one hand, red on the other, stained for life like his body. Everything was for life, you never got big, you never came back, you never could climb in and be truly, truly warm again.

Fifty-One

"Where's this one from?"

"The farm."

"This one?"

"The farm, too." Mar balanced the angel in her hands, shook it across the air between her and Gerhardt. Its tiny legs were anchored with wires under the satin skirt. If you shook it right, they moved like a person's.

He grabbed it from her. "How much junk did you bring to town with you?"

"I don't remember."

But she did. Two suitcases, in the attic with the boarders' discards. The cardboard boxes in the closet under the stairs. A library's worth of books. A barrel with the dishes packed in sawdust. The ornaments had been in a box, all of them that were left. The angel, which Gerhardt was still holding. The clock with the wire hands. The zigzag tree. Her Santa Claus, and Mrs. Santa. Jimmy's horse. He had always wanted to unwrap it himself, and if anyone else got it by mistake, they had to hand it over or he'd run outside. Right out into the snow. Because of the horse's legs, cutting a rectangle against the tissue wrapping, she always knew and could shove it over his way so he'd think it was his by nature. Or maybe he had known.

"You want the angel on top?"

"Don't break my mother's chair."

"I don't need a chair. You think I'm some little guy?"

"Well." Mar handed him the angel. In his boots, heavy-heeled, he truly didn't need the chair.

"Your mother's asleep?"

"I don't know." The door was closed. No light. But her mother could stay awake all night if she chose to.

Gerhardt stepped back, checked the angel. "She don't like me."

"She never thinks about you."

"How do you know?"

Because then she'd like you, Mar thought, or hate you, and you'd know it either way. "I know," she said.

"I visited her two, three times this fall. When I got out of the army. Stopped in like she was family or something. Brought her that big pike I caught. Only time she looked at me was when I teased her."

"Here." Mar held the tinsel string in her hand. "Take one end."

"That woman is not fond of me."

"She's fond enough of you. Why should it matter what she feels?"

The tinsel was too short. "Nobody can understand women," Gerhardt said. They yanked, gently, one on each end. Gerhardt knotted his end to a branch.

"Looks dumb, that does."

"Yes." Mar stopped. "No." She took his hand, surprising him, pulled it down to her side, moved him across the room to the window. "Look at it from here. That's enough for tonight."

Outside, the snow had stopped. Time for the baby to be born. She never had believed in those palm trees. It was cold, cold enough to crust over the drifts, and little star-sparkles glinted on all the outside surfaces. On the farm, it had swept on forever, the seen and unseen worlds.

"It's nothing but snow."

"I know."

"You figure that tree's done?"

"It's good enough."

Gerhardt put his arms around her. "You lose some weight?" he asked.

"I don't weigh myself."

"Seems like you lost a few pounds." He kissed her. Around the corner of his head, the snow and the night cut the window precisely in half.

Fifty-Two

"I have always wondered how you managed to read so many when you were always in the kitchen." Mr. Keopek's words fell into the right patterns now, but his accent still marked him. Talking with him was like a musical exercise.

"Reading them the second time is easier."

"I see you have the Goethe."

"Just *Faust*. I used to wish Mar had been named Gretchen."

"Not a good omen for a girl."

"But the name is lovely." Susan leaned back in the recliner, raised her teacup to watch the light filter through the translucent china. Mar and Gerhardt had gone together to buy her the chair, which curved back with her in it as if she were visiting the dentist. It would be almost impossible to escape without spilling. Every time she sat in it, she resigned herself.

Mr. Keopek set his cup down. It rattled against its saucer. "For us, in Europe, Goethe was the one against whom we modeled the others. And then the war. I brought the *Wahlverwandtschaften* with me, and *Wilhelm Meister*. In the first year, I would read them and wonder if the evil rested there as well." He took his cup again. "I was never to find it," he said. "Only the wisdom. And the fine words."

"Perhaps Goethe was German only by accident."

Mr. Keopek thought. "No. Had he not been born so, he would have chosen it. Because of the national sorrow. Because to be seeking the perfect was his nature. And the rage against those who could not give it."

"You almost sound German yourself."

"That I am not. But they have a power. It would be idle to ignore it."

Susan shifted, easing her legs down. If she worked hard at it, perhaps she could make a graceful exit. "You read a great deal too," she said. "When I dust your room, I admire your library."

"Hardly a library."

"More than most."

"Perhaps." Mr. Keopek folded his hands in his lap. "You know that you are welcome to read anything that I have if you should desire. I would be honored."

"I only read English."

"The two bottom shelves are all of them written in English."

"Perhaps I might. Thank you." She had already finished the bottom shelf, reading in snatches after she got back from Dr. Collins's the days when Mr. Keopek worked the late shift. He was so neat that it was easy to replace the books in the perfect line in which they had been left.

"I find that few Americans read."

"Oh, I don't think that's true."

"Nevertheless, it has been my experience. Your daughter, for instance. She is seldom seen with a book."

"Mar has other interests."

"I am sure."

"She has kept things together here while I work."

"That is true. She has educated me with her gingerbread and also her spice cake. I find them delicious."

"Mar likes to bake."

Outside, a swarm of cedar waxwings ravaged the mountain ash. Their fat, busy forms clattered among the drying leaves. It was over the Peterson bird book that the tea party had originated. Mr. Keopek was ignorant of every bird species except eagles and ducks.

"Will you obtain further boarders?"

"I haven't given it much thought."

"In these new days, the people stay in one place for such short times."

"I suppose I could if I looked for some."

"At the plant, the men often rent their own small homes in other houses. I have forgotten the word."

"Apartments."

"That is right." He finished his tea. "I myself have not been tempted by this," he said. "I would not be able to feed myself, I fear. I would miss the gingerbread."

Susan had edged out of the chair to safety. "Women fill that need well," she said as she took his teacup.

Mr. Keopek stood up, too. "You have preferred not to marry again?" he asked.

"I made my choice."

"Yet you remain a woman of attraction."

Susan was halfway to the kitchen. She held her elbows to her sides to keep the teacups quiet.

"Thank you," she said.

Fifty-Three

"You're her mother."

"No need to tell me that." Susan cracked the eighth egg, pried the shell pieces apart with her thumbnails.

"I guess so." Gerhardt handed her the next two eggs, his boots edging along the stool braces. "But you don't act like a regular mother, that's for sure. Not like *my* mother."

Susan reached for the last eggs. Lots of nerve he had, that one. "The Kauffmanns are probably different than most of the rest of us," she said.

"That don't sound like a compliment." He caught the last egg-shell as she tossed it toward the garbage can, set it on the peak of his head like a dunce cap. "We're not all that different. Old-time Germans, sure. Dance hard, drink hard. Not so different from anyone else."

"If you Germans work hard all day long, what are you doing here now?" A dozen eggs separated. Not a speck of yellow in white or white in yellow. Perfect.

"The Kauffmanns take time off. Crops get along without us."

"I believe you." She noticed the dunce cap, laughed, and wiped a long floury streak across her chin. "Get off that stool. If Mar isn't here to whip these whites, then it's my job, and I can't do it standing up. Go over on the rocker."

"Where's Mar?"

"How would I know? Finishing the baking at the Collinses. Mrs. Collins is having her church circle tonight. Doing their washing. Doing their ironing. At the library. On the way home." Across the white disk in the bowl, froth bubbles broke and reformed. Susan's whisk glittered.

Gerhardt sat, one boot nudging the linoleum. His mother had a rocker, too. He edged his weight down against the padding, tested it, speeded up the rhythm, feeling the rug behind him where the rockers held on.

"Hot day."

"Not my choice to bake. I must have had angel food on the brain. Mr. Keopek likes it."

"He the only boarder left?"

"For now."

"You can afford to go it alone?"

"What a thing to ask." The bowl surged with white.

"Looks good."

"Looks like egg whites. Last thing Mar needs is a cake."

"I'll eat it."

"You'll never touch this cake," Susan said as she set her face toward his, set her whisking hand between them. His cheekbones gleamed.

"Maybe I only like devil's food." The eggshell edged its way down over his flat hair, balanced on his ear, tumbled into his hand. He crushed it, then tossed it into the garbage across the room.

"I'm not baking for you."

"Come on now, Mrs. Carson. Come on." He swabbed at the sweat infiltrating his eyebrows, then smelled his fist. His blond hair margined his skin, which was pulled too tight over his skull to wrinkle. Whipping the egg whites so fast that the bowl clanged in a steady murmur, Susan thought of her own face, her mind moving over it in a secret exploratory dance. Still tight, but with the little bags under the jaw, bags soft as puddings. She arched her neck, pulling up. Hardly an extra ounce anywhere else. Or perhaps only a little.

Susan glanced out the window, checking the sky. Still blue. No wind. Even the tiny-leafed bridal wreath in the yard stood unmoving. Was it hot? Her dress stuck to her. It was hot.

"Come on."

She touched the egg-white iceberg.

"You make me feel like some dumb kid. I'm no kid."

"Not exactly aged, either."

"No kid."

No, no kid, Susan thought. She looked out the window again. "I have to hurry. If it storms, I want this cake in the oven beforehand. If we lose the power, that's the end. And this is storm weather."

"Radio said more than a 50 percent chance." Gerhardt caught the rocker on the backswing and held it, chest curved out, belt buckle in the light. "How long will Mar be?"

"Another hour. I don't know."

"What do you think she's doing?"

"Baking for the Collinses. And ironing their curtains. The downstairs ones. They wash them twice a year and spread them out on the bushes so the sun can bleach them. Then, when they're dry, they bring them in, iron them, and put them right back up."

"Sounds like the old days."

"If you have money, you can have whatever days you want."

"I guess."

The curtains would be in by now, safe, but Susan looked out the window anyway. A line of grey had rolled up the edge of the sky and was thickening across the backyard and behind the Ramsey house with its shrubbery trimmed into green umbrellas. Beyond Red Dog. Susan punctured the whites with her forefinger and licked it. No flavor at all, then a distant sweetness. She glanced at Gerhardt, his German face balanced neatly in his hands like a plate.

"Mrs. Carson."

She didn't answer. Sharply, she swirled the whites into the dry ingredients, streaking them together. Her rubber spatula cut through, blended, cut through again. The bowl filled with an airy puff.

"Susan."

"What?"

"Jesus, I feel funny saying this." One big hand touched its mate. She surged the batter into the round tube pan, easing the clinging bits off the sides of the bowl.

Gerhardt's hands hooked into his belt. "Look. Maybe you don't want me here. It's your business. But every time I take that girl of yours out, I feel like you watch me all the way to the car. And then some. Like you hate me. No, that's not it. I had girls before. When I was in the army in Germany, those fräuleins really liked us guys in uniform. Anything I didn't learn on the farm, I learned there. Mar's OK. She never says all that much. But . . ." He pulled up his pants legs, twitched them down again. His ankles were whiter than a woman's.

Susan put the cake into the oven.

"Shit, this is crazy."

Susan shut the oven.

"It's crazy. But I know you and her work for that Dr. Collins. I thought maybe you had some pill. Something. That you snuck into me. With the coffee I drink here. Or the lemonade. My people, my grandmother on my dad's side, they used to witch all the time. Jesus, in her house, up in the china closet behind her Haviland, she had little jars of crazy stuff—feathers, stones from the crick, white ones, threads tied in knots like a chain. She knew I knew they were there, that old lady. But we never talked about it."

"Why not?"

"Why not?" Gerhardt looked out the window at the clouds, boiling at the bottom of the sky. "She'd of thought I was the crazy one. It was none of my business."

"Did she collect arrowheads?" Around the top edge of the oven where the seal had cracked, wisps of steam drifted into the kitchen.

Gerhardt stood up. "Arrowheads?" He moved into the hall, to the window facing east. "Why? My grandma was Kraut all the way through. No Indian in her."

"Sorry." Susan moved Gerhardt and Mar up against each other in her mind, tried to align them. How tall was Mar? Five feet? No, taller than that. But not much. None of her children would have been tall.

But he was. As he stood at the hall window on the worn purple rug, he made a line with the two flower pictures, hung up high so the boarders wouldn't scrape against them. He'd rolled his sleeves up, even though that yellow shirt with the sprigs on it was no farm shirt. Come calling. Under the wadded fold-overs, his arms were like fishes, dark on the tops, white-bellied. Highways of veins ran along them, pushing up through the taut skin. In his neck, his pulse was beating.

Thunder. But the sun was still spilling into the annual border. Gloriosa daisies exchanged gold.

"It's going to storm." He didn't look at her.

"Ten more minutes."

"What?"

"Ten more minutes. For the cake."

"It rains in the oven?"

It wasn't worth an answer.

"It rains in the oven?" he asked again. Crooked grin the same as always, he grabbed for the oven handle as if he intended to check for himself. So she swatted at him with both hands waving, and he swung his elbows up on the sides of his head with his lower arms cutting across his face to protect it. Above them, his half eyes, split horizontally, glittered at her. He had that bony German forehead. She swatted again.

"Got to hit better than that."

"What I really need you to do, Gerhardt Kauffmann, is to go find that Mar. Call the Collins house. Call the library and see if she's there. Walk her home." Susan shook her egg whisk at the window, drawing lines in the clotted kitchen air. "A storm is coming on, no doubt about it."

"She can make it on her own." He grabbed for the oven again, except that Susan was in the way. Because she was trying to open it herself without getting blasted off her feet by the escaping heat. Because it was so hot in the kitchen, building for the rain. She bent sideways, but her back arched and her rear stuck up. Gerhardt brushed against her as he tried to get by.

"Angel food," he said, and dialed the Collins house. Mar had already left.

The cake came out of the oven looking like dirty snow on top, brown filigree with cracks through which the white showed itself. Susan set it neatly on the counter.

"It needs to cool."

"How long?"

"An hour. Or less. So it will come out of the pan easier."

"Then who gets to eat it?"

Susan looked at him. "Just stop it," she said. "I can't listen to you anymore. You try to take over my kitchen. Go find Mar."

"But it's going to rain."

"That's why I tell you to leave *now*." She turned down the hall, over the purple velvet with its backing showing through in the center trough, and opened the front door. The wind hit her. "Go on, Gerhardt Kauffmann. Get wet. If Mar brings you back for cake, that's another story. You won't get a thing now. You might as well go."

"Hell!" He pulled back his upper lip, showing his front teeth. Thumb sucker, that one. A mother could always tell. "It's raining already," he said, his feet planted. "You got everything inside? Want me to go fetch stuff?"

"I thought you didn't want to go out in it."

"I would for a good reason. Not just because you're mad. That's no reason. Mar's got sense enough to duck in someplace, find her way home when it lets up. Don't you figure?"

What Susan figured was that the weather was changing even as the rain fingered the kitchen window, browning the chipped sidewalk back to the clothesline. If the rain held—and they needed it because the annuals she had planted along the walk were rolling back their leaves at midday now to conserve moisture—if the rain held, then she wouldn't have to set the sprinkler, wouldn't have its damp sparklers touching the lawn with unnatural wet running like fudge through the hollows, leaving the sculptured muck in patterns between plants, the bush verbena, the peony, the primroses. If the rain held. The drops on the window were deceiving because the old ones bobbled, loosened, ran into the new, and you couldn't tell which was which. Gerhardt was watching her watch them. She should shut him into the living room with Mar on the sofa. But Mar wasn't there. She was waiting out the storm at the library. She was somewhere else.

A flowerpot she had left sitting on the porch railing took off. Marveling, Susan watched it zoom horizontally through the yard and smash against the maple at the edge of the fence. It clung there like a boil for a moment, melded into the trunk, then tumbled into the dark mat of begonias around the roots.

"Jesus, that is some wind."

Susan caught at the edge of the sink. Outside, the plants were leaning flat, trying to be grass. Trees streamed like green lace. The glass in the window sighed, caught its breath, deepened its sigh. She placed her palm against it, holding it in. It breathed against her.

"Jesus!" His voice cracked like a teenager's. Like Jimmy, shouting on the racetrack, whip falling. Postcards had no voice. "Mrs. Carson, we'd better . . ." Something. "Come on. See those clouds? When they look like that . . . Midsummer is the worst." His hand balanced on the shelf of her back. "Basement!"

She couldn't let go of the glass for fear it would shatter. Wind was surging through every kitchen crack, keyhole, door molding, the shivering edges of the window. Rain plowed the ground. Even the broken flowerpot had dissolved in blackness.

"All right."

"Let's get going!"

Together, Gerhardt holding back at first, then surging ahead so their shoulders jammed, they clattered down the stairs between the magazines heaped at the sides. She could never throw them all out. At the bottom, the damp caught the both of them, cement walls spotted with moisture. Gerhardt hesitated, pulled back.

"Where?" He was shouting. She caught his elbow.

"Underneath." They turned back around the edge of the stairs, jacked up on two-by-fours. Underneath there was darkness, cement dust on the floor, bits of cobwebs murky in the damp. No light through the window above the laundry tubs. Strange. It was afternoon, and the western sun always shot through. But of course. The storm.

Under the window, nailed down to hold it in place from where it had warped, water beaded. One bead advanced, ruptured, sent a spring down the wall. A tiny lake grew at the floor joint, advanced, ruptured, edged toward the drain. More drops.

They stepped under the stairs. The wind was screaming. Water poured down the wall now, waves of rain hitting the outside and dashing through the line where the nailed woods met. What must it be like upstairs? The kitchen window faced west too. The kitchen would be swept away.

Susan lunged for the stairs. Her body stayed, one arm wedged. Gerhardt had both hands around her elbow.

"You can't go!" He must have been screaming.

"My cake!"

"Shit! Who cares?" He drove his arm around her belly, anchoring her. "This whole place is going to go!"

"Where?"

He looked at her as if she'd lost her mind. "Where?"

"*Where?*" Both of them were screaming.

"This is a *tornado*, you crazy lady. Mar is stuck out in some goddamn tornado!"

Susan stood skewered. Displacing the blur of her nose in her vision, the angel food spun around the streets of Manatee. She kicked at Gerhardt.

"Goddamn!" He didn't let go. "Get under them stairs!" He pulled her around, pushed her down to the damp concrete on her hands and knees, her hair working loose and into her mouth when she turned around and tried to scream at him. "You lost your mind? If you go up there and the wind takes the house, you've had it." His voice cracked.

Madly, Susan thought of the fruit cellar, all the jars black in the blotted-out light. Pears, plums, boysenberry jelly. But she couldn't give in. Twisting, she turned her mouth against Gerhardt's upper arm and put her teeth on him. Then, as his muscle tensed, before he yelled, she went at his shoulder. All cloth, no blood, hardly worth the trouble. Troops were marching on the stairway, fife and drum. Something metal hit the window. Water shot into the room in a square. When it spattered off the floor, the spray drenched her hair.

"You bitch!" Spreading both hands like shovels, Gerhardt forced her cheek down against the cement.

For a moment they lay there, him on her, matched all the way down except where her feet petered out just above his ankles. She stretched her toes, willed growth. Under his hands, her wrists were braceleted into the concrete. Her breasts flattened, shoved back into her lungs. The drain couldn't take the water fast enough, it was creeping up along the fingers of her right hand, sliming the floor under her. Across the room, the laundry tubs danced. The wringer turned. Gerhardt's breath smelled of mints. Did he smoke behind the barn and hide it? Those Kauffmanns, fit to try anything.

The roar stopped, a train in the station. She was lying in water, a good inch, her damp hair snaked over the top of her cheek. Under Gerhardt's skull, hard on hers, she wrenched her face sideways, one eye free. The ceiling was all in one piece. That meant the kitchen floor was still there. Gerhardt pulled himself up on his hands, roofing her over. The reversed stairs angled above them both.

The cake.

She slid out from under, anchored, spun for the stairs. Water splashed into her shoe. No light to speak of, just the line under the door at the top. She scuttled up.

"The cake!"

"The cake?" He was coming behind her, grabbing at her heels with his fingers so fast she couldn't trample them down. "Oh right, the cake! The cake, by God! Beat Mar to it! Susan Carson, we'll eat that goddamn cake. If the wind didn't get it, we will. Right down the old mackazoo; right down the gullet. You bite that cake like you went for me, lady. I wanna see that. I wanna see where that mouth of Mar's came from."

They tore into the kitchen together, slamming through the doorway at the top of the stairs, door snarling into the wall, then crashing shut. You'd think we were the same age, Susan gasped to herself, and then stopped when she realized that it didn't matter in the least how much the same age they were or weren't because they both had their tongues set for something sweet, something that hadn't even been taken out of the pan yet, the syrup in the heart of the storm. The kitchen window had shattered across the counter, probably a tree limb or another flowerpot flying, and Gerhardt swept the glass into a glittering dam by the stove. He cut his middle finger, blood trickled down his palm. He held it up like a stop sign, laughing. She laughed back.

But she couldn't find the knife. Just the paring one. The big one must be in the silverware drawer. No. In its pan, the cake rose smooth as a pregnant cloud. Rim, inner rim, upside down, out on a china plate. But no, no. Not this time.

As if they had been planning it, all their hands plunged thick into the riches, fingers plowing froth, handfuls dredged up. Wonderful. Luscious. Great duck-paddles of sweet. Feeding each other, plastering their faces. His Adam's apple raced up and down. They choked, coughed, grabbed, and wedged. One whole side of the pan was free now, and she swooped her forefinger down it, gouging a silver pathway in the brown. It clotted under her nail, she scraped it out between her two bottom teeth. He did the same.

"You are a goddamn witch, Susan!"

"Gerhardt Kauffmann. Goddamn German!"

"Woo-ee!" He turned around, grabbed the pan like a silver discus, and set it on his head. "Woo-ee!" He kicked off with one leg and spun in a circle, hands on his hips. The pan fell off, bouncing next to her. She anchored her hands on her hips too, clutching cloth, and kicked it across the room. It banged into the cupboard, then rolled like a hubcap back to his feet. They both sprang for it, tripped, fell. Cake crumbs layered his hair. Jerking back her chin so her jaw was as smooth as a girl's, she plunged her mouth against his.

Fifty-Four

"Jesus Christ, you gotta marry me."

Mar wiped the pink glass. Her mother had unpacked the dessert set out of the barrel two years ago and put it in the cupboard. It was too valuable to use for everyday, but you still had to wash it every year to prevent the dust from gathering. It had come from North Dakota, from the original place, from her grandparents'. Like the bookcase.

The dishes sat on the counter, summer air soaking up any drop the dish towel had missed. Small plates, goblets, pitcher, cream-and-sugar, cookie server. Mar wiped.

"Put that thing down."

"Please, Gerhardt."

"Put that thing down!"

"I have no intention of marrying you just like that."

"Like what?"

"Like you're asking."

"You want me on my knees?"

Mar wiped another glass. Five. Then six. It was amazing that they were all still there.

"You drive me crazy, Mar."

"I'm not doing anything."

"We've been going together since we was kids."

"It hasn't been that long."

"Even in Germany, I thought about you."

"I bet."

"I need a wife, Mar."

Mar put her index finger through the glass handle of the cookie server, lifted it off the counter. It was some special kind of glass, but she didn't know its name. She set the server down under the cupboard, turning it on its base. Not for anything chunky like brownies. Little macaroons. Lemon bars, crusted with powdered sugar. Ladyfingers.

"Mar, I'm asking."

"I certainly know that."

"You don't wanna live here forever."

"I get along here."

"We could live in the place next to my folks. Melchor wants to sell out. My dad talked to him. We wouldn't have to live *with* my folks if you didn't want."

"I know Melchor's place. The kitchen looks like a pigpen."

"Hell, we could rent the Adams place for a hundred fifty. Less if I went shares with him."

"You'd actually leave your parents?" The sun hit the pink dishes, testing each one.

"Jesus, Mar, I'm not a rug rat anymore."

Mar began the careful climb up the kitchen stepladder, a pink glass in each hand. "Your mother doesn't like me," she said.

"Hell, *your* mother doesn't like . . ." He caught himself.

"Like you either?" Against the back of the cupboard, the glasses glinted like chalices.

"I didn't say that."

"You always have before."

"Shit." She didn't wince. "Shit," Gerhardt said again.

"I don't want any of those nine-month babies," said Mar. She started carefully down the ladder.

Gerhardt put his head in his hands.

"I don't know if I want any babies at all."

"Jesus, Mar, anything you say."

"I don't want one of those big German weddings, either."

"All right."

"You'd have to let me come back into town if Mother or the Collinses needed help."

"All right. Hell, Mar, what is this?"

"I'm just saying what I want."

"You want your ma to live with us?" His mouth fell open. The words had just slid out.

"She wouldn't want to."

"I guess not."

"Would she?"

"What?"

"Would she?"

Fifty-Five

"Take off all your clothes except your shoes, please. The robe fastens in back." Rebecca Cassiday, the nurse, looked over her shoulder at Susan as she turned to leave the examining room, one hand flittering like a hummingbird on the periphery of the door-frame. "But you *know* all that," she said, her red lips twisting up at the corners. "I feel foolish even saying it."

"It's what you're paid to do," replied Susan, starting methodically on the buttons of her blouse from the top down. For how many things in life had that been a justification? Though the pay was seldom in the official currency of the realm, God only knew. But the world was set up so there was compensation for everything. Out of loneliness was born independence. Out of pain came the next generation. Out of age came security, of a sort. So they said. And out of passion?

Blood answered to blood. No wonder her monthlies had come in again.

Outside, a cold front had begun, or as cold a front as could arrive in the midst of summer. The chilling wall of air had formed at Hudson Bay, marched through Winnipeg and down the border between Minnesota and North Dakota, then over to Manatee. The sky was a blue that cut the eye, piercing down between the trees and rooftops of the houses across the street. Susan could imagine it peopled with fierce fairies, merciless in their judgments, mad with energy. When the tornado came, they rode the thunderbolts, spread themselves in the flood, approved what couldn't be forgiven. One paid for the pleasures they brought. One paid for everything. Only the earth forgave, absorbed. Only the soil accepted whatever came to it.

But, of course, that was nonsense. Susan laid her blouse on the chair by the examining table, unzipped her skirt and slipped out of it. Around her waist under her slip, the extra flesh formed an uneven circle. But not so much. Really not so much. Gerhardt hadn't said a word about it. But then, he was used to Mar.

She put her face in her hands. The encyclopedias didn't have any answers to this one.

"Right there!" came Dr. Collins's voice from the hall. It was a slow afternoon; otherwise he couldn't have given her an appointment. Although she did have some privileges, having worked there as long as she had. The gown was as idiotic on her as it was on every patient, bunched under her breasts, open all the way down the back. She wrenched it closed under her rear on the unrolled paper covering the examining table. Her splayed feet looked back at her, every toe an affront. But she hadn't had to take off her shoes. Now she remembered.

Well. Better let him see it all. The time for secrets was past.

Then he came in, stethoscope swinging. She hadn't realized it would feel so odd to be his patient. Through the gap under her buttocks where the gown was once again seeping away, the paper crinkled as she shifted her weight. The blue sky blazed through the window, colored the dotted-swiss curtains a deeper green where they crossed the glass. The curtains had been her original idea. No use pretending that the people who balanced on this miserable examining table weren't aware of the kindnesses arranged for their eyes.

"Not feeling well?"

Confronted with that direct question, Susan found herself without an easy answer. Except for the renewed flow and a profound unease, she was without pain. It was as if the countries of her body were in the process of realignment.

Dr. Collins saw her lack of answer as embarrassment and changed his tactics. Susan knew his every move, could have predicted one after the other, could have recognized Monday's more energetic probing and Friday's end-of-the-week dimness. "Concerned about something?" he asked, his stethoscope ready.

She drew back her chin. "My body," she said.

"All of it?" He was grateful for the humor.

"The newly activated parts."

He drew back, looked at her. The intent of the remark went past him, but something in the afterwash caught his attention. It was as if he were running through his anatomy book, looking for the classification. There was no alphabetical listing to help him. He lowered his eyes as he stepped forward. Susan kept hers straight on what was now the top of his forehead.

"Short of breath?"

"Seldom." His stethoscope probed delicately, fingers tapping her flesh in widening circles. Susan braced herself erect on the table, concentrating on holding back any response.

"Simply time for a checkup?" He still wasn't looking directly at her.

"Yes." She felt no embarrassment, but it was impossible to speak in a way that would reveal anything.

"Lungs good." His voice came from around her shoulder, his fingers discreetly probing down the knobs of her spine. "Any back problems?"

"No." Her back was a permanent fixture in the residence of her body. Women who complained about their backs were despicable.

"Headaches? Sore throats? Any problems with sleeping?" They were standard questions, hardly worthy of being entered on the chart. The fact that he didn't know why she was there seemed not to matter to him as he moved on along the path where he felt confident, the list of inquiries welded into his brain by medical school and Manatee practice. Susan recognized that she was not an individual to him. All the responsibility for being an individual was her own. She was using him. She was using him as she had used the others. She was using him as she had used Gerhardt three weeks ago.

Dr. Collins, his swatch of reddish grey hair dipping over his forehead to the bridge of his nose, where it touched and then swung loose, had stepped back from the examining table and seated himself in the little chair by the Formica desk. His white lab coat bulged up over the chair back as if wings were about to sprout from it. He uncapped his fountain pen, a Parker with his initials in gold along the side, and began to write on the chart sheet. "No problems that I can recognize, Susan," he said. "You're in good health for a woman your age." He paused, his pen arrested above the paper. "Susan May Carson," he said. "Maiden name?"

"McIntire."

"Scotch?"

"Yes."

"Parents born here."

"Not here."

"In the old country?"

"No. In the East. In Massachusetts."

The pen had stopped writing. "So they moved out here?"

"Yes. To North Dakota."

"Still living?"

Susan stopped. "No," she said. Then, "They died when I was thirteen."

"Epidemic?"

She hadn't meant to say more. She had never said any more to anyone, not ever. She was a middle-aged woman now, moving toward agedness, and she didn't respect him or any man. All that had happened a long time ago. She had borne it. She had dealt with it.

"No."

He looked at her.

"Someone killed them," she said, knowing that it had been the marker that had started it all.

"Good Lord," said Dr. Collins, holding the Parker upright and rolling it between both palms.

"And after that, it was never the same." The gown splitting down her back was driving her crazy, so she gathered it up into a wad on her lap and drove it between her legs. Let him look at her hinter parts and marvel. "I went to live with neighbors. I went to normal school in Belfontaine, but I didn't graduate. I met Richard and married him. I had three children. Frankie died. I had four abortions and never bled to death. EuraBella knew how to do it. Richard didn't want to stop. I didn't want him inside me. I didn't want to be half of a person. I don't want to now, so why did I do it? I want to do it on my own."

Dr. Collins had his eyes straight down at the chart. The pen was fastened to the front pocket of his white coat. He didn't move, although it was past closing time. Rebecca Cassiday would have locked the files and left.

"I don't understand about love," said Susan, knowing what was coming next, as it always did in every examination a man gave, lying back on the crunchy paper and lifting her legs into the stirrups. "It's not in the encyclopedia. But sometimes you feed each other. Sometimes you're empty in there." She bent her knees outward, hunched her buttocks down toward the drop-off where the table ended. "Only women understand," she said.

Fifty-Six

"They won't know where I am." Susan sat on the love seat in Rosa Bellamy's parlor, holding a teacup on her knee. From the rocking chair, Rosa had set her mending aside. It was knitting, actually, at least today, and the product appeared to be a scarf of undetermined length. It wound around the top of the basket like a curled-up cat, with one end hanging over the edge and spilling down along the leg of the end table. A man would have had to be ten feet tall to wear it.

"*They* are not that important."

"I can always say that I'm at the Rebecca Circle."

Rosa smiled. "Of course," she nodded. "An excuse for anything."

"In actuality, I've come from the doctor."

"Is something wrong?"

For a moment, Susan lowered her eyes. "I must have defined it that way," she said, "or else I wouldn't have gone."

"Something that can be fixed?"

"It is within my powers."

Rosa reached for the teapot, a fat china sphere with pagodas circling it. Stretching, she gentled a stream into Susan's cup. "You always talk in mysteries, my dear," she said. "Whenever you come, I feel like I need some special dictionary to translate your words. Not your words, so much—they're clear enough. But the words you don't say. They hang in the air like spirits. I'd have to be far more than a Methodist minister's wife to bring them to earth."

"I suppose I find it simpler not to commit myself to something I can't take back."

"That's why I still don't understand why you committed yourself to our friendship."

"Yes, you do."

Now it was Rosa's turn to lower her eyes. "Yes, I do," she said. "But who would have guessed that the Rebecca Circle would have led to this?"

"What I have trouble understanding is why I joined that group of silly women in the first place."

"You were carrying out my husband's directions."

"I have *never* carried out a man's directions."

"Yet you were married for a long time."

"And still am, as much as I know."

Rosa stood up. She moved in front of Susan until the vertical line of her body was exactly centered, so that from the window, only one woman could have been seen. "I think there is more than one kind of marriage," she said.

"I think so, too."

"That friend of yours. Lucianne. She ran a thread through your life more than any man."

"She did indeed. And we are still in touch."

"A strange expression. However, she isn't in Manatee."

"No, she isn't."

For a long moment, they looked at each other. Rosa held out her hands. "My husband won't be home until late this evening," she said.

"And now that I think of it, I believe that Mar was having supper with Gerhardt's family. I suspect that they are moving toward marriage."

"How does that make you feel?"

"Relieved."

"There is more to that word than one might think at first." Rosa pulled Susan to her feet.

"You are far too wise for a minister's wife."

"I am not inhibited by my husband's profession."

"I appreciate an uninhibited woman."

There was a pause. Hands together, they looked at each other. Then, leaning back and half turning, Rosa pulled the curtain.

Fifty-Seven

Mar's decision to be married had come on with the speed of a summer storm, but the resources of Manatee's dry goods store had served her well. The dress had to be expanded a considerable degree; nevertheless, it still had a certain maidenly charm lying flat across the bed in the upstairs room that had been Mr. Rawlings's. The skirt was full, the bodice attached subtly behind a swath of belted lace, and the neckline, also lace edged, made a gracious sweep downward for a modest distance. Considering that it had been a last-minute purchase, as last minute as the obligatory instructions from Reverend Bellamy and the arrival of Elizabeth from Minneapolis to serve as maid of honor, it could be rated as a success.

"It really is a success, Mar. It's just amazing that Metzgers had one like it available."

Sitting on the rocker next to the bed, Mar knew exactly how she was supposed to feel on this, the morning of her wedding. Some of her did feel that way. Elizabeth had been delighted to stop being a secretary for two days and to stand up for her at the ceremony. All the rituals were being finished off.

Mar looked over at Elizabeth, circling the dress as if it might make a break for freedom. "What did you do with your yellow tooth?" she asked.

"I had it capped."

"Why?"

"Good heavens, Mar! Why would I want that awful tooth sitting in the front of my mouth for the rest of my life? Besides, the boy I was dating had a brother who was a dentist. He only charged thirty dollars, and he did a real good job."

"I've got horribly healthy teeth." Mar opened her mouth wide and pulled back the corners with both forefingers. Then she stuck her tongue out.

"You'll need them with Gerhardt!"

"I'm not going to *bite* him."

"Keep the possibility in reserve."

The two of them started to giggle, choked it back, then giggled more. It was amazing that their friendship had resumed with so little fuss. Actually, thought Mar, they had never been real friends, simply schoolgirls whose lives had overlapped. But Elizabeth *had* been willing to come down with hardly any notice. Right now, she stood picking loose threads off the hem of Mar's dress as her giggles subsided, a perfect assistant.

"You remember Gerhardt, don't you?" Mar's chest was still trembling with the aftermath of laughter.

"How could I forget? He always reminded me of Kaiser Wilhelm."

"Elizabeth, that's silly."

"All he needed was one of those hats with the point on the top. Jab, jab, jab."

"Elizabeth!"

"Only tonight he won't do it with his hat!" Elizabeth buried her head in the chenille bedspread over the pillow, her giggles starting up again.

"Gerhardt is a good man." Mar stopped, feeling the need for an adjective that would pin Gerhardt down for all time. "Ordinary," she said finally. "But true."

"Ordinary but true! It sounds like something by Les Paul and Mary Ford!"

"Elizabeth, Minneapolis has ruined you."

"No, it hasn't!" But she was still laughing. "Unless we're all ruined. Because we got older." Elizabeth twisted and giggled. "And you'll feel older yet after that Gerhardt gets his hands on you tonight."

Mar felt a surge of wit. It was exhilarating. "It's not his hands I'm thinking about," she said.

"Mar! What would your churchgoing mother say?"

"I have no idea. She doesn't go to church all that often, either. Just to Circle sometimes. Or to talk to the minister's wife at the parsonage."

And, as if by signal, her mother came in with hardly more than a brush of knuckles on the bedroom door. She had arranged a little lunch on a tray, two of the pink plates, lemonade in the goblets, tuna fish on rolls open-faced in ruffled carpets of lettuce. It had a ceremonial appearance.

"Not long to go." Susan set the tray on the bedside table.

"She'll be ready, Mrs. Carson." Elizabeth reached for her sandwich and nibbled at it. "Have we forgotten anything?"

"Ask the bride."

"She can't think of anything." Elizabeth nickered her teeth

against the soft roll.

"What about my wedding bouquet?"

Susan rose to her feet. "I never gave it a thought," she said. Across her face passed a wave of concern, as if the failure might be attributed directly to her.

"The florist isn't open on Saturday," said Mar matter-of-factly.

Elizabeth sealed the breach. "We'll think of something," she said. "Look at the dress, Mrs. Carson. It really is almost like the one in the June *Vogue.*"

The three women moved toward the bed where the dress lay. Its satiny glow illumined the chenille spread around it. No one said anything for a moment, then Susan reached out one hand and lifted the lace where it had been tacked into the side seams of the bodice. "It was a good choice," she said.

"Do you still have yours, Mrs. Carson?"

Susan raised her hand, then held it in midair as if ready to balance some object on it. Only there was no object. She examined both sides carefully. "We just wore our Sunday clothes," she said.

"Just as well, Mother. I certainly could never have had your dress expanded to fit me."

For a moment the three looked at each other, faces blank. Then all three broke into laughter, and they kept it up until they spilled on the margin of coverlet, framing the dress with their bodies. Elizabeth choked, cleared her throat, then buried her head in the pillow, howling. Mar and Susan held on to each other.

"It's a crazy world, isn't it?" As if this were the answer to everything, they kept on laughing until they couldn't keep it up anymore.

"Reverend Bellamy will think you're crazy if you don't have any flowers."

"Flowers for the wedding bower!"

"So it won't turn sour!"

Susan got up. Her apron was a mass of wrinkles down her front. "You can have some from the garden," she said. "They're still nice. Come look."

The three of them hurried down the stairs, hairpins tumbling into their collars, fringes flying, buttons coming loose from buttonholes as if they had taken off on their own. They tore outside, rounded the corner of the house. Maybe it could come out all right. Maybe on this day they could be what they were supposed to be to each other.

And the late August flowers spilled everywhere. The tall delphiniums were propped against the fence so they wouldn't topple, double blues and whites, lavender-pinks. Johnny-jump-ups tangled at their feet, untrimmed, unpicked, and beyond them were the gloriosa daisies, hybrid black-eyed Susans, the center of each flower a brown nipple for the bees. Some joe-pye weed and Queen Anne's lace, weeds that were prettier than most flowers. Late daylilies, though they wouldn't keep once you picked them, and the columbine going at it again, insatiable. Best of all, the annuals, lusty petunias bitter on the fingers, bitter marigolds, bitter zinnias, the ones never touched by early frost, the ones you could count on.

And the pansies, sweet, sweet, faces from the underworld, sweet.

Fifty-Eight

"Please."

"You are crazy."

"No. Oh hell, maybe. I can't forget. I see angel food at the Methodist bazaar, I can't think straight. It don't make no sense."

"I believe that."

"You always act like you're looking down at me. Like I don't matter. Except that one time. I mattered *then*."

"Yes."

"I want it again, Susan."

"How could I?"

"Nobody'd know."

"Yes."

"Nobody'd need to know. You ain't going to get pregnant. Mar's home on the farm, cleaning. She cleans that house like she was building it up from scratch. When I track in, she *likes* it. It gives her something new to clean up."

"Cleaning makes a woman feel she's in charge of something."

"I guess."

"It's important to be in charge of as much as possible. Even if you have to act crazy. Even if you have to crawl."

"Hell, I feel like I'm not even in charge of where I set my feet down."

"Maybe you could change that if you tried."

"What'd you think I'm doing now?"

Susan opened the cookie jar. She had baked three days ago, but not a double batch. There were only a few chocolate chips left, their margins crumbling in the bottom reaches of the fat china panda on the counter. She took out two and gave one to Gerhardt. He held it in his palm and stared at it.

"It was the storm."

"Sure, Susan. And more than the storm."

"It was the window breaking."

"Right. And I could put my fist through it this time if that was what you needed."

"No. We can't. I won't. Eat your cookie."

"Fucking cookie."

"That language doesn't scare me. You know that."
"I know that. You're beyond scaring."
"Yes."

Fifty-Nine

The stores hadn't used to set up Christmas so early, not in the small towns like Manatee. Every holiday had its assigned place. Halloween blossomed appropriately at Woolworth in mid-October with cat masks and Lone Rangers swinging from hangers in the front window. The orange-and-yellow corn candies, the only ones that had ever made Mar throw up, appeared in paper bags at Smiths Grocery Store, heaped on the counter by the cash register. For the sanitary parents who wanted the candy individually wrapped, there were the miniature Baby Ruths.

Then Thanksgiving had brought pilgrims, including the ones in front of the Methodist Church, cut out of plywood and lined along the walk. Miles Standish (they had their names painted down their fronts, the Reverend Bellamy's idea) had weathered; John Alden had held up. Kindergartners brought home brown-paper turkeys, their tails curled strips of construction paper, their eyes beady raisins. Smiths lined cans of cranberry sauce in pyramids at the end of the center aisle, smooth and lumpy varieties together, perfectly balanced. Susan had always used to make her own. Now, when Gerhardt and Mar came, she spatulaed the solid red cylinder out of the can and dumped it quivering on the blue-glass serving dish.

Manatee didn't always have snow for Christmas because the winds from the west blew off the November attempts most of the time, but it always had cold, thermometers swallowing their tongues, air like a sharp headband. But this year the first snow had come the week before Thanksgiving, gobs of it pivoting down through the streetlights, roofing the Methodist pilgrims. It had been so wet that it had stuck to the ground, and even with the temperature rising the last days of the month, most of it had stayed. Then, on December fourth, when she'd cashed Mr. Keopek's rent check, the only check now, it had snowed again, first the sleety kind that hissed against the windows, then the thick white blossoms of chill. And that had stayed, too. So now that Christmas was only a week away, the decorations legitimate, snowbanks lined Manatee's main street. Even the postman, when he brought her Jimmy's Christmas postcard—horses eating from the hand of a girl in a silver robe— had complained about tromping through the unshoveled walks of those townspeople who weren't responsible.

The entrance to Barnwells Dry Goods Store was edged with plastic Santas. There was hardly any room to pass between them. Susan edged sideways, pushed inside, her purse in front of her like a shield. Over the door, small lights blinked in a line that was woven across the wall from the electric outlet.

"Doing your shopping late this year, Mrs. Carson?" The clerk was merry beyond the demands of the season. Fingers trotting, she was lining up costume jewelry in the showcase.

"Not too late." The sale shirts were right in front of her. In the chill from the doorway, even her wallet seemed to stiffen in her fingers. Barnwells faced northwest, and the wind refused to be kept out.

"Family coming home?"

"Yes."

"Saw your girl the other day. Not too much longer."

"What?" Susan placed the chosen shirt on the counter along with the necessary paper money. Shirts were neutral gifts. Even Gerhardt would recognize that.

"They're staying on the farm? Good place for kids."

Susan pushed the bills forward. "What kids?" she asked, guessing the rest of the conversation, perverse in playing it out.

"I have eight grandchildren of my own."

"No sign of it for me." Susan placed three quarters on the bills, weighing them down where the draft couldn't move them. Mar had been big enough to look pregnant since high school.

The clerk, eyebrows together, stopped with her hands over the cash drawer. "But . . . ," she said, too caught in her own embarrassment to go further.

Susan didn't assist her. She speculated about grabbing a fistful of quarter rolls. Then she could chunk that gossipy head with them.

"She isn't . . . ?" The clerk's finger got caught under the clamp in the dollar drawer. She was anchored by it, twitching. It had been a good business day. Under the metal, her flesh was safely cushioned by greenbacks.

"My daughter is just a husky young woman." Even Mar said "fat," but that was her business.

"Oh well." The drawer finally clanged shut. "They wait nowadays, most of them." The clerk handed over the change. "Merry Christmas," she said, recovering herself.

Susan tucked the shirt box into her shopping bag, square with organized purchases. In her other hand she carried her purse, small, but heavy so she wasn't too badly overbalanced. The shop-keepers salted the ice in front of their stores, chopped out what didn't melt. But they never got it all. She was used to walking on frozen silt, though, used to the ridges against the soles of her shoes, used to her heels coming down on ice hummocks. She hadn't fallen in years. Even if she were to go around by the parsonage, she'd be able to keep her balance.

It got dark early now. The shortest day tomorrow. People who passed her slipped through the dark like they belonged. You got used to it.

Her packages heavy on her arm, Susan turned down her own street. Red Dog had died in the summer, asprawl on the sidewalk after attacking a poodle. His heart had gotten him. His melancholy ghost followed her as she approached her house, its windows blossoming with light. Even Mr. Keopek's room had light glinting around the drawn shade. She'd left the others on herself. It was her own celebration.

"Christmas shopping?" Mrs. Ramsey was reshaping the snow-banks along her fence. She held a child's shovel in her mittens, handle weighted with the heaviness of the snow she was heaving.

"Finishing up."

"The children coming in for the day?"

"So they say." Susan held her key like a tiny pistol.

"Lucky they're not too far away. If the weather's bad, they'll still make it. Gregory's trapped in the Twin Cities if that happens. Wouldn't want him on the road." The little shovel balanced an ice chunk like a cherry on the bank of snow.

"It's not a problem when they're four miles outside of town."

"That's certainly right."

Susan pushed the door into the hall, splashing the outside dark-ness with the gleam. It was stupid to have put up a tree, but she had wanted one. Even without its lights turned on, it made its presence known.

Inside, she unloaded, unzipped her boots, hung up her coat. She had almost the whole rack to herself. Mr. Keopek's jacket hung on the short hook against the post, its wool arms entwined. It would embarrass him to see it. She pulled the arms apart, smoothed them down decorously over the pockets. He must be upstairs, lying without weight on his bed, the coverlet unwrinkled, the mattress un-bent. His bed was the only one in the house with a flat mattress. The other boarders, before they had left, had channeled theirs with wear. Her own waved like the ocean.

Susan took her parcels to the tree. Mr. and Mrs. Santa hung exactly at eye level, their strings tangled. She straightened them. The angel was around by the wall. Jimmy's horse was still in the box, and the box in the closet under the stairs. She hadn't even needed to unwrap the tissue to know which one it was, nor to feel it, either. It was the perfect shape of the insides of her clasped hands.

Purposefully, Susan went for the upright vacuum in the pantry. It sucked up the stray needles scattered beyond the protective sheet, roaring. Of course it was no surprise when she heard the footsteps on the stairs, since he must have heard her through the ceiling as she'd intended. "Mrs. Carson?" he said, with that little twist that made a melody of the syllables.

"Yes."

"I heard you come in." Five years ago, he wouldn't have gotten the tense right. "You're getting ready," he said, his English accurate as a native's.

Susan started putting things under the tree. She'd wrap them later. The plaid work shirt for Gerhardt. Bedroom slippers for Mar, fuzzy pink. The new *Better Homes and Gardens Cookbook.* New bread pans. Mar never dried hers; they rusted within a year. Her bread came out of the oven with orange stripes. These were aluminum, good for generations. Mr. Keopek was watching.

"For him. For her."

"Yes."

"It's good to have family."

"Where are yours?" Her words ran out without thought. Of course, he must have left them behind.

Mr. Keopek looked down. Susan was taking out the last package, a big cylinder. "Still in my country. Only a niece now. Her husband and children."

Susan knew the feel of the envelopes that came for him, soft like tissue paper. The letters on the return address had little signs above them. They came more often than did the postcards from Jimmy.

"My sister died. After the war." The pink tip of his lips quivered at the midpoint of his mustache.

"Don't you ever want to see your niece?"

"I go next month."

Susan raised her hands to her hair. "Next month?" It would still be winter.

"I sail January eighth."

"Would you like me to paint your room while you're gone?"

Mr. Keopek nudged her shoulder with his hand. There was an

envelope in it. She reached out.

"This is the rent. Early, for January. Because I leave, and you have no time to find another one."

"Then you're not coming back?"

He twisted his hands together, but his voice was calm. "I think I go live there now. The trouble is gone. They build the houses back up. I help with the children, read books in my language, go to cafés. They are family, after all. I think about my family."

Susan started to get up, then knelt again, catching her breath. She reached out to the final gift. "Look at this, Mr. Keopek," she said, hanging on to the season, to the moment kept under her control. No use thinking about what was going to happen. It wasn't in her hands.

He knelt beside her.

"They were on sale."

He held the round cover as she handed it to him.

"I always thought you could build a tower almost as tall as you were yourself if you got the bottom balanced right."

Mr. Keopek's smile hoisted his mustache right into his nostrils. "Like the Eiffel, I think."

"Or the Empire State Building." Susan poured the Tinkertoy pieces out onto the floor, then swept them together with her hand.

"Here." He inserted sticks. "We make a square. Then we go on up."

"We'll stick them in the corners, then across again." It was easier than sponge cake, dishes, knitting, hems. "The next floor will go up a little ways inside."

"You have enough?"

"I bought the biggest set."

"And to whom does this belong?"

"What?" She had the base for the third level. It really wasn't hard at all. She wouldn't even have to skimp.

"This belongs to your child?"

Mar wouldn't have touched a Tinkertoy, of course. Gerhardt would stomp and laugh.

"Your big girl?" He was building the final level, his fingernails ticking the wooden disks.

"Of course not."

"Your grandchild?"

"Maybe some day, before I die."

Mr. Keopek placed the peak of the tower where it belonged,

anchored it in the final structure. He finished it off with a final stick, a spool, one of the green paper blades. "They last, these Tinkertoy," he said. "Oh, yes."

Sixty

"Thirty more miles, lady. The worst is over. No new snowstorms now." A tight roll of flesh overlapped his blue collar, bearing down as he spoke. In the rearview mirror, the bones of his forehead caught the light from the sun that was just beginning to struggle out from under the morning horizon's layer of cloud. The snow, unreeling in front of the bus and along each side, woke up to a pink as artificial as food coloring. The headlights of the bus had disappeared into the morning white of the highway.

"How much further to Alcottsville now?"

"Like I said. Twenty-five. Why not make a trip of it, go all the way to Wichita? Way the place is growing, they'll be the same thing couple years down the line." He wedged his hand into his pocket, withdrew the round snuff tin, opened it against the rim of the steering wheel. "No turning back progress."

Susan shifted, flexing her knees. "Sorry. Just to Alcottsville. The main hotel there."

"The Palace. Right downtown. We pull up in front. Twenty minutes, maybe." His neck was so thick that when he tried to turn back toward her, he couldn't get his head further than a profile. "You need a room?" he asked.

"I'm being met."

"Not much going on in Alcottsville with Wichita so near. Church camp on the lake. The County Fair. Grandstand at Burnette burned down four years ago. Now they have the fair at the Alcottsville racetrack and put up tents. Nobody in Burnette will vote in a bond issue for rebuilding. Even in 1956, good year, they couldn't get it passed."

Outside the window, a schoolhouse appeared, one single structure in the pink snow. The pathway to the door was shoveled just wide enough for one. Down the road, a yellow bus moved toward it. Susan watched.

"Not many of those little schools left." The driver was shoving the can back into his pocket.

"Not these days."

Behind them both, a few tousled heads wobbled over the backs of the seats. The bus hadn't ever been crowded, not in Manatee in

the bare light of Wednesday's dawn, not at any of the small towns
along the way. A farm boy with his duffel, cold but not showing it.
A fine old woman with the wrinkles on her forehead wrenched
back under her scarf. That was at Jefferson, Iowa, where the Amish
had an outpost. The driver had told her that. "Good people," he'd
said, his jaws working.

Susan couldn't remember when she'd last been on a bus. During
the war? Further back? The volleyball team at normal school? No.
That one time to Fletchersville, to wait for Richard. And would it
have mattered if he had come?

The window again. Blurred by the tinted glass, little houses set
back from the road began to jump alongside the bus. The land was
open, almost prairie, and the owners had gone to work to protect
their privacy. Skinny saplings lined the morning sky to the north
and west. Along the road, several of the owners had planted pines
at compromised distances to leave room for the future giants they
would become, but also to fill up as much grassy margin as possible
now. Where the wind had swept the snow free, the black arrows
aimed skyward.

"You're being met?" the driver asked, as if he hadn't heard the
first time.

"Yes I am." She could have sat in the back, after all. But then she
would have had only the views to each side. Up by the windshield,
through which the sun was now glowing, was the best place to be.

"Pretty early to be met."

"Not in farm country."

"Ranch country out here." His uniform cap, Susan realized, covered every possibility of hair. And he had shaved off his sideburns.
She imagined him bald as an egg. "Ranch country," she said back.

Then they were rolling down the main street of Alcottsville.
Café, gas stations, Happy Hamburgers, two taverns kitty-corner
from each other, grain-and-seed store. The hotel was further, perky
with its brick facade. It faced east; the sun had flattened its windows into golden squares. The bus pulled up.

"Need any help with that?" He would probably miss her. They
had done the heartland of America together.

"No, I can manage."

She hadn't brought much, Susan thought, as she stepped down,
her toe landing precisely on the oval where the ice had been cleared
bare to the cement sidewalk. If she were going to stay any time,
she'd have to buy some more underclothes. A long-sleeved sweater.

It was colder than she had thought, even this far south. Her right stocking had developed a run, straight down from the knee, disappearing into her shoe. She had no bathrobe.

The woman standing in the hotel doorway filled it like a statue. Her coat was the best wool, fur collared. On her head was a hat of the same fur, rich and brown in the early light.

"Your stocking has a run," said Lucianne.

"I know it." They held each other. The fur tickled. From somewhere down the street, blurred words sounded like a radio. A door slammed. The words stopped.

"I have breakfast ordered." Lucianne took her hand, her suitcase.

"Is there a real restaurant here?"

"Several. I chose the local café. They're bringing it over when I signal. Which is now." She raised her arm in what would have been a salute had she been a man. Across the street behind a plate-glass window, a flicker waved back.

"They were watching?"

"For five dollars, even a short-order cook will raise his eyes from the grill." Lucianne swept through the hotel lobby like a ship and up the carpeted stairs. "This place has known better days," she said, moving down the hall. "But they haven't given up. Our room has been redecorated. Hand-painted around the molding. They were trying for a rose arbor but without significant artistic triumph. But I give the Palace Hotel credit for trying."

Lucianne opened the door. The molding was entwined with spotty images of roses.

"Are you tired?"

"Try another word."

"Exhausted? Comatose?"

"Tired."

"After that bus ride, does it seem like this is really happening?"

"It's happening."

"Well, the two of us always did make things happen, Susan." Lucianne spread her coat over the bed by the window and smoothed out the creases. "They said it wouldn't wrinkle. I should have known. Anything will wrinkle in a car trip of more than an hour. I was right not to stock it."

"You were right to buy one for yourself. You look beautiful." Susan began a slow inspection of her friend: the powdered cheeks, the careful eyes, the hair barely moving upward as the fur hat joined the coat on the bed. Lucianne moved like a queen. She had gained weight, and all it did was expand her dignity. She crossed the room as if a carpet had been laid for her.

"Thank you, Susan. I got it free. So I like it even better. There are some advantages to the retail trade."

There was a knock on the door. Breakfast. The boy who brought it was most likely ten or twelve. He held two brown bags, tightly folded and rolled, in his arms. Tiny eyes peered over their tops as he stood dumbfounded.

"You're no busboy," said Lucianne. "Give it here." She transferred the bags, moving across the room to the round table under the swag lamp. The boy stood with his arms hanging.

"Why aren't you in school?"

His mouth opened, but nothing came out.

"It's not a holiday, is it?"

An edge of pink tongue curled up to touch his upper teeth.

"Spare me. Go back to your child labor." Lucianne thrust a dollar into his hand. His tongue convulsed as he hopped for the hallway.

"That'll keep him. More than his weekly allowance, I'm sure." Lucianne sailed toward the table. "Well?" She eyed Susan. "Eat. I'm about to talk. You heard it all over the phone, but this is the second performance. Be fortified."

"I can't swallow." Susan put her hands on each side of her plate.

"Yes, you can. Bite of egg, bite of toast. Strawberry jelly. Remember how my mother used to make it?"

"Lucianne."

"Yes."

"Tell me."

"That's what we're here for."

"Tell me now."

Lucianne patted her mouth with the napkin. Her lipstick remained unchanged. "Well. I was traveling. *Not* a holiday. Looking for possible retail outlets. We're saturating the heartland. No end to what's possible. The president of the company gives me a free hand. Kansas is still Indian territory as far as he's concerned, but he's willing to listen. The population has doubled in the last ten years, at least in the Wichita area. So I drove down."

"You have a car?"

"I certainly didn't drive a horse and buggy. Though I might as well have. I'd gotten an early start and was about five miles north of Alcottsville when the steering went. I sailed into the ditch as if I'd planned it. Not even a thump, there was so much snow. When I got out, I was wading up to my rear."

"Snow angel."

Lucianne took Susan's hand. "Yes," she said.

"Were you hurt?"

"They would have had to drop me from Sputnik to do any damage. Just look at me. But by the time a car came by to pick me up, I was so cold that my fingers had turned blue. This man insisted I go have a doctor check me over, so he took me into town to find one."

"Here?"

"On the edge. The regional clinic. Twenty beds and outpatients. I was their first customer of the day, and of course I was fine. By then I was turning pink again."

"Tell me the rest."

"I already did, on the phone."

"Tell me again how you found him."

"Right." Lucianne put her fingers, nails buffed, around her coffee cup. "I will. The clinic was part of the hospital, and when I left, I turned the wrong way. Instead of going to the exit, I ended up walking along the main corridor. It was so early that nothing much was happening. The breakfast cart had just started out from the kitchen. No strawberry jelly, I'm sure. All the doors were shut except for one. You know me. I couldn't help looking."

Susan bent her head. Her eyes were closed.

"I knew him right away."

Susan reached for her own coffee. The cup danced on the saucer. She took her hand away. "How?" she asked.

Smiling, Lucianne broke the last piece of toast into quarters, arranged them on her friend's plate. "Susan, he looks just like you. Then and now. Nothing has changed since he was four, except that he got some bristles on his chin. He's stretched out a little in size, but not all that much."

Outside, a morning snowplow began churning at the margins of the street. Still, it was impossible to hear everything in the room.

"Believe me, Susan, it was like meeting someone I'd seen just last year. And I hadn't seen you or him for . . . how many?"

"Many."

"And it didn't matter. I walked in. His name was on the foot of the bed. Jimmy Carson. Did you even put 'James' on his birth certificate?"

"I don't remember."

"I introduced myself. My voice was shaking. I sounded like the air coming out of a balloon. His leg was in traction, and I found myself talking to it. His face kept disappearing behind the plaster. I don't think he was even surprised when I told him who I was. He seemed like the kind of person who could accept anything."

"No." Susan shook her head. "When he couldn't accept it, he left it."

"Didn't you ever try to find him?"

"No. I thought about him. That was enough."

"You only had Mar left."

"He should have his freedom."

"What kind of freedom is that, following the horses around the country, no family, no security? Mailing you postcards from every midwestern racetrack?"

"It's what he chose." Susan's hands held each other. "It was the best thing I could give him. To make his own choice."

"Susan, I've never argued with you. More than anyone I've ever known, you've earned the right to do what you want. Which you don't exercise very often. But he is your son. You should be with him."

"He is my son. That's why he has to make his own choices."

The two of them were silent. Outside, the snowplow came back, aimlessly scraping. The wind had picked up, and swishes of snow shot straight up and out into the air from the edges of the metal.

"Lucianne?"

"Yes? What?"

"You never married."

"No, I didn't."

"Aren't you lonely?"

"I live with someone."

"Who?"

"A woman. Sarah Northbrook. She's a secretary for the president of Allied Stores."

Susan looked straight into the eyes of her friend. "I envy you," she said.

"Well, you always were my first choice."

Susan smiled. "Thank you. You were mine, too."

Between their hands, the toast crumbs clotted on the breakfast plates. Lucianne's coffee, a black circle in her cup, lay lidded with a tint like oil. Their eyes held together.

"You'll see him, won't you?"

"I did come all this way, didn't I?"

"He knows I called you."

"You were never any good about secrets, Lucianne."
"Oh, I don't know. I've done pretty well."

Sixty-One

"Ma, I could never stand that Civil War. War of the Roses. What-
ever it was. I just climbed out and went. I don't know."
   "You could have hurt yourself."
   "Filly made up for it now, anyway."
   "How long?"
   "How long what?"
   "How long will you stay in that bed?"
   "Doc said ten days. I've been here six. You came halfway along."
   "I was on the bus the morning after Lucianne called."
   "Right. I figured."
   "You figured right, Jimmy."
   "How's that Mar?"
   "Married."
   "Hell. Well, I knew she would be. Gerhardt?"
   "What?"
   "That Gerhardt. She was sweet on him way back."
   "That Gerhardt."
   "Any kids?"
   "Not yet. This summer."
   "I'll make some uncle."
   "Yes."
   "Wouldn't mind being an uncle."
   "Yes."
   "Some little guy comes on the bus, I could put him up. Got a
trailer now, Ma. Real decent. Out behind the stables. Ottersons.
They own the track, too. Real money in that."
   "Who's in the trailer now?"
   "Now?"
   "Yes."
   "Tilly's keeping it up for me."
   "Tilly?"
   "Yeah."
   "A girl."
   "Yeah, Ma, a girl. I'm not a kid anymore."
   "I know."
   "You ever hear from him?"

"Your father?"

"Yeah."

"Not for years. After we moved into town, he came by a few times. He saw you and Mar. You wouldn't remember anymore. And he and I talked."

"What about?"

"Oh. Money. The farm. What he was going to do."

"Did he want us back?"

"Did he what?"

"Want us back."

"I wouldn't have gone."

"I kept thinking I'd find him somewheres. He liked the horses, too."

"Yes he did."

"Maybe he's dead now."

"He might be."

"I never found him."

"I know. Come home, Jimmy."

"Ma?"

"Come home. Back to Manatee."

"What'd I do in Manatee?"

"Stay with me until your leg heals. Get a job. Help Gerhardt and Mar with the farm. Play with your nephew when he's born."

"Jesus, Ma."

"I never asked you before."

"I never gave you a return address."

"That's right."

"Ma, it's like this. Make your bed, lie in it. I figure I just got one life. The horses, they let you in on another piece of living. I like that. I want to do it my own way. People think I'm crazy, that's OK. Go if I want, come if I want. Be a free spirit."

"Even if you can't walk?"

"Hell, once I get this cast off, I'll walk. Don't have to walk to ride, anyway."

"Could you visit?"

"Maybe someday."

"Someday?"

"Someday, Ma."

Sixty-Two

Diane. Or Hilde. Or one after the other. And Gerhardt if it turned out to be a boy, of course, because the Germans always wanted it that way, no matter what someone else might want. Unless he'd let her change his mind. She had lived with him long enough to make that happen.

A stretch of time. Waiting. Plum in a jar. Beneath her skin, it rolled like the sea. Surged and struck. Rested. Surged again. Bigger and bigger.

First had been fall. Then winter, spring, summer, fall again. And over. And over. To the little farm by his parents'. His aunts, his uncles, Gretchen, Hedwig, Mathilda, Kepler, Hochmut, Lowmut. The oldest ones gone.

Something had happened to her mother. The bus. Where? And back again, not the same. When they visited every week, she was waiting at the window. But not for them. Gerhardt said she was crazy. *He* looked crazy.

Not crazy. Waiting.

Then.

Wet spring, boots clogged in the old kitchen. Manure floating in the pasture, cows bellowing on the knoll under the elms, udders swishing the water. River gone mad, eating roads, stubble, dark cake as wide as the world. Mother coming out, first the walk from town, then wading, then half swimming, like a lake fish. Smiling up at us, her coat adrift behind her. Got her inside, one at each shoulder. So heavy wet. With us through the night. Gerhardt stood at the window, face a lowlands map.

In the morning, it was going down. Sludge everywhere, cows bellowing a chorus. Mother up, wrapped in the Hudson's Bay blanket like an Indian. Made bread, loaves and loaves. Stacked everywhere. Thirty pounds of flour, gone. Fed us all.

Sixty-Three

Through the kitchen window, over the double sink scrubbed down through the white porcelain to its grey underbelly, she saw the hospital lights. Not very many of them, because of the trees along the fence and then the Ramsey house, its edge like cardboard across the sky. But a corner of light.

Susan filled both sink holes with soapy water, moved her hands from one to the other. Time. Twelve hours was time enough. But maybe not for Mar's first. Still.

She turned, turned back, let the water out. The drains gargled it down. Pipes slid it to the sea, so far away, past the potato farms, the stubble in the cornfields, the boundary states, laced by the Mississippi, the great blue finger. Minnesota, Wisconsin, Chicago burning underneath.

She knew. How things came out. Mar's body from hers, Jimmy's the same. And before. But no more. She had said no more, no more, never, gone where she couldn't be reached. They grew up, grew out. Jimmy gone through that window, postcard now and then, free spirit. Wouldn't come home, even though she'd asked. And Mar, never leaving, growing thick. Almost an old maid. Until he. Germans liked them square. Under the stairs. Orphans of the storm. Didn't count.

She'd done what was right. Made the wedding bouquet. Stood up with them, given Mar away. The minister's wife had watched from the pew while her husband did the ceremony. Rosa Bellamy. Who would have guessed their time together? Secrets could be kept, and not just by Lucianne.

And the years of nothing. Why hadn't she lost it? You were supposed to lose it, weren't you? Not to go on wanting.

Mar was having a baby. Behind the golden windows.

Susan looked down. Under her frantic rag, the glitter was wearing off the Formica of the counter. She was on her way down to the pressed board filler. Her wrist ached.

She dropped the rag into the sink, snapped her wrist into life. Her skirt was damp in front. The rest of her was dry, legs, arms, breasts, teeth like shelled kernels jammed into her gums. Sandpaper rubbed between her legs. Her ears hummed.

Standing on the front porch, she listened for the phone. Nothing. Not yet.

Should she go by the parsonage? No. Not tonight.

Susan looked up. On the farm, the night sky had been without boundaries. She remembered. Stars like white raisins. Even in this little town, there were too many lights, so the stars came through only at the very peak, crowded breathlessly against each other. Orion with his belt and knife. The Dipper, pouring black. A galaxy. She reached out her hands, her damp stomach against the porch railing, arching over the wood. Why did a body hold everything that had marked it? Why did the stars dance?

She was still asking herself the same questions as she began walking toward the lights, though she knew perfectly well she wouldn't be privy to the answers even if there were any. The street signs were no guide. Myrtle Avenue, named no doubt for some pioneer lady. Sharp Street, then McConnell and Douglas. Other Celts. Nagoponock. The Indians were everywhere. Retzlaff Lane. Elwin's grandfather, progenitor of all those Catholic hordes. She thought of Elwin whenever she spun a seed rack and with every Halloween pee. Then the little park with the white Virgin on her pedestal, pruned shrubs at her base as long as Mrs. Hempstead continued horticulture as her vision of civic pride.

In front of Susan, the hospital rose. An old remodeled building faced with rectangular slabs of fake brick not quite matching where the rectangles met. Grillwork over the door, looped with leftover Christmas lights even in this warm season. When she pushed down on the handle of the entrance door, it opened without a sound.

Inside, the carpet had darkened, its orange mottling dirtying into a grey. A sofa in crunchy plastic. Two chairs. Magazines on the table, but someone had been messing with them, and they swirled across the smudged veneer. *Life. Collier's. Reader's Digest.* All those picture people jammed in the pages, breathing paper, choking. She felt her own throat. Under her chin, as her hand edged upward, the skin was softer every year, hanging from her jaw line in bunches. She looked up. The bones came clear to her fingers as they always did. The schoolroom clock on the wall said two. The elevator. Open. Fourth floor.

She had been born at home, of course. Home? But her own had been born here. What women did. Men couldn't. The light overhead blurred through its layer of dead gnats inside the glass. Men couldn't, so they ran away. Could run away. To pay you back. Because you could.

A waiting room with chairs. Linoleum. Her legs were losing their linkages, coming apart. Down, bending where she always bent. Breath. Hands crossed in front, advancing, retreating. Daisy petals. Golden center. Snow angels. All gone. Gone.

Hospital quiet surrounded her. She cataloged occasional sounds. Down the hall, a chair scraped as someone got up, pushed back from something. *Click-click.* A door, air sucked as it swung, then held. Star voices. Tapping in the pipes. A magic tunnel. The door again. Then a high whistle. The chair. The door. The tap in the pipes. The whistle, on and on. Straight out from the lungs, no windpipe, no throat, straight through the ribs, spreading like blood. Into a scream. No words, no lips, no tongue between lips, nothing touching. All alone. All alone riding, hanging on. Hang on, Mar, she said, for the first time ever. Hang on, daughter. Hang on.

She slept. She woke, head bent back so far on the puffy upholstery that she couldn't pull her jaw closed. Dull light on the table, dull light near the end of the hall, coloring the doorway. Red caravans marched across the backs of her eyes, then fragmented.

Gerhardt came in. He was crying. Her legs crunched at the knees when she got up.

"Is she all right?"

He pushed his face into her neck.

"Answer me, you fool."

He put his hands down across the small of her back. "Yes. A girl. Eight pounds. Diane."

"Not so little." She could taste his shirt.

"No."

In the hallway, the loudspeaker blatted.

"Will you come with me?" His voice shook.

"Where?"

"Back to your house."

"Mar?"

"She's sleeping." Behind his words, the loudspeaker blatted again.

"The baby?"

"Sleeping, too. In the nursery." He stepped back. Brown work boots, laced in zigzags. Perfect. Damn German. He must have come from the fields. On the flat surface of his face, the tears had left no lines.

Susan held out her hands.

"Then will you?"

She pulled her jaw back. Under her skirt, blue with flecks of gold, she tightened. Then she nodded.

They walked into the hall discreetly. Side by side. His farm boots clattered, heavy slaps on tiles. Someone getting beaten. She could tiptoe it, she could. The nurse at the desk looked up, opened her mouth like a perch. Glub. Nothing. EXIT light, door swinging in. Out. Bare stairs. Down. Then down faster. Swinging around the corners. Both. He ahead. They'd break every bone. If they let go. If they swung loose.

They reached the bottom together. She wasn't any more out of breath than he was, and that's what you got for working yourself to death, on the farm, off the farm, cooking for boarders who sucked down smooth mashed potatoes like vacuum cleaners, wouldn't know a lump if it hung between their legs. Washing dishes, drying dishes, damp towels worse than diapers, postcards, horses, Dr. Collins's hands in all the wrong places, didn't she wish, pushing and cutting, shoving, arranging, hitting, stroking, hands hers, her own, all she had, sold the rest, auctioned it off, but every morning, noon, evening, still the air going in and out, still the breath that proved she hadn't made it up, and now she could stand up to that big German, her daughter's husband, just two bodies, through the big space out, down the steps, over the curb, and together on the summer sidewalk striping the town of Manatee with an innocent white even at this ungodly hour. Even the parsonage would be asleep. No one else. Only him.

"I didn't think it would come this soon." She put her hand through the arch of his arm.

"Mar was napping. The cat was lying on her belly. Could hardly stay balanced, Mar was so big. I was cultivating the garden, trying to stay ahead of the goddamn weeds. I kept checking on her. Finally threw that cat out the window, and it got stuck in the eaves trough, would you believe it? Had to climb to get it loose. Then I heard Mar yell. Cat's probably dead by now, I never did get it out. We went right in."

"What time?"

"When I called. Suppertime. Doctor was delivering across town, they said. We stayed in one of those little rooms until he got here."

All those little rooms. Susan dug her hands straight down into the pockets of her skirt. The left pocket ripped, seam gaping. She plugged the hole with her middle finger, wiggled it reassuringly back and forth against her hip. Above, so far above that the light filtered through her raised eyelashes, Orion strode on his knees, humbled, sword-tool swinging loose, shoulders coat-hangered against the black.

"Do you want some coffee?"

"What?"

"Coffee." They had turned the corner, starlight slicing the dark between them. But already the edges of the black globe were cutting loose from the earth, grey striping down between buildings. As the great ball rolled through space, words and phrases a preacher could have used, the light rose in its path, laid a creamy hand across the dark, lifted the shutter of the sky, brought day.

She hadn't locked the door, nor even shut it properly. One hand above the knob and it slid open. Gerhardt stood behind her, cupping her back in his space. She shut the door. "I'll start the coffee," she said.

"Wait."

"Why?" She was already filling the pot, setting it on the burner.

"Just wait." His hands, separate from the rest of him, slid under her arms and over. Breastplates. The old words from a normal school textbook. Lucianne laughing. A woman standing against the wind, spear in hand. Amazon.

She moved, then stopped. "No coffee?"

"You're crazy, woman."

"Yes." Easier to think of it that way.

"You come live with us now."

"What?"

"You come live with us. Sell this place. Help with the baby if you want. We don't care what you act like. Crawl in a ditch, hang from the rafters. It's all right, Susan, I promise you it's all right."

The coffeepot bubbled of its own accord. An old dream. The farm coffeepot, chirping. Sparrows in the kitchen. Sparrows? Her mother laughing, peeling, moving her hands. The little head, beak, feathers soft as fingertips. Shadow bird, magic from her mother's fingers. All around the air had been full of bird murmurs. Woodrow Wilson, asleep under her porch, murmuring, too.

She pulled Gerhardt's head down to hers. Orion's belt. The new life. Dark skirt of sky, edged with dawn.

Sixty-Four

"How many of these do you want?" Mar balanced the books in her arms. Squatted on the carpet, one-year-old Diane burrowed against her mother's calves.

"All of them."

"Gerhardt can build an extra set of shelves in the hall."

"Yes."

"Although we already have a whole wall of them in your room."

"That's good." Susan put her hand on Diane's hair, a thick sheet of rusty gold. The little girl laughed.

"Should we sort out the closet next?"

"Tomorrow." On the opposite wall of the living room, a branch ticked away against the outside screen. Never to change them again. The new owners had three big boys. Someone else could wrestle the ladder up against the siding. The oldest boy had freckles in a mat across his cheeks and nose. The younger two just had speckles.

"I can't help then. I'm canning."

"That's all right."

"It's heavy lifting."

"That's all right." Suddenly Mar's presence seemed the largest obstacle to the move. Diane could be boxed away like the Shakespeare, tickled under her round chin, fed gingersnaps and orange juice. She was too young to try to help.

"Should I go?"

Susan listened to the branch against the house.

"Mother, should I go? Gerhardt plans to come with the pickup after church on Sunday. After waiting so long for the house to sell, there's no point waiting longer. I could come Saturday to help you finish."

The branch staccatoed like drums.

"Mother?"

"Go on home."

"Mother, are you all right?"

Susan laid her two hands on the two tallest stacks of books. She hardly needed to stoop. The piles were so tall that they stood up like buildings.

Mar turned away, Diane in her arms. The little girl looked back at her grandmother, her face a perfect oval balanced on Mar's shoulder. She was too young to wink. Still. One hand opened next to her ear, pointed like a star.

Once the car had pulled out of the driveway, once the disappearing sound said "safe, safe," Susan turned back to the books. Over the years, she had read them all again and again. Even the encyclopedias. Well-made books aged less than any object, more tightly bound than flesh, immune to scratches, dents, lines of decay. Edges of pages yellowed with a fine honor. Bindings held. The new paperbacks crumpled as if on signal from the finger of time. These old ones lasted.

Susan rested her hands on the piles, the encyclopedias, as if she were growing from them. A box didn't hold many. They didn't become spare with age. She lifted each one in both hands, hefted it like flesh, touched the binding, placed it down.

A-ANA, ANA-ATH. ATH-BOI. FAL-FYZ. Filigree. Fir. Fire. Frankincense. G-GOT. Galilee, Gypsies. A wandering folk. Ply an endless variety of trades. Giraffe. HIR-IND. Hottentots. The generic name. Huns. Hunting.

One pile done. Hands on her back, Susan shifted her weight, tightened her muscles, let them out. She pulled the next box closer. INF-KAN. Infinity. KAO-LON. LOU-MEM. And on. ROT-SIA. Rotifera. Sacrifice. To conciliate the favor of a deity on whom the worshipper has no right to count.

Salt Lake City. Saxe-Meningen.

The heavy books solidified the boxes. When she heaved one off the floor, the bottom curved downward. She packed the remaining spaces with napkins, tablecloths, dish towels, things with no weight.

One more box. The books were out of alphabetical order. PHY-PRO. Physiology. Pilgrimages. Pilgrims were entitled to shelter, fire, and water in all convents on their road. Resting stations were erected for them on all the great lines of travel.

That was only right.

Sixty-Five

The grass was a mass of riches, tubal, tiger-eyed, a thousand slashes of every conceivable green lined against each other like generations, spearing the air, spearing the earth, rooted so firmly that every sweep of the palm bent the blades but never marked them. Yet they couldn't be properly pulled up, could only be broken off for sucking, whistling, tickling, book-marking, dragonfly wings that pirouetted, spun, fell through the June air.

Underneath, the roots started up again without anyone's even knowing. If you lay down with your nose deep in the grass, you could taste the salt near the bottom, and you didn't have to cry your own tears. If you pressed yourself close to it, you could almost join the ones who were pushing it up. The grass would hold you to it no matter how fast the globe spun under you.

Susan was reading to Diane from Walt Whitman. He knew about grass. The book didn't have any pictures, but Diane was patient and had learned how to turn each page by the lower corner, without crumpling. Her fat fingers walked to their post with a weighty two-year-old responsibility, and she knew not to suck them beforehand. When she had turned the page properly, she would look up at her grandmother, and they would smile at each other.

They could sit in the grass for hours, reading.

Sixty-Six

All the Methodist ministers from the western district of the state were at that yearly meeting in Minneapolis. So the coast was clear. Mar was asleep with the new baby; she never let him out of her sight since he'd rolled off the bed. Diane was with her Grandma Kauffmann, sleeping over. Gerhardt was at the board meeting of the cheese factory. Although they'd finish up by ten, he'd end up going with Herbert Mueller to their favorite tavern on the other side of Manatee. He did it every time. Good thing he'd taken the pickup. Susan wasn't crazy enough to try a stick shift for the first time out.

Susan opened the doors of the shed where Gerhardt kept the town car. He favored Chrysler models, but the last one had been a lemon, and he had revenged himself by driving thirty miles into Fort Simon and buying a Ford for cash. She'd heard talk about it at church, but it hadn't surprised her. Nothing surprised her about Gerhardt.

The key was in its hole. She had a flashlight. All the levels of speed were marked. If you could read, you could drive. It must be like cooking.

Outside, through the rear window, a perfect rectangle of the farm lay framed out behind her. The moon was full, heavy in the lower layer of the sky. Some might call it the Man in the Moon, but she knew better. They must be watching it down in Cuba, too, while all those Russians got ready to fire those missiles. They wouldn't reach as far as Manatee, she was sure of that. But she was prepared for any disruption. They could raise most of their own food, did already. They'd miss salt, but their blood pressures would profit. It would be best for Mar, who had put on even more weight after Diane and Luke.

The car shot backward through the open door, skimming by the elm trunk on one side and the wheelbarrow on the other, abandoned where Gerhardt had finished raking the day before. She stopped it before the bumper went through the fence. "Shit!" she said, to herself but loud enough to be heard if anyone had been listening.

But no lights came on in the house. Luke was an exhausting baby, and Mar slept hard. Already, he pulled dishes off shelves, explored bleach bottles under the sink, hitched himself across the living room to decimate his mother's sewing basket. He had just taken his first step, and she had seen it, and he had seen her seeing it. It was a secret between them. But he had decided that hitching on his bottom was quicker and less suspicious. At night, the back end of his stretch suit or overalls was a uniform grey, clotted with wisps of hair or unidentified crumbs. Diane had crawled in a normal way, starting at eight months. Luke was deviating by his own choice.

The car had edged its way down the driveway, lights sweeping into the bare branches of the October trees. At the entrance to the country road, she found her hand reaching for the turn signal, just like Gerhardt would have done. Ridiculous! Who would see? She wrenched the wheel to the right, then back to the left as the car plunged around the corner and straight for the ditch. Amazing how quick her reflexes still were.

Nobody was on the road, of course. After the first mile, driving began to seem like something she had done for a long time, like baking or mending. Through the windshield, the moon rested in a basket of grey clouds. The rest of the sky was pure and bare, with all the stars in place. On the horizon, tiny Manatee sent a small band of light from the Mobil station, the streetlights in the center of town. All the house lights would be off. The firemen would be napping on their cots, as snug as children.

Experimentally, Susan practiced braking. The car responded. Past the last country crossroads, she jammed the brake to the floor. The steering wheel banged into her belly, but she hung on. The car screamed, locked its wheels, shuddered to the right, held the road, stalled. It stopped more quickly than she would have thought. Power under control. That was it. She turned the key in the ignition and started up again.

By the time Susan steered the car down the main street of Manatee, she had no doubt about her capacity to drive. It was simply a matter of push and let go. The hood of the car, extending like a plateau out in front of the windshield, cleared the way for her, and when she reached her destination and pulled near the curb, she had already become familiar enough with the breadth of the machine to bring it to rest neatly. The moonlight helped, no doubt, striping the sidewalk white, the boulevard black, and the curb white again. Simple. But if Mar saw her, her eyes would get that my-mother-is-crazy look, and her lips would snap shut on the first thing that came to them.

But Susan felt no guilt. It had all washed away in the moonlight. She had paid for her privileges. The ledger balanced.

Although the gate to the parsonage appeared to be closed, Susan guessed that it wasn't. Her fingers nudged the metal, which pushed away from the upright pole without having to be unhooked. She opened it, walked through. The crabapple tree was a witching stick, bare in the October light, its black branches bristly as an upended broom. She moved through the grass, some of it still green, and around to the back of the house where the little addition which was the sewing room stuck out into the yard. She tapped on the window with her forefinger, three times. It wasn't that late. Three times more.

The window opened. Rosa's arms came out, warm and white under the puffed sleeves of her nightgown. Her face was a light oval behind the upper glass, though even through that transparent skin between them, her smile glowed.

"Susan!"

"Let me in."

"It's so late!"

"But you were waiting."

"The moon was so bright I couldn't sleep."

"Ridiculous. You're missing that husband of yours."

"How can you say a thing like that? You know I pray that the yearly ministers' meeting will last twice as long as it does."

"I'm going to the front door. Like an invited guest. Let me in."

The front door was open when Susan got there, and Rosa stood in the hall with her arms outstretched. They embraced. Every item was familiar to Susan as she walked with her friend to the kitchen. The pot was already boiling.

"So you must have expected me."

"Nonsense. The electric stove is unbelievably quick."

"And did the cups fly down from the cupboard?"

"I confess to having set them out. But it was a matter of seeing how they looked against the green placemats."

"Would your husband have approved?"

"You know he never drinks tea. Or coffee either. A pure man who doesn't believe in stimulants of any sort."

The two women looked at each other, and both burst into laughter at the same time. Rosa set the tea to steep under a tea cozy shaped like a fat rooster.

"What time is it?"

"Eleven. Not so late."

"I have another hour."

"Enough. How did you get here?"

"I drove."

Rosa stood up, her hands on her hips. The creases at the corners of her eyes tightened. "I didn't know you had a license," she said.

"For some things I have a license."

"I've missed you since you moved out with Mar. But I knew you were safe. We've been so many things to each other in the past years that I felt as if I had only to look inside myself and I'd find you anyway. So I could wait."

Susan removed the rooster, her eyes focusing on the stitching around the comb. She looked over at Rosa. "Very nice sewing," she said.

They both howled with laughter.

"I often wondered why you chose my husband to come to for consolation that day."

Slowly, Susan poured her tea. "I was walking past," she said. "I'd visited Frankie's grave. Jimmy hadn't sent a postcard for almost a year. Your Decoration Day peony was just coming up, like the one I'd planted before in the cemetery. I'd remembered that ministers were supposed to talk to people. It made perfect sense at the time."

"Until you heard him give his prerecorded consolation speech."

"Listening to him go on and on made me realize more than ever how much we have to solve our own problems in this world."

Rosa paused, her lips just above the rim of her cup. "What did he say to make you scream?"

Susan dipped a finger into the tea and caught two leaves on it. "Two means a double life," she said, dotting them onto her wrist. "Actually, it was when he said 'God He.' The good Reverend Bellamy, your husband, kept ending one sentence with 'God' and then starting the next one with 'He.' I don't picture God as a man, myself. 'God He' began to sound pretty silly. *Godhe, godhe, godhe.* Like a new species of birdcall. After all that, I couldn't just say good-bye. I had to scream my way out."

"But you'd been crying."

"I've had enough to cry about."

"People in town think you're odd."

"No doubt they're right."

"Doesn't anyone know what good friends we are?"

"I very much doubt it. I've always slipped in."

"How is it living with Mar and Gerhardt?"

Susan picked up her teacup and replaced it on the saucer.

"Easier if I don't talk," she said. "Easier if I'm acting crazy. Eccentric. That way I can preserve my freedom. No one can come too close." She ran her finger around the rim of the teacup. "I like Diane," she said quietly. "I'll like Luke once Mar lets him out of her sight. He and I seem to have something in common, though I don't know exactly what."

"Did you *really* go to bed with Gerhardt?"

"There was no bed involved, at least not the first time. But yes, I did."

For a moment, the edge of a smile teased around Rosa's mouth. She crooked her little finger out from the handle of her teacup like a French lady might have done. "Do you miss it?" she asked.

Susan put the rooster back over the teapot with a gesture so firm that no fowl could have escaped under any circumstances. "It didn't matter all that much, Rosa," she said. "At the time, it was like a wind blew through me. Halloween night all over again. It was the same the night Diane was born. He still thinks he can get it sometimes, of course, but I've turned it off. And he's afraid of me. Old Amazon woman, I am."

"You know the conference Martin's at."

"Yes. I read about it in the bulletin. That's how I chose my night to visit."

"This may be the time they transfer us. They've put it off for so long. That's not like the Methodists."

"When would you go?"

"In the spring, probably. But they may decide to let us die here."

"I'd rather you went than have you die here."

"Yes. I know that."

Sixty-Seven

When Mar first woke up, she didn't know why. Luke, a warm damp ball pressed against her spine, hadn't moved, and Gerhardt wasn't home yet. Those cheese factory meetings left everyone with a terrible thirst, and he and Herbert were the worst of the lot. Though it was almost the only time he did any serious drinking. In that sense, he kept good hold of himself. She appreciated that.

With one hand, disentangled from the covers and then carefully inserted again, she felt down inside Luke's diapers. He was sopping, and he had soaked through right across the front of his nightie. Everything he drank went right through him. But his eyes didn't even flicker as she probed, and only his damp mouth opened further against the sheet, then shut with a little snap as if her were nibbling at her. He was going to be a blond, and a curly-head, too. You couldn't tell a thing from that black bristle they were born with. Already the curls were clustered together on his head like little love knots.

Mar shifted herself onto her back and further up on the pillow. One of her breasts escaped from the elastic around the neck of her nightgown and hung over the top like a one-sided bib. She tucked it back in, where it settled companionably against its mate. Gerhardt was always at them every chance he got. But she could have guessed that from when they had been courting. She didn't mind.

Outside, the moon had centered itself in the window as formal as a pendant on a chain. The October moons were always the biggest. You could see them from everywhere in the world, except the side where it was day. Nice to remember a little geography from junior high. With the children, she sometimes felt her mind had melted into soup. Only her mother had time to read things.

Her mother. They got along all right. But she hardly ever talked. Not nasty, just silent. Sometimes Gerhardt would go after her and after her until he'd force her to say something. Only it never made him happy. What he mostly liked to do was eat her mother's baking. He could go through a whole cake by himself and not take more than an hour at it.

Luke started to suck in his sleep, but it was just a reflex. She never had to feed him until dawn. He was a good baby, though not as good as Diane had been. But boys were like that. They got into things. You just had to watch them.

She heard a car outside. It sounded near, but then further away. Probably a stranger. No one to worry about. She could go back to sleep.

Sixty-Eight

"What's that?"

"The farm where Daddy grew up."

"I know that farm. Who's that?"

"Where?"

"Right here, Mom."

"That's a tree."

"No!"

"Here, Diane, let me look. All right. I think that's Grandma Kauffmann. Just part of her. She was hanging up clothes."

"Who's that over there?"

"Daddy. When he was little."

"Next page, Mom. Who's this one?"

"Grandma Carson."

"Was she crazy then?"

"You know she's not crazy."

"I mean funny-crazy, Mom. Not like bad people. Like when she and Baby Luke ate the grass."

"They didn't eat the grass."

"You said, Mom."

"She took him outside to sleep on the blanket for his nap. They were both lying down and looking at the grass together."

"I saw them. Their heads were very far down. When was that, Mom?"

"This summer. July. It doesn't matter."

"What's that one?"

"It's the house in town where Grandma used to live."

"Grandma Kauffmann?"

"No. Grandma Carson. You've seen it, Diane."

"It's big."

"She used to rent out rooms to people."

"Did they eat her food?"

"Yes."

"I like apple crisp when it doesn't have yuck in it. Grandma Carson makes it good."

"When you're bigger, you can make it yourself."

"I'm four."

"Four and a quarter."

"Luke's almost two."

"Yes. You're twice his age."

"Am I twice bigger?"

"It doesn't work like that."

"You be bigger than Grandma Carson."

"Yes."

"Is that why she has the little room?"

"Not really. I was little once, too, Diane."

"Show me a picture."

"Over here."

"But you were already bigger than me. I want a *little* picture."

"I don't think we have any."

"Why not?"

"Maybe we didn't have a camera when I was little."

"Were you poor?"

"I can't remember."

"Was your daddy poor?"

"I don't remember."

"Did he buy you Merry Sunshine stockings that folded over two times?"

"I don't think so."

"Then he wasn't a good daddy, was he?"

Sixty-Nine

The day was not going to be long enough. There had been so much spring rain that the sky itself had been washed free of color, and although the sun was shining, yellowing its corner like a kindergarten drawing, west in the sky lay a pasty grey, backing to the cottonwoods along the far bank of the river. Even now, the air held a memory of rain, moist against their cheeks as they shoveled sand into the burlap bags, twisted them shut, pummeled them onto the little wagon that Diane was piloting. Luke trotted around all sides of it like a lunatic caboose.

"It's no use, Gerhardt." Mar held her spade upright in the mud.

"Goddamn, we can hold it. I'm not wading out to the barn this spring."

"It's not like the house would be flooded."

"*None* of my land is going to be flooded."

No use arguing. And they really wouldn't know, anyway, to be completely honest about it, until the night was over and the crest had passed. So they might as well act as if they had some power over the river water, as if acting could create that power whether they had it or not.

Diane was hauling the wagon back with Luke sitting inside. He hung onto both side rails, bracing himself against the humps that jolted his bottom into the air. The two of them could as well have been knocking together on the river current itself, riding the tree limbs that surged down even now, the shingles, the pieces of plywood from the factory over in Menger County.

"Goddamn!" The big spade handle cracked in Gerhardt's hands with a snap so loud that both Luke and Diane turned toward it.

"There's another one in the shed."

He stamped off. In the muddy ground, his footprints cut ovals, lay pure, oozed water from their bottoms, began to fill. All the earth was saturated with moisture everywhere.

Diane shoved Luke out of the wagon, making sure he landed on his feet. The tongues of his boots lolled open. He teetered in them, perfectly happy to be erect, perfectly happy to be a part of any family activity where he could think he was helping. Under his knitted cap, tight down around his ears like a sailor's, his blond curls hung loose. Every shake of his head set them bouncing. He looked with joy at the sandbags spread damply across the ground, and planted one loose boot in the middle of the nearest one. The watery sun polished his forehead.

"You take him away, Diane."

Diane looked up at her mother, obedience and fire battling each other in her eyes, then edged over to her brother. Luke was leaping on the sandbags, burying the two on which his feet were balanced deeper and deeper into the mud.

"It's getting late. He should eat."

"Grandma's making supper when she gets back." Diane raised her chin just enough to free it from the scarf around her neck.

"She's taking her own sweet time about it." Gerhardt tramped toward them, his voice plowing ahead, the replacement shovel tucked under his arm like a bayonet. He charged past his own footprints, making a parallel row. The yellow sun, diffuse and cool, balanced on his shoulder as he bent down.

"It's not her fault."

Gerhardt snorted. "I figure another foot of bank in the middle there," he said, turning. "The water won't go over that. Keep filling."

"How can you be so sure?"

"I know what that river will do."

"But we had eight feet of snow to melt this spring, besides the rain." Mar could take her own side on any subject at all. She could hold her own through her mother's entire *Britannica.*

"Jesus, Mar." Only his head and shoulders stuck out over the heaped sandbags as he wrestled them into a tighter wall. "Have mercy on me." From where Mar stood, it looked as if he were beating at the bags with his head, which, when you came right down to it, might have worked even better. She began a slow smile, felt the evening wind against her face. With both hands, she reached down to button her plaid jacket, frayed and old, good only for mud time. The bottom two buttons wouldn't close. Already.

She looked down. Diane stood facing her, not an arm's length away. She reached out her gloved hands, the knit faces on the backs stretching and grinning as her fingers extended. She pulled at her mother's jacket, too.

"It won't close, Mom."

"That's right. Not anymore."

Diane dropped her eyes, then looked up again and grinned. "Let me, Mom," she said as she took the smaller spade from her mother and bent down over the nearest open sandbag.

"Go watch your brother." Luke was heading for his father, the empty wagon banging along behind him. He was holding the handle with both hands behind his back; the wagon looked like a distorted tail sticking out beneath his jacket.

"I already did watch him."

"Why is your grandma so late?"

"She said six o'clock." Diane pulled her wrist out and looked at her watch, for which she was far too young, but for which she had campaigned with a determination even a full-blooded German had to admire.

"Isn't it time yet?" Mar straightened her back, forcing her pelvis hard against the palms of her open hands.

"My own watch says five forty-five."

"And I suppose that's right, isn't it?"

"I set it this morning."

Sometimes it was hard to believe that Diane was only finishing kindergarten. She seemed ageless. Her red hair roofed a head full of eternal wisdom. And then there were Luke's blond curls. For the next one, she'd better plan on Indian black.

"Dr. Collins doesn't usually work this late." Mar turned her head toward where Gerhardt was climbing over the sandbagged riverbank.

"The old bastard probably learned that money doesn't grow on trees." Gerhardt cast his gaze on Diane, on Luke, but they were busy upending the wagon and banging on the bottom to get the sand out of it. Mar watched him with something akin to tenderness, even in the chilly evening with the unfilled sandbags carpeting the mud and the voice of the river slapping below the reinforced bank. The two of them looked at each other, at their children. Mar rested her hands on her belly. Gerhardt tried to look at something else. For him, the whole process of pregnancy seemed as much a mystery as a July hailstorm, a January thaw. With the third one, women got big quick. Everyone knew that.

"It was silly to make her go in for a checkup, Gerhardt. Just because I went in yesterday. She isn't sick any more than I am. She's just fifty-seven years old. We're none of us children anymore."

"That woman will never be old."

"She only went because you kept after her. And when I had the x-ray yesterday, they'd had the cancellation."

"Probably gave in just to see that Collins again." Gerhardt shaded his eyes against the sun, which was losing what little light it had as it tumbled toward the rim of the earth.

"I think she saw enough of him in the old days."

Luke, as golden haired as any angel, came up and took her hand. Diane was approaching from the other side. Mar looked at the sky and realized it was dark. Just like that.

"It's dark."

"You don't have to tell me that." The four of them stood listening. Out of the dimness, the slap-slap of the river against the bank was dulled, softened by the fat sandbags blanketing its force.

"Hungry, Mom." Luke hung tight, chained to her hand.

"I am too." Diane's fingers flirted with her mother's.

"What about me?" Gerhardt banged his belly with the flat of both hands, leaned back against the night, his shovel upright in the muck beside him. Against his tight skin, the slaps reproduced the sound of the river. "I could eat any damn thing on the table."

"No sauerbraten tonight."

"Don't need sauerbraten, woman."

"Sauerkraut?"

"Krauts are always sour."

Diane reached around the front of her mother and poked Luke in the chest. He giggled fiercely, then dropped into the mud. Once down, he attached himself to his mother's ankle. Mar felt his damp mouth against her leg like a brand.

Down the country road, back a good ways but still visible, lights appeared. First they lit the sky, a halo against the top of the hill, then swung over it with two yellow eyes. Mar detached Luke, hoisted him up. He stood on her stomach, leaning out, then plastered himself to her chest.

"Maybe that's her."

"Jesus, she was supposed to call so I could pick her up."

"With you looking like a drowned cat."

"Cow." Gerhardt grinned.

"We couldn't have heard the phone, anyway."

"Weren't you going to find out your results today, too?" He knew that already. It was silly to ask.

"Yes. Dr. Collins said he'd call."

"Hell, they should have figured that picture out yesterday."

"The doctor who reads x-rays only comes in on Tuesdays."

"So they'll know today?"

"Yes."

"So we're missing all the goddamn news by being out here sandbagging."

"That's right.

Down the road, the lights dipped under an overhang from the low rise where the creek branch crossed under a bridge that the highway people had been planning to repair for almost ten years. Then they came up again, lighting the cloud layer along the horizon. Down below the house, down where the driveway branched off by the clump of ash and elder, they sliced through the dusk. They'd turned in.

Gerhardt swung around. "They've turned in."

"Dr. Collins is probably bringing her back."

"Don't suppose he learned much about sandbagging in medical school."

"I don't suppose he did, Gerhardt."

"Think he'll have your results?" He could never quit. Her exasperated look sent him rocking heavily from boot to boot. He bent down to grab Luke from Mar while the little boy screamed with glee and pulled away. He ran in circles like a puppy, Gerhardt reaching after him at every curve. Diane held her mother's hand, watched, tried to disapprove. She looked up at her mother, who smiled down. Diane mimicked her. The circles of light moved on toward the house, where they reflected off the back door. Then they went out.

"Someone brought her."

"That goddamn Collins."

"I don't know why he makes you so angry." Mar captured Luke and turned toward the house.

"Work a woman into the ground, he would."

"I never saw him handling sandbags with one."

Gerhardt coughed, then shook his head. Mar did too. Already moving, Diane was on her way to the yard where two figures stood next to the silent car. Gerhardt left his shovel standing upright by the pile of empty sandbags and started down toward the house too. Mar followed with Luke balanced against her, his sturdy shoulders tight against her right arm as it encircled him.

"I brought her home." Under the yard light, Dr. Collins's red hair became truly grey, not just the brindled red it showed in the daytime.

Susan stood next to him.

"Healthier than I am." He scratched his head. "Wish I had her back at the office with me, making my life easier. The assistant I've got now can't tell an Ellis from a Humperdinck. That's what happens when you come out from Pennsylvania. Too far to ever settle in properly."

Susan stepped away from the car. "We're all strangers," she said.

Dr. Collins moved his eyes away from her. "You folks working after dark?" he asked, his voice doubtful.

"River's supposed to break the banks before dawn." Gerhardt spoke in profile so his words slid past the front of Dr. Collins's head. "Sandbagging."

"Not much to flood up there, anyway."

Gerhardt's eyes snapped. Mar felt the shock wave. "A man has to protect his own," he said. "So it's only pasture. I'm not having the cattle stranded out on the back hill *this* year." The flood of words tangled on his tongue, and he grabbed Luke away from Mar, holding him flat in the air like a plate. Luke giggled and convulsed. Gerhardt sat him on his shoulders, muddy boots marking his windbreaker in stairsteps as Luke pulled his feet up to rest on his father's collarbone.

"Well, Mar." Dr. Collins had one hand on his car as if to make sure he could get away on his own terms.

"Yes."

"Don't you want your news?"

"What did you find?" Any bigger hospital would have had the results yesterday. He had probably held them back on purpose.

Dr. Collins leaned against his car. He had never seemed a particularly humorous man to Mar, even though life in Manatee had given him plenty to be happy about. He owned the biggest house in town, went to Chicago to see the Cubs play, sent his children to colleges in the East. Even his nasty wife was getting laugh wrinkles around her eyes in the last years, now that she could truly afford anything she might want. She drove a Mercedes, the only one in Manatee. All the repair parts had to be imported from Minneapolis, at least, or maybe that was Chicago too.

"I thought you'd be calling me to check."

"You said you'd let me know. And I was sandbagging." It was just another baby, another fat German.

"Twins," said Susan. She was holding Diane by her hand. "Clear as day on the x-ray."

"What?"

"Jesus." Gerhardt bent his head back, whanging it against Luke's. Both of them bit their lips.

Diane clapped her hands. "Mom, I can take care of them both!"

"Well, your mother got ahead of me on the telling of that piece of news." Dr. Collins opened the door of his car, his face holding a gritty smile. He drove a Cadillac, the smaller model.

"Yes, she did." Mar couldn't help smiling.

"Yes, I did," said Susan.

Seventy

It had turned incredibly cold, not surprising for February, of course, but still a change from last week's January thaw. The wood-and-oil burner in the basement of the farmhouse churned all night long trying to keep the chill out, until it took on a human personality and Luke started to refer to it as "Jeffrey." "Jeffrey is breathing hard," he'd say, head lifted from his picture book or from the Tinkertoy pieces that he'd gotten for Christmas, of which he had an accounting for every piece, "Jeffrey needs to be fed," and "If Jeffrey gets too tired, he won't be able to sleep." Finally, Diane had taken it up too, and she discussed Jeffrey with her mother when they did the dishes or set the table, until finally Mar let out a scream like a steam whistle and said, "There is no Jeffrey! That is the FURNACE!" After that, Luke and Diane kept it pretty much to themselves, though at night, deep under quilts in their upstairs bedroom, they'd go on with their story making. Susan slept on the other side of the wall, which was little more than cardboard. Their whispers were like an inside wind, and she went to sleep, when she slept, with the soft sound swirling around her.

It was the wrong time to get a dog. For one thing, the twins were too little, and at the worst possible age. They crawled and toddled and destroyed with a single-minded passion, interchangeable, indestructible. Mar had color-coded them with cord necklaces which they couldn't get off, so that she could tell Charles from Christian without stripping them down to their bare bottoms, where Charles had two small moles like spatters of ink. They were worse than puppies themselves, untrained, demanding of attention. When Susan held them both on her lap (it was impossible to hold just one, because the other one would beat at him and scream), they churned against her. They pulled her hair down and stuffed her braid into their mouths. They stamped on her stomach with their Buster Brown shoes. If she put her hands to sorting them out, they shoved their mouths against her bare skin, something like affection, but always on the edge of a bite. They were the German-looking ones with their square heads and their skimpy, blond hair. Gerhardt's genes had triumphed completely.

On the puppy day, the seven of them set out together in the new

Valiant, which had replaced the Ford when Gerhardt had worn off his resentment. Mar sat in front with the twins on her lap, immobilized in their snowsuits, their cheeks fat above the plaid neckscarves. Susan sat between Luke and Diane in back. Their breath frosted over the insides of the windows before they had even reached the crossroads. Gerhardt hit the fan, the defroster, the windshield wipers all at once.

"Herbert should have drowned that bitch before she ever got bred."

"Gerhardt, please." The puppy had not been a mutual decision.

"Last thing we need on the farm is a dog." The car skidded on an unsanded patch of ice. Gerhardt swabbed at his window with the heel of his hand, uncovering a square of white and grey. The cold outside was so fierce that even with the heater going, the inside of the glass was like a frozen slab.

"It will be good for the children." The twins looked straight ahead, mummified by their wrappings. "He'll guard the place at night."

"From what?"

"Oh, anyone who comes by. He'll bark." Mar readjusted the twins, shifting on the seat so their solid bodies left her room to breathe. "It's time, Gerhardt. We have everything else. A dog will be a real pet."

"What kind of dog is it?" Luke liked to classify.

"What color of dog is it?" Diane had licked her lips with anticipation for so long that in the February cold they were chapped an unnatural red.

"Jesus, who knows?" Gerhardt bent over the wheel, pressing it into his chest. "It has to sleep in the barn, you know. Can't come in the house. You kids have to feed it, give it water. I'm having no part of this job."

Luke and Diane looked at each other across Susan, whose eyes were pointed as straight ahead as the twins'. They had won. Too late for Christmas, but still a victory. They had promised everything. Luke had already made the bed in the hay, had set aside bones from last week's pot roast. Only the bitter cold kept the smell under control. He had known enough not to save them under his bed—his first impulse. Diane was knitting a collar with her tightest stitch. They had read the twins the Golden Book about Pokey Puppy, Diane holding down Christian, Luke wedged against Charles. Or perhaps it had been the other way around. They had made every preparation they could possibly think of.

Gerhardt turned up the driveway to Herbert Mueller's place, what they were coming to call a farmette. Awful word, not in the encyclopedia. The car charged along between the plowed drifts and entered the yard at a speed not appropriate for the terrain. Susan felt her foot jab against the floor as if she were braking. But Gerhardt wrested the machine to a stop just short of the garage, the twins bobbing toward the dashboard like Kewpie dolls and back again. "Bump!" they both said, clutching at each other. "Bump!"

"Probably all died by now anyway." Gerhardt wrenched the leather earflaps of his cap down as he stepped out into the icy air.

"No, they haven't." Diane couldn't be threatened. Holding her face straight up to the light, she climbed down onto the chunks of snow, moved around the back of the car and met Luke halfway. They joined their mittened hands and started walking toward the door, which was already opening.

"Great day for a puppy!" Herbert Mueller's belly stuck forward with such emphasis that a perfect oval of undershirt was outlined by the straining buttons. Behind him, Mrs. Mueller beamed and bounced. "Come in!" she said, jiggling up and down on her fluffy house slippers. "Come in, don't freeze! We have strudel! Apple and blueberry!"

Behind them came a bark, snappish and abrupt. It was followed by high-pitched yapping. Luke's mouth opened with joy. Gently, Diane reached out a red mitten under his chin and tipped his jaw up until his lips came together. "Your tongue will freeze off," she said.

Inside, the puppies were ensconced on a chaise lounge pad spread across the warmest end of the kitchen. Herbert Mueller had rigged plywood board around it, high enough to keep them in, but low enough so the mother, a long-haired mystery of a dog named Delicious, could leap out when she chose. With a fine sense of theater, Delicious was spreading herself among her brood, one line of tits erect as buttons. The puppies, six of them, arranged themselves.

"I like the spotted one." Diane reached down and touched the one at the far end.

"Don't really need that milk anymore," said Herbert, a flush of embarrassment on his face. "Eat me out of house and home with that Puppy Chow. Just showing off, Delicious is."

"I like the one with the ear," said Luke. The middle puppy had a brown triangle of ear laid against its mother's belly, where it rose up and down with her breathing. "I like that soft ear." He had his hands folded in front of his jacket as if he were praying.

Across the room, both twins were tearing into the strudel on the table without even having tried to take off their mittens. Mrs. Mueller's face beamed above them like the hunter's moon. She was slicing as fast as she could. "Eat! Eat!" she said. Mar attempted to interfere, but the nearest twin grabbed her leg with one arm and began to rub the blueberry strudel into her coat. She pried him loose. The second twin was climbing into the end chair, hands outstretched toward the pan. His face was covered with crumbs from one cheek to the other.

"The minister wants this one." Herbert reached down and wiggled the head of one of the puppies. "Thinks it'll make a watchdog. I said why not? Should be pretty good-sized. Look at those feet." He extended one fat paw out across his forefinger. "Don't know about watchdog, though, when I think about it. Delicious always was a pushover. Don't know that she'd have any tough puppies."

"What about the father?" Diane's bright face looked up at him.

Herbert cleared his throat, looked over at Gerhardt, who was leaning against the sink, his whole upper body inclined back toward the door as if he would have liked to topple right out and back to the car. "Don't rightly know," Herbert finally said. "Guess he had gumption enough to find the farm and do his job. Guess he must have been smart enough not to do it when I was around to take the shotgun to him. Guess that all says something. I don't know exactly what."

Luke and Diane were carefully unscrewing each puppy from its mother's tit. They passed each candidate between them, checking out bellies, paws, ears, the dampness of pink noses. Two were singled out, a short-haired brown one, and a long-haired one with a fringe of fur on his bottom. His tail, also fringed, curled up beyond his back. The two children sat on the floor, snowsuited legs spread, boot soles meeting, and placed the two puppies between them for a scientific evaluation. Behind them, the twins sat on Mar's lap, stuffing strudel into their mouths. Mrs. Mueller watched them with rapture.

"This one wouldn't need combing."

"This one would. But she's very curious." The puppy was nosing the toe of Diane's boot. "That's a good sign."

"It's a he."

"How can you tell?"

"His pisser is right up front."

"Luke!" But Luke had the long-haired puppy up under his chin. The pink nose nuzzled the line of his jaw. Luke put his hand over the furry head as if he were building a protective roof.

"I want this one."

"Is it all right with your sister? Diane?"

"I like them both." Diane was being mature. "If he wants that one, it's all right."

"What will you name it?"

From the corner of the kitchen where she'd been standing, completely bundled against the cold, not a button undone, Susan stepped forward. The chill of her wool coat moved with her. "Harry Truman," she said, holding her hands out. "And I'll take him."

Seventy-One

It had been such a hot month that Susan hadn't had to worry. He'd be warm enough. Even July had had some chilly nights, and last winter when he'd been new, she had hardly slept at all for worrying. Horses never died, no matter how cold it got. They just placed themselves against the wind and waited. But a puppy was so small.

Of course, he wasn't a puppy anymore. But not full-grown either. His legs had gotten disproportionately long, and his tail had developed a fringe so luxuriant that it looked like a creamy flag sweeping along the driveway or through the second crop of alfalfa. It hadn't taken him long to learn to escape the depredations of the twins, and he had developed a fierce growl to keep them on their own turf. With Luke and Diane, he was friendly and serviceable. Mar had taken over the role of food-giver, which he appreciated. When he felt shortchanged, he would pick up his food dish and deposit it at her feet, then sit on his haunches and beg. He followed Gerhardt to and from the fields, but at arm's length. None of these relationships overlapped, and when a new person passed by him, someone watching him closely could see his new role slip into place behind the yellow-brown liquid wall of his eyes.

What Susan did was this. During the day, she didn't pay him all that much attention. The others took care of that. But at night when everyone was sleeping, she got up and went quietly out to the barn. Usually he heard her coming, but he never barked. Instead he would come out the hayloft door through the missing board, his creamy fur speckled with bits of straw, and stand next to her waiting for her signal. It was like he knew what she wanted before she even said it. He'd sit up, or roll over, or fetch, but what he most liked to do was sit next to her in the trampled grass where the hay loader was parked and look straight ahead with her into the dark. His tail lay along the ground like a pure, narrow rug, and unlike most dogs, he enjoyed having her pet it, enjoyed having the snarls worked out. He kept it remarkably clean for a farm dog.

When she knew it was time for them both to go back to sleep, she always said the same thing. "Good night, Harry Truman," she'd say. "Sleep tight. Don't let the bedbugs bite." Then he'd roll onto his

back, feet curled above him, and fix her in his eye. The little "woof"
he made was hardly audible, but he always made it. Then he'd
scramble to his feet and slip back into the hayloft. Susan would
watch the tip of creamy tail disappear like a light being turned off,
then she'd move quickly back through the dampening grass,
through the door, up the stairs, past Luke and Diane's room from
which their deep breathing whispered like the earth itself, and back
to her own bed. Out the window it seemed the moon was always
shining, tucked safely into the black of the sky. Even when she
woke up the next morning, after dreams she couldn't remember,
she knew that Harry Truman had woken up safe too.

Seventy-Two

They filled a whole pew in the Methodist church. But that was because the twins wouldn't stay in the nursery. When they had been willing to, then there had been more room in the pew, and the three purses could sit fat in a row on the seat, hers pink plastic with DIANE written down the middle. The clasp was worn grey from all the times she'd opened it and closed it. If Jesus hadn't been born like the cows, in blood and slime, then maybe Mary would have found him in her purse. But not plastic. They didn't have it then. Something like Grandma's carpetbag. A pure baby, silver as a napkin holder. A savior.

Reverend Manchester was talking. He was the new one. The old one had been Reverend Bellamy. It was the Mercy of the Multitudes that Reverend Manchester was saying. She could recite it just as good herself.

Luke was picking his nose. No, just rubbing. She knew the danger line, and so did he. Her mother handed him a Sunday handkerchief with violets in lumpy embroidery all around the edge.

Cleft for me. Let me hide myself in thee. The water and the blood. Through thy riverside.

Luke handed the handkerchief back.

If she looked just right, she could see her father's watch. Her father was looking at it, too. His wrists always stuck out no matter how much her mother yanked down his suit sleeves.

Diane checked the flowers by the altar. From Mrs. Hempstead's garden. She was the only one with any left, and that was because she hung them with blankets every night of the early freezes, then watched out her upstairs window to make sure. Harry Truman had dug up all their own asters in August. He never learned.

Now her father's hands were behind his back, both of them. She couldn't see how much his wrists showed.

Take my life and make me pure. In the garden.

Her mother had a twin on each side. She was reading the responsive reading, holding the book out against the back of the pew in front of her. Her lips moved, but her words floated in a river of words from everyone. The twins were blubbing like frogs with their mouths. They couldn't read yet, of course. They were so dumb, they'd never be able to.

With the cross of Jesus. Going on before. Conceived in the Hold of the Spear, born of the Virgiemare, crucified dead and berry. God Almighty. God's Nightie.

The fat farmers, strong as bookends, straddled the aisle and sent the offering plates down one way. Her father wouldn't touch theirs, so her mother reached over him to take it from the Aschenbremers. She had an envelope with lilies on it.

When the plate got to her, Diane opened her own purse, balanced on one knee while the plate rested on the other. Her quarter was down in the corner, hiding like a mother cat. She dredged it out, dropped it in. Shouldn't clink. Like the communion wafer. Just let it soak in your spit. If you put your teeth together, Jesus felt it. In the sky, red polka dots would spring on the white folds. Twitching with pain, He'd yell "Ow!" Rain would fall.

The plate went around to the row behind them. Diane's hand was still hidden in her purse. She scrabbled with her fingernails against the lining on one side, catching her breath against the thrill. When she got big, she'd buy silk panties. In New York.

Then she felt the other side of the purse where the postcards were. There must be forty or fifty now. Her grandma had handed them over one by one when they picked blackberries or shelled peas or baked. Two of them had been hidden under her plate. Sometimes her grandma just gave them like a normal person. The old ones had brownish pictures, or colored ones that faded. The pillowcase was no good for hiding them because her mother washed it. The purse was private. It was a good place.

But Uncle Jimmy sure couldn't spell.

And her Grandma Carson, sitting next to her, ramrod straight, eyes shut, not getting up even now when they were singing the last hymn so loud that God would have to listen whether he had better things to do or not, didn't care one bit.

Seventy-Three

There's a land that is fairer than day,
And by faith we can see it afar,
For the Father waits over the way,
To prepare us a dwelling place there.

"Why you sing that song, Grandma?"
"Shhh. Because I like it. Lie down. The two of you."

In the sweet
Bye and Bye
We shall meet on that beautiful shore.
In the sweet
Bye and Bye
We shall meet on that beautiful shore.

"But there's no shore here, Grandma. No shore!"
"I know that."
"Then why you sing that song, Grandma?"
"Go to sleep."

Seventy-Four

"I'll never buy another Jersey cross, goddammit. Head like a deer, butt like a weasel. We'll lose this calf for sure. And her too."

"The vet's on the way." Mar knelt in the straw next to her husband. Overhead, the loose bulb dimly outlined the barn ceiling. Harry Truman had come down from the hayloft and was poised behind them, eyes alert, mouth open. He had developed a taste for afterbirths in previous calvings, and although he had been lambasted for it, it didn't seem to have made any difference.

"Luke could be helping me."

"Gerhardt, he's nine years old. He has school tomorrow. The bus comes at seven. Let him sleep."

"I never got to sleep when a calving went bad."

"Maybe the world has progressed since then."

"Hell of a progress."

It had been a warm spring day, unseasonably warm except that all the seasonal rules turned themselves inside out in April. All the snow was gone. The river had been satisfied with a modest rise, dabbling at the bottom half of the old sandbagged reinforcement.

Mar shifted her knees, put her right hand against the warm pelvis of the Jersey cross. They'd only had her since Thanksgiving. As the calf inside her had grown, her smooth brown flanks had blown outward like balloons. Up front, her gentle head peered back at her own bulk with a look of mild surprise. Even now, straining to birth, she regarded her hindquarters with puzzlement. When her muscles relaxed, she nuzzled the hay in the trough.

"Christ, if I lose another one, that's it for the year. The tax man can walk away with this place."

"It's not as bad as all that."

"Four kids, and the cows are dropping like flies."

Mar rose to press her hand tight against the brown flank, then her whole arm. She wished her weight against the calf inside. Under the Jersey's tail, the pink circle gaped. Before it sucked tight again, pointed hooves slid out into the cool air of the barn. Then they disappeared.

"Goddammit. If I use the pulley, I'll have her insides out on the floor."

"Wait for the vet."

"He's probably lost in a ditch somewhere. College never did much for that boy." Gerhardt rolled up his sleeve, anchored himself behind the cow. When she finished straining the next time, he spiraled his hand inside her, his mouth thin. The Jersey bellowed, banging her head against the sides of the stanchion. Gerhardt burrowed, retrieved his hand. The cow bent her head to the hay.

Mar looked at him. "Diane won the prize for the whole junior high," she said.

"Prize for what?"

"Recipes. She put them in a book and drew pictures for each one. The county agent judged. They get ten dollars for a prize."

"Won't buy another cow." But he grinned.

"Mother helped her with it."

"Glad she can do something right, your mother."

"Gerhardt."

"First thing wrong with this cow is the name that woman gave it."

"You didn't have to enter it in the book."

"Shit. I come out to get the book down that same week, and she's already got it in. Bad luck to name a cow after a real woman. Mary Queen of Scots. Jesus."

"She looked royal when we bought her."

"She looked like somebody's idea of trouble."

The cow, true to both sides of her nature, rolled a rich brown eye and rattled the stanchion again. The tiny white horns clanged. Her rear end lifted, jutted outward. The black hooves tasted the air. Alert, Harry Truman lifted his ears. Damp rose on his tongue.

Mar rubbed the Jersey's flank. "We used to know some people. Two ladies. They named one of their animals that, it seems to me. A long time ago."

"Sounds like a goddamn canary." The Jersey bellowed.

"It wasn't a canary."

"Your mother hardly talks to me no more."

"She talks to the children."

"She acts like I got no right in my own house."

"She doesn't talk to me all that much either, Gerhardt. She's set us aside."

"You think she's losing her mind?"

"I don't know."

"I suppose next she'll be . . ." He dug inside the cow.

"Whatever."

Gerhardt clung to the slippery hooves, balancing his weight against the little cow's body. A black nose touched the air between the hooves. Gerhardt grappled for the chin beneath it with his left hand. He lost it. The cow groaned.

"I could never make that woman happy."

"Maybe you weren't meant to, Gerhardt. Did you ever think of that?"

Seventy-Five

If it should rain a lot, then they couldn't go. If it should rain just a little, they'd go anyway and spend the picnic in the log shelter. Everybody would want to eat right away so they could get home and get dry, and even the firewood in the WPA fireplace would be damp. When the Reverend Manchester fanned it with his straw hat, the smoke would choke a horse.

A lot of rain had been the story last year, when it had surprised them by coming down like Noah, great silver streams pouring down off the edges of the shelter roof and splashing on the cement floor. All the Sunday school classes, teachers too, had clustered around the picnic table with the Kauffmanns in the middle of the circle. Diane had played checkers with Luke, and how had he known to bring the set along? First she had won, and then he had, thinking about his moves so hard that there had been sweat drops all along the sides of his face where the blond curls started. Mom had shivered, the skin on her upper arms wobbling. Grandma had gone off for a walk in the middle of it. Their father had left early, stamping through the muck to the pickup. "You can go home with the preacher," he'd said. "I have enough of this God-given misery already." The two big ruts from his rear tires had been almost filled with rainwater by the time they had gotten a ride back to the farm.

This year was probably going to be different. Now the sun was out. Diane stirred the German potato salad again, trying to arrange the crumbled bits of bacon so they came out even across the steamy vinegar sauce. Underneath, the potato slices pressed against each other. This was their potluck dish, and she had made it herself. Last winter Grandma had shown her how to, doing it with Diane planted next to her on the stool, then letting Diane do it herself while she kept an eye on things. After that, she had sat across the room cutting up string for the pot holder loom while Diane did it all on her own. They had given the extra away to a neighbor, there had been so much that time.

"Give me a bite." Luke clattered across the floor with his yard boots on, mouth wide.

"Take off your boots."

"I deserve." He opened his mouth further, pink-ribbed lining as festive as Christmas.

"Nope."

"Yup."

"Nope."

"The twins can cook better than you can." It was the ultimate insult.

"No they can't." Diane lowered her eyes with a snap. She could cook better than anyone except Grandma.

The argument had ended. Luke settled himself on the floor by the doorway and began to wrench his boots loose. "I'll wear my new ones," he said, as if she hadn't known. His socks had matching holes along the insteps for no good reason. Diane had to laugh, then cover her mouth with both hands.

"Don't laugh at me."

"Will if I want to." He was already shoving his feet into the new boots. She softened. "Bring me the dish, Luke, the one with the glass cover. When you're done. We can get this ready now and then find the twins."

He obeyed. "Mom has them in the pickup already," he said as he moved next to her. The Corning Ware dish had blue flowers on it, printed by some machine that had made them all exactly the same.

"Dad?"

Diane spooned the last of the steaming vinegar sauce into the dish, then stirred it around to fill as near the edges as possible. She hated the possibility of not having enough. When she had grown up thin as a model, not like her mother, she'd have her own home in the East, built next to a bridge over any river of her choice, dishes full all along the kitchen counters, a spoon in each.

"What about Dad?"

"He's in town with the Valiant."

"Won't he come?"

"Luke, you know what he thinks about Sunday school and all that."

"He came last year."

"And went home in a snit right in the middle of the rain."

"Maybe he'll come later today."

"I hope you have a prayer for it." Diane wrapped the dish in a checked dish towel, tying it across the top, then wrapped it the other way with a second towel and made another knot. The dish swung in her hand as she hoisted it.

Outside, the midwestern sun had heaved itself high enough in the sky to escape the clouds that clustered around the horizon, a low bank layered above the green that supported it. Harry Truman came running as the door slammed behind them. They walked down the porch's tippy boards, down the blacktop pathway which was their newest compromise between cement and dirt, down to the packed ridges of the driveway, up to the rear of the truck. Its tailgate was down. The rusted metal bottom of the box was ridged with patching welds and cluttered with all the farm junk that never got put away, including a pack of worn boat cushions heaped up against the back of the cab. Diane had been at that auction with her father and watched him bid on them. "Why in hell did I want those things?" he'd asked when he shoved the money at the cashier. "Why in hell?"

Their mother was wedged into the driver's seat, the twins packed next to her. "In the back," she said through her half-open window. "That miserable dog tried to bite Christian. We're going to have to tie him up."

"But we're going to bounce in back, Mom. The potato salad will spill!"

"Hold it tight. If you sat up here, these two would have it all over everything."

"I'll hold it while you get in." Luke squatted on the tailgate, arms stretched out for the potato salad. Diane put the dish into his hands and climbed up, stepping daintily except for the first heave. They kicked the cushions into place against the back of the cab and sat down. Luke hung on to the salad. As the truck pulled out of the driveway, cutting over the humped-up turf at the turn, they looked at each other. They were thinking the same thing.

"Will Grandma come?"

"She always comes."

"I know. But will she come with us?"

"If she wants to. She'll be by the crossroads."

"Why doesn't she come with us from our house?"

"Because she likes to walk."

"But she lives with us."

The dust rose behind the pickup. "She doesn't like to be tied down," Diane said.

Luke giggled.

"What's funny?"

"I tied her down."

"Hold that bowl straight." Diane reached out her hand.

"I tied her down when we played in the woods. In the sugar bush. In March."

"She probably tied *you* down."

"Nope. She gave me the rope. We were boiling the sap. Dad had gone back to feed the stock. She'd been helping him with the buckets before I came. She took the rope from the shed and told me to tie her up."

"Grandma did?"

"Yup. I tied her to one of the maples. She wanted me to do it tight." The wind lifted his curls.

"How did she get loose?"

"I came back and untied her."

Diane moved to the sideboard and leaned over to look ahead. The wind pulled the shorter hairs out of her braids and stuck them across her mouth. Up the road was the place. She saw the stump, or not the stump actually, but the red dress, a dot at this distance. No one but her would know it was a dress. No one but her would know who was inside it. And Luke.

"Grandma likes picnics," Luke said. He had the potato salad between his legs.

"She's ready for this one."

"Can you see her?"

"Yes I can."

"I'll bet Mom can too. Mom wouldn't leave her behind."

"That would be hard to do when she's just about sitting in the road."

"On the stump."

"That's the same." The truck was slowing down, but not with the sudden jerk of brakes grabbing. Their mother was lifting her foot up from the gas pedal as she got nearer.

"She's slowing down."

"She sure is."

"Hang on, Luke." Their grandma sat on the stump as proud as Queen Victoria. She had her hair tied on top of her head like an Indian wigwam.

The truck stopped with a jerk after all, and both the twins hit the back of the front seat. They roared in unison. Diane looked down over the edge of the truck box at the cookie jar between her grandma's knees, half on the stump, half off. It was the panda one, black and white. Anything could be inside, but chocolate chips were the best. Her grandma called them Toll-House cookies.

"Ready?"

Muffled by the truck cab, even with the side window open to ventilate the twins, their mother's voice sounded raspy. "Get in,

Mother."

Grandma still sat there.

"Get in."

Along the road flirted a little gust of wind, something extra on top of the steady drone blowing from the east that had brought the day in. Diane could see the tiny whirlwind coming toward them, gathering dust and flower lint, seeds and bits of the land. It spun along, then veered to one side just short of her grandmother, plundering through the field. The tops of the grass bent as it passed.

Under her and Luke, the truck jiggled. Inside the cab, her mother's voice was going up and down, and the twins were beating on the windshield when they weren't thumping at each other, their bullet heads like two puffballs where she could see them through the glass. The truck box shook again, and Luke, who had put the potato salad down in the corner wedged against the boat cushions, slid one leg over the edge, then the other, and dropped to the roadway. One twin beat on the window, the part that was closed, then rolled it all the way down and stuck both arms out. Luke's curly blond head, his part browned like a crayon line, slid across her vision, then dipped as he moved. Diane heaved herself up to watch. He squatted down next to Grandma, facing front, then rose and whispered something in her ear. They clasped hands. Luke took the cookie jar against his hip, then pulled Grandma up, his muscles braced.

Inside the truck cab, their mother was swatting the twins. They wanted cookies, but Grandma never let them have any, not when they yelled.

"It's a nice day, Grandma."

"Persephone," Grandma said. "No. Too late for her."

Both of them were climbing over the tailgate. Luke's advancing leg had jeans on, Grandma's was brown like doughnuts, covered with lisle stocking. The big lump under her knee was from having babies. When she had her stocking off, it was blue as a robin's egg, and twisted. Blue snakes.

The three of them sat in a row. Luke handed Grandma the cookie jar, and she took off the top of the panda's head. In each hand she put a cookie. The three of them lined up against the boat cushions as the truck jolted down the road, protesting as their mother went through first, second, third, too fast for the motor to keep up. They swung back against the cab, then forward, facing out to the curving fields, new hay tender as God's nightie, a farm driveway, red flag up on the mailbox because whoever lived there, and

Diane thought it was a Kepler or a Hebelmeister, was sending out something, saying, "I'm here, I'm alive, and I'm going to touch you whether you like it or not. We're all family here on this earth."

Seventy-Six

"Jesus Christ, man, you won't get away with that in this town!"

As if he hadn't heard a word, Gerhardt shook out the last drops, giving the tip a little flick at the end to make sure nothing was hanging on. Then he tucked it back inside his overalls and snapped the opening together with a satisfying meeting of metal. They might not like it, all right, but nobody was going to do more than talk, not in Manatee.

"Well, I did."

"Crazy German." Herbert gestured toward the wall, brown outdoor paneling now zigzagged with darker brown. "Preacher'll get you for that."

They should hire that Herbert Mueller to pass the plate and pee in it, too, Gerhardt thought, as he edged himself around, then strode toward where the Valiant was parked against the curb. "Shit," he said, reaching for the door. Let the preacher hear.

Herbert caught up with him. "Want a drink?" he asked.

"Bar's not open yet."

"Just as of now it should be." Herbert kept an old railroader's watch in his pocket, and he began to tug it out. Gerhardt watched with half an eye as the struggling fingers worked down into the pocket stretched tight against Herbert's watermelon belly.

"Jesus Christ, man, let it go. By the time you get it out, anybody'd be dead of thirst."

"Here it comes." The watch popped loose. Herbert held it to the sun.

"Christ, how much do you weigh?" Gerhardt wiped his mouth with his hand. "Can't you buy some pants that fit?"

"How many times will I be pulling out that watch with you giving me trouble about it?" Herbert laughed, then saw Gerhardt's glare. "All right, so you don't want a beer. Go do whatever you got to do for yourself. By the time you're fifty, you'll have a belly, too."

Gerhardt turned around, this time for real, and grabbed the Valiant's door handle. Even with the dust on it from the drive into town, the old car looked decent, stating that Gerhardt Kauffmann was doing all right, crops in the clear, machinery running, nobody in the family sick, unless you counted sick-in-the-head, kids to carry on the name. Standing upright, he scratched his crotch, a good hard satisfying dig, and then slid into the car, pulling out the key from his overalls and sticking it into the ignition all in one motion. He scratched again, gunned the motor, held it in neutral, relished the car struggling to race ahead. He spurted it loose in front of the Superette with its little herd of carts fenced in by the door. Nobody with any sense bought anything except groceries in Manatee. All the good stuff was for sale somewhere else.

Once Gerhardt got outside of town, though, past the bare brick school on its blacktop platter, he slowed down. Before he reached the crossroads by the church, he'd have to decide, or else just sit there like a fool, motor running, and think it over. Better think it over now. If he didn't go, then Mar would be sour, and the kids would look up at him when they thought he wasn't watching, catching his eyes and dropping theirs. God, he hated that! And if he did go, then there'd be all the people, not to speak of those goddamned hot dogs, black on one side and split open, as well as the heat, and the creak of the playground swings going back and forth. Someone was always swinging at the Sunday school picnic. There must be some kind of special reward in heaven for saying grace with the mosquitoes sucking at you and the horseflies marching around the salad bowl rim. Then there was Jesus, hovering over the split-log roof like a partridge. And Luke's teacher, city sharp. And all the rest of them.

Shit.

Coming from the east, a growing wind stirred the hot air in the car. Gerhardt leaned over to open the passenger window, let it pass through, dry him off, but the seat was too wide for him to reach. Braking hard, steering so the car held to the ruts in the gravel, he stopped, slid over to the other side, reached out to crank the glass down. The window handle jammed halfway, then came loose in his hand.

"Goddamn!"

Through the rearview mirror, he saw a spurt of June dust behind him. Never had he felt less like waving a friendly country greeting when a car passed. Maybe he could wrench the Valiant through the ditch and into the field, huddle under the spring wheat. Pity it wasn't August corn, peckered out. But with his luck, he'd never get the car free again, and how to explain that?

It was the Hochhalter Plymouth. And picnic bound, no doubt. Gerhardt propped his left elbow on the shelf of the door so they'd see his hand when they went by. Let them think it was a neighborly wave. But even as he plotted inside himself, the Plymouth slowed, disappearing into and then emerging from its ball of cloudy dust. It stopped directly behind him.

Jesus Christ!

The dust subsided. Gerhardt put his head on the steering wheel, then lifted it. Even a drink wouldn't have helped, he thought, as Robert Hochhalter thrust himself out into the roadway and came toward the Valiant.

"I figured somebody would be on this road, but I didn't figure I'd find him stopped." Robert leaned against Gerhardt's open window, his mouth barely moving but his Adam's apple making up for it. He was so bald that not even sideburns stuck out below his Cenex cap. "You all right?"

"Yes."

Robert scratched his neck, then his cheek where stubble caught at the corner of his mouth. He dug at it with a serious finger.

Behind the Valiant, in Robert's car, a grey shadow flexed across the windshield. Gerhardt caught it in the mirror, flicking his eye there and back. A kid? His wife? Who knew?

"Driving somewhere?" Robert scratched under his chin, his head tilted back.

"To the picnic." Gerhardt's skin stretched so tight across his forehead that he felt his skull scrunch together.

"Figured." In the great plain of silence, the early grasshoppers clattered in the grass by the edge of the road. Even the still country air had a hum built into it. "Could you drop her?"

"What?" In Gerhardt's mind, a great swatch of blue swept clear with a tiny figure cutting down it, tumbling in spirals, skirt up, slip up, legs apart. Shit. "What?" he said again.

"Drop Missy off at the picnic. The wife has got a doctor's appointment in town, wants me along." His meaty face colored, then faded. "Hate to lose the time. Doctors are always late, for sure."

"She in the car?" The grey shadow.

"Missy. Her and the chocolate cake." One hand massaged his mouth and chin, leaving bands of white on the brown. The grasshoppers rustled.

"Well." Gerhardt's mind was so blank that he couldn't even remember what Missy looked like. Smaller than Diane? Bigger than Luke? "All right," he said as he reached over to clear off the other seat even though there was nothing on it. "Anytime." But Robert had left, was walking back along the gravel, was opening the door of his own car. A few words. Preceded by an aluminum pan covered

with a crinkled sheet of tinfoil, Missy slid out in front of her father.
Her hair was pulled up into a ponytail. Was that the right word?
Her T-shirt, shadows on each side under the little ovals, said "Grain
Is Great." Instead of blue jeans, she had on a pair of shorts too tight
for decency. The cake pan was so broad that she needed both hands
to keep it stable, and she stood outside Gerhardt's car itching with
restless helplessness. The window cut her off at the lips, over which
her tongue was working. A brown arm. Her father opened the door
for her.

"Want me to pick you up afterward?"

"*Daddy.*" A princess's scorn. "I'll get a ride with Mrs. Kimm. She
goes right by."

"Well." The cake straddled her knees. "All right." A grasshopper
chorus. "Thanks, Gerhardt." Another pause, the grasshoppers saw-
ing ferociously. "See you." Robert seemed unable to stop touching
the car door, fingertips against it even as his arm straightened and
braced him away. "All right," he said again. He took off the cap and
checked its innards, his bald head gleaming. Gerhardt checked the
back of his own head, edged his fingers up to the top. Safe, for a
while.

They drove off. Six miles, he figured, more or less. He wasn't
committed; he could drop her off at the park entrance, cake in her
hands, and then go on. Or drop her off at the shelter and pull away.
Or he could stay if the weather held this year, and if the old lady
would maybe talk to him, and Mar didn't talk to him too much.
Gerhardt squinted through the haze around the edge of the world
ahead of him.

"Penny for your thoughts?"

"Penny for what?"

"I'm sorry." Missy's profile looking out the window was all
angles, like a piece of machinery.

"I didn't hear what you said."

"Penny for your thoughts."

"Not thinking much, I guess." The third mile came up on the
dial.

"Daddy shouldn't have asked you. He just doesn't much like the
Sunday school picnic. He'd *rather* sit around some doctor's office."
She was caressing the edges of the tinfoil with her thumbs.

"Well, shit, I don't think much of it, either." Gerhardt turned to
see if the "shit" had shocked her, but she was smiling full into his
face, each tooth neatly separated from the next one by a tiny vertical space. When she saw him looking, she pulled up one hand and

covered her mouth, then turned away.

"Sorry." He felt like a teenager.

"That's all right. Just not the Lord's name."

"What?"

"I don't mind *some* swearing. Luke and Diane say 'shit,' you know. I do too." With her shoulders back, her little breasts stuck out. Gerhardt pulled his eyes away.

"You and Diane in the same grade?"

"I'll be a sophomore. She's behind me one." Missy stopped and rubbed her nose, balancing the cake on her knees. She looked older than Diane somehow, but wasn't that as it should be?

"All right." They rode without talking through the next piece of countryside. Every time the car hit a loose rock in the road, Gerhardt jolted back. The Valiant shook, chugged on.

Missy cleared her throat. "Do you like chocolate cake?" she asked. She was lifting a corner of the tinfoil between her thumb and forefinger.

"What?"

"Do you like chocolate cake?" She inserted one finger and enlarged the little triangle of opening. "I baked it just before Dad and I started out."

"Well." He wanted to ask her about the frosting but felt embarrassed. A kid's question. But it mattered, all that sweetness mattered, layered along the top of your mouth where you could spread it out. He looked out the window, looked at the same farmland he'd seen since he was a boy. That didn't change either.

". . . make it with melted chocolate, not cocoa," she was saying. "It was almost too warm to spread." Her little voice nuzzled into the afternoon.

Gerhardt looked at her, marveling. The car swerved toward the ditch, and by the time he faced out over the hood again, leaving the chocolate, the tinfoil, the warmth of the wire whisk he could still see the old lady using, both his right tires were off the edge of the road. "Goddamn," he said hopelessly, struggling for control of the car, tightening the muscles in his shoulders so he could hold his arms firm against the bucking steering wheel. The car slid into the ditch. He heard Missy grunt, make some little noise of surprise or of acceptance. The tinfoil crinkled. He ground the brakes into the floorboards and, riding the last buck, manhandled the car into silence. They were stuck.

"Shit!" Gerhardt started the motor, forced the car forward. It swayed and pushed against itself, roared and swayed again. Stalled.

Again. Once more. He didn't dare look at Missy. Dust rose from behind. The car stalled again. He ground the key. A hacking cough, hiccup. Nothing.

"Are we stuck?" He heard her breathing.

"Yeah."

"We'll be late."

"Yeah." No use trying the motor again. Once it was flooded, that was it until the temperature dropped.

"Are we near enough to walk?"

"No." She must have known that. Or was she just too goddamn buried in that stupid cake?

"Can you get it going again?"

"Maybe." His lungs were boarded in. "When she cools off." His chest felt grafted to his spine. Crazily, he pumped his arms back and forth, forcing the air in.

"Well, how long do we have to wait?" She lifted the cake pan from her thighs, squelching the aluminum free. "It's pretty hot, for June especially." Arms outstretched, she balanced the cake on the dashboard, her right palm flat against it to keep it from sliding off. Although her hair was pulling loose down the side of her face, she still had a solid noodle of ponytail left.

"Until I can be sure that the motor isn't flooded anymore."

Missy—could that really be her name?—swung herself around, cake between her hands, and edged herself up so she could reach over and put it on the backseat. "It's too hot to hold that thing anymore," she said. She looked at him, deferential, teasing. "Shouldn't we get out?" she asked. Holding her withered ponytail like a rudder, she opened the car door, the handle firm in her hand.

Gerhardt joined her. The sky was so empty, there wasn't even a bird, or a jet trail. They were at the beginning of a round hill, the Hilton church property, with a dirt road veining up it, and the little country church, white and peeling, settled in just over the crest. Every idiot in this country built on hills. From where they were standing, he could see the steeple, a thrust of greyish shingles, and the tops of the three arched windows.

"I'm glad I don't go to that church." Missy was standing tiptoe, craning up against the sun. "Daddy's car would never make it up that driveway." She giggled. Suddenly she truly looked older than Diane, a lot older, a little crotch-tickler, seething inside.

The hardness pushed at his overalls. Christ. Not looking at him, she started up the hill. Contracting his groin, Gerhardt focused on her back. "Where're you going?" he asked, as stupid a question as anyone could come up with.

"Up."

"I wouldn't do that. The car . . ."

She looked at him over her shoulder, her cheeks pushed up by her smile. "You can come, too." Then she was running up the driveway, shouting back to him. "When we get down, the car will start. The cake is for dessert, anyway. If we're late, it doesn't matter."

It had been forever since he'd gone up a hill that fast, chasing a half-grown morsel, back to high school and the crazy horsing around on the weekends when you got loose enough to chase out with your dad's old car and gun it down some dark road with all the squealing and clutching of friends in the backseat and some little bag of juice up against you in front and both of you so itchy you didn't dare grab anywhere too hard for fear it would come off in your hands. More than a few times he'd parked the old heap and gone off into the night, stumbling over grass humps and cow pies, chasing some girl who never ran too fast. He'd had them on river-banks and on roadsides, maybe not all of them, not all the way, but enough. And in Germany, he'd had them any way he wanted. More than he got now. More than he'd had in a long time.

He was halfway up the drive, the church floating clear. God, he wasn't that old at forty-two, but he wasn't thirteen, either, or four-teen, or fifteen, or whatever she was, trotting up the gravel with a little jump of her shorts, wrinkling from one side to the other as her buns switched back and forth. He kept right after, magnetized. A monarch butterfly, the only kind he knew the name of, sampled the thistles along the top edge of the drive, touching one, then the next, moving its wings for balance.

They were standing at the top.

"Wow, this is higher than I thought!" She held both arms over her head and waved her fingers in flutters, like the butterfly. "Wow, I can see the trees where the park is."

"The park's the other way."

She didn't pay any attention. Instead she turned and started walking up along the side of the hilltop lawn and then around the corner of the church in back. The untrimmed grass sprang up from under her feet.

Gerhardt held his hands at his side. Below him the car sat in the early summer heat, its pockmarked top smooth in the light. He couldn't just leave her. The cake would be melting in the backseat, brown fingers on the upholstery. But he couldn't go back.

Hell, she was just a kid.

Over his head, the sky crinkled. Missy must be in the graveyard. He circled around the corner of the church like she had, his body bent back against his own momentum. At first he couldn't even see her, but he wasn't looking right. She was sitting on a marble bench in front of a tall monument, pretty fancy for a two-bit country churchyard. Sandstrom. Swedes always thought they were better than anyone else. Whoever did the mowing hadn't been able to get up close enough, and the tall dried grasses were brushing the edges of the marble slab. Her feet were hidden.

"There's bugs in that grass." It was the only thing he could think of to say.

"Who cares?"

"Well."

"I mean, I know about bugs." She swayed her feet back and forth. Her ankles were pinched in like somebody had molded them with thumb and forefinger. Above them, her legs fattened out.

"Was Diane born here?" She rubbed a spot on her chin. Her eyes were focused low, and Gerhardt's hands, caught in their gaze, hung like blocks from his wrists.

"Well." His lost hands seemed to want to wave in the hilltop breeze, so he had to hold them steady. "She was. All of them were. I was, too, matter of fact."

"I guess I knew that, the way people talk around here." She had wet one finger with her tongue and was wiping the corner of the marble bench. "My dad's lived here all his life except when he was in the army." She had cleared a little white half-circle and was picking at the edge with her fingernail. She looked up. "Were you in the army?"

He couldn't remember. Yes he could. "I was," he said, but his voice rose, and she looked at him as if he had asked a question instead of answering one. "Yes," he said, putting things right.

"If they draft women, I'm not going. Never. Women shouldn't have to fight." She pushed back her hair and looked as if she expected him to argue.

"I guess." His mouth was dry. Breathing through it like a grounded fish, he stepped to the bench, hesitated, went on to the monument itself.

"There weren't any Sandstroms in school, but I think one plays on the Hilsdahl team." Her voice followed him. "It'd be like the pyramids, hauling that stone up this hill."

Gerhardt concentrated on that. The Sandstrom monument was a

pointed spire settled on a square base, both marble, grained with grey and lichen that was grey, too. He bent down and looked closely; the lichen patterns had little orange cups sticking up from them. Flowers? There were names, too, carved in an ornate script with the letters half worn off. Orlanel, died in 1911. A woman? Jessie and Corrie, 1913. Twins? There were no months, so he couldn't tell the season.

When her voice lifted out of the heat and the insect hum, he wasn't ready for it, even though he hadn't forgotten her. "Penny for your thoughts," she said, again, and pulled her knees up under her chin, feet on the bench. He was so clumsy sitting down next to her that he missed the end of the bench halfway and had to reanchor himself. At first she was soft, then rigid, and when he pulled her up to him, not knowing what to expect, but sure she was being given to him for something, he heard a little grunt, and then he was rolled off the bench onto the grave so fast he couldn't get his legs under him, and she was nagging at him too, the same sound he'd heard in his head for what seemed like his whole life. "Behave yourself!" she yelled, really letting him know. "Behave yourself!" That wasn't the worst he could have heard, but it was bad enough. He'd done the worst thing already, and it would last him, yes it would. It would last him for all the years right up until the end.

Seventy-Seven

Most of the real prairie was gone. He'd seen pictures, Luke had, of the way it used to be, with the grass so thick and even that it was like water, closing after each step. Even a herd of buffalo hadn't been able to tramp it down for long—a few days maybe, and then it would rise upward toward the sun again, expanding in the warmth.

The Prairie Pioneers Park had been formed years ago, mostly to preserve a little chunk of prairie that the Holcomb family had never plowed. They'd donated the land, old Mrs. Holcomb sitting like a stack of doughnuts on the platform on the Fourth of July. His grandma had said. There was even a metal sign like a historical marker where the road entered. The county mowed along the main road, then left the hay to dry in the windrows. But beyond the mowed part, there was real prairie, not as much as there had been, of course, because there was a whole playground there now, even the plastic horses on springs, and then a little basketball court, only with just one basket. And a wading pool. The county had fought about the wading pool, and it was true that no one used it much except to throw candy bar wrappers in. Boys just going into high school snuck out there early in the night, hitching rides with big brothers or bicycling if the roads weren't muddy, and practiced pissing from one edge to the other. No one in Luke's grade had ever been able to do it, but four years ago Maynard Franklin was said to have done it, if you believed his cousin. He'd drunk two bottles of Coke first and said it was the carbon dioxide. Jet propulsion, he'd said.

"Poopy Lukey, poopy Lukey!" Scrambling out from opposite ends of the shelter, the twins ran toward him. When they had been babies, he had swung them around one in each arm. Not anymore.

"Poopy Lukey!"

"Be quiet." He walked away.

"Poopy Lukey pillbox!" Both of them had spit running down their chins, and one was hitting himself on the chest. Luke still couldn't tell Charles from Christian most of the time.

"Don't go any farther, you two. Mom will be angry." He could see the edge of her in the shelter, sitting down at the center table. No one was next to her.

"Lukey poopy." Only one was shouting while the other jumped up and down. They stayed too far away from him to grab.

"Go back, you two. Mom needs you."

"Doesn't."

"How do you know?"

"She's talking to Diane."

"Then Grandma needs you."

"She ain't there."

"Where is she, then?"

"On the swing." They pivoted on their outside feet and started back. Though they were the shortest second graders and the dumbest too, they still had begun to outgrow their jeans. Above the sagging socks, each one had a band of ankle.

Luke turned too and began to trek toward the playground. What if there had been two of *him*? He knew how the egg divided and all, but how could there be doubles of anybody? Was it peaceful to be able to see yourself every time you turned your head? Then if you died, your parents only cried half as much. When he cooled off in the trough on the farm, he would lie on the rough bottom as long as his breath could hold and think about never coming up. Even then, though, they'd still have to fish out the part of him that was his body and dispose of it. Grandma would braid an eagle feather into his wet hair and sing "Oh! Susanna." Did you really go to Louisiana when you died? Of course not. You went to the Pioneer Home Graveyard and fertilized the prairie. Bodies didn't rise again; the preacher was crazy. Goldenrod and buffalo grass, with the sun making blond curls over it.

He crossed the entrance road. Two cars, dust stained, turned in front of him. One was Luke's teacher, her husband in the backseat with their daughters and a gigantic hamper, while their black Lab, the only purebred in the parish, sat in front, lapping at the windshield. He was bigger than Harry Truman. At first his teacher waved hard, then she slowed the car down and rolled open her window.

"You're all settled in already, Luke." The Lab lapped frantically at her cheek, and she shoved him back, her hand a white starfish on the steaming black coat. "Did you spend the night?"

"No."

"The morning then?" She was the only Sunday school teacher he'd ever had who made jokes with children.

"No."

"What you need, Luke, is something to eat. Your word fuel is burned up." She had come from New Jersey and thought people were supposed to talk. Only an outsider would think that.

"I guess."

Laughing, his teacher swatted her hair with the hand that wasn't holding off the Lab "Want a ride to the shelter, Luke?"

"No thank you." Pickle juice sat in his throat. He thought good thoughts, beatitudes, commandments, and sweetened his voice. "I'm going down to the playground." But then she would think he was a kid. "To look for Grandma." But then she would think Grandma was even crazier than they all knew she was. Except him. He couldn't get it right. Eyes rolling, he turned away from the car and marched off. She could think whatever she damn pleased.

It wasn't far. First the entrance road, and he was past that already. Then the short grass, and then a line of poplars, pruned down to stumps by the County Parks but sprouting again. Luke edged between two of them. A little swamp off to one side. The strip of unmowed prairie grass, so thick that when he saw a mouse, it was running on top. Then the playground.

She sat on the lowest swing, a brown hand around each rope. Her feet were in the dirt, rubbing little channels, erasing them, rubbing them again. Her housedress was pulled up around her hips, circling like an inner tube. Nuzzling down beneath were the tips of her garters, holding up her brown stockings. She had something in her hand. When she saw him, she held it out.

"What's that, Grandma?"

"Arrowhead." It was like a tiny white knife on her palm.

"Did you bring it in the cookie jar?"

She laughed. Luke settled in the dirt beside the swing. He put his hands on the cross bars at the end of the swing set and stretched out the muscles in his arms. The old lady—she wasn't *old* old, not like Santa Claus or God—went on swinging in her gentle furrow, not looking at him, not looking at anyone. "Did they eat up the German potato salad?" she asked.

"Not yet. Everybody isn't here." There'd be two dozen families anyway, and no one would want to start early. It wouldn't be polite.

"Did she put in enough bacon?"

"She did it just like you taught her." His voice cracked.

"Men think they can control everything, but they can't," she said, pumping up.

Luke got up and went behind her. Her back curved out toward him. He gave her a good shove, his hands solid. Through the quiet thickness of the air, he heard the twins, or someone about their age, yelling faintly back at the shelter. By the second shove, they'd stopped, and he heard a car come in, something with a rattling muffler. It sounded like a Ford. There wouldn't be too many more. With the third shove, he spread both hands like fans and touched her flat, pushing outward so she could really go high, sky-high.

When she swung back toward him this time, he caught her around the waist with one arm and grabbed one chain with the other. She lit in his embrace, not very wide at all. The swing swerved crooked, and he hopped along the ground to control it, then pulled his other leg up next to her, tunneling his toes along where the chains were riveted to the metal triangles sticking out from the edges of the board seat. She was so small across the bottom, not like his mother, not even like the way Diane was getting to be, that he could tuck his boots along both sides of her and give a ferocious pump with both knees bent so low that the backs of his thighs pressed against his calves, then sprang away. Wobbling like one of those half-hit fouls in the softball park with people hooting through their teeth, the swing soared up, nearly hitting the metal pole on top, then righted itself. They reached so high that they might have gone over, might have tangled around the bar, might have twisted up like fishing line, knotted and then swinging loose, but they didn't. Back down again, with a pressure that forced him forward against her back, his knees and shoulder blades tightening. So far back that when he looked straight out he could see the hill behind which their farm rested. There was a bouquet of lilac sliced into the green because it was that time of year. Then down in a great swoop, his knees bent again, then coming up to hold her just under the shoulders so she wouldn't fall, her own body bending just enough to share the momentum. He would war-paint his face with potato salad, slice the cookies with arrowheads, cut the chains with a blade of air and a branch of lavender. Then, when he came home she would hold him against her at the kitchen table and tell him that all the generations pass so one perfect one can come, and he would be it, he would, swinging, swinging into the sky.

Seventy-Eight

They were in the swamp. Voices far away. Cattails like Indian feathers. Muck.

Squash. Splash. That a nest? Wove right in there. Can't have it.

"Mine!"

"No, mine!"

"Bastard."

Keep jumping. Keep jumping. You too?

"Wanna drink."

"Baby."

"Ain't."

"Pants-full baby."

"You live in a shithouse."

"You too."

Prairieparkswamp. Didn't get no ice cream. Not yet. Want it. *Want* it. SweetJesuswantit. Come on. Come on back. Come *on*. Hear 'em?

"Where is?"

Too far gone.

"We ain't lost."

"I don't hear 'em."

"Crybaby."

"Crybaby you. Pisser."

"What's that?"

"Nothin'."

"Is too."

"No it ain't."

"My shoe gone!"

"Dummy."

"Where'd it go?"

"Turtle ate it."

"Mom'll be mad, she will. Luke. Diane, all them'll be mad. They'll all be mad at us."

"Night's comin'."

"No it ain't."

"I'm cold."

"Shut up, you. My feet's wet."

"Don't like this. Don't. Wanna go home!"

"Go home, me too."

"Won't never find us."

A rustle, not very loud. Then louder. Muskratbeaver? Bears? Mama?

"Grandma!"

She reached out to them. "You two can't even drown clean," she said, and wiped their noses before anything else. "This way," she said, and pushed them both along to where the cattails turned to grass and the sky came through like always. "Double trouble," she said, but she was smiling, and she pushed their hard heads together until they rubbed like sandpaper. By the time they got to the shelter by themselves, all they got was an everyday scolding from Mama, like before and before, and the swing down in the playground was creaking.

Seventy-Nine

The pickup bounded against the rutted road. She'd get a moment to herself, Mar would, with not a one of them home yet to harass her, if she just made it up the driveway and missed the ditch, if she could just do that and nothing else. It wasn't raining. The sky was as blue as life itself. She'd survived the picnic, got through it all again. If she hurried, she'd have a genuine private moment.

They'd cleaned out the German potato salad, down to the casserole bottom. Everyone had praised Diane. But that crazy child had barely been civil, biting her lip and mumbling.

"Why can't you be nice?"

"I didn't make enough."

"You're not obliged to feed the whole Methodist Church."

"I don't like running out."

And you'd never know she gave a thought to food in her life, skinny like she was. Might as well eat nothing at all.

The rest of them could get back on their own. The Fenstermeisters had a minibus, secondhand from the Hilsdahl schools. The twins could kick each other in back, her mother could queen the front seat with her cookie jar on her head. Luke and Diane would sit quiet while Mrs. Fenstermeister held to the middle of the gravel road like a tank. No one would talk about the AWOL mother. After all, maybe her stomach had been upset. Some people couldn't handle charred hot dogs. No one would mention Gerhardt.

At the turn to their farm property, Mar stopped at the mailbox. A Sears catalog was sticking out, fat and promising with its shiny ladies beaming at each other on the cover. There was a *Reader's Digest* award notification. Maybe it was true, after all. Someone had to win them. Then the creamery statement. The Kauffmanns were holding their own this month. The *Missionary Message*, one corner torn off. Some savage must have taken a bite. The church should tend to its own right here, where people knew what they wanted and didn't have to be saved with extra effort.

Mar roared up the driveway, holding the mail in one hand as she steered. Smells from the cut lawn caught her nose before she'd even gotten the car properly stopped. Luke never forgot, whether they paid him or not. The old mower was his horse, his airplane. When he hadn't been looking back, she'd seen his lips moving as she watched out the window. Harry Truman always walked next to him, orderly as a soldier. Harry Truman was checking her out at that very moment in a much less orderly way.

Smiling, Mar dropped the mail on the long counter by the sink. The papers spewed like a shuffled deck of cards. One postcard fell out. She picked it up.

It had been at least a year. He was almost middle-aged like she was. Their mother was almost an old woman.

Why bother with those almosts?

The postmark was smeared, but it couldn't have been mailed from too far away, because Jimmy had dated it the twenty-third, and it was only the twenty-fifth now. Or maybe he knew how to speed the mail along. He'd always known how to keep things moving.

The picture, as she turned the card over, was pretty much the same as always. But this one had both a mare and a foal, not just one, both brown as satin with seven white feet between them. They stood side by side like silhouettes of each other. In the square cut out by their legs, the grass was so green that you could eat it yourself.

Mar turned the postcard back again. They kept forwarding them from in town. Didn't her mother write back with the new address? Or couldn't he read well enough to tell that the address had changed? Or didn't her mother know where he actually was? It probably didn't matter.

How long could Jimmy keep riding? Maybe he was just mucking out stables now. He wouldn't mind. Or maybe he'd found someone to take care of him until he died, a widow maybe, lusty and good at listening, with enough of a nest egg so it wouldn't matter if he never earned a cent.

Mar set the card down on the catalog, moved it over to the counter surface, picked it up again. He only wrote to their mother.

He must really love her, in his way.

In his crazy way, from out there wherever he was.

Eighty

Smells. Something from back then, back with the others, running on the flat land. The brown masters. Pulling the travois, the buckskin thongs matting his fur. Bare bones, ground by the big teeth. Gut shriveled inside his skin. All there.

Even outside. Even outside in the cold. The smell when the door opened. Through the wood itself. Wet in his nostrils, soaking it up. All the tricks. Fetch, roll, sit, stay. Sit, roll, stay, fetch. Watching the house. Watching.

"Luke, that damn dog is out there in the yard doing tricks."

First the heat. Warm air like when the grass began. Through the door, circling his head. The voice of meat, on and on, brown and sweet. All day long, always the same. The window open. He stood on his hind toes, but couldn't. Jumped. Tongue on the wood.

"Harry Truman! Stop it! I have to shut this now!"

They were making it all day. They were making it all day. They were making it all day.

He howled. His own voice was a surprise. Again. Like something from before. The cold air in, and then out warm. The fur lifted on his ears. Underneath, in the soft part, a sound like singing. Again, again.

"Shut up! Shut up, Harry!"

Finally there was nothing left to do but run. Round and round. First he tried it one way, under the willow, next to the stones the house sat on. Then he reversed himself and tried it the other, nose plowing the dead grass. White was in the air, his paws ached with the chill. The smell was almost gone on one side, but full force on the other. He couldn't lose it. He couldn't leave it. He drank his water dish empty. His belly sloshed as he tore through the cold. No good. Empty. Empty. Empty.

Night came. The hay was too far. He lay flat in the grass by the steps, spittle on the black fringes of his gums. She came out without calling, and the door didn't quite shut behind her. There was no sound. In her hands she had it all, in a bowl the size of the earth. She set it in front of him.

"There, there." His body shook as he gulped, but he could still hear her, still feel the fingers on his top fur. "There, there. I took some of the good pieces, too. That's from the breast. The stuffing has gizzard in it and the gravy on top. Diane made a lot. That's mincemeat. We mashed the potatoes, both kinds. That's rutabaga. You wouldn't like that if it was all you had. That's the drum-stick . . . careful of those bones. Slow down, Harry Truman. Slow down."

After he was done, she filled his water dish again. He put his greasy face in her hand. She had worked out the snarl under his collar. The moon rose.

Eighty-One

"What's that, Grandma?"

"It's what I'm sewing."

"But what is it?"

Susan moved her hands out from her lap and took Charles by the shoulders. That was so she could regulate his distance from her. The blue sweep of fabric on her lap glistened in the light from the window, through which she could see Christian and his father gassing up the Valiant. They each had one hand on the hose from the pump by the garage, although it took only one person to do it. Gerhardt had his other hand on the top of the car, patting its red roof as if it had grown skin. Christian had his other hand in his pocket. They faced in opposite directions.

"It's a dress I'm making for Diane."

"If she wins a blue ribbon today?"

"If she does or doesn't."

"What if Christian and me win? We did them pictures. With cows. For the art part."

Susan replaced her hands in her lap. She had always liked cooking better than sewing, always. But it was simply a matter of will. "I'll sew your ribbons to your collarbones," she said, but her smile didn't threaten. She took up the dress again.

"Diane says she don't care if she wins or not."

"It's her right to say that."

"All them fair people is crazy Frenchies, anyway."

"Mrs. Bouchard was French a long time ago."

Charles edged nearer her lap, fended off by her knees beneath her skirt. "She ain't now?" he asked, leaning forward into the sweep of blue.

"Everybody's something," said Susan, pulling the fabric back.

Outside, the handle clanged back into the gas pump. Christian had hoisted himself up on the hood and begun on the windshield, swabbing with the dustrag. Last week the rag had been his pajama bottom, or Charles's pajama bottom, rotting in the drawer from disuse. Both twins slept buck naked, even in winter, woven together under their quilts. The only use to which their pajamas had ever been put was to wrap Harry Truman for space travel. He had almost bitten Christian when he broke away, and he wouldn't come near either twin anymore.

"When we goin' to the fair?"

"When your father calls."

"How come we don't sleep at the fair? Mom does. Luke and Diane does. Right with Luke's calf."

"Because there's no room in the pickup for more than three."

"How come you and me and Christian can't be three?"

"Eeney, meeny, miney," said Susan, ending the discussion. Talk led nowhere. "Moe," she added, putting the last stitch in the waist-band and getting up. Through the window, she saw Gerhardt's mouth open, then close again. He must know she was watching. He cared less about the fair than anybody, but if Diane took blue rib-bons for her baking, he would rub her between her shoulder blades and sputter. Luke's prowess in anything embarrassed him.

"Coming?" Gerhardt's voice rose in the air. Sewing basket under her arm, Susan followed Charles down the porch steps and into the backseat of the Valiant. Against the rear window, a sleepy bumble-bee nuzzled the smudged glass, his wings pressed tight to his furry back. As the car jolted down the driveway, he lost his footing, flut-tered higher. His buzz was gone in the rushing air.

The fairground was on the other side of Manatee. The second generation of settlers had built it, first a frame barn for the cattle, the roof peaked against the winter snows. Then a second barn for pigs and sheep. After that, when people had begun to look to the fair for something to entertain themselves with, a grandstand for the harness races. Pretty rickety, that Manatee Fairgrounds grand-stand, but they kept propping it up every year with metal braces under the ramps that sagged. Then a 4-H house with built-in booths and bulletin boards around the walls. Folding tables stacked in back after the year's fair. All open now. All set up. Diane had graduated out of 4-H into the adult division this year, even though she still qualified as a teenager. She had set her teeth against child-hood. "If I can't win as a grown-up, they can keep any ribbon they'd want to give me," she'd said, quietly ferocious, as she slammed the cutter down into the baking powder biscuit dough.

Diane's biscuits were fat and perfect every time. Luke ate them so hot from the oven that he always burned the top of his mouth. The twins waited for five minutes or so, their eyes on the clock over the sink. Diane didn't like their eagerness either. Pies had to wait for supper absolutely, although the tarts from the leftover crust were fair game any time. Currant jelly for Charles and Christian, its red bubbles poking up through the trinity of holes. Blackberry jelly for Luke. Gerhardt was too embarrassed to have a preference, would eat anything. Mar tried to keep her weight down.

They were turning into the fairgrounds. Gerhardt bent over the wheel with his head turtled between his shoulders. Pulses beat in the twins' necks. Christian showed the gatekeeper the exhibitor's pass bent between his fingers. The Valiant bounded along the center track, then turned by the lot where the tractors—John Deere, Harvester, Steiger—stood to be admired. Next came the exhibit halls where Gerhardt slid between a pair of posts and parked by the nearest door. Inside, the rest of them would be waiting.

"Maybe they ate Luke's calf." Charles's eyes blinked.

"No one's eating that calf."

"You said, Dad."

"Luke won't sell it unless he wants to."

"He don't wanna?"

"Not from what I heard."

"He win any ribbons?" The twins said it together.

"Jesus. You guys saw. A red on the calf. On that goddamn 4-H thing, too. The root sample stuff."

"No blues?"

"What you kids know about blue ribbons?" Gerhardt jerked his hands off the wheel, grabbed the back of his neck with both fists, kneaded the muscles. The twins spilled out and into the building. Under his heavy fingers, Gerhardt's head rolled back and forth.

Centering herself on the backseat, Susan looked out both windows, rotating her own head with precision. Then, leaning back, she took her sewing out of its basket, withdrew the needle from its neat pucker in the collar. She began on the sash, overcasting the stitches as evenly as possible, thinking about Diane. Diane had won blue ribbons before, two last year, for pickles and brownies. But she had been in the Teen Group then. The competition was harder as an adult. Tuesday night she'd been up until three A.M. baking. The oven had been still warm at breakfast. They'd moved everything in the truck the first day, then gone back for Luke's calf.

"I gotta get out of here."

Susan's needle rounded a corner.

With a wrench that sent the Valiant's body rocking on its springs, Gerhardt backed the car toward the access road. A horse trailer blocked the way.

"Jesus Christ!"

Whoever owned the trailer wasn't by it. It seemed to sink into the dust by the minute. Gerhardt withered in his seat.

"No use," Susan said.

"You're talking?" Gerhardt turned around, arms sprawling loose.

"When I have something to say."

Another bumblebee hummed against the side window, sluggish in the spell of the warm glass. Susan folded the fabric of the sash inside itself, continued overcasting. The sweep of color caught the light through the rear window in a silky vertical design like a meadow of blue ribbons.

"You think she'll win a blue?" Gerhardt's voice came out his nose on the air of his last breath.

"If she doesn't this year, she will next."

The bumblebee crawled on the edge of the open window. Dimmed by captivity, he hesitated at the layer of new air, his stinger wobbling hesitantly from his furry behind. Susan ticked him with her sewing needle, and he shook himself on the rim of the glass. She pushed him with her finger. His soft rump awakened her skin as he tumbled out into the brightness.

Finally the horse trailer was pulling over into the area by the stalls, jacking itself carefully into place. Gerhardt jammed the Valiant into reverse, then spun it around facing the midway. Ahead of him, the rides stood poised with their passengers. There weren't many. Gerhardt banged the car down the exhibitors' track to the side, his knee rocking upward into the dashboard. He was breathing through his mouth.

"Where are we going?" Susan leaned forward on her arms, the blue dress draped carefully over the seat on the other side.

"You tell me."

"I think we're going nowhere, Gerhardt." She hadn't sounded so sane in years, and she knew it.

He spun the car through the smaller of the two gates to the fairgrounds. A rounded woman who could well have been Mrs. Bouchard, fine and French in origin, stood talking to a small cluster of other round women who leaned toward her as if in a slight breeze. Gerhardt dusted their nylons as he pulled away.

"I feel like I'm goin' to get old and die and have not a goddamn thing in this world."

Susan smoothed the dress. "You should read more," she said.

He looked back to one side of her, driving blind.

"I could lend you whatever encyclopedia you needed."

"You're crazy like a fox, woman."

Smiling, she smoothed the blue dress, silky under her hand.

With a spin of the Valiant's rear tires, Gerhardt pulled into the big fair parking lot across the entrance road. The car settled into its tracks as if someone had shot it. Even the radiator sent out a gust of steam in relief. He leaned back.

"What do you think of Luke?"

"He's Luke."

"Got his own mind, right?"

"You could say that."

"You ever regret anything, Susan?" This time he looked right at her. The mirror reflected the bristles on the back of his head. They were speckled with grey, almost as much as hers. Some Germans had a gene for early greying.

"There was nothing I could help."

"Me either."

"That's right."

If was as if a chapter had been concluded. With a flourish, the two of them stepped out of the car, joining arms once their feet hit the parking lot. They walked back through the fair gate, Susan's elbow linked into Gerhardt's as if for support, but her feet in their sturdy old woman's shoes were solid on the dusty midway. They marched as if a band were clearing the way for them. Before them on the cluttered fairgrounds, the only ride running was the merry-go-round, its music thick with whistles up and down the scale as a mother and three children got off, all four so blond that they appeared to have no eyebrows. One little girl looked back at them.

Inside his booth, the ticket seller had his fingers spread on the wooden shelf as if he were dealing them out instead of selling tickets. His eyes focused lightly to one side of the opening. When Gerhardt laid the money straight through to him, he felt it before he gave the change, slowly, ritualistically, then smiled back at them both. Gerhardt jammed the coins into his pocket.

Together they made a processional up the ramp onto the platform of the ride. The merry-go-round quivered. A violin started, or something like it, as the recording ground into action again.

"Mar says her brother was always one for the horses," stated Gerhardt as he took Susan's arm.

"Jimmy used to be."

"Mar says he still is."

"I don't know how she'd know." They were making a slow circle as the movement built, looking for the perfect steed.

"Bet he never rode one this color." They held themselves in front of a horse of bubble-gum pink, its mouth twisted around a lavender bit. Gerhardt bent down, held his hands in a cup one on top of the other. Susan stepped in, then rose with their combined momentum. Her hands held to the pole as the horse rose and fell.

Gerhardt stood beside her, his hands in his pockets, swaying. "What if Diane don't win a blue?" he asked while the music scratched and banged out of the calliope, just a tape deck somewhere in the middle, but still the right sound. It was some song Susan knew, like a folk song, something with a long-ago name. There was thyme in it, and a lover. The name raced ahead of her, always the same distance away, but she could never catch up.

"The blue dress is so she won't mind," Susan said, bending her head down to him. "A blue ribbon dress." She couldn't tell if he heard her or not because voices sometimes didn't get through, and it didn't matter, anyway, not when the air on every side of them was full of violins and trombones and guitars and harmonicas and drums and all the other instruments that carried them and the horses away and away and away.

Eighty-Two

Jimmy'd always dreamed it would be like this. Blue sky, bowl blue, holding the sun within it. The track a golden oval, all the dust watered down, the grass in the middle so perfect that the horses didn't dare eat it. People filling the stands, jammed together, even the kids caught with their popcorn hands halfway to their mouths. The farm ladies standing up, for once, and the farm husbands beside them, slamming one horny fist into the other because they'd never seen a finish like it with the little bay tearing down the backstretch like she was off to meet her lover. And a few important people too, more than a few, but standing up themselves, suits and silk dresses, one lady with a feather in her hat, a feather that swooped down across her forehead. The fronds blew in a sweet breeze as she cheered him on.

Before, there'd always been something wrong, or at least something not right—a second place, the prize money already spent by the owner, who everyone knew was a gambler anyway, rain clouds clotting in the sky over the grandstand, gypsy trailers camped in the middle next to the portable toilets. For all the years of his life. Although he had chosen it, he knew that. Made his bed. Free spirit. But it hadn't been the way he'd thought it would be.

Jimmy stood at the finish line, leaning on his crutches, a little man with legs that would never take him anywhere important again, but that was the way all the second-rate jockeys ended up. It didn't matter, though, because the sky was as blue as it could ever be, bluer even, and the grass glittered like emeralds, like bolts of the king's velvet, and the people were yelling so loud as the little bay, the little one he mucked out for, pulled ahead in the stretch, that you couldn't really tell what they were yelling except that it was a noise like thunder, and he could hear his name in it as well as any other. And that one family up there, the tall farmer, the woman with the feather, the grown daughter next to her, they looked real familiar, all of them, like he'd known them a long time, like they'd be coming down afterward, tripping in their hurry and laughing, and they'd hold his hands, all grabbing each together, as they put the horseshoe of roses around his shoulders, as they crowned him and loved him and honored him just the way he'd always dreamed.

Eighty-Three

"Mother."

There was no answer.

"Mother?"

Still no answer, but a presence in the air. Spring had eaten through everything. For once, they could hide the Easter baskets outside at church. For once the children wouldn't have to wear boots.

"Mother?"

"Mother!"

Mar stepped outside, her sweater around her shoulders. She hardly needed it. The sun, powerful as a voice, was calling up the dandelions. The grass shimmered. Where Gerhardt had plowed the garden plot, the soil lay rough in chocolate chunks, rich and solid. The winter moisture was being pulled up into the air even as she walked. It could almost be planting time for the lettuce, the early peas, perhaps the beets. Though a frost might well come before Decoration Day. There was no way of knowing.

Susan was at the far end of the garden, down where the currant bushes formed a barricade in front of the barbed wire fence. She knelt in the dirt, her housedress pushed aside in a circle around her. Her bare knees had worn their own channels, her toes had dug in even deeper. In front of her, her hands made fan-shaped patterns in the brown compacted dirt working its way up in walls between her fingers. The walls broke, resurrected themselves. She went on.

"Mother! What are you doing?"

Susan didn't answer. Mar looked at her across the rectangle of brown as if they were separated by something impenetrable. Lying between them along the edge was a bundle of pointed sticks, around which loops of aging twine had been tied. Gerhardt or Luke had been thinking about planting too.

"Can't you answer me?"

Susan looked up. She might choose not to talk, but there was never a moment when her mind wasn't awake. She centered her gaze on Mar's face as if it were the only thing to be focused on in the vast sweep of springtime. She raised her hands, brown paws as clotted as Harry Truman's. She smiled.

"What answer do you want?"

"What on earth are you doing?"

"That's right. I'm doing it on earth." Susan smiled again. As Mar approached her, she rose, striped with the rich brown from her knees down to her feet. "Don't touch me," she said. "I'll mark you."

"Don't you think it's too early to plant?"

"It depends."

"On what, Mother?" The exasperation trespassed on the edge of Mar's voice.

"On what happens."

Mar opened her mouth, then closed it. The rich damp soil had edged up over the soles of her shoes on the sides like a layer of fudge. She scraped one against the other, teetering. Her ankles stayed small no matter what. They must have their own metabolism. That was the only way to explain it.

Susan reached out. "Mar," she said.

"What?"

"We only do what we have to."

"What in the world does that mean?"

Susan was looking at the dirt. "I only found one," she said.

"One what?'

"One arrowhead."

"Here?"

"No."

"There never were any Indian camps near Manatee, I don't think."

"That's what Gerhardt told me." Susan settled down to her knees again.

"Mother." Mar caught her breath. "Mother, I want to ask you something."

Susan was quietly digging.

"Why did you leave the farm?"

"We're on the farm right now."

"Not this farm. The other one." Mar noticed her voice was shaking, and when she noticed it, it shook more. She put one hand on her throat as if that would make a difference.

"I know what farm you mean."

"Why did we go? Why did you leave him? And where is he now?" Mar struggled to get the words out.

"Your father?" Susan was deepening the hole with two fingers, spiraling down into the soil.

Mar couldn't answer.

Something slid into the hole, so small that one could hardly recognize its presence. Susan began to tamp it over. "He's probably dead," she said. "Jimmy too. Both of them are probably dead. And we go on anyway. Women always go on. Women always go on, Mar. All of us. We share surprising things. Sometimes we even love each other."

Mar nodded. Her knees were loosening under her.

"Remember, you're my daughter. You can love me or hate me or both. It's all right." Susan stretched out her hands, mucky as they were. Mar lifted hers. As the spring wind rose, fickle as all beginnings, they reached toward each other, surrounded by the earth stretching away beyond imaginings.

Eighty-Four

He liked the big ones. They always got off the bus first, and they always saw him first. They would rub his fur the wrong way and the right way both. He had been waiting by the mailbox for so long that he didn't mind. He jumped and jumped, today and all the days. When his paws were wet, he tried not to, but it was no use. He had to reach all their parts or they wouldn't belong to him.

He didn't like the two who were the same. They got off last, and they threw things. Or they tried to get on his back. Or they gave him things from their boxes and then took them back when his mouth was open. He was as good as he could be, but he knew it wasn't good enough. He made the noises and put his teeth together. He tried not to be where they were. But if he wasn't there, then he couldn't have the big ones. He wanted them so much.

On the day when there was smoke in the air and in his nose, he waited in the sun so long that he went to sleep. Inside his head there were people with sharp things, and they were riding. He ran with them. The sharp things went from them through the air, but he could go just as fast. When they stuck, the big ones with fur tried to run. He jumped at them. He could feel the fur in his mouth. He tore down through it. His legs crackled through the grass.

Today the two got off first. One of them came fast and put his foot down. He couldn't get away because his fur was under the foot. So he opened his mouth and put it together. When the other one came, he did it again. He heard their voices, but they were the wrong ones. He smelled the sharp smell and kept at it.

The big ones came down, and they hit him. He cried, but he was happy too. He rolled over and sat up. But they ran to the house and didn't pet him. He went to the water where the frogs were. It was almost, almost, almost. Then he chased where the earth was dry and in pieces. The noise of it was wonderful. He ran and ran. There was no fur but his own.

"God, it was a miracle he didn't go for their throats."

"You know they always tease him, Dad."

Gerhardt looked as if pieces of him were about to fly loose. "I don't give a shit," he said. "This is it. If they hadn't had those jackets on, we'd be laying down a fortune for that Dr. Collins. That dog has had it."

Christian and Charles stood together next to the kitchen table, looking down at their bellies. They had yanked up their T-shirts, their jackets lay in a heap on the floor. Christian had a line of teeth marks as straight as a ruler, but they hadn't broken the skin. Charles was bleeding in two places. They almost never cried anymore, but their noses were running in identical lines.

Mar came from the bathroom with a washcloth, alcohol, Band-Aids. It was hard to know how she felt. Diane and Luke stood to each side of her, ready to help if they were needed, but there was really nothing to do. Diane kept snapping the expansion band on her wristwatch until Luke pulled her hand away. If anyone was going to argue with his father, he was the one.

"He never bit anyone before."

"You know damn well that he came mighty near."

"We could keep him tied up."

"Jesus Christ, Luke. We tried that and tried that. Lot of good it did. He chewed his way through everything except the snow chains. He was a bad bargain from the day he was born."

Gerhardt was walking toward the entryway. Luke cast his eyes around. "He's really Grandma's dog," he said. "She talks to him."

"The fucking only one she does talk to."

Mar didn't even raise her head from working on the twins. There was no use arguing, and she knew it. When Diane's mouth came open, Mar lifted her hand. Then she turned toward the door to the living room where her mother was standing. She might have been standing there for hours, but she had given no sign. She was wearing the corduroy barn jacket.

"I'll do it," Susan said.

"Do what?"

"What has to be done." She started across the kitchen to the entryway where Gerhardt was taking the shotgun from the wall. "Give that to me, Gerhardt," she said. "You were never a good shot."

Stunned, he handed it over. She took it from him and walked out into the yard. Everyone watched her. No one could tell if she was crying or not.

Eighty-Five

It was the coldest January since the war, the real war, all the old farmers said. Every day, squeezing out from under the patchworks, Luke gritted his teeth, plunging with one deep breath held to breaking down to the kitchen where the woodstove, long outmoded, seemed to be the only thing that could create a permanent puddle of heat. The combination wood-and-oil burner in the basement heaved with effort, the pipes under the floors rattling as the warm air surged through, evaporating into the chill. Diane stayed at the office in town past closing time, typing next to the radiator, then caught a ride home with one of the ladies from the late shift at the hospital. The twins fought over the extra suit of long underwear and came down to breakfast snarling. They tried not to go to school at all.

This morning there were waffles on the table, steaming under the inverted bowl. Luke caught the smell as he slicked back his hair in the bathroom mirror, inspected his face for pimples. Clean. They all grew on his shoulders. In the summer, in the fields, the sun had dried them up until they had become an uneven mottling beneath his tan. Now they had come back, sore against his undershirt. Though no one could see them.

"Hurry up, son." He hadn't known his dad was there.

"Where's Mom?"

"Shoving jars around in the fruit cellar."

"Now?" Luke took a waffle, neat geometry of four squares dangling off his plate. Even this near the stove, the butter was a yellow brick. He slivered off a chunk, chopped it onto the waffle, squeezed the honey bear's head for the sweetening. Sluggishly, a brown stream hung on the fat lips, formed a globe, dropped like amber on his plate. He mashed it in with his fork.

"I guess." His father watched the window where the milk truck would drive up. On Tuesdays and Fridays. But this was the weekend.

"Where's Diane?"

"With Grandma."

"She's up?"

"Never sleeps." His father slid his face forward, watched him eat.

Luke wadded waffle chunks into the furnace of his mouth, dissolved them. The snow had reached the top wire of the electric fence, hanging safe now that the cows were in the barn for the winter. Every week a little more, not counting blizzards that came down like the wrath of God. When he drove at night, tiny finger drifts danced across even the highway into town.

"Where's the twins?"

"Out messing with the silage."

"I slept late."

"Saturday."

Luke took another waffle.

"I heard you did good this semester in school." The words dropped out of Gerhardt's mouth like pebbles bounding off the oilcloth on the table. He put his hands in his lap, wrapped them around each other.

"I guess."

"Simmons called. Said he wanted us to know personally. Personally. Before the report card."

"Mom didn't tell me."

"I answered."

Luke upended the honey bear, wringing its neck with both hands. The plastic squeaked.

"Said you should think about college after next year. Maybe the university."

"I don't know."

"Said there's an FFA scholarship if you go into ag. You don't have to *go* into it, just say you're going to. You can change. Simmons said that."

"Ag's OK."

Gerhardt picked up the waffle cover, holding it between his hands like a Frisbee. "Weather's bad today," he said, putting the waffle cover back down. It teetered on the plate, one side off balance. Luke straightened it.

"Diane's upstairs?"

"Was."

"Mom's in the basement?"

"I guess."

Outside, the north wind had picked up. The windbreak protected the house, always had once the Russian olives had gotten to any size, but three of them had died out opposite the kitchen window, and the wind reached through. The thermometer hung on the frame shook with the first gust, then set up a running vibration against the glass. Gerhardt plunged to his feet.

"Oughtta fix that." Over his flannel shirt, he zipped up the first jacket hung by the door. The zipper wouldn't close. It was Christian's, or Charles's. Gerhardt tugged futilely, his eyes wild. He left it open, pulled on his plaid cap. The earflaps stood out like cloth wings.

"I can do it." Luke stood up.

"No, no." The door was open, Gerhardt blocking the draft to the kitchen, arms out as if someone were being held back behind him. "No," he said again. "Finish your breakfast. Finish it, goddammit."

Luke sat down. Above his head, the steps creaked. Diane came in.

"That was Dad?"

"Yeah."

"I thought he finished the chores already."

"He's going to fix the thermometer."

"What?"

"The thermometer."

"What's wrong with it?"

"It's too cold." Luke grinned at his sister.

"Does he think he's God?"

Luke swabbed a thumb over his plate, churning up a gob of honey. Crumbs studded it like pollen. He stood up, tiptoeing toward his sister, who was bent over the sink. She had the hot water running, steam rising into the cold air of the kitchen, her hands plunged into it. Beneath her pulled-up hair, her neck was as soft as pillow slips, milkweed fluff, Red Cross cotton blowing in April. He blotted the honey on her top vertebra.

"Luke!"

"*I'm* God!"

Eighty-Six

She was crawling along the side of the road—crawling fast. Her knees churned piston-like under the faded cotton skirt of her housedress, or at least they had at first, but now they were slowing, a hesitation as they lifted, a tentative plunge to the earth again. But it didn't matter on Rural Route 82, between the Kepler and the Hebelmeister farms, down where the grass was. It didn't matter how you crawled.

Now her hair was in her mouth. She spat out as much as she could. She couldn't spare a hand to pull it back to stay.

The milkweed was starting to fill its pods again, new green children, fat and popping their sides. Who would guess, if she hadn't already seen it a hundred times, that those rich nipples would dry out and peel back, send their froth out on the wind to populate the ditches for the next lifetime?

From the way she was crawling, she couldn't see the sky. The top of her head soaked up the heat like a platter, cooking her skull down to where her ears started. The dust was in her mouth again. She'd reached the crossroads where the twins had run the old pickup off the bank and through the sunflowers, twisting those dumb golden faces so they'd broken out of their daily sweep and had to follow the sun the next morning all upside down and torn.

Susan's eyes tightened. She pulled herself up and out to the road edge, then looked both ways. Silly when there hadn't been a truck or a car by in the last hour, for sure, and certainly not in the last ten minutes, or the dust would still be billowing out over the fields. No one ever drove this road except the Keplers or the Hebelmeisters, coming back from town, going to it. Or the milk truck. Or the Saturday night farm children, still children to her even though they did it all the time (she watched the television when the rest were asleep, she knew how they did things now). Drunk as lords, most of them, just like the twins had been.

She liked it close to the earth. The trick was to pleasure yourself in the things you could touch.

A sound. Susan looked up. In the distance, their new red pickup was coming slowly, motor turning over with a polite rhythm. From the ditch, she couldn't see if Luke was driving, but, of course, he would be, and he'd know enough, as he always did, not to look for her directly like the others, but to watch the grass tops and see where they moved against the wind.

She slid back into the ditch to give him a challenge, but kept her head up, watching. In front of the sky, the truck moved like a toy on a track. Closer. She let her lower legs cleave to the ground. Closer yet. Now it was next to her, following along her pathway so slowly that the dust didn't even spread out behind it. Luke had the window open and his whole left arm down the side of the door, his blue shirt sleeve rolled to a wad under his shoulder. Through the bearded grass, she couldn't see particularly well, but he seemed to be looking straight ahead. She knew better, though. He always had her in his eye no matter where she was.

"Grandma." He stretched it out. "Grandma, it's hot. Why today?" His fingers tickled the red paint. "I wish you'd explain yourself."

She knew the game and kept crawling.

"Have I got to come get you, Grandma?" The motor struggled. "Or are you coming in to me? Mom will be at the end of her rope when she finds out. She hates it when you act like this."

It was still his turn.

"They think your mind is going, right over the hill. Nobody in their right mind goes out crawling in ditches."

It was the game she knew. Luke and she had invented it. Eyes shut, Susan put her hands in front of her chest as she rolled over on her back in the dry grasses. Along the sides of her arms, the stalks rose up. A twig forest. She pushed her feet out straight, then pulled together and pointed her toes upward, black-laced shoes dusty, brown lisle stockings resting on all the crushed weeds. Her skirt was crumpled under her but smooth on top, faded pink flowers on the blue cotton. She flapped her hands in front of her chest, making a little wind. "Woof-woof," she said. She peeked out of the edge of her road eye.

"Grandma." Luke had his chin on the window rim and his eyes on the horizon.

"Woof-woof," she said again. Her lips made a breeze. "Woof-woof."

"Grandma." The radio was playing, first the end of a twangy song and then the grain market reports. Prices were up. They had four bins full from last season.

"Woof." She let her hands fall, fingers overlapping. They lay on her flat breasts. All of a unit, she waited for Luke, waited for the pickup to unlock him. This was the second part of the game.

For a time the only noise was the motor, switched over and churning as it idled. He'd turned the radio off. Then the latch clicked, the hinges creaked, and Luke's farm boots with the buckskin laces landed in the roadside dust with a thunk. He'd left the truck door open. The grass rustled as he stepped into it. "Grandma, you and me could win some kind of contest with this act," he stated as he knelt beside her, one hard knee bumping her hip.

Susan opened her eyes and looked straight up at the sun. Forbidden. If she were blinded, then she wouldn't be able to see the dust or the grain elevator in Manatee, or Luke's blue eyes settling on the cords in her neck.

The sun looked back, a golden hole. Overhead, above the grass but still low enough so she could feel it, a breeze tasted the dense air. The sweat on Luke's forehead pulsed, then one dribble set off on its way down. With one square brown hand he swabbed it off. "Woof," he said.

She got up. Or rather, she made a getting-up gesture that Luke interpreted as she reached out to pull herself up by whatever was there, which was mostly grass and no help at all. Luke slid his arm behind her shoulders and set her upright. Then he waited while she shook out the dizziness and lifted her chin so he knew it was time for the next step. This time he slid his arm underneath, then rose with her and stood so she could lean against him, swaying. When he had been a little boy, he had smelled of dust and pee all summer long. Now he smelled like machinery oil and an edge of spice. He was so tall.

"What's next, Grandma? We can do it together." She'd never make it up the bank even on her hands and knees. Blasted county ditches, dug so deep that a crawling woman was trapped in one. And still the twins could go catapulting off over the ditch like a sailplane, twisting a golden stew among the sunflowers.

She moved the axis of her shoulders toward Luke. He put his arm around her. He didn't have on his own work boots after all, but rather his father's, the ones Gerhardt couldn't wedge on his feet anymore since his bunions had started. Luke had small feet compared to the rest of him; they fitted into the crevices of the ditch bank and let him spring upward holding her. He sat her against the hood of the pickup, metal heating through her skirt, opened the door, then slid her through and onto the seat, her spine straight down, bottom and thighs out again, knees bent where they should be. Her hand reached out for the door handle, but Luke reached out and shut the door himself. Then he walked around in front, stopping to gather a handful of gnat wings from the grill and sprinkle them free.

Neither one of them did more than incline their thoughts after they heard the second pickup coming. Luke was gathering another handful of gnat carcasses and flicking them out of his palm with his thumb. She had her eyes open to the metal ceiling, hearing the drone of the intruder as if the air were being strummed by hands she couldn't see. Dust poured out back on the road, but she wasn't looking at that either. Luke was reaching for his third handful of gnats before he took the trouble to identify the noise as the Blue Bomb, owned by the Hebelmeister family and driven by whoever couldn't get their 1967 Chrysler started for the trip into town. There was no way of knowing, when the pickup started to jack-knife down the packed hump in the middle of the road, that it wasn't going to get control again, that it was going to hit the ditch on the other side and then spring back, that whoever was driving was letting out a monotonous line of curses that nobody could hear because the windows had been jammed shut for years. When Luke let the last gnats out on the wind and looked into the racket, the truck was already upon them, and when it plunged into them, he spun into the air higher than his childhood dreams of flying. Through the wavering blue, fragments of sound, he spread out wide, gliding on the wind, then folded over and landed on his back, angel wings in the black dirt. The blue pickup had bitten into the red one and was steaming across its gearshift, windshield edged with teeth, hot nose in a knot of metal. From the edge of the road, its driver, a round boy, pumpkin faced, walked in circles and shook his head. "My shoes are gone," he whined. "Find my shoes, Mama." He was passing a piece of aerial from one hand to the other.

But already, even before the impact, Susan had placed her mind back on the earth. She was crawling down the row in the soil, moving toward something both from before and to come. It was hot, so her dress was open. Things happen, and you can't be blamed. Things happen.

Eighty-Seven

Her breasts were mountains. When she raised her arms to hang the bottle on its little silver bar, the white cloth filled Luke's eyes, breasts and snow, rocks pure as sugar, summer sunlight over the grain fields.

"You aren't going to die, you know."

"Your mother brought some cookies."

"You're a strong young man."

When she left, her breasts were on the bed. No, those were his knees, stretching the white fabric. He thought about lowering them, decided on it, thought again, making trailways down from his brain. They moved, the right one slower than the left. He told his hands to help, but only one heard. Somewhere behind his eyes, a road had been blocked off. He sent the driver on down a new way, but he got confused.

The door opened.

"How do you feel today?"

"I brought some cookies."

"He's going to keep the red one and use it for parts."

The air moved. Flies must be a problem in a hospital with all that blood. Maybe that was what he felt across his chest under its wrapping, a colony of flies swarming and sizzling.

"It's a nice day, Luke."

"Do you feel better?"

Somewhere in the stiffness across his shoulders, in his humped knees that he knew were knees now when he looked at the sheet, in the clear liquid that trickled down the tube into whatever was under the adhesive tape on his arm, there was something. He needed to ask something. The visitor had moved around to the foot of the bed and was holding the crank handle like an eggbeater, ready to fragment the air into mush.

Then she was gone, down the hall with its Indian designs on the walls. The question slipped back, and he cut it off, arrowhead sharp. In all his life he'd never found one. But he knew what they looked like.

When the Indians died, the Great Spirit came and took their souls. No, that wasn't how he'd learned it. Their families wrapped them up and put them in trees, like flocks of birds settling in for the night. You could see a Death Tree for miles across the prairie. Inside the wrappings were whatever they had needed during life, a bone toy for a child, a spear for a warrior, some bit of beadwork for a young woman cut off before her prime. And what for the old? Did their old women ever die?

He could see the Death Tree so clearly that when the familiar figure stopped at the doorway again, he thought she was in it, strangely upright and not dark enough for an Indian. She was wearing the dress from the VFW dance last month. From his pillow on the elevated bed, he looked down at her, so he must be in the Death Tree too.

"Hi, Luke."

He smiled, but he couldn't tell if his mouth was right.

"I'm sitting down." Diane pulled the straight chair out from next to the bed. "You get to lie down, so it's only fair I should sit." She took his hand, lying surprisingly on the sheet. She interlocked their fingers. "That doesn't hurt, does it? The doctor said you landed on the other side."

"No, it doesn't hurt."

"Did you get the cookies?"

He couldn't remember. He didn't say anything.

"Well, there weren't all that many after the twins got at them. But they were good." Her fingers were as hot as the pickup's hood under the sun.

The branches waved. He'd forgotten her name. He should know it if they were going to be bound in the Death Tree forever.

"It really wasn't your fault, you know. The Hebelmeister kid lost control. You had pulled almost all the way off the road."

But all the way off would have been in the ditch. "Not all the way off," he said, choking.

"Pretty near."

"Not all the way off."

She had her hand under his elbow and was moving his arm up and down like priming one of those old pumps no one had anymore. She said his name. It sounded like always.

"I couldn't get too close until she gave the signal. Then it was all right to come up close." What had happened to his voice? "If they bury her with the Prairie Pioneers, she should be on the edge. As near the ditch as they can find room." His hand was full of gnats' wings, rustling and throbbing.

Diane put his arm down on the sheet and laid her fingers over it, rubbing a little. She must feel that she'd have to say it, whatever it was, through touch, because she didn't have any words coming out, at least not words that he could register in his mind. Maybe he wasn't thinking right; maybe when he'd flown, his mind had shrunk back to where the words hadn't grown. There were reasons for all those silly phrases; they were all around you. Like a movie, they sped by you all the time, vehicles for what you saw if you could just get your mouth around them fast enough; they beat at the back of his throat and begged to be let out. When he finally found the key, they had already withered.

"Luke, honey, don't cry. She isn't dead. I mean, it's just like she's asleep. She might wake up. If she doesn't, they're planning on putting her in the Eksjo Home next week, the nursing part, and that's a nice place, you know that. You can see her as soon as you get out. Maybe she'll open her eyes for you. She always liked you best, Luke. Better than the twins or me. Better than anyone else in this world."

Eighty-Eight

"Can't do it."

"Whadiyamean?"

"Can't do it, Charlie-Parlie."

"Could if you tried."

"You say."

"I say. Who else?"

"Luke, maybe."

"Luke? He don't know nothing."

"Does too."

"Ain't even here."

"Comin' back, though."

"Grandma saw you, she'd spit."

"Grandma ain't seein' nobody."

"*If.*"

"If what?"

"If she did."

"Think she will?"

"Ma says nobody knows."

"Dad don't know, for sure."

"Still has her mind, Ma says. Maybe."

"You think? She don't say nothing now."

"Never did. Not much."

"Remember back when that last tornado come?"

"Sure."

"Grandma made us go hide in the ditch. Told us about them fairies."

"Myths."

"You mean them gods?"

"Not just gods. People from back then."

"Lotta shit."

"*You* say."

"I say. Me. Christian Kauffmann. Me Christian, you Charlie."

"Big chief."

"Ugh."

"Stop that."

"How come?"

"We're too big."
"Nobody's looking."
"How you know?"
"Got eyes."
"So's Grandma. Don't do *her* no good."
"Charlie?"
"What?"
"Come on."
"I won't."
"Savin' it?"
"Shut up."
"Make me."
"Wish you'd died in that truck."
"Wish you had, too. No I don't."
"You don't?"
"Not in them sunflowers. I hate 'em."
"Not as bad as buckwheat."
"Or soybeans."
"Or beets. Shit, I hate them beets."
"Come on."
"Fourteen's too big."
"Bigger'n yours."
"Whadiyamean?"
"Mine's bigger."
"Shit. Same."
"Bigger."
"Who you kidding?"

Eighty-Nine

Out in the barn where the weathered boards shut off everything from the house, Gerhardt sat, shifted the tobacco in his mouth, looked at the old machines. It was his domain. Whenever there was an old corn planter, combine, field rake abandoned on some hill, stark against the sky, he would swoop down on it, putt-putting with his tractor down the dirt roads, jolting his kidneys, so he could hitch it up and wrench it back to his collection. Over the years, he had created a metal tangle that spilled down from the barn wall through the pasture to the machine shed, weeds pushing up between wheels, twining around steering rods, clotting attachments. The green wave rose every spring around the old machines.

Then one day he would awaken in the morning, pull on his dirty overalls from the night before, stamp downstairs to where his scythe hung on the wall by the out-of-date calendar, and stalk through the damp grass to where the battle was scheduled to begin. He always won, goddammit. Clanking and thunking, he'd spend the day beating off the vegetation, notching his blade a hundred times on steering gears, engine blocks, horse hitches, the impact aching through his wrist and up his arm, tightening his shoulder muscles until his slices got shorter and shorter, and his temper shorter with them. Places he couldn't get at, underneath and between, he spat at, marking them as conquered, goddammit. His rusted, welded kingdom rose out of the grass like a tribe of monsters.

Gerhardt let a sleek stream of tobacco juice loose into the right-hand bucket on the old corn planter rig. His mouth tasted thick. Served him right for chewing before breakfast. In the morning dew, the stubble he'd scythed down last week still gleamed moist. He held back the urge to slice at it again.

"Breakfast." A word on the wind.

The door slammed, but not as loud as he would have done it. Someone was coming up the hill toward the barn, built right where he'd wanted it, with stubborn disregard of its location above the house, threatening the water supply with pollution. There was enough else to worry about.

"Dad." Luke was standing next to him, but not too near.

"Goddammit, what?"

"Breakfast." Luke rubbed his shoulder.

"Sowbelly again?"

"That's right. Ma's got the eggs done."

"Hard as that rock by now."

"I guess."

"Shoulder hurt?"

Luke was silent. "Not much," he said finally. He kicked the corn planter with his boot, knocking off the fringe of rust edging its frail metal brake. "I ate already. I'm going into town with the pickup."

"Nothing's open but the café."

"Will be by the time I get there." Luke started back to the house. His jeans were wet to the knees, getting wetter from the heavy grass slapping against them. The door slammed again.

Gerhardt got up and started back to the house himself, picking his way along the ruts where he'd hauled the manure out for so many years that the grass didn't grow there anymore. Goddamn breakfast. No matter what Mar did with the eggs, steaming them in the cast-iron pan for ten minutes even, he could always find some little bubble of yolk wobbling in a corner. She used to look hurt about it, grey hair steamy at the edges, wisping around her solid face. She'd started to grey early, not like her mother. Not like Susan.

The screen door was open, grease and the KCTM morning grain markets both coming through. Gerhardt marched up the steps. He looked in, squinting against the dark.

"Gerhardt, come and eat."

Around the corner of the house, Luke was backing out into the driveway with the new truck. He swung it in a fierce turn, then headed down the farm road, swaying on the humps.

"Food is getting cold." With her thumb and forefinger, Mar pinched in her cheeks, pursing out the edges of her mouth. She was loading eggs on his plate like cordwood.

"Goddammit, I know it." The pickup was crossing the bridge, a faint rattle coming back to him.

"Eggs are getting cold, Gerhardt."

Without acknowledging what she said, he looked down at his boots. Worn brown, the color scratched down to the light heart of the leather, these boots were on their way out. Another year of knocking against fences and slogging through the spring muck would crack them right through to his toes, white and twisted as rootstock.

Gerhardt opened his mouth, started to say something. No use.

He swung around and clumped down the steps.

"Gerhardt!"

"Going to town."

"Come back here. You have to eat." Mar's forehead was cross-hatched against the screen.

"Going to town." Goddammit, Luke had the pickup. The Valiant was up on a jack, waiting to have the right rear wheel replaced. A rangy orange tomcat was sleeping on its hood, stretched across the windshield wipers up against the glass. His front paws kneaded the metal, one after the other, then pulled back into the warm fur. A small fly forded the brown dribble from the corner of one shut eye, then buzzed off.

Stamping around the upended rear of the Valiant, Gerhardt lunged out into the wet grass at the edge of the farmyard driveway. The old John Deere was sitting by the gasoline pump right where he'd left it yesterday after cutting. Fifteen miles an hour on the straightaway, twenty if you gunned it and hung on over the culverts. He climbed into the seat, balancing on the metal, and turned the key. A sputter, then a clanking roar, the two cylinders choking on their own gas. He stalled it, then started it up again, nursing the fuel along. Everything needed tuning up, cleaning out, changing, rearranging, replacing, refueling, painting, God knows what. Diane worked all day in town, Luke was silent as snow. Who knew what the twins were doing? In the garden, the squash was beating out the quack grass, but everything else was being taken over.

On the gravel road in front of the farm, the tractor stalled again, heaving its front wheel off the ground in protest. Furious, Gerhardt kicked the accelerator pedal, feeling his toes cringe through the hardened leather. Unexplainably, the tractor started up, hesitated, then took off with a roar that made the heat waves shake in his clouded vision. He steered with both hands, shook one loose to scratch his crotch, replaced it on the wheel, feeling the vibrations up into his shoulders. The railroad ties in the culvert bridge shook and rattled. Up to the four corners, all the entering roads were hidden by yellow grass, headed out to deceive some town fool who didn't know what real grain was.

Once he had made the right turn and started up the hill toward Manatee, he pressed down hard on the gas. The John Deere gave a strangled roar and lurched ahead, lifting him off the metal seat and then dashing him back again. In another ten minutes, his overalls, a faded blue except for the seams, were heavy with road dust, blown back at him in the two streams his rear wheels tore out of the gravel. His boots were white. The tractor was moving so fast now that its front wheel kept leaving the ground in little throbs, clattering down, holding, thrusting upward again. Past the Strong- heart place, goddamn Indians who didn't even have the sense to turn Methodist. Then the two houses the retired teachers had built, two little garages in between, almost touching each other. You'd think they'd have had enough of lining up in the classroom. Louise and Josh's house. She was a bitch; no wonder Mar liked her. A thicket of wild plum that the highway department chopped down every few years, with Mrs. Furstenberg waddling down her drive- way when she heard the road grader coming, screaming in Platt- deutsch and waving her feather duster. One year the old lady had stuck it right in the front wheel, turkey feathers shredding all over the alfalfa, blowing with the milkweed fluff. All for a few goddamn plums, rock hard or rotten, take your pick.

The tractor hit a rock, convulsed, and chugged on. Up ahead, a snapping turtle, big as a dishpan, was crossing the road. When the tractor vibrations sent their message through its horny feet, it hesi- tated. Gerhardt hit it with a crunch like walking on saltines, swore, wrenched the tractor past it in a cloud of even heavier dust. The sweat had stained his shirt in a triangle down his back, his collar rubbed against his neck. Goddamn everything—turtle, morning heat, prairie summer, everything. Goddamn hills humping along the sides of the road and shutting him in.

You couldn't see the nursing home from the road because of the way the Loeffler brothers had set it over the crest of the hill, wind- breaking the north blasts and cutting down on the road dust. He knew where it was, though, and he didn't need the big mailbox, two old ones stuck together with a line of welded metal beads, or the black letters on the wooden rectangle above it. He didn't even need the driveway, though he turned the tractor up it, flattening the clump of alfalfa that had pushed through the first crack in the blacktop, because he could have shot right through the grass if he'd had to. Along the fringes were two rows of straggly petunias, a flower he happened to know because Diane raised them every goddamn summer. He gunned the John Deere just over the edge, flattening a square of big white ones, flowers like ear trumpets. Foot down on the gas pedal, pushing so hard his bunions hurt, he charged into the parking lot, past the long-nosed Chevys, Fords, Plymouths—no foreign midgets here—and braked with such a jolt that his overall buckles clinked against the steering wheel as he bounced off it. The tractor roar still shaking inside his head, he dropped stiff-legged from the seat, pulled his Cenex cap down over the sweaty white top of his forehead, and rocketed to the door, wrenching it open and then shut behind him all in one gesture. The hall was dark against the early morning sun, pee smell slicing through the dust, and as he started down toward the dayroom and Room 137 just beyond it, his own voice, set high and whimpery against its own nature, cut through the smell and the tiled floor and even the mummy heads wobbling above their chairs where the TV blathered, and he heard the words without noticing his mouth was even moving: "Goddammit, Susan, you witch, wasn't there nothing I could of done to keep you halfway content in my house where you belong?" There was a lot else to say, years' worth, but when he tried to get it out, tried to set it free because he couldn't keep his jaws around it anymore, all that he heard, over and over again, was "Goddammit, goddammit, goddammit."

Ninety

One thousand calories. One thousand, and then if you ate the oatmeal, one thousand two hundred. Do that for a week and you lost five pounds. Two weeks, ten pounds. Three weeks . . . but it didn't work like that. Once the water was gone, you just sat there. They called it a plateau. And finally, if you were lucky, the slow march downward. Inside, all the organs, their fatty blankets disappearing, would huddle into their corners, tight like fists, keeping out of each other's way. Stomach, liver, spleen, gall bladder, damp and pink, all of them seeing each other for the first time across the great plains where the fat had gone. When you put your hands on your belly, the loose skin would bundle up in your fingers. They said it shrank within a year, but some people had it cut off, sewed up like a zipper. She'd read that, too.

"Mar?"

She hadn't heard the steps on the porch. Could she have been reading that hard? One thousand two hundred calories, and they'd send a chart. Sighing, she shut the magazine and put it under Friday's paper next to the eggs, greasy golden rocks. "Come in," she said.

"For a minute I didn't think you were here, the place was so quiet."

"But you didn't knock."

"Who knocks? This is the country." Against the rectangle of light from the yard, crosshatched by the screen, the tall figure stretched its arms into a cross, waved, and then came in, destroying the screen, the light, the perfect angles of the wall and the kitchen. Louise, who couldn't walk across the yard without flattening some fragile stem, and then laughing about it as she looked back at the destruction.

"It's early."

"I know. My watch is finally fixed." Louise bent over the stove, hefting the coffee pot. The black liquid splashed up against the Pyrex, first one side, then the other, then back again. "You saved some for me."

"He didn't eat."

"Teeth hurt, or just mad at the world?"

"I have no idea."

"Men." The coffee curved over the top of the cup and slid down into a burner. "Where's a towel?"

"In the drawer." Louise was so skinny that the sun shown through the sides of her blouse hanging loose on her body. The first time Mar had seen her, talking to the preacher after the Methodist services, she'd been so embarrassed by Louise's thinness that she had taken a gigantic breath and pulled in her own stomach as hard as she could. Of course she'd only been able to hold it halfway down the steps to the dusty walk, gasping out a feeble peep of appreciation to the preacher as she passed. But Louise was younger. Six years. Or seven. In the growing heat of the kitchen, she couldn't get the arithmetic clear in her head.

"This is cowboy coffee, Mar. I'll be wired until winter."

"Should I make another pot?"

"Oh good Lord, no. I like being wired." Louise stuck out her tongue, wiggling fingers like Reddy Kilowatt. "When the Rural Electric comes by again, they can just hook me up. Pazaam!"

It was impossible not to laugh. "You're crazy," Mar grinned, easing herself into a kitchen chair. They were all oak, worn dark through the years from when her mother had kept them lined up along the dining room paneling in the boardinghouse, glistening with lemon oil.

"Crazy as a fox, as they say far east of here." Louise put her coffee cup on the drainboard, stopping to look out the window through the Swedish ivy in its hanging glass. "Do you realize that if you look out this window, there's not a living thing to be seen that isn't *green*? Nothing's changed in a hundred years. I couldn't believe this place when Josh and I moved here." She pinched an ivy leaf, but not enough to crack it. "All they need to do is hire the buffalo to come back, Mar. Sell it to the coyotes and prairie dogs. It's Indian country still."

"Oh, Louise." Secretly, Mar held out her forefingers, measuring Louise's width across the hips. Her own bottom pouched out over the chair seat.

"You need a crazy friend."

"Seems like I have enough crazies. The twins. Gerhardt most of the time. My mother."

"How is she?"

"The same."

"What does that mean?" Louise was looking out the window again.

"We don't know. Eksjo Home says there's no change."

Louise had hunched herself up on the counter, the ivy batting gently against her frazzled hair. "Well, she's either lying there like a vegetable or else she knows what's going on. My mother sat in her own shit for two years before she died, but she knew what she was doing. I think she saved it up for us when we came in. I used to gag before I got past the reception desk."

"My mother isn't like that."

"Be grateful. At least she's not disrupting your life." Louise slid down, her feet in their loafers paddling on the linoleum. "Let's walk down to visit her."

"Louise!"

"Why not? I don't mean walk the whole way. We'll hitch a ride at the crossroads with someone going into town. Then we can walk the last haul up that ridiculous driveway."

"But we go on Sundays."

"Is that the eleventh commandment?"

"But I have the canning to do, and the kitchen floor."

"Mar." Louise leaned one pointed hip against the counter. "It's a beautiful morning. Fall is almost here. You deserve something better than tomato pulp. We're free women. Josh is in town, Gerhardt is off somewhere, your kids have eaten and disappeared." She put her skinny hand under Mar's chin and tapped the padding beneath the line of the jaw. "Two old ladies off to see the world."

"You're crazy."

"Right." Louise pulled her up. "We'll totter down together."

Without even stopping to check the stove burners, Mar followed Louise out the door and down the steps. They started off on the farm driveway where three months of summer dust had coated the edging rocks into a uniform tan. Louise kicked one shaped like a darning egg, skittering it into the grass. Where the drive curved under the willow tree, split between its two main trunks and held together with an iron rod, a quick morning breeze whisked by them, ballooning Louise's blouse, then letting it cling flat again. Only a tornado could pry my clothes loose, thought Mar. I must be crazy doing this. I'll never make it past the culvert.

"Got doubts?"

"Doubts?" Mar chewed on her tongue, then felt her mouth purse up with laughter. "I got doubts? I'm too *fat* to have doubts!" She giggled.

Louise took two giant steps to the other side of the drive, put her hands on her pelvis, and jiggled herself up and down. "And a sense of humor, too," she whistled out. "How about sharing the wealth? I could use a layer here, and maybe one down here as well." Her hands circled her body like airplanes. "And bigger feets. Ah needs biggah feets!" She dug her heels into the dust, then her toes, spewing the sand to each side.

"Anybody sees us, we go to the Mental."

"Good business for the county."

"They don't need it."

"No business like good business." Louise was chugging her arms up and down, drum major style. "Come on, Mar, we'll get picked up in ten minutes. Who could resist us?"

Here where the road led up to the culvert, the edges were humped with overgrown hay, too narrow to be worth mowing. The road itself was narrow, too. The two women, arms linked at the elbows, adjusted their paces to each other. Mar shut her mouth so she couldn't hear her own breath snuffling out through her throat, but it whimpered through her nostrils instead. Wheezy old woman already. Louise whistled between her teeth without any breath at all.

When they had taken her mother to the Eksjo Home, or rather when they had followed the ambulance there, Mar hadn't even been upset. Luke being all right was all that mattered. But what she had thought about was her mother's skin, so thin and soft that when she had finally patted the veined hand on the stretcher, the skin had moved into little humps under her finger and then stayed there. A stubborn, impossible woman. Yet, somewhere out of the beginnings, back on the farm at the bottom of her memories, there had been someone who sat in the sandpile with her and Jimmy, making patty-cake buns with rocks for raisins. And then the hard lumps of dirt had sat on the shelf in the pantry along with the loaves of bread and even a cranberry pie.

"Here he comes. Look beautiful." Louise struck a magazine pose, buckling her shoulders back. "Wave them arms!" Through the dust, a seedy Cadillac, muffler gone, braked and skidded, then jerked down to a stop twenty feet ahead of them, spotting the road with loose gravel.

"Ladies, I take it you want a lift." Gregory Helmcroft, Copenhagen in cheek, opened the door and watched Louise slide across the seat toward him. Should she get in back, Mar thought, wondering both whether she could fit through the door into the back and whether she'd flatten them all in front? Louise answered the question by pulling her in beside the two of them.

At first they drove quietly, except for the gurgling of the motor.

It was probably about ready for Gerhardt's collection. Then Gregory shifted his cud and looked down at Louise's shoulder, his white eyelashes slicing against his cheeks. "Goin' into town?" he asked.

"We're going to the home to visit Grandma." Louise shifted her bottom, nudged Mar.

"How's she doing?"

"The same." Her own voice and Louise's said the words together.

"There for good?"

"We don't know." This time Mar got in first. "It depends on how she does. She sleeps all the time."

"We all come to it, like it or not." Gregory rolled down the window on his side and spat out into the sunshine. "How come Gerhardt ain't going?"

"He's busy." Another mile and they'd be past the wild plums, then less than that beyond the Eksjo driveway. "We all go to see her on Sundays."

"She's gonna bust her gut seein' you today, then." The plums passed in a blur. "Old lady won't know what hit her, gettin' the two of you today." He must have been drinking, early or not. Nobody talked that much without a little grease in the gullet.

The big metal mailbox cut the sky up ahead. "You can let us off right here," Louise said, shifting herself on the seat. Mar felt a ripple as her flesh compacted. "It'll be good exercise to walk up the driveway."

"Can drive you up just as easy."

"There's no need."

"All right, ladies." He pulled the Cadillac sideways into the drive, near enough to the mailbox so his front tire flattened the weeds at its base. "You have a good day, now."

With Louise pressing against her, Mar worked herself to the edge of the seat, then plopped down on the driveway. For a moment her ankles trembled and rocked inward; she held them rigid by sheer mental force. The hill stretched upward, waiting.

"See. No rape, no pillage. We saved a good long walk." Louise had hooked elbows with her again as they plodded toward the home.

"My floor is still dirty."

"Gerhardt can lick it clean, that old goat."

"We'll be sorry we did this, Louise."

"I can't imagine why. Even in Manatee, you're supposed to visit the sick."

"She's not *sick*." It came out in spite of herself. "If she was sick, she'd be home like normal with us." Mar's words tottered. "For all I know, she hears every word we say and just lies there on purpose."

"Mar." Louise slowed her pace.

"Who's to know whether she can open her eyes or not? There's probably nothing she likes well enough to make her want to look at it!" Mar's breath wheezed. A rotting spice smell pushed at her nose; she noticed the petunias lying twisted at her feet. Had a bear gone through? They were supposed to be killed off, but you never knew.

"Mar, you just have to trust things." Louise's voice was soft. "She's a strange old lady, but we're all what we've been made. Nobody's to blame for life."

"I guess not." But Louise's mother had at least sat still and let herself be visited, shit and all. She hadn't gone off looking for God knows what. Louise didn't know what she was talking about, even if they were friends. Louise could just stand there and ooze like those petunias.

"Mar?"

If she said anything in response, she'd never get her breath.

"Mar, are you all right? Should we stop and rest?" Louise batted at a dragonfly zapping her hair, and it retreated with a chatter of wings. They were supposed to breed in June, not September.

"No! You got me into this!"

Now the upper story of the home showed over the rounded crest of the hill where the bulldozers had smoothed the dirt like over a new grave. Three more steps and the windows of the first floor came up. Two more and they showed their sills, along with the tops of the cars in the parking lot, some of them catching the sunlight in little blips like those flying saucers people kept thinking they saw. Was Dr. Arnold there? He'd married the Collins girl, and they'd kept the practice in the family. That blue Continental, the only one with white sidewalls among all the dulled Chevys and Plymouths, was pulled up along the front entrance. Someone must be doing yard work, because a John Deere was wedged into a parking space a few slots down, so thick with dust that you could hardly tell the color of its paint. It looked like some of those old machines out back, tangled in the grass until Gerhardt had his pruning day.

They were at the door. Who should get the knob first? Mar pulled it toward her, then shut the door behind them after winding her arm up and back so Louise could squeeze through. A Berger girl, all trussed up in a little striped uniform, came by from the reception office with an armful of sheets. She smiled, then skittered away.

"What room?" Louise was waving the neck of her blouse, encouraging a breeze down her front.

"137, unless they've moved her."

"This way?"

"Yes."

"My God, you'd think they could get ride of this *smell,* considering what they charge in these places." An old man, stooped so low that his head looked back at their waistlines, shuffled past them toward the front door. He was drooling, but his eyes were as bright and evil as a storybook king's. Louise clicked her teeth and looked straight ahead.

Everyone in the reception area was watching *The Price Is Right,* if you could count as watching all that vague leaning toward a flicker and a rough edge of voices. Two women with braids on their heads, round as dumplings in their wheelchairs, were knitting together on two ends of a huge maroon rectangle, needles talking through the wool. They looked like twins.

Louise and Mar, the two of them, arms linked, headed off down the corridor. Room 131, with no one in it but the beds unmade. Room 133, where an old, old lady sat tied in a chair, her hands patting her lap like drumsticks. Someone had put a pink bow in her hair, and it had slid down over one eye. Room 135, where an aide was feeding something in a bed, something so flat the sheet could simply have been lifted a little from the air underneath it. Oh, it was awful to be old, awful to be shrunk down so even your bones retreated into little chicken sticks, awful to not want things anymore, even the things you couldn't have, awful to just go on forever like nothing had changed. By the time they were that old, thin Louise and fat Mar would be dried out into twins, knitting toothless together in the main room of the Eksjo Nursing Home.

The door to Room 137 was shut, but not latched. Both of them stood there, catching breath and balance.

"This is hers?"

"That's right."

"She's in there now?'

"Oh yes."

"Well." Louise put her arm around Mar's broad back. "Let's go in. We did a lot of walking to get here."

Although Louise had made the suggestion, it was Mar who opened the door, moving it inch by inch over the linoleum, green and cream, cream and green squares reaching further and further across the space ahead. Whoever was in the nearest bed was asleep, a waxwing tuft of white hair on the pillow, an inch of faded skin below it. Moving her eyes like a slow swing, Mar looked up at the other bed, the one next to the window, the one with the grey chenille spread folded back and wrinkled, the one where Gerhardt, her husband, was lying with his back to the door and his arms around the thin, unmoving body of the bed's rightful occupant.

Ninety-One

They kept going higher. They weren't on the ground anymore. That was all right, too. She wouldn't be dropped. She was rising like milkweed fluff on the very breath of a wind.

The sky was dark. Someone was beside her. She was being held. That was all right. She was going back inside until the last light was gone. It was like that. This time it was like that.

They were all there, but she didn't have to have them if she didn't want. They would let her choose. Although she didn't have to do that, either. She could do it by herself this time. That was all right. This time she could do it herself.

All the noise was just the wind. Her skirts swirled around her. The stars took her up.

About the Author

Mary Gardner was born in Wisconsin and has lived in North Dakota and Minnesota as well as a number of other states. She is a teacher and writer whose first novel, *Keeping Warm,* was published by Atheneum in 1987. Currently she is on leave of absence from the University of Pittsburgh/Greensburg. She has three grown children.

Quality Books from Papier-Mache Press

At Papier-Mache Press our goal is to produce attractive, accessible books that deal with contemporary personal, social, and political issues. Our titles have found an enthusiastic audience in general interest, women's, new age, and religious bookstores, as well as in gift stores, mail order catalogs, and libraries. Many of our books have also been used by teachers for women's studies, creative writing, and gerontology classes, and by therapists and family counselors to help clients explore personal issues such as aging and relationships.

If you are interested in finding out more about our titles, ask your local bookstores which Papier-Mache items they carry. Or, if you would like to receive a complete catalog of books, posters, and shirts from Papier-Mache Press, please send a self-addressed stamped envelope to:

Papier-Mache Press
135 Aviation Way #14
Watsonville, CA 95076